"Nonstop action, eroticism and intrigu
in the terrain of swashbuckling au
—Richard Bernstein, *New York Ti*

The Devil's Oasis

A Novel

BARTLE BULL

Author of *A Café on the Nile*

Acclaim for Bartle Bull's
The Devil's Oasis

"*The Devil's Oasis* bears the imaginative stamp of Mr. Bull's previous [novels]—*The White Rhino Hotel* and *A Café on the Nile*—their intricate plotting, their lusty sense of character and their geographical and linguistic authenticity . . . Nonstop action, eroticism and intrigue."
—Richard Bernstein, *New York Times*

"Bartle Bull . . . wisks us off to Cairo, where crepuscular shadows stalk the British empire and skulduggery is rife. . . . A World War II page-turner that's part *Masterpiece Theater*, part *Raiders of the Lost Ark*, part *Casablanca*."
—*Washington Post*

"This smoky, boozy café society buzzes with the intrigues of complex personal alliances as World War II comes to North Africa. The military history of the Allies' fight against Rommel in Egypt and Libya have been scrupulously researched."
—*Philadelphia Inquirer*

"It's an all-out, gung-ho war adventure, with much of the period glamour of *The English Patient*. . . . Exotic adventure fiction doesn't come much better."
—*Publishers Weekly* (starred review)

"All of the colorful characters from Bull's *A Café on the Nile* are back in his latest saga of war and intrigue in the cafés and nightclubs of Cairo . . . . Brilliantly rendered. . . . Highly recommended."
—*Library Journal*

"Stunning. . . . Bull is a master storyteller, interweaving authentically detailed military history with a continually evolving human drama."
—*Booklist*

The Devil's Oasis

BARTLE BULL

CARROLL & GRAF PUBLISHERS
NEW YORK

THE DEVIL'S OASIS

Carroll & Graf Publishers
An Imprint of Avalon Publishing Group Incorporated
161 William Street, 16th Floor
New York, NY 10038

First Carroll & Graf cloth edition 2001
First Carroll & Graf trade paperback edition 2002

Chapter illustrations and map by Indre Bileris

Library of Congress Cataloging-in-Publication Data is available.

ISBN: 0-7867-0990-1

Printed in the United States of America
Distributed by Publishers Group West

For Romia

What are we to do? It is simple. We must beat the English. They are opponents fit for our own steel. They pretend they are not trained for war, and indeed one sees it is true. But they are good men at the art of war, or the game of war.

—General Erwin Rommel, 1941

If a man were to be cross-examined as to his wartime doings, it would be enough for him to say that he had fought with the 8th Army.

—Winston Churchill, 1942

— The Characters —

Olivio Fonseca Alavedo *A dwarf, the Goan proprietor of the Cataract Café in Cairo*

Saffron Alavedo *A daughter of Olivio Alavedo*

Giscard de Neuville *A French archeologist, Gwenn Rider's lover*

Gamal, Munir and Ramzi *Three brothers employed by de Neuville*

Mustafa Bey Hafiz *The Inspector General of the* Service des Antiquités

Dr. August Hänger *A Swiss specialist in dwarfism, originally German*

Makanyanga *A Wakamba, from Kenya. Anton Rider's head safari man*

Jacques Nordhouse *A captain in the French Foreign Legion*

Lord Penfold *An elderly Englishman, resident in Kenya*

Anton Rider *A professional safari hunter from Kenya, raised by gypsies in England*

Denby Rider *The second son of Gwenn and Anton Rider*

Gwenn Rider *A Welsh lady living in Cairo. A surgeon, she is the separated wife of Anton Rider*

Wellington Rider *The first son of Gwenn and Anton Rider*

Erwin Rommel *The general commanding the* Afrika Korps, *the German army in North Africa*

Tariq *A Nubian employed by Olivio Alavedo*

Ernst von Decken *A German soldier of fortune. An old Africa hand and friend of Anton Rider*

Harriet von Decken *The American wife of Ernst von Decken*

The Devil's Oasis

— *Prologue* —

3 September 1939

The dwarf peered out from the darkened bar into the upturned faces of his guests seated on the broad deck of the Cataract Café. Directly over the bald dome of his head, the golden beam of the film projector played on the large cinema screen mounted above the bar on the vessel s quarterdeck. Cigars and cigarettes flickered like fireflies in the warm evening. With pleasure Olivio Alavedo noted the diplomats and bankers, the landowners and officers, the grandes dames and the young belles, the White Russians and the Greeks. His eye hesitated when he made out the people he envied most, those rare couples, the true lovers, whispering in French no doubt, alone in the night.

Only one couple troubled him. Seated to one side near the front, erect and graceful in a white shantung suit, was the wife of his friend Anton Rider. A tall slender woman with wavy tawny hair and a sculpted face with full lips and strong cheekbones, she inclined towards her companion and caught his eye with the quiet smile of an intimacy shared. Setting down his black cigarette holder, taking her hand without resistance, the elegant grey-haired man kept his head turned to Gwenn Rider even after she faced back towards the film. Olivio turned away.

To starboard the coals of a hookah cast shadows against the gunwale as the Inspector General of the *Service des Antiquités* bent over his water pipe. To port the wide river flowed smoothly, grey and sluggish, reflecting here and there the gently swinging lantern hanging from the mast of a passing *felucca* or *qayyasa*. Olivio watched an ibis flying upstream in the gloom. His favorite moon, a hunchbacked crescent, was climbing slowly through the sky above the square stern of the caravel. The dwarf sniffed deeply and inhaled the musty smell of the Nile, blending with the tobacco of his guests.

"How can you ask me if I love you?" cried the indignant voice of Rita Hayworth from the speakers.

How, indeed, Olivio wondered, could one trust the love of such a woman? Fortunately, there was so much more to women than fidelity.

For a moment his mind turned and he thought of how different his crew would be if, instead of being a café, his caravel were a true Portuguese sailing ship of the fifteenth century. A vessel as compact, as agile, as enduring as he himself. The sort of craft that had carried his ancestors south along the Atlantic coast of Africa, around the Cape and across the Indian Ocean to Goa. Instead of diplomats in black tie, Alexandrine bankers in *stamboulines*, British colonels in starched white mess jackets and Circassian beauties slinking in the silks of Paris, there would be bearded officers cursing orders from the quarterdeck and barefoot lascars sweating at the ropes as three patched lateen sails stretched and snapped overhead and the ship's rounded bow surged through the seas. What if Vasco de Gama were at the helm, not he?

Just then the bar telephone rang.

Olivio Fonseca Alavedo lifted the black earpiece. He listened, pinching the open loop of his free earlobe with his other hand. This news would change the world. He crossed himself, a thing he rarely did. The dwarf hung up the instrument, instantly calculating all that this bulletin might mean. He reached beneath the bar and tore a telegraph form from a pad. He wrote the date, 3 September 1939, and considered what he would tell Anton Rider.

Would this be the end of a world, or the beginning? Which of the people before him would live or die, suffer or survive? Who would be enriched or impoverished, honored or disgraced? Would treachery or loyalty be rewarded? Regardless, it would mean an ocean of opportunity. The dwarf felt his lips go dry. He moistened them with swift movements of his thick pointed tongue. If only he were younger, and in health. His mind retained the passionate energy of youth, but his body was cursed by the accelerated aging and progressive debilitations that harried and brought down most dwarfs.

The little man stared out again into the half-light of the crowded deck, searching for his eldest daughter, Saffron, now seventeen. First he saw the twins, the girls who kept him young. Rosemary and Cardamom were seated on the deck against the starboard gunwale, whispering and tormenting each other with pokes and pinches. Then he spotted Saffron at a third-row table, her head cast back a bit in laughter, her coal-dark eyes glittering, a light smile on her lips as she watched the film. She was seated between two admirers, Italians, he guessed. He did not trust the devils. Yet he was more troubled by a different and unrevealed attachment of his daughter, to a man far too young and far too poor.

The tone of Saffron's coloring, a rich glowing honey that borrowed more from India and Portugal than from Africa, was lost in the dimness. But the bright Latin shawl that covered her shoulders could not hide her startling deep-chested figure, the gift of her Kenyan mother. Still more dangerous, he was certain that even as Saffron had her mother's magnificent lips and breasts and high tight round derrière, so too must his daughter be hot beneath the skin, tinder waiting for some unworthy man to light.

Olivio Alavedo sighed and stepped carefully along the shelf behind the bar. His back was bowed and tight as a newly coopered barrel. His tiny feet were in torment even before he took each step. The palms of his hands were ridged and tight with the thickening cords of Dupuytren's contraction. At the end of the shelf he stopped and glanced down at the stack of fliers for next week's film: *The Sun Never Sets*, starring his favorite actor, Douglas Fairbanks, Jr. "Warm-blooded men! Desperate women! Caught in the merciless maelstrom of expanding empire!"

The dwarf lowered his head and sniffed the dense sweet smell that rose from a bowl of ripe figs. The petals of their skins were already separating of their own accord. Then he whispered instructions to his Sudanese servant.

As the film continued overhead, Tariq set a magnificent new Mullard radio receiver onto a café table that he placed at the entrance to the bar. Lifting the skirt of his *gallabiyyah* in one hand, the burly Nubian crept along the gunwale to convey his master's orders to the projectionist, the dwarf's second daughter, Ginger.

Olivio checked his pocket watch, squinting with his one eye to make out the time in the projector's glow. He waited two minutes until just before the hour struck, then nodded to Ginger.

The film stuttered to a halt. The deck lamps blazed. Olivio adjusted the grey tarbush on his round head and advanced to the radio set as his guests shielded their eyes and muttered and complained. Did they think Rita Hayworth was more important than the future of the world?

The little man raised his hands. The crowd stilled.

"I bring you news," he said. "News from London." Many, he knew, had been waiting for this moment. He tuned to the BBC and turned the radio to full volume.

The strains of "God Save the King" broke through the brittle static. The anthem stopped. The soft air of the Nile seemed to chill as the Prime Minister addressed them from Westminster.

"I am speaking to you from the Cabinet room at Ten Downing Street. Three days ago Germany invaded the peaceful nation of Poland," declared the reedy voice of Neville Chamberlain.

"This morning the British ambassador to Berlin handed to the German government a final note stating that unless we heard from them by eleven, that they were prepared at once to withdraw their troops from Poland, a state of war would exist between us."

The Prime Minister paused. Olivio heard no sound from the crowded deck of the Café. Only the traffic of the embankment and the cry of a boatman cut the night before Chamberlain continued.

"I have to tell you now that no such undertaking has been received, and that consequently this country is at war with Germany."

Gasps and cries and the scraping of chairs obscured the words that followed.

"God Save the King," said the Prime Minister in a stronger voice. The national anthem rose again.

Perhaps half the crowd, civilian and military, women and men, New Zealand and Indian and Canadian, British and South African and Australian and Rhodesian, stood and sang together. Even the dwarf, never aroused by patriotism or other distant loyalties, felt a prickle charge his spine. His skin chilled.

Noisily pushing back their chairs, the German ambassador and his entourage quickly made their way between the tables and stalked up the canopied gangway to the Nile embankment. Several Egyptian officers put down their colored fruit drinks and hurried after the departing Germans.

Watching the ambassador enter his black Mercedes, Olivio recalled the last Great War in Africa. A small, greatly outnumbered German army had fought across four countries for over four years, never defeated, the last Germans in the world to surrender in 1918. What would these Germans do in Africa this time? As the magnificent motor car pulled away, the dwarf noticed the chancellery flag snapping in the wind. The black swastika on the red field was illuminated by the glow of light rising from his Café.

"God save our gracious king, God Save the King," carried clearly across the darkened Nile.

"Good shot, Denby," said Wellington Rider to his younger brother as one dove fell at the edge of the canal and the other flew into the palms, "but you could have had the pair if you'd swung right on through them."

Approaching the fifteen-year-old, Wellington gripped his brother's right shoulder in one strong hand and the shotgun with the other. "Always keep the gun in tight to your shoulder, like this, and put your weight on your front foot, so the recoil doesn't knock you back and spoil the second shot. Here, load up and we'll try again."

"Don't have any more cartridges," Denby said, looking up at his brother, conscious of their father watching from behind them.

"Here you go." Anton Rider ground out his cigar with his boot heel and took a handful of shells from the old bush jacket set on the palm stump beside him. Anton always liked shooting in the Faiyum. Only fifty miles south of Cairo, the vast southern oasis, fed by canals for two thousand years, was green and thick with geese and duck and dove. In the evenings there were always cards and girls and dinners, all in a way more sporty and relaxed than in the capital or Alexandria. Denby ran over and Anton gave his son six more 16s. "Put the rest in your pocket. We'll try a bit farther down the canal."

Anton sat again and watched his boys with regret, as he often did. Regret that he had not seen more of them as they grew up, regret that their mother had left him and they did not live together, regret that his own foolishness had caused it all. And now, in his pocket, was more bad news.

He took out the cable and read again the message from Olivio. War. In due course, if it proved serious, he would go himself. In a way, it was what he had always been prepared for, far more than most men. What else was a professional hunter good for, after a lifetime of shooting and tracking and organizing expeditions in the bush? Especially with the safari business dead for the duration.

Last time, he had been just too young to go. Ever since, he'd felt he had missed something that he should have done. For years, he'd been hearing about all the young men who'd been killed in the German war, a lost generation almost his own. This time, at thirty-eight, he himself was perhaps a bit too old. But if England was in it, he would do his share, though he dreaded the drill and discipline of any decent British regiment. While on safari in '35, he had tangled with the Italian army during the war in Abyssinia. He had some idea what war in Africa would be like. The Alpini and the Bersaglieri had hounded him halfway across Ethiopia, trying to catch his safari and destroy the film his clients had taken of the Italian army using poison gas. Two American clients and several old friends from his safari staff had been killed during the pursuit before the rest of them escaped into Kenya. If the Italians were going to be in the next one, Anton had a few accounts to correct.

And what of Wellie? The boy was big and solid, dreading more school, and already talking of joining the army, though he was about to leave for university in England. Friendly with one or two of the young subalterns, Wellington was keen on the Hussars, part of the Cairo Cavalry Brigade. The 11th had been stationed in Egypt for five years, constantly on maneuvres in the Western Desert, using trucks and armored cars instead of horses, learning to navigate in the wilderness and live on the move. On leave in Cairo, bronzed and fit from the desert, Hussar officers were part of the smart young set, polo at the Gezira Club, dances at the embassies, and wild nights with other sorts of girls from the Birka and Shari Clot Bey. Not a bad life, Anton thought, for a young man, but there would be more to this war than social life in Cairo.

Anton knew how the boy's mother would hate it all, especially the military side. Gwenn would blame him, saying it was his example, his influence, his giving both boys a sense of adventure rather than a sense of purpose. She was right, of course.

"What is it, Daddy?" said Wellie, suddenly beside him. Anton folded the cable, then changed his mind and handed it to the older boy. Denby strolled over, grinning. Two more small soft grey birds swung in his hand by their feet. The boy glanced warily at a large black water buffalo that stood chewing under a nearby palm tree.

"Don't worry," said Anton. "These chaps aren't like the Cape buffs in Kenya."

"Grand news!" exclaimed Wellington, looking up, his face flush, nearly as red as his hair. "Ripping! I'll have to go home and sign up."

"Home?" said Anton, always feeling Nairobi was home, if he had one. He rested one hand on Denby's head.

"England, Daddy," said Wellington, passing back the telegram. "That's where you've got to train and join the regiments. And I'm nineteen. It's time I did something. I'll talk to my chums in the 11th and get a letter to take to England."

"No, you won't," Anton said. He understood perfectly. He himself had run off to Africa twenty years before. And he guessed what Wellie wasn't saying. Perhaps he'd rather be based in Cairo, where young Saffron Alavedo lived, than at school in Cambridge without her. The two young people had known each other all their lives. Though they still seemed to regard each other as little more than childhood playmates, it was clear to all who knew them that soon they would see something more in one another.

"I'm already packed," said Wellington.

"You're not packed for that," said Anton firmly, shaking his head. The boy already saw himself in uniform, his head out the top of an armored car, field glasses swinging from his neck, the Hussars' pennant flying from the antenna as the engine roared and sand flew up behind him.

"You know your mother wants you to go to university. You're off to Cambridge next week." And I've already paid for the first term, Anton thought. He was damned short of money. Now he was hoping he could squeeze in one more well-paid safari before the war came to Africa.

"You never went to university," said Wellie as Denby looked from one to the other with wonderment. "Didn't you come out to Africa at eighteen? And spend years bashing about on your own, hunting and digging for gold? You told me you never really went to school at all . . ."

"I didn't, but your mother doesn't want you to be like me," said Anton, disliking the sad truth of it. He'd wandered first as a boy in England, living in a *vardo* with his own mother and her gypsy lover, drifting from village to village with a few books for schooling, mostly Dickens, on a shelf above the wagon door. "And she's right."

"I can always do university when the war's over," said Wellington. "But I've got to join up now. There are only a few places for lieutenants,

Everyone I know will be signing up." He took the shotgun from his brother, broke it and checked the barrels against the blue.

"I already did that, Wellie," said Denby crossly, feeling ignored. "You know I always do that."

"Good lad, Den." Anton paused and put one heavy arm across the shoulder of his younger son. "But it's always best to check."

Wellington grinned down at Denby and the three started back to the dirt path, kicking stones as they walked. A pair of mourning chats rose from a nest. The small black and white birds darted and circled and skimmed about as they waited for the three to pass.

Anton picked up a large flat stone and handed it to Denby. "Now how about a quick game of duck-on-a-rock?"

Denby ran on ahead, stacking up seven stones, one atop the other. Wellington gathered up a few throwing stones. Anton drew a line in the dirt with the toe of his boot, then a second closer to the target.

"Your go." Wellington handed his brother a rock as Denby hurried back, eager to throw, determined to knock over the most stones and win. Carefully, all concentration, the younger boy took position with his left toe against the forward line.

"Thank you for the farm, *Liebling*," Ernst von Decken said, gruffly but sincerely, putting aside the resentment that often accompanies gratitude. He reached between their deck chairs and took his wife's free hand in his hard fingers, a rare concession in public. With the other hand, she turned another page of *The Undiscovered Self*.

"*Danke*." He kissed her hand, admiring the smooth long slender legs that were stretched out the length of the chair, the perfect ankles crossed. Then he paused and squinted over the rail of the *Coburg*, annoyed that Harriet was not appreciating his attention. Frowning with concentration, his wife clenched her marking pencil in her teeth. At least this Jung fellow was German, Ernst thought, or something like it.

Zanzibar was retreating behind them to starboard, its spicey scent lost in the salt air. And the last of what used to be German East Africa was falling away to port. Soon the nine-thousand-ton vessel would steam past Mombasa, Malindi and Lamu. British East Africa would also be behind them. But at last he had fulfilled his father's requirement. Thanks to this beautiful difficult American wife, after twenty-one years in British hands, Gephardt Farm belonged once more to the von Deckens.

"It's nothing." Harriet closed the pencil in her book. She tossed her head and ran her fingers through her red curls. At least this little present would keep her rough German in hand a while longer. "Your farm was even lovelier than you'd told me. In the mornings Kilimanjaro was inside our bedroom window." And in the warm dozy afternoons, she thought, as we made love in the hammock, I could smell the sweet rotten apples breezing up from the old orchard below the verandah.

"Herr von Decken," interrupted a lean Arab steward, bowing in the crisp white uniform with the green-and-brown-striped sash of the Hamburg & Orient Line. "A cablegram, *mein Herr*. From Berlin."

"It is not your concern from where my messages come," Ernst said without looking at the man. "Two schnapps. Quickly, boy. *Pesi, pesi!*"

He released his wife's hand and ripped the cable from the tan envelope, aware that her eyes were on the text. Fortunately, after four years she still had not learned German. Were these Americans waiting for the whole world to learn their language?

4 SEPTEMBER 1939

VERTRAULICH.
HOSTILITIES EXPECTED IMMINENTLY STOP ALL GERMAN SHIPS ARE ORDERED TO NEUTRAL PORTS TO EVADE ENEMY ACTION OR SEIZURES STOP ALL VESSELS IN GULF OF ADEN AND RED SEA MUST STEAM FOR ITALIAN PORT OF MASSAWA STOP GERMAN CREW AND NATIONALS OF MILITARY AGE TO REPORT TO CONSUL IN MASSAWA OR ASMARA STOP HEIL HITLER STOP

Ernst stood and limped to the rail, glancing down at the rounded peg that emerged from his right pant cuff. Crippled or not, he would fight to stop the damned *Engländeren* from stealing his farm again. This time Germany must win in Africa.

"What is it?" Harriet asked with rare tenderness, joining him shoulder to shoulder, smelling his powerful salty odor on the warm breeze.

"War."

"We'll be all right," she said after a moment, touching his strong arm, feeling his excitement. "We just have to get home."

"This is home." Ernst spread both of his hands towards the African coast. "I am German, and an African. I have to fight." He stared past the flapping swastika on the sternmast as Tanganyika disappeared to the south.

"Back there, just north of Tanga," he said, "I killed my first Englishman in '14. Had to shoot him a second time when he got up. Soon it will be time to shoot a few more." Von Decken took a schnapps from the steward's tray while his wife signed the chit.

"Tanga was the last battle we won out here. After that, there were too damn many of them. Australians. South Africans. Britishers. Indians. Rhodesians. *Schwarzes*. Even Portuguese. But old von Lettow led them a chase, by God. Ten to one and the bastards never caught us." Ernst knocked back the drink and dropped the glass over the side. "Hope Africa gets another German general like that old fox."

"All that's over." Harriet's voice firmed to match his. "We both have American passports. No one will stop us." She hesitated, admiring his brown lined hard-set face, his thick steel-grey hair. She knew this was her last chance, still wanting to reconcile her spoiled world with his unbending independence. For five years she'd tried to compromise, although never quite enough, giving up much of the horse and party life of Lexington and Aiken and Saratoga, instead trying to enjoy the lonely colonial life he loved. She wanted what she'd married, but she didn't want to give up anything to have it.

"It's not your turn, Ernst. Please. You fought your war. We'll go home to Lexington. You can run the horse farm. Everyone loves you there." Well, a few anyway, she thought, and some perhaps too much. "When it's over, we'll come back here, to Gephardt Farm."

Her husband looked out at Africa and did not reply. The ship's engines throbbed beneath the metal deck. The water seemed to hiss ever so slightly as it slid by.

"And how can you want to fight for that ghastly little man with the black mustache?" she said contemptuously, pulling away a bit without meaning to.

"You do not understand," he said at last, shaking his head. He was thinking of his dead comrades of the *Schutztruppe*, white and black, the men he had fought with and carried, sick and wounded, through the bush for four years. Always they'd been hungry and on the run from the British, chewing strips of leather and drinking the blood of birds, picking at their infected unhealing wounds, singing *Haya Safari* as they marched in endless winding columns, the spotted hyena following patiently like sharks after a hospital ship. Four years.

"I don't give one damn about Adolf Hitler and his gang. Our men will be fighting for Germany. For Africa. For each other, as they always do." He looked her in the eye. "And for you and me and my father."

Used to getting her way with everyone but Ernst, Harriet started to speak, to insist, then stopped, knowing it was hopeless.

"And I'm not going to let these damned Britishers steal my . . . our farm a second time."

"Ernst." She took his arm with both hands. "The army won't even take . . ." She paused, knowing Ernst von Decken could do more on one foot than most men on two.

"I must," he said. "How many Germans know Africa as I do?"

"If you go to fight," she said in a low steady voice, turning and gripping the rail with tight white knuckles, "I'll go home alone, and I may never come back."

"You know I have no choice," he said, looking at her with more distant eyes, certain she was already gone. "And you are my wife, *Frau* von Decken. You, too, are German."

Gwenn Rider closed her eyes and clutched the safety strap as Omar made his usual unhesitating turn across the frantic traffic of Heliopolis and braked the venerable Renault taxi to a shaky stop before her building. One of Olivio's new green Sunbeams was waiting in front of them. Anton must have just brought the boys home, she realized, sorry she hadn't been able to get back from the hospital first. As usual, the surgeries and her rounds had taken longer than she'd thought. Bracing herself for the encounter, Gwenn felt that mixture of irritation and regret that always characterized her meetings with her estranged husband.

Part of her still loved him, she sometimes thought, or was that just the memory of affection?

Meeting on the boat to Kenya twenty years ago, they had shared the upcountry highland life and struggles, then married at last and tried to make the farm work. But Anton was always eager to get away, preferring the adventures of safari life to the cruel grind of farming in Africa. At first she put up with his need for freedom, even his occasional foolishness with women, understanding both in a handsome husband eight years younger.

But finally the loneliness and the hopelessness of the farm had worn her down, made everything unacceptable, and she'd left him. It was the boys that finally induced her to leave. She didn't want their lives to be limited by hers and Anton's. And now, with Giscard, she'd made things even more difficult to undo, if she ever wanted to. Giscard was only her second affair, but she knew that two long public romances were harder to tolerate and forget than Anton's many furtive flings.

Determined not to hesitate at her own doorstep, she strode swiftly up the walk. She found the door ajar to the first floor flat she shared with her sons. Wellington's shotgun, a fine old Holland, a gift from his godfather, Adam Penfold, lay open across the hall table.

"Don't go yet, Daddy," she heard Denby say from the kitchen as she came down the hall. She tried not to feel resentful. She knew how much Denby loved these rare days with his brother and father.

"Evening, Mummy," said Wellie cheerfully. "How're the patients?" A lager already in hand, he let Gwenn kiss him on the cheek as she entered the kitchen. Still exhausted from the surgery, Gwenn raised her chin and ran her fingers through her short hair. She feared she must be looking more old and tired than she should. For an instant she forgot herself as she looked into Anton's eyes, eyes you could see across a room, blue as robins' eggs against his tan. She noticed the familiar bump on the bridge of his prominent nose, and the slight unruliness of his dark wavy hair. No longer the tall rangy boy he'd been when they first met, Anton looked heavier now, but powerful and still quite fit, with an easy physical confidence that both women and men seemed to understand. Unfortunately, in Cairo, and even in Nairobi, he never had patience for the social life that was required to make one's way in the world.

"Oh, hullo," said Anton awkwardly, turning from the sink to face her with blood on his hands. He smiled, hoping for a moment of easy understanding. "Just showing Denby how to clean the birds, so they won't be wasted."

"Of course," Gwenn said, trying to keep the anger from her voice. Once a hunter herself, she didn't think it was the shooting that she minded, though that was part of it. Somehow, on days like this, all three assumed they shared something she never could, some little bit of wildness, of tribal adventure, that tied them together. Anton seemed to forget that the flat was hers, and not hers and his together. Whenever she saw him here with the boys, he seemed more at home than she did.

"I got three doves," Denby said proudly, looking up from the sink, his shirtfront a mess of feathers and blood. "I cleaned this one by myself."

"Good boy." Gwenn smiled despite herself. "Why don't you all finish up in here and I'll see you in the sitting room."

Driven from her own kitchen, she went upstairs and washed her face and hands and changed into comfortable shoes. She glanced at her short, surgeon's nails. She hoped she could get Anton out of the house before Giscard came by. Neither man would understand.

"I've got some news, mum," Wellington said eagerly as soon as she came downstairs.

Gwenn sensed it was trouble. "Let's sit down and talk about it." Her elder son sat on the edge of the seat opposite her as Anton and Denby entered the living room.

Anton was helping Denby dry his filthy hands on a clean tea towel. The boy's shirt was still a mess, and there was a smear of blood on his cheek. But his blue eyes shone with pleasure and excitement. She herself was sometimes torn by her family's separation, and she knew Denby was happy that, briefly, they were all together.

"I'll be off to England in a few days . . ." said Wellington.

"I know," Gwenn interrupted. "Of course, to go to university."

"No, mum." Wellington, flushing, shook his head. "To sign up and train with the Cherrypickers. The Eleventh Hussars. It's only eighteen weeks. First Bulford Camp, then Salisbury Plain," he said in a rush. "I'm sure Bingham and Gates will be coming, too."

She felt she had been struck across the face. "No, you can't." She turned her head towards Anton, then looked back at Wellington. "Darling, you can't. You don't know what this means . . . It's not a lark. It's your life . . ."

"I've thought about it, and . . ."

"I've seen two wars. In Flanders and Ethiopia. You don't know what it's like. Your father was in Ethiopia. Anton . . ." She looked at her husband and her voice hardened. "Anton, you tell him. Tell him he can't do it."

"I talked to him earlier, Gwennie. I told him he should go to Cambridge. But he . . ."

"Daddy did his best, Mum. He told me, but I've got to."

"No, you do not."

"Course, I'll have to put off university until this flap is over, but I promise to get back to it. They'll keep my place . . ."

Wellington paused, seeing the dismay chill his mother's face. He was reminded what his schooling meant to her, the endless effort, her scrimp-ing, her sense of the future. He leaned across and took her hand in both of his as her lips narrowed. "I promise, Mum. I promise."

"Promise? Promise, Wellington? How do you know what's going to happen? What the university will do? How long this war is going to take? The last one was four years, more." Gwenn felt her face tighten. She was annoyed that Wellie was trying to spare her. Why couldn't he use the word 'war'?

"Don't you see?" she said. "You're going to war when you don't have to. Thousands of people will be killed, maybe millions. Poland's just the beginning. It could go on for years. Who knows what'll happen to all those boys in the Hussars? Do you know what happened last time? Do you? None of the first ones lived. Every junior officer in those regiments was replaced three times."

"Mum, if it's like that, then they'll make me go anyway. The whole world will be in it." He glanced at his father for support.

"Wellington," said Anton, understanding both too well. "Let's take a few more days to think about it. Two or three weeks. Let's see what's going to happen. You can do that for your mother."

"No," said Wellington quietly, shaking his head. "I'm sorry. I can't sit here while all my friends are signing up."

Gwenn was unable to speak, feeling she'd lost him already, that she was with his ghost. Wellington's hands already felt cold on hers, but she knew it was not him, but her. All she had seen in the Great War flashed before her. Her overloaded ambulance, wheels spinning, settling hopelessly into the mud behind the trenches as the French .75s popped away endlessly. Groaning casualties, a sea of them, lying waiting in the shell-pitted fields by the road, like birds after a violent storm. The puffy remains of an observation balloon rolling back and forth over them in the wind like a loose grey shroud, until it tangled in a hedgerow. The road itself lined with blackened shattered trees, a parade of desolation. Many of the dying boys had looked younger than Wellington today. It had been the same in Ethiopia, seventeen years later. Not the trenches, but the same poison gas, and the swarms of wounded overwhelming the field hospital after the Ital-ian bombers had passed. What would this new war be like? How could it not be worse? Every new invention would find its brutal application.

"*Mon trésor?*" called a Frenchman's confident voice from the hall. Every-one was quiet as the swift sharp steps approached. Anton stood.

"I brought you flowers," the newcomer said, barely hesitating before he smiled. "Good evening, Wellington, Denby. I see you got some big game. *Bravo! Bien fait!*"

So this is the man, Anton thought.

"Thank you, aren't they lovely?" Gwenn said quietly. She rose and exchanged kisses as she took the yellow roses, touching the Frenchman's cheek with the fingers of one hand. He was always so considerate. "This is Anton. Giscard de Neuville, Anton Rider."

"*Enchanté*," Giscard said as Anton gripped his hand and looked him in the eye with a nod. "Would you like me to leave you with your family, Gwenn?" He spoke like an Englishman, with almost no accent.

"No, no, we just need a few minutes," she said, struggling to collect herself. "Please make yourself a drink. You know where everything is. Maybe you could put the roses in water for me." She could feel the tension between the two men. Cairo wasn't big enough for both of them, let alone her flat.

Giscard folded the jacket of his grey suit and hung it over the back of a chair before walking to the pantry with the flowers. He was shorter than Anton, with very pale skin and a small mouth and bright flitting eyes surrounded by deep lines. His handshake was firm enough, in a tight wiry way, but the skin of his hand was smooth like a girl's. Lean and fit for a man in his fifties, his grey hair was shiny and carefully parted and combed straight back in neat lines above his wide high forehead. He carried himself with refinement.

"You haven't even been called up," Gwenn said urgently, turning back to Wellington. "This is nonsense. You can't. You're just nineteen, you're still a boy. There's been no call-up. There isn't even a war out here. This isn't Poland. They're expecting you in Cambridge in two weeks."

"Mum, I've got to. Please. Everyone's going to go. If I wait to be called up, I won't be able to choose my regiment. Who knows where they'll send me then? At least this way I'll be back out here in Egypt with the Hussars, don't you see?"

She faced Anton, all the old anger returning.

"It's you," she heard herself say, her cold voice not her own. "You've made Wellington like this. You never wanted him to go to university." She paused, her green eyes hard. "You just want him to be like you."

"That is not true." Anton shook his head. But he understood why Wellington had to go. Soon he'd be doing the same.

"Mum, no . . ."

"It is true," Gwenn said, not taking her eyes from Anton's. She knew she was going too far. Anger and sadness mixed in her uncontrollably. "Now, if he lives through it, he'll know nothing else but shooting and violence and killing things. Just like you. You . . ."

Then she saw Denby's face as he leaned back against the wall, his eyes full of tears, his lips trembling, and she stopped. Denby, soundless, began to shake.

"Gwenn," Anton said in a low voice, stepping closer to Denby, furious that the Frenchman was listening in the pantry. "No matter what you think of me, Wellie has to be who he wants to be." He put one hand on Denby's shoulder. "Didn't you yourself leave the boys and go off to be a doctor in the war in Ethiopia?"

Gwenn clenched her teeth. Her face reddened. She stared at Anton.

"You're letting him ruin his life," she said, at the same time feeling she was dooming them all with her words. "If anything happens, it will be your fault."

"May I get anyone a drink?" said Giscard amiably from the doorway, a vase in one hand, his cocktail in the other.

"Good evening," said Anton, nodding to the room. He bent and kissed Denby on the cheek and roughed his hair as the boy, steadier now, tried to smile up at his father with shining eyes. Anton picked up his dusty bush jacket in his fist and walked to the door to the hall. There he paused and turned and looked at de Neuville, then at his wife before he spoke to her.

"You insist that Wellington do what you want. Do you believe you are doing what the boys want?"

June 1940

"Welcome to you, your lordship," called the dwarf with rare merry delight as his guest arrived for early cocktails. He watched his oldest friend descend the gangway. Tall and angular, a man of wrinkled easy elegance with a craggy face and fierce grey eyebrows, the old Englishman favored his right leg as he approached. His cane tapped smartly with every step. Wounded in the Great War while serving with the East African Mounted Rifles, Adam Penfold had spent months as a prisoner of the Germans in Tanganyika and Northern Rhodesia before going home to his farm and hotel in the Kenya highlands. There he had struggled on until the lean days of the early '30s drove him to give up and move to Cairo.

The heat of the day was past. A gentle breeze rose from the Nile as Penfold joined Olivio on the poop deck of the Cataract Café. Noticing the newspapers stuffed into his jacket pocket, Alavedo prepared himself for Penfold's favorite ritual, sharing with the dwarf his commentary on the news of the day. Old papers were often shuffled in his pocket with the latest edition, and the dwarf was obliged to endure repetition. But Olivio took pleasure in extending to this man the patience that he enjoyed denying to others. Mercifully, the news had grown more interesting, always the second gift of war.

"Good evening, ladies," said Penfold to Rosemary and Cardamom. He was not about to guess which twin was which. The two curtsied and continued to braid each other's hair with colored ribbons. When he thought the dwarf was not watching, Penfold slipped each of the eleven-year-olds a sweet. Then the Englishman raised his chin and pulled several copies of the *Egyptian Gazette* from his pocket. He studied them through his spectacles with watery pale blue eyes.

The dwarf glanced down. He saw the pointed upturned nose of a rat in the river. He watched the animal swim through the sweet rotting fruit and the oily film that washed along the edge of the embankment.

"GERMAN SUBMARINE SINKS BRITISH LINER," Penfold read aloud. "FIFTEEN HUNDRED TAKE TO BOATS—THREE HUNDRED AMERICANS ON BOARD LINER *ATHENIA*." Penfold looked up, aware of his little friend's habit of inattention. "You see? What did I tell you? It's just like '14. Wretched Hun hasn't learned a thing. We shall just have to thrash 'im all over again."

"No doubt, my lord, no doubt." The dwarf turned his head as best he could and watched Saffron descend the gangway to the boat as his friend continued. She seemed to be dressed for an evening of glamorous mischief. From a distance Saffron reminded him of his first child, Clove, who had died four years before in the boat fire that had destroyed the original Cataract Café.

"BRITISH EVACUATE THREE HUNDRED THOUSAND AT DUNKIRK. FRENCH PREMIER BROADCASTS FINAL APPEAL TO AMERICA. GERMANS TAKE PARIS. Just the place for 'em. RUSSIANS OCCUPY PART OF POLAND BUT REAFFIRM NEUTRALITY. Now, that's a neat one." Penfold paused, glancing at his companion over the top of his eyeglasses.

Was he not aware that Olivio was too attached to his own concerns to share his interest in such distant foolish events?

As if reading the dwarf's mind, Penfold squinted at several pages before continuing. He wondered what the world would be like after this next war. He thought of what had followed the last one. The loss of civility, the orgy of materialism, the lack of time for dalliance and purposeless conversation. He sighed and turned to the Markets page.

"Aha, there we are. Here's something for you, old boy. WAR BRINGS BOOM IN COTTON FUTURES."

The dwarf leaned forward.

"BUT EGYPT INTENDS TO STOP PROFITEERING," Penfold read. "Should hope so."

"Profiteering?" cried the dwarf, shocked. "Does the army not require uniforms? Are these brave men to burn by day and freeze by night? Profiteering, they call it? What is an honest man to do?" He was astounded again by the alarming innocence of his friend, long ago his own employer when the dwarf was a barman in Nanyuki at the old White Rhino Hotel.

"Here's something on the lighter side," said Penfold. "Fifteenth installment of Agatha Christie's *Ten Little Niggers*. Would you like me to read it to you? It's not too long today . . ."

"Ah, I think not, just for the moment, my lord, if you don't mind."

"Here's Saffron now." Penfold spilled his gin as he folded the *Egyptian Gazette*. "My, my."

"Are you off to a dancing lesson, my child?" said the dwarf when Saffron, her figure promising as a ripe peach, bent to kiss her father. A new perfume, he noticed.

"No, Father, that's not what she's doing!" cried the twins as one. "She's going to a dance."

"Shouldn't you girls be doing your French?" snapped Saffron. "It's almost bedtime."

She smiled and kissed the older man's cheek. "Good evening, Lord Penfold. Yes, Papa, I'm going to a charity thing for one of Gwenn Rider's causes. See if I can help. She asked me to come along." She moved from side to side and the skirt of her lavender silk dress swirled with her. "Do you like my dress?"

"Too lovely, my dear." She was not dressed and perfumed for a ladies' charity tea. But Saffron was always careful, Olivio was certain, not to tell her father a direct lie. He himself tried to accord his children the same respect, whenever possible. No doubt the event would be crawling with hard-drinking young British officers, wild and randy from the front.

"Speaking of Gwenn, I believe young Wellington's about back from England," added Penfold. "Should be any day now. I saw some of his Hussars lifting a glass between chukkas at the Club." The dwarf watched Saffron for her reaction to this alarming news, but he had taught her too well.

"Oh, my," said Rosemary to Cardamom, raising her eyebrows and batting her eyes.

Dr. Hänger's dark, almost black eyes glared up at her across the top of his surgical mask as Gwenn reached towards the tray of instruments offered by the nurse. Deferring, she withdrew her hand and watched the Swiss orthopedist select a long scalpel, one of his personal instruments, period-ically sent to Sölingen for resharpening. He made the final incision near the base of the child's spine. "Ach! German steel," he muttered to himself, nodding sharply.

Even shrouded in cap and gown and mask, August Hänger's presence was distinct. Long furry white sideburns and knobby cheekbones framed the peaked dark eyebrows that were set beneath the three deep lines that crossed his forehead. Rectangular gold spectacles pinched his prominent beak-like nose. A short angular man, even in the surgery he wore black wing-tipped shoes. The white collar of his shirt, tall and stiff as porcelain, emerged from his gown.

Gwenn resented his manner but respected his expertise. She followed with admiration as the Swiss specialist worked to straighten the young girl's back. He was equally adept with muscle, cartilage and bone, delicate as an angel with nerves and vessels, celebrated for his "good hands," sure and never hes-itating. Once the human skin was opened, Hänger worked with an intensity of concentration that Gwenn had never seen. Not in a surgery, not in war-time, not in making love. He delighted in complicated cases.

Schooled in Heidelberg and Zürich, contemptuous of lesser educations, he took no interest in the training of younger physicians. Whenever pos-sible, the senior doctor preferred to operate alone. Increasingly, however, he was accepting Gwenn Rider into his surgery at King Fuad Hospital to assist with difficult cases. At first, she knew, he did so only to honor the insistent recommendation of the physician's most important patient here in Cairo: the man who had lured Hänger to Egypt, her small friend, Olivio Alavedo. But the doctor was an old man, over seventy, and she sensed he was wary of his own fatigue. A man of merciless punctuality, he also ap-preciated her respect for his schedule.

Dr. Hänger held out his arms. The nurse pulled off his blood-slick gloves. He washed his hands, dried them, then flexed the fingers of both hands, rapidly curling and uncurling them, before snapping them like gunshots, a ceremony that concluded every operation. Gwenn knew the surgeon used to suffer from arthritis. In the desert air of Egypt, he had found relief from the stiffening damp of Switzerland. Vinegar mixed with warm water and lemon juice was his favored regimen.

The nurse opened the door. Two Egyptian orderlies removed the gurney and the girl.

"Join me, my child," Hänger said to Gwenn, not unkindly for one so severe. He removed his cap and replaced his gown with a perfectly pressed white cotton coat, so starched, she thought, that it could have stood on its own. Save for a narrow ruff of even white hair that met his sideburns, his head was bald. Together, they set off on his rounds.

"I am concerned," he said in the corridor, his hands locked behind his back as they walked, "concerned about your friend."

"Olivio?"

"Yes, Herr Alavedo. He is, ah, he is zo much himself."

"Of course," said Gwenn, already uncomfortable.

"He has stopped my regime," said Hänger, ignoring her. "No more does he rest and eat as I direct. No more does he abstain. No more does he exercise and stretch. If he continues so, his body like a clamp will tighten. Though he has the will of a giant and the sexual mission of a youth, for a dwarf he is old, more than old, ancient, fifty-five. Ze little men cannot live so long. All the distortions of his body, from his twisted feet to his bent neck, the lordosis, everything, should have killed him long ago. Now, he understands pain." The doctor paused, as if expecting Gwenn to speak.

"Will you help him, *Frau Doktor* Rider? Will you tell your dwarf to obey me?"

"I cannot tell Mr. Alavedo what to do," she said as they stopped at the first patient's bed. "Who can? But I will speak to him, of course."

Visiting briefly, they passed from patient to patient.

At the end of one corridor, Gwenn paused to spend time with an elderly amputee. Hänger tapped one foot impatiently, then drew her aside.

"You must learn not to be so sentimental." Exasperation crept into the doctor's normally steady voice. "Remember: we are all of us dying. Zience, not zympathy, is a doctor's business." He paused near the desk of the floor nurse.

"Matron," he said to the apprehensive woman, "your ward again is filthy. Everywhere I see it. Dust. Disorder. Have this floor scrubbed at once." He turned to Gwenn. "These natives are useless. Useless."

The two surgeons reached the foot of the bed of an English soldier. His pelvis and hips were in heavy plaster. His left leg was raised in traction.

"Morning, sir, ma'am," said the young man with determined cheerfulness. "Thanks for patching me up."

"Not at all," said Hänger, almost smiling, glancing at the uniform that

hung on a hook by the door. "My pleasure. How did this happen to you?
There is no fighting yet."

"Our scout car rolled over in a steep wadi, then bumped all the way
down to the bottom. Lucky it wasn't worse."

"Sounds like reconnaissance duty," said Hänger. For once he was unhurried. He examined the surgical plaster, reminded by the pelvic wound
of another operation, sixteen years before.

The Nazi leader Hermann Göring, shot in the groin by the *Landespolizei*
during the Hitler Putsch in Munich in 1923, had been rushed across the
border in secrecy to a clinic in Austria. August Hänger, himself half
German, though long resident in Switzerland, had been vacationing with
an old colleague in Innsbruck. He was proud to help save the celebrated
aviator of the Great War, the ace who had shot down twenty-two French
and British and American aircraft, the commander of Baron von Richth-
ofen's own squadron. It had been a delicate operation: one testicle lost, one
saved. Now a field marshall and the commander of the Luftwaffe, the
distinguished Nazi pilot had remained appreciative, and occasionally in
touch. Apparently he was interested in the ancient art of Egypt.

"You must be in armor?" the doctor added.

"Yes, sir," said the lad with pride. "Seventh Hussars, part of Seventh
Armored now. All part of the new Eighth Army. They've just had us out
testing the new Dingos."

"Daimlers, no?" said Hänger, taking his time while Gwenn adjusted the
cable of the traction and tried not to listen.

"Right you are, sir, armored scout cars, and straight off the boat."

"How are they?"

"Bit top-heavy, and thirsty on the petrol, but nippy enough and pretty
tough," said the soldier, eager to talk. "And hot as a baker's oven in the
sun. I'd rather be on horseback."

Ready to move on, hating the idea of young men in uniform, Gwenn
hesitated as the two men spoke. She was surprised by the doctor's interest.
Liking the boy, she thought of Wellington, fearing what would happen to
him once the war came to Egypt.

"Where were you when it happened?" continued Hänger.

"Up near Bir Bayly . . ."

"Really?" said the surgeon. "Really? That far west?"

"Yes, sir, we've been scouting and mapping the desert near Cyrenaica, right up to the Libyan border, trying to sort out all the soft sandy parts from the hard rocky bits that will support trucks and armor. Almost got it done. Sometimes we even see the Italians watching us, just across the wire. The chaps say one day we'll be going on an Eyetie hunt, instead of chasing those little desert gazelles."

"Splendid, young man," said Hänger. "Splendid. An 'Eyetie Hunt!' Doctor Rider and I will examine you again tomorrow."

"That's it, then, Doctor," sighed Gwenn, eager to get home, anxious to sit with Denby while he had his dinner.

"For today," said Hänger, walking slowly down the hall with his hands behind his back, occasionally nodding to passing orderlies and nurses. "For today. But when this war comes to Africa, these surgeries will be going all night, stopping only to wash them out. You'll see. Men will be lying along both walls of these corridors, waiting for us."

"Good evening, Marko." Gwenn smiled at the Maltese head waiter as she hurried into a private dining room at the Gezira Sporting Club. Hating to be late, she had changed for dinner at the hospital, hurriedly cleaning away the smell of blood and antiseptic before slipping into her evening dress. She'd done her hair and lipstick in the car, thinking of her sons and gossiping with Omar as he hurtled along Shari Qasr al-Ayni and across the bridge to the large island in the Nile.

She was thrilled that Wellington had come home from England that morning, although now he was that much closer to the fighting that was coming. Her son was proud and handsome in his new uniform, and she had tried to make him feel that she was delighted, too.

Giscard met her at the door. Elegant and assured, the Frenchman welcomed her with a quick smile.

"We were just sitting down, trésor," he said, no reproach in his voice as he brushed her cheek with a kiss. "How charming you look. Let me present you to our guests."

"Of course," said Gwenn, knowing how important these evenings were to Giscard, and that later they'd be going on to a charity party of hers. "Sorry I'm late, but some operations never seem to end."

"I'm certain you did your best." Giscard smiled again and led Gwenn by the arm, introducing her with care.

Gwenn barely heard the names. She was still dispelling the endless con-

centration of the operating room. She tried to do her duty while she and
Giscard toured the room arm in arm. Catching her breath, she finished a
glass of champagne and went to her seat at the far end of the long
table.

"*Ravi, Madame*," said Mustafa Bey Hafiz, the Inspector General of the
Service des Antiquités, as he held her chair. At first Gwenn thought that
the heavy man was bowing to her in deference. Then she recalled that he
was permanently stooped. The arched weight gathered on his back was
nearly as substantial as his belly. Taking his seat, leaning close to her until
she smelled his sweet cologne, the Egyptian immediately pressed her with
conversation. She was careful not to reveal her antipathy.

Sometimes, at moments like this, she felt that perhaps Anton was right
after all, that all this tedious socializing meant nothing. A drink or a
breakfast by a camp fire, or even sharing a silence outdoors, was worth
more than all the elegance and talk of Cairo. She recalled, before they were
married, lying on a blanket with Anton between two cedars near their fly
camp, watching the big tuskers trek across from Mount Kenya to the
Aberdares. Yellow wild flowers and tiny forest mushrooms grew right before their noses, seeming tall as lampposts. From time to time they heard
small trees snap like twigs as the elephant eased slowly through the forest
all around them. From nearby came the deep relaxed rumbling of an elephant's digestion. A cow entered the clearing before them with slow swinging steps, shepherding her stumbling calf with gentle stroking movements
of her trunk.

Gwenn was troubled by what she had said to Anton when she blamed
him for Wellington's signing up. She ignored the chatter of the guests as
her mind wandered. At the far end of the table, the French ambassador
rose and began a toast, something about the long friendship between France
and Egypt, beginning with the invasion of Napoleon.

Gwenn knew that the same rough combative streak that she had de-
nounced in Anton had saved her own life more than once. She thought of
the moment twenty years ago that she tried always to forget: hearing her
screams one night in the passageway on the boat to Kenya, Anton had
burst into her cabin as a huge Irishman was raping her. Never having seen
her before, Anton, eighteen, had seized the big man around his head,
twisting violently until the rapist withdrew screaming from her body.
Anton had defended himself with his gypsy knife. She still remembered
the horror of the Irishman's pale sweating body, matted with moist red

hair and belted with fat and muscle, hammering her down against the steel deck.

Later, she had lain curled against the wall of her bunk. Shaking, withdrawn and alone, she'd thought with astonishment of how the boy had saved her. He had risked everything for her without hesitation. A short time later, he had returned to her cabin with a bucket and soap and a towel, urging her to bolt the door after him. The next day, awkward and shy, he had avoided her when she saw him carrying a stack of filthy trays in the steerage dining cabin. She dreaded having to relive the horror, so she missed the first opportunity to thank him properly. When finally she spoke to him, she had begun to cry. "I'm Anton Rider," he'd said, twisting a dish towel in his hands. Unable to speak, bursting with shame, she'd turned away and left him. Several days later, the Irishman and his brother had attacked Anton and dragged him into the donkey boiler room and burned him against a steampipe. Only much later did Anton tell her how he'd received that scar.

Light applause and the clinking of glasses interrupted Gwenn's thoughts.

"And how is your Monsieur de Neuville's dig progressing, Dr. Rider?" asked Mustafa Bey eagerly. The Inspector General turned towards her in his chair, bending over her like a heavy bird eating seeds. "Have they found a new chamber?"

"I'm not sure," Gwenn replied. Giscard, like most archeologists, hated to discuss such details until the work was complete. And this was a man with whom to be careful. Not only was his position one of influence, as the functionary responsible for the oversight of all permits and foreign concessions, but he was rumored to have self-serving, even corrupt interests in the same field. No doubt he was already fully informed by the resident government inspector at the dig.

She glanced down the table and saw Giscard smiling at the lady on his left. How distinguished he looked, Gwenn thought. Very much her own type of man: slender, with full grey hair and a lined intelligent face, and a man who did not have to be preoccupied with making money. She admired Giscard's scholarship, and his knowledge of the world. "I haven't had time to visit the ruins," she said. "Things are so busy at the hospital."

"I believe the land adjacent to this dig belongs to a curious friend of yours, this Olivio Fonseca Alavedo. Am I not correct?" The inspector's face seemed to shine, as if about to pour with sweat.

"I believe so," said Gwenn, observing an expression of distaste. Was her little friend the cause, or was the food? "The bisque is not to your taste, Inspector?"

"Doctor Hänger denies me shellfish, you know," said the Egyptian, toying with his spoon. "These Swiss are so careful."

"Of course," Gwenn said, wishing she were at home with Denby and Wellington. "He'll be back here with his regiment before you know it," Anton had said reassuringly the day Wellie had left for England. "It's your fault," she had replied, not altogether fairly, knowing Anton was still the same man she'd chosen. "And he'll end up useless, just like you." Two days later, Anton had left on safari to Somaliland. Catching her thoughts, regretting her words, Gwenn heard her neighbor talk at her again.

"But about our host's work. Egypt is fortunate to have independent scholars like Monsieur de Neuville here to assist us so generously. The Louvre will take one or two interesting pieces, with our compliments, and the rest will always belong to Cairo." The Bey smiled. "But today, alas, everyone's attention seems to be turning from civilization to war." He wagged one short overly manicured finger. "And if this war ever visits us here in Egypt, you will be busier still, Dr. Rider."

"Easy, Bingham," said Wellington, looking out over the crowded dance floor of the Casino Loutfallah, searching the crowd for a particular girl. He had returned that morning from training camp in England, and was proud of his new rig, long tight trousers in Cherrypicker red and trim tunic jacket scalloped at the back. "It's Leap Year, and in your condition any of these NAAFI girls could make you hers forever."

"Right you are. Chap has to be careful." Bingham's bright eyes darted around the room. A slender gangly young man, he was already bald. He took the drink offered him by Michael Gates.

"They say the dollies always look their best when you come back from the blue," Bingham continued, not taking his eyes from the floor. "Sort of like those lake mirages we always hope are real." He spilled his drink as two dancers jostled him at the edge of the floor. "Look at them. WAAFS, WRNS, ATS, nurses, all the girls of all the services, all of them out here trying to look after us and bring one of us home alive to mum and dad. More big game from Africa."

Downing their gins, the three Hussars circled the edge of the dance floor until they stood near the band and ordered fresh drinks from a passing bar boy. Behind the band, a broad banner proclaimed the evening: LEAP YEAR BALL OF THE WOMEN'S HEALTH IMPROVEMENT ASSOCIATION. A leader of the struggle against tuberculosis in Egypt, the Association was a cause close to the heart of Wellington's mother. But the young soldiers were not here because of their interest in suppressing communicable lung diseases in the villages. On the opposite wall, another banner urged the dancers: LEND TO DEFEND- BUY BRITISH DEFENCE BONDS- THROUGH BARCLAYS BANK (DOMINION COLONIAL AND OVERSEAS).

"Always prefer these AT bints myself," said Bingham eagerly, handing his drink to Wellington. "Bashing away at those old teleprinters at GHQ all day gives 'em useful fingers. Haw, haw!" He squared his thin shoulders and sauntered over to a pair of uniformed ladies. One appeared to be either crying or laughing hysterically. Wellington poured Bingham's drink into his own glass and set down the empty on the edge of the bandstand.

Just then Wellington saw his mother dancing on the far side of the crowded floor. She'd cried that morning when he came home. Looking more fresh and young than she had been recently, Gwenn Rider was doing a two-step with her French friend. She seemed to be enjoying herself. A bit annoyed, Wellie was glad his father was on safari.

The tune changed to a jitterbug, and the dancers changed with the music. Gwenn and others of her generation left the floor. The women collected their pocket books and searched for free tables. The men looked for drinks and lit cigars. Bingham led the hysterical lady onto the floor. She matched him enthusiastically as he jitterbugged in his tight scarlet trousers. The crown of his head glistened.

Wellington saw Saffron. She was even more lovely than he remembered when he'd thought about her in England, no longer the gawky little creature he had known when she was young. "Leave me alone," he used to say when she followed him around too much. He had even avoided her at dancing school.

The girl stood between two columns across the room, engrossed with her companion. A tall lieutenant wearing the chequered insignia of the Scots Guards, the officer appeared to be a few years older than Wellington. The sandy-haired man threw back his head and laughed. Wellington felt sick as Saffron smiled and laughed gaily with him. Covering her laugh, she raised the fingertips of her right hand to her mouth and touched her upper lip with the tip of her tongue. She seemed to be steaming.

Wellington stared, hardly breathing as they danced, the Englishman a trifle stiff, Saffron as if the music were written for her. The skirt of her lavender dress swished about her legs with every step. Each movement seemed to emphasize her chest.

Aware of Wellington's gaze, Saffron was careful how she danced with her companion. She knew Wellington would be divine in uniform, and he was. Sometimes she thought he would never look at her except as an annoying playmate. A little jealousy might be helpful, she thought, but if she appeared too involved with her escort, Wellington might look elsewhere. For years she had admired him, the handsome carefree older boy who always seemed to lead his friends and hers. She remembered one awkward moment when they were young. Unable to afford the lunch treat that all their friends were sharing on the Tea Island in the Zoological Gardens, Wellington had said he had already eaten. They had exchanged an understanding glance, sharing the truth of it. Realizing how hungry he must be, she'd thought of paying for his, but knew he'd rather starve. Except for that red hair, he was so like his father.

The tune changed to a crab-walk. Wellington saw Bingham's girl clap her hands ecstatically and lead him in a series of sharp sideways rushes across the floor as she taught her long-legged Hussar the latest step.

Saffron's lieutenant smiled engagingly and looked at the other dancers and threw up his hands. The two left the dance floor holding hands. Saffron stood to one side as her escort joined the throng struggling to get drinks from the bar. She stood alone for a moment, looking at the ceiling, but thinking of her father. Would he ever accept a suitor like Wellington, very likable but without fortune or position?

Wellington walked across the floor directly to her as the music changed again. A fox trot, *Mountain Greenery*.

"Will you dance with me, Saffron?"

"Wellie! You're back!" she cried, as if startled, pleasure in her eyes. They kissed on the cheek.

"Shall we dance?" He seemed desperate to steal her before the Guards officer returned.

She hesitated, glancing towards the bar as Wellington took her hand.

"I love you in your new uniform," Saffron said, liking the pressure of his hand on her back. She felt herself catching the excitement of the evening, the extra intensity the war had brought to every party, everyone keen to make the most of each moment. For many of her friends, the present had become more important than the future. She was lucky, she thought, to be with someone she knew so well.

"I love you in that dress," Wellington said, his cheek nearly touching hers.

She allowed him to hold her closely.

Wellington closed his eyes and smelled her light perfume. Her thick hair swung against his cheek. Her heavy breasts touched his chest.

The lieutenant stood staring at them with a drink in either hand as the band played *I'm Getting Sentimental Over You*.

— 2 —

"Gently, you fools!" ordered the dwarf from his brocade cushion under the shade of the broad tent canopy. At his feet rested a copper tray bearing a frosty pitcher of fresh lemon juice and dark honey, proud products of his nearby farms in the valley of the Nile. From the striped Arab tent behind him, he heard the impatient rustling of a lady's garments. No hurry, he thought. A little waiting would enhance her ardor. It was hardship enough to be away from the pleasures of Cairo, from the intrigues and opportunities that enriched each day at the Cataract Café. Here in the wild, with only wretched villages nearby, a gentleman was obliged to bring his necessaries with him.

Jamila, the dwarf's favorite in a number of regards, seemed suitable for this adventure in the field. A wise resourceful lady who appreciated even his most peculiar courtesies, she would not fuss and trouble him when he had other obligations. A Circassian, like the finest of her class, she was superior in one most accommodating way. She enjoyed an unrivalled command over every part of her body, however intimate, as if each muscle and organ were an independent servant waiting to execute her will. Though smooth and soft to the touch, beneath the skin she was firm and limber as an adder. Cocking her hips, Jamila could bend a thin gold coin in her navel with one ripple and snap of her belly.

The sweating Nubians toiled before him in the desert sun. Some emerged from the long sloping trench with baskets of sand and rock slung from poles across their shoulders. Others shoveled sand against coarse wire-mesh screens while an overseer watched for any precious fragments that might not pass the grid. Near the end of the trench that was close to Olivio's tent, two men worked at a more delicate task under the dwarf's own eye.

"Gently," he called out with ferocity, "or I will bury your children in the sand. Watch them, Tariq!" He thought of what his enemies would do if they could catch him now. All that he had achieved in Egypt would be lost: lands, position, influence, fortune, the very future of his line.

With measured taps of large wooden mallets, the two men drove the flattened ends of shovels between the stones that formed a sunken wall along one side of the trench. Tariq stood behind them, slapping a *qurbash* against his thigh with sharp cracks. Expanding the entrance, the workers extracted a stone from its place, first one end thumping a bit forward, then the other.

Like every man working on the excavation at Al Lahun, these two laborers came from Shoboka, Tariq's ancient village in the Sudan. Tariq had been careful to register each man with the Sudan Agency in Cairo, as the law required. But a higher and less forgiving authority concerned Tariq more than did those distant bureaucrats. The massive Nubian was responsible to his small master. He was answerable for the work of these men and, even more, for their discretion.

Olivio craned forward, his mouth slightly open as the first stone came free. How long he had waited for this private excavation. He moistened his lips.

The shorter man set down his blade and mallet and seized the large protruding stone in both hands as his companion wedged it free. The muscles on his broad bare back rose and hardened into thick black cords when he took the entire weight of the stone across his arms. Dust and grit clung to his sweaty shoulders like a sand-grey mantle.

Just then the second worker cried out and jumped back from the wall.

"Allah, spare me!" the man screamed, hurling his shovel at the ground. "A scorpion!"

Olivio saw the lobster-like arachnid slithering on the sand between the two men. Its jointed tail curled up to strike. Its claws arched in two trembling crescents.

With the speed of a cobra, Tariq flicked his rhinoceros hide whip. The long horsehair lash snapped like a gunshot. It caught the scorpion amidships and flung its torn body in the air. The short man dropped the stone and screamed.

His right foot crushed, the man collapsed back against the near wall of the trench and slid to the ground moaning and hollering.

"Have this fool taken to the clinic in Faiyum," said the dwarf with bitter reluctance. He was annoyed by this untimely nonsense. "But be certain, Tariq, on your life be certain he speaks to no man of how and where this happened."

The dwarf put aside his irritation with this interruption to his work. He rose with a groan and entered the tent. He closed his eyelids while he inhaled the rich perfume that enveloped him.

Not at all embarrassed by his hard protruding belly and low scrotum, Olivio raised both arms above his head and permitted Jamila to undress him. He reflected on what he had discovered behind the wall. It was a tomb, for the ancients favored burial here on the west bank of the Nile, where the sun began its nightly journey across the underworld.

The dwarf enjoyed breathing the cool dead air of the tomb, lifting a lamp as the shadows danced across the relics, unwrapping a swaddled mummy and touching bones that were older than Rome, lifting in his hands some small treasure, jewelry or sculpture, scarab or carving, above all the image of the dwarf-god, Bes. While tiny creatures, lizards and beetles and rodents, scuttled about in the cool shadows of the past, he himself touched immortality.

He lay face down on the divan while Jamila straddled his thick yellow body and rubbed almond oil into his aching flesh and joints. From time to time she indulged herself and teased him with some arcane arousing gesture.

Like so many things that developed into something richer, this dig had begun innocently enough. While extending an irrigation canal on his new farm at the edge of the desert near Al Lahun, his men had unearthed a few stones of an ancient wall. Recognizing its antiquity, Olivio immediately had stopped the work and directed Tariq to procure ten trusted clansmen from the Sudan. He wanted men without relationships in Egypt, men who could be isolated in their own work camp, and fed and paid beyond their experience. To keep them in camp, they had been provided with two women, to cook, to wash their robes, and to attend to their other needs.

A rectangular, almost square mastaba, it was not nearly as large as certain of the important tombs he had visited and studied in the burial grounds of Memphis. The secret structure was late enough to be of stone, not mud brick, but early enough to be a flat-walled flat-roofed rectangle, not a pyramid, perhaps from the middle of the third millennium before Christ, Olivio estimated with rough scholarship. But close enough to the truth, he thought, and a prize important enough to be priceless, yet not so great as to invite disaster, provided he was careful and blessed with luck.

Some, he knew, particularly his dearest friend, Lord Penfold, would protest in horror at his scheme to make this treasure his. But what else was an honest man to do? Step aside while others made it theirs?

He thought of how his own ancestors had looted the temples of Goa and shipped their art home to Lisbon. Were not the capitals, the museums, the great houses of Europe and the Americas filled with the looted bones of every civilization? Were not London and Paris the very graveyards of the world's stolen art? Had not the ancient Egyptians themselves, Menes and Amenemhet and Rameses, pillaged the lands of their enemies in Nubia and as far as their armies could march or sail? In today's Cairo, who was more corrupt than the government that would seize these treasures? And what if now, in war, the filthy Italians or, worse, the distant Huns, were to invade Egypt? What then? What would they not steal? Already, German archeologists, nothing more than grave-robbers with degrees and round spectacles, had sacked the wreckage of Troy more thoroughly than Agamemnon himself, disinterring and laying out the ancient ruin stone by stone, digging and sifting it, meter by meter, while wooden crates stood by in rows, already stencilled with the word *Berlin*. Why should Olivio Fonseca Alavedo not preserve what he found on his own dearly purchased land? Why not?

The dwarf dozed as Jamila's fingers lightened their touch and released him into repose. But his mind woke him after a bit, sensing that there was more to do. He rose, his body looser, more youthful after the attentions of Jamila. He splashed himself with water from a bowl, then pulled on a robe and wriggled his feet into a pair of brocade slippers. He stepped out and stood under the fly of the tent while his eyes adjusted to the light and his staff observed that he was once again in command.

"*Ya bey.*" Tariq bowed and preceded his master as he walked slowly down the trench toward the tomb. "You will find the men at work." He raised the heavy canvas tarpaulin that covered the doorway and Alavedo entered the musty tomb.

"Leave me," said the dwarf. The lamplight cast a huge shadow of his round head upon the wall.

Tariq drove the two Nubian diggers out through the gloom and left his master inside.

Already, with his own hands, Olivio Alavedo had cleaned the low wide chair that had reposed at the far end of the mastaba. Centered in the straight seat back was a carving of a dwarf with the head of a lion, the god Bes in its strong protective form. How suitable, he thought. The short legs of the chair, almost comfortable for a man of his own height, had the bent knees and clawed feet of a lion. He had cleaned, and filled with oil, the four stone mortuary lamps they had found at the corners of the sarcophagus.

The dwarf seated himself in the boxwood and ebony chair, now artfully reinforced with molded boards and fitted leather strapping. He was astonished, nonetheless, that it still might hold even his modest weight. He leaned back. He folded his small hands in his lap, like a pharaoh receiving at court.

When last, thousands of years ago, had a man sat in this sepulchral throne? When, if ever, had these lamps cast light?

If he were younger, he would already have opened and examined every treasure of this tomb. The weapons, for both war and sport, the instruments of medicine, music and astronomy, the games, the garments, every furnishing and ornament and jewel, all would have already felt his touch, been revived by his attentions. But now, despite the cruel limit of his own time, he approached nearly everything with patience and preparation, whether it was a matter of the senses or the purse, love or revenge.

Each day he awoke in his tent, like Saladin or Alexander on campaign, ignoring the stiffness and pains that wracked his body like their wounds. If alone, he waited for the sun to warm the eastern wall of the heavy black-and-white-striped fabric, his mind scheming with the promise of the day's discovery. Tariq would bring him his first rich coffee and, when he was adhering to Dr. Hänger's orders, his first juice, the pulpy nectar of his own mangoes. If he were attended, he would tickle Jamila's belly with his toes, and she would know with which enlivening ceremony to begin the morning.

Once in the tomb, it was his idea each day to bring the mastaba to life, or somehow to make real the ancient vision of the after-life. The mastaba itself was equipped with everything required to build around the deceased a second fully equipped existence. Why should this existence not be his? With what genius, with what energy, had the ancients not labored to see that each sense would be satisfied as it had been in life itself? Flagons of wine would refresh the sense of taste. Incense would again satisfy the nose. To the extent possible, the dwarf intended, and sought, to personify these resurrections. When here, he intended to live as the deceased himself had intended to live again. He would relish the art, indeed all their arts. He would dress in the garments intended to be worn. He would contrive to drink the wine and smell the odors of life and death. Breaking the hard wax seal in the bottom of one flagon, he had found a thin red crust, the very distillation of distillation. If a few drops of essence, taken from the anal gland of a civet cat, could produce one gallon of precious perfume, why could not this preserved maroon essence yield, with a dash of water from a desert well, one sip of wine?

Rather than strip and despoil this ruin, as other men would do, Olivio Fonseca Alavedo would make it live. Where other men, fancying themselves archeologists or scientists, scholars or collectors, approached antiquities with an academic eye and a desiccated spirit, he would himself enjoy them as their creators would have wished.

About two things, however, he had a higher curiosity: how had these wizards intended to revive their sexual potency? And what secrets had they which might defeat or delay the relentless progression of his own deformities? If they understood the heavens, the fulcrum and the brain, why not also lordosis and talepsis, the blight and bane of dwarves?

Today would be a special treat. He would be pitting his mind against the masters of the past.

Olivio wiggled to the front of the chair, then reached to the top of the nearby chest. There lay a rectangular board, inlaid with small ovals of ivory and ebony, each one with a rounded depression or basin at its center. Resting on this board was a box of some light wood, possibly camphor. The box was filled with ten round stones of two different shades, dark and light. Inside the lid of the box were painted designs representing the game to be played with the stones. The object seemed to be to finish with one stone at either end of the board.

The dwarf laid the board across the arms of the chair. He set out the stones and slowly began to play, tapping his tiny feet together with excitement and frustration as the contest revived his mind and he challenged the intellects of the greatest of ancient civilizations.

On stag, wrapped in his sheepskin greatcoat, Wellington sat on the hard sand with his back against a rear wheel of the Rolls Royce. He was watching the immense desert sky, recalling what his father had taught him of the heavens, waiting for the eastern stars to disappear as the first light softened the cold night. He pulled on his cigarette, against the rules of night sentry duty, but still tolerated since they were not yet engaged.

He cupped the friendly tobacco in his hands to conceal the glow, thinking again of the last time he'd seen Saffron in Cairo. She said it was best not to meet at the Café. He'd met her at Groppi's on Shari al-Manakh. She was elegant and grown-up in a smart French frock. Her olive skin was a warm contrast to the cool white of the dress. They bribed their way to a fine table against the wall in the garden. They sat sipping Pimm's and nibbling pastries, finally holding hands as he tried to explain to her why he was so excited about his regiment and its long history in Egypt.

Then the shock, worse than a mine going off under your Rolls. He glanced at the mirror behind Saffron's head and saw a new party enter the fashionable restaurant: old Lord Penfold, and beside him, being ushered in with as much fuss as if he were King Faruq himself, Mr. Alavedo, on a rare outing from his own Café. Had the dwarf known, and come to teach them both a lesson? Had Groppi's called him? Or was it just the gods of chance? For an instant, their eyes met in the mirror. The dwarf was not startled. Nor did he reveal anything. He just stared evenly into the looking glass with that grey unblinking all-seeing eye. Wellington felt diminished, as if he were shrinking inside his own uniform. He knew that although Mr. Alavedo liked him well enough, and indeed loved his mother and father, he did not think a soldier, young and uneducated and penniless, suitable for his daughter. Wellington released Saffron's hand and hurried to the entrance. "Won't you join us, sir?" he said to Mr. Alavedo. And the two men did. Lord Penfold with awkward friendship, Mr. Alavedo with calm distance. Wellie smiled as he recalled Mr. Alavedo hectoring the waiter over the temperature of his *tilleul*, demanding that boiling water be poured directly onto the lime tea. And he remembered Saffron casting her charm over all three men as she set them at their ease. Wellie was pleased that he had not shirked, that he had risen and faced the matter directly, as his father had always taught him.

The cigarette burned his fingers. Wellington wormed it into the sand. He watched a slim grey and brown lizard emerge from a cluster of rocks. The animal switched its head from side to side, then scuttled off. Wellie rose, shivering, and relieved himself. Only Orion and Ursa Major and Gemini were still sharp to the eye.

Quite an honor, he thought. After seven months, the real war had finally begun in Europe. In an hour, maybe two, he and his mates would fire the first shots of the war in North Africa. Meanwhile, German columns were racing across France, the British Expeditionary Force was being pressed back towards the Channel, and Europe swarmed with refugees.

Yesterday morning the 11th Hussars had moved out from their forward base south of Sidi Barrani, near an old camel track junction now known as Picadilly Circus. Last night, one day after Italy declared war on England, the Hussars had crossed into Libya. First, the sappers had cut through the Italian fence, a two-hundred-mile entanglement sixteen feet high and thirty feet wide with triple rows of concertina barbed wire attached to metal stakes, originally intended to contain the rebellious Senussi tribes and stop gun-running from Egypt into Libya. At dawn, the Cherrypickers would be attacking *Ridotta Maddalena*, one of a chain of Italian strongpoints scattered across Cyrenaica from Fort Capuzzo near the coast to the oasis of Kufra in the far south.

Fourteen more armored cars, both Morrises and the older heavier Rolls Royces, left-overs from the Great War, were gathered nearby in the usual tight night-time laager. Clustered by troops in groups of three, black shadows against the blue-black sky, they reminded Wellington of families of elephants gathered near a waterhole, asleep on their feet. He wondered what it had been like the last time his regiment had fought in Egypt, against Napoleon a hundred and forty years ago. Six hundred men, galloping spur to spur, hurling themselves at the French dragoons, breaking Napoleon's cavalry, sabres slashing, horses crashing down, then, most officers lost, turning and gathering without command and charging back through the scattered French to finish the job.

"I'll take over, Rider," said Lieutenant Mosby-Brown, quietly at his side, surprisingly silent in the field for a home-bred Englishman. Sporting a fly-whisk and mustache, the young officer wore a paisley scarf and heavy tan corduroys. "You start the brew-up. We'll kick the lads up in ten."

"Right, ho." Hungry as a hyena, Wellington took a pile of scrub brush that was lashed to his Rolls, splashed some petrol on it and started a small blaze in a pit he had already scraped into the desert with a spade from the car. He used a bayonet to open tins of bacon. He did not want to damage the tip of his *choori*, the slender gypsy knife his father had given him the day he signed up. "My own step-father gave me this in '15, the day he left for France. Told me it would come in handy." Knowing his father loved it, Wellie had examined the blade with care, noting the hollow just before the tip. "Did it?" he'd asked. "You'll see," his father said.

Wellington threw the slabs of fatty bacon into a large pan and shoved the big black brew-tin into the edge of the flames. He set a box of precious eggs nearby.

Soon the tin was jumping with boiling water. The men stood about with khaki blankets across their shoulders, muttering "to Africa" as they peed at the edge of camp. Wellie threw handsful of tea leaves into the tin. Johnny Bingham strolled over to see how it was coming. He held a string of bangers in one hand, pinched no doubt from some other crew.

"Hopeless," said Bingham with his sharp crusty voice. "How'd you ever catch a girl, Rider? Can't even boil tea. Why didn't you start it sooner?"

"You're welcome." Wellington lifted the steaming tin from the fire by the bit of wire that hung from two holes punched at the top of the cut-off ration box, then stepped aside while the leaves settled. "Where's Gates?"

"Still sleeping under his Rolls. Reckon we'll leave him there. Maybe the Wops can wake him." Bingham knelt over the pan and tossed in the bangers. He began fiddling about with the sausages and bacon.

"Your first time in a kitchen, sir? Allow me," said one burly driver, a grey-haired sergeant with twenty years' service. He leaned over Bingham and took the fork from his hand. "You have to separate the bits of bacon there, one piece at a time, sir, that's it."

"Roll them sausages, so they're not all burned on the one side," said a gunner, wiping his hands with some sand. He'd just cleaned his Bren with an oily rag. "No, no, you have to cut 'em apart first."

"Don't let those two darlin's spoil the eggs as well," muttered a third old trooper to another, cocking his head towards the young second lieutenants. "Nice and slow with them eggs, now. These bleedin' fresh chicos will poison us even before they get us all killed."

"Worse than camp in England," said Bingham quietly to Wellington. "These old jockeys think they know it all."

"Maybe they do," said Wellington.

The men stamped their feet as they waited in line for tea. One sergeant bent down and threw two wooden matches into the brew tin to gather any floating leaves. Then they shuffled past with their enamelled tin mugs before dumping in masses of sugar and long pours of tinned condensed milk.

"Stupid sods," said one man. "How'd they expect us to carry on without any burgoo? A bloke needs porridge in his belly to do any proper fighting."

Breakfasting by troop and rank, like tables of form boys at school, scraping their mess tins clean, clutching steaming mugs between their hands for warmth, the Cherrypickers shivered and gobbled their food and smoked hungrily, aware of the old tradition of a hot meal before battle. Some older desert hands wore black wool Balaclavas over their heads against the morning cold.

Each car commander then checked his engine, his tires, his wireless, his machine gun as he waited for word to mount up. Resisting the morning, stiff as old men, some of the Rolls Royces had to be started by hand. Wellington saw Bingham turning the long crank handle that hung down between the forward springs and wheels of his Rolls. Once the engine caught, he spread open the two metal doors that covered the sand screen in front of the radiator.

Captain Blake came around, car by car, man by man, speaking in his low calm voice as he slapped a hippo-hide swagger stick against his tall cavalry boots.

"How's she running? . . . Fifteen miles to Fort Maddalena . . . Then we hold up while the air boys pay them a breakfast call . . . Keep in formation as we go in . . . First six cars circle to the back . . . You'll have the sun in your eyes . . . This should give 'em a bit of a start . . . Old Benito thought he was going to get the kick-off . . . First blood . . . Spent five years prepping for this show . . . Right lads . . . Whips out. Saddle up and good luck . . . Tally ho!"

Good man, Blake, Wellington thought. Said to be a wizard at polo.

The rim of the rising sun was huge and blood-orange through the dust that stormed up behind them. The first troop, three armored cars of A Squadron, 11th Hussars, churned through the gritty desert. The surface of the limestone terrain changed often, switching from soft and sandy to hard or stony, first flat, then rough or undulating. The colors varied with the light, yellows and tans and greys and browns and russets, but the air was always clean, somehow fresher even than at sea, and in the mornings, cool.

Wellington gripped the edge of the bouncing steel turret with both hands, exhilarated by the charge. His rust-colored beret with its red Cherrypicker band was tight on his forehead.

Two gazelle suddenly rose from the desert to the right. Males, perhaps two feet at the shoulder, they bolted directly in front of Wellington's car. He admired the double curves of their lyre-shaped horns as they galloped away. With their sandy-reddish-brown coats and white bellies, they reminded him of the Tommies he used to hunt with his father as a boy. He remembered the excitement of hurrying back to their camp fire in the early morning, the Thompson's gazelle slung across his father's shoulders, held in front by its thin legs.

Wellington glanced at the two vehicles to his right. Just forward in the center, the leading car approached the rocky ridge behind which they should find the Italian fort. The scout car's four wheels were hidden by the dust, like the oars of a war galley with their blades concealed beneath the water line. The box-like steel cabin bounced violently on unforgiving springs.

On the antenna near Wellington's head, like a pennant on a lance, snapped the new battle flag of the 7th Armored Division: a scarlet jerboa set in a white circle in a scarlet field. Unlike his mates, Wellington had actually seen one of the small desert rats in the flesh. As a boy, he had trapped and stuffed a jerboa himself, rather pleased at the time how he had skinned and eviscerated and dried and rebuilt the little creature. It had a long tail and extraordinarily powerful rear legs, made for jumping, rather like a wallaby or hare or miniature kangaroo. "Fine job," his father had said when he finally came home from safari. "You've got it all right but the eyes. Those things are popping out like hippo's eyes."

Wellington grinned and removed Saffron's blue silk ribbon from his pocket. He tied it about the aerial just below the flag. He remembered Saffron with her hair loose, swinging like a velvet curtain when she moved her head, sweeping his face with a thousand touches the first time he kissed her. "Such a bother," she'd murmured when he'd mentioned it. "It always gets in my eyes," she said, taking off the ribbon and tossing her head to please him. "Here, take it, Wellie. Now you have something so you won't forget me."

The cars stopped. The lieutenant jumped down and lay on his belly in a cleft in the ridge, scanning forward with long field glasses.

Suddenly the sound of engines rose from the east. In minutes a flight of Blenheims made a run at Fort Maddalena. Turning in a wide arc, the three long-nosed twin-engined light bombers came by for a second pass. Each aircraft dropped another five bombs on its way home.

"Bloody useless," said Mosby-Brown. He climbed onto his car and led the attack over the crest.

The small white fort was before them. It had thick low walls and rounded corner towers pocked with firing slits. Something between a Foreign Legion outpost and a lesser Irish castle, Wellington thought as he checked the banana-shaped magazine on his machine gun. In the bright low light, the fort's shadow ran on to the horizon. Several tents were spread before the walls. A few camels and a truck stood nearby. As the scout cars closed, men ran from the tents to a small door in the walls. Columns of dust rose where the bombs had struck home, damaging but not destroying the fortifications.

Wellington's car bounced and jarred violently across the rocky outcrops that broke the hard sand surface, then dashed around the fort. Light weapons fired from the walls. Wellington flinched, then straightened his shoulders when he saw Mosby-Brown erect in his car, gesturing orders as he advanced.

The first three cars slowed opposite the main gate. Hard desert dust churned around them, sparkling in the dawn sunlight. The Hussars closed to eighty yards and opened fire with their mounted machine guns. Squinting into the rising sun, Wellington clenched his teeth and squeezed the trigger, concentrating on the main gate itself. A group of Italian soldiers was struggling to close two heavy doors while several others knelt and fired rifles at the armored cars. Not conscious of the buck and noise of his weapon, but smelling the sharp bite of the cordite, he swung twice through the groups of Italians, seeing men fall and struggle to retreat inside. His Bren was empty. As his driver handed him up more 30-round clips, he saw a white flag rise on the wall before them.

The first battle of North Africa was over. Already the desert was warming. Wellington took off his coat. He waved at Bingham.

"Not much of a match," hollered Bingham, climbing onto Wellington's car and clapping him on the back. His eyes were shining through the grit that covered his face. "Hardly had time to get one's eye in." He took off his dusty beret and scratched his shiny scalp with both hands.

"Doubt that they'll all be like this," said Wellie.

"Don't shoot. He's no good."

The rifle cracked and echoed across the narrow rocky valley. A hundred and fifty yards away a tall massive antelope stumbled and then moved off swiftly on three legs.

"I told you once before," said Anton harshly, though he knew it was no way to speak to a client. "Never shoot unless you know you've got a kill."

"Stop telling me what to do!" screamed the heavy red-faced Oklahoman. She ejected a cartridge and reloaded her .375 with a hard slap of the bolt. "I've been hunting all my life."

"Shooting and hunting are two different things." Anton rose and checked his own rifle. "I asked you both never to shoot at a running animal unless you've already hit it. Now we've got a wounded oryx on our hands, and it's almost dark."

"If you hadn't yelled at me, I would've dropped him," the woman replied with hot anger. "You know I wanted a good oryx."

"I tried to stop you because his head's no good. His right horn's missing, probably broken off brawling for a mate."

"How could I see that from the side, in profile at this distance?"

"You didn't have to," said Anton. "I told you not to shoot." He loathed this trophy madness, and he was fed up with pandering to clients. After this nonsense, war would be a picnic.

"Don't speak to my wife like that," bawled an angry American voice behind him. The man stood, stumbling on loose rock, and wiped his face on his sleeve. "I'm paying you good money to find animals and run this damn safari in Somaliland, Rider, not to boss us around."

"Please take Mr. and Mrs. Gaines back to camp, Kieti," said Anton to the gunbearer, barely containing his anger.

He studied the rapidly disappearing antelope through his field glasses. "Can't leave a wounded animal. Have to finish what you start. This old boy's got one hoof hanging by the skin, but these oryx are tough. And he's a fine one, apart from the head. Must be four hundred pounds or more. I'll bet over two and half feet of horn. He'll run from here to the Gulf on three legs."

"Ndio," nodded Kieti.

"Let's go, Makanyanga."

Rider and the big Wakamba tracker set off at a trot. Anton knew that Makanyanga enjoyed testing his pace.

After an hour's hard dusty chase in the falling light, stumbling through thorn bush and rocky outcrops, Anton and Makanyanga came to a small pool set in a low basin of sand and stone. Anton held up a hand. The two men lay down behind an acacia bush and watched the shadows that moved in the bush across the water. There was no need to speak. The two had hunted together for years.

As they settled themselves, the last of the light vanished from the clear African sky. A yellow half moon rose behind them. Tough shooting, Anton thought. He smelled the dust and pinched the hard black pellet of a gerunuk's spoor between his fingers. He saw two brown furry points moving through the low scrub a few yards to his right. He watched the two ears twitch and turn from side to side. A bat-eared fox emerged from the scrub and slunk to the pool.

Makanyanga touched the right sleeve of Anton's bush jacket. Across the water Anton discerned a tall antelope, perhaps four feet at the shoulder. It stepped from the bush and walked forward haltingly. In the gloom its profile reminded Anton of the unicorn, whose legend the oryx is said to have spawned. Unable to make out the animal's tan and black markings, Anton saw its long ringed horn, pointed and nearly straight, outlined against the star-filled blue-black sky. The beisa oryx limped to the pool and lowered its head. The reflection of the moon was shattered as the water stirred. Anton shouldered his rifle.

Suddenly there was a rush of sound. A pale figure streaked from the bush and leaped onto the shoulder of the wounded antelope. Heavier than the lioness, the oryx stumbled forward into the water, tossing its powerful shoulders and raising its head. Anton heard the harsh coughy breathing of the lioness as it fell on its feet in the shallow water, then instantly turned with its back to the shore to face its large prey. The oryx lowered its head and drove forward, spearing the lioness in the side with its sharp horn. Growling and spitting, the lioness fell backwards with the oryx still thrusting towards her.

A large dark shadow tore from the bush with a roar that thundered low across the water. The oryx raised its head to face its new enemy. The lion reared back on its hind legs at the edge of the pool. With one swift slamming blow, it swung its right paw across the face of the antelope. Anton heard the creature's neck crack like a gunshot. The oryx dropped at the water's edge. The lion fell on it and dragged the still struggling beast into the bush.

"Reckon that chap did the job for us," said Anton to Makanyanga. "And now we don't have to carry all that heavy meat home for the boys. The lions got their dinner." He pointed back the way they came. "We'll sleep up there on the hill and get back to camp at first light."

He lay awake for hours under the vast bright African night, staring up at his old favorites, Phoenix, Peacock, Al Na'ir. From time to time he heard a scurried rustling in the bush nearby. Once the long rumbling roar of a distant lion rolled towards him along the ground.

In the night his thoughts turned to the mistakes he had made in the past. He knew well why Gwenn had left him. The combination of infidelity, absence and insecurity was more than any self-respecting woman would bear. While she'd struggled with the farm, he'd enjoyed himself on safari, often too much, with clients who were all too eager. But finally, he thought, it wasn't what he did that drove his wife away. It was Gwenn herself. It was her need to build her own life that drew Gwenn to Cairo, to medical school and the hospital, even to this lover she had chosen. Once or twice they'd almost made it back together, finding in each other for a time what they both enjoyed, knowing in their hearts that they could never share as much with anyone else. But the differences soon returned as well, his wildness and sense of freedom, her need for steadiness and security. As they grew older, her demands seemed better suited to the future than did his. Back in Cairo, he promised himself, he must try once more. He could not imagine spending the rest of his life with any other woman.

He thought he understood how Gwenn felt about the war, and why, but every day he was more determined to go himself. It was time he did something that mattered. And he was proud of Wellington.

When Anton awoke, chilled and trembling in the early morning, he heard the insistent call of an unrequited bou-bou, waiting to be answered. Rider sat up and smelled meat sizzling on a small fire nearby.

"Well done, Makanyanga," he said. He knew the tracker's magic with snares.

"Every camp needs one true hunter." The Wakamba grinned and turned the stick on which the little animal was spitted. "My bwana is a child in the bush."

Anton saw the small brown skin lying flat on a nearby rock. "Just one Abyssinian hare, eh, Makanyanga? Pity there's none for you," he said, stretching, "but it's better than nothing."

Just then a low buzzing sound reached them from the west. Anton and Makanyanga stood with their backs to the rising sun and watched the sky as the noise grew louder. First three aircraft broke the horizon, then two more flights, nine planes in all, flying on a line to the north.

"Capronis," said Anton, shaking his head. He recognized the distinctive three-engined bombers. "Italians. Flying into British Somaliland, by God, probably bound for Berbera. Looks like the war's finally hotted up." He wondered if the "phony war" in Europe was over, too, the months of near peace that had followed Hitler's invasion of Poland. Whatever the Krauts were up to, it looked like Mussolini had his hands in it now. "Soon enough, it will be my turn to sign up," he told Makanyanga. "This time I'm not missing the fun."

"Then Makanyanga will come, too. I will teach my bwana how to kill."

They heard the crump-crump, crump-crump of distant bombs as the planes crossed the next valley two or three miles to the northeast.

Anton split the hare in two with his belt knife. "Better eat up, there's a war on." He passed a piece to Makanyanga and eagerly began to chew the stringy charred meat. The engines stilled in the distance, and a different sound, wailing and whining, rose ghost-like from the adjacent valley.

"What white devils are coming now?" Makanyanga raised his shoulders and eyebrows in surprise.

"Bagpipes," said Anton, hearing the sound for the first time in Africa, amazed at how far it carried. "They're on our side. The Italians must've been bombing the Black Watch near Laferug."

Anton smothered the small fire and stamped out the coals. "Time to get back to camp and introduce Mr. and Mrs. Gaines to the war. Then we'd best dash back to Berbera and sail for Suez." At least I've made a few quid, he thought.

For months the *Coburg* had been anchored off Massawa. The noisy inner harbor was thick with lighters and dhows plowing through the oil slicks and garbage that littered the water. Battered tramps and converted liners and a few old Italian warships were tied end-on to the crowded docks. Eight more small German vessels, taking sanctuary in the Italian port, were berthed at secondary piers or anchored just outside the port. The *Schwan des Osten*, a filthy tramp, perhaps six thousand tons, was anchored beside the *Coburg*. Her hull was rusting at the waterline. Paint peeled from her stubby funnel. Shrill boat whistles and deep horns cut through the music of an Italian military band playing ashore in Eritrea.

Ernst von Decken remembered the day Harriet had left him.

He had worn his borrowed tropical Italian service gear: sand-colored four-pocket "sahariana" tunic, riding breeches and one tall brown boot. There were swastika flashes on his armband and sun helmet. Ernst stood at the end of the dock and waved his helmet at the *Demetrea*. The old Greek passenger-freighter sounded her horn and steamed away for Suez. Standing near the ship's captain, Harriet waved back at her husband from the bridge, blowing a kiss, he thought. Ernst could not make out her face.

"Don't worry about me," Harriet had whispered early that morning, touching him as she spoke, pleasing him for the last time. He ran hard hands slowly over her body, as if trying to memorize her. Then he lowered his head, scratching her thighs mercilessly as he prepared her with wicked kisses. "I have a schoolfriend in Cairo," she said after a time, stretching like a cat. "Her husband can arrange everything. And Gwenn should be there, your friend Anton's wife."

"*Capitano, prego . . .*" the impatient Italian lieutenant repeated again at his elbow, recalling Ernst to the present. "The General is waiting to escort you to your volunteers."

"Damned *Spaghettifresser*," Ernst muttered, turning to follow the little man. He squared his big shoulders and limped slowly towards the Italian staff car. Five years before, he'd had a violent run-in with their army in Ethiopia, but in all the Italian military only one officer could possibly identify him. He paused a short distance from the vehicle, forcing the Italian general to step down in order to address him. After all, he was himself a German officer, a veteran of the Schutztruppe.

The lieutenant held open a rear door of the tan canvas-topped Fiat. Ernst heard the senior officer curse as he bent forward and set one polished boot on the foot plate before stepping down. Tossing a cigar into the dust, the general thrust out an arm for the lieutenant's assistance.

Unable to click his heels in the Prussian manner, Ernst saluted when the man descended.

"Welcome to *Africa Orientale Italiana!*" The red-faced officer shook the German's hand, looking up at him, smiling warmly. "Here are your orders, Captain von Decken, directly from O.K.H., your Army High Command in Berlin." He handed Ernst an envelope. "I understand you are an old hand at campaigning in Africa."

"Thank you, General Galtieri." Ernst noted the ornate silver eagle on the general's cap badge, a silver cross on the eagle's chest. What a shame, he thought, the Italians couldn't fight the way they dressed. He hoped the

Germans would not have to do their fighting for them. All the same, he wished his own uniform had been cut by a proper military tailor in Potsdam. With only one foot, he needed all the help with the ladies he could get.

"Join me in our new Fiat," Galtieri said proudly. "A *Torpedo Militare 508*, specially designed for the next colonial wars. Screens to keep sand from the engine, spare tanks, high clearance, low gear ratios. *Perfezione!*"

"Thank you, General," said Ernst, tapping his stump on the ground. "She'll be just what I'll need with this leg of mine if my men and I are to be of use to you fighting the Britishers."

"That may not be possible, *Capitano* . . ."

"Forgive me, sir, while I read my orders," Ernst said abruptly. He scanned the long message. Sounds too much like the last war out here, he thought: making do, undersupplied, assigned to drain enemy strength, little hope of local victory, no chance of recognition. But clear orders to use all available Germans to stiffen the Italian fight against the British in East Africa. In exchange for German support, this Italian army in Eritrea was to arm and equip Ernst's small German force. He knew the Italians had a quarter million men in Ethiopia and Eritrea. Now united with Ethiopia, Eritrea was one of the five provinces of Africa Orientale Italiana.

"Here we are, sir." The lieutenant pulled up in the thick dust of an immense open square near the harbor. Two large stone buildings, with long shaded verandahs on both stories, flanked the plaza, powerful symbols of commerce in Italy's oldest colony. One side of the square was open to the sea.

Ernst stood on the bottom step in front of one of the buildings, sweating and tapping his toe. His hands clasped behind his back, he studied the men before him. Jaded as he was, he felt the excitement of this adventure, proud to be the first German to take the field again in Africa.

Perhaps two hundred men, mostly sailors from the German vessels, were being organized into loose formations by what looked to be two ill-trained junior officers, reportedly from the military guard of the German embassy in Addis.

"*Achtung! Achtung!*" cried the two young officers, goose-stepping between the ranks, dressing their men to order as von Decken watched. Some of the men wore Italian-issue wide khaki shorts, others plus-four trousers and puttees. All wore saharianas. Some appeared too old for war, others too soft and heavy-bellied.

Ernst stepped down and examined one man's weapon. It was the 6.5mm version of the Mannlicher-Carcano rather than the new harder-hitting 7.5mm model. Typical Italian incompetence.

Ernst closed his eyes and shook his head. After scouring up a few more volunteers from the bars and hotels, pressing into service any Germans he could find, he would take this lot up into the hills above Massawa and prepare them for a little soldiering.

The two lieutenants turned to face him. Their men stood in silent uneven ranks behind them.

"Heil Hitler!" both officers cried, stamping their boots. The men with weapons attempted to present arms. The others gave the Nazi salute. Here and there, Ernst recognized an old soldier by the man's crisp drill.

Von Decken wished he had a few dozen of his old askaris. They'd been uncomplaining enduring men from Tanganyika, mostly Manyemwesis, blacker than the devil's soul. Unpaid throughout the war, in '27 the survivors had been paid at last. With General von Lettow back in Germany, tirelessly protesting the outrage, finally, nine years after the war was over, a Hamburg banker had been dispatched to Dar es Salaam to pay off the loyal askaris. But the barefoot veterans were too shy to enter the Kaiserhof Hotel to seek their money, and the banker did not know how to identify the old askaris among all the other needy Africans. So finally the banker had set up a table outdoors, down by the docks, and he'd brought a broomstick from the hotel. The men lined up. Every African who could perform the German rifle drill with the broomstick got his pay. And in '35, when von Lettow returned to Dar, his old black comrades were waiting for him at the dock, hundreds of them. Singing *Haya Safari*, his askaris carried him on their shoulders to the Kaiserhof Hotel. They said it was the only time the old soldier ever shed a tear. How Ernst wished he'd been there, he thought, as he looked about him now.

Uniformed Italians and white-robed Eritreans clustered around the Germans in the square. Barefoot children played in the dust. A few clerks and women looked down from the verandahs of the vast commercial buildings. Ernst glanced up and caught the eye of one slender black beauty. Her clear features and dark eyes were framed by a white cotton shawl. Fanning herself slowly with a straw heart-shaped fan, she gazed down at him with cool regard.

"*Kameraden!* Men of the German Volunteer Motorized Company in Eritrea!" von Decken thundered from the steps. He paused and looked over the men out to sea, where he had watched the *Demetrea* disappear into the heat haze.

"It is twenty years since we Germans have fought for the fatherland in *Afrika*. Today we begin again."

— 3 —

"How about one of your famous tomato omelettes to start the day?" said Anton, pleased to be back in the only place in Cairo where he felt at home. He knew well that Olivio liked to bedevil the kitchen early in the morning. "Trifle on the soft side, if you don't mind. Four eggs."

"For you, Mr. Anton, we will do better," said the dwarf. He was seated in the captain's chair on the poop deck of the Cataract Café. A twinkle brightened his single eye. "Hen's eggs will not do. No, no. Our celebrated *Omelette Surprise* will launch your day." The little man favored nautical terms when on the boat. "If you can determine all the ingredients, we will credit you with witchcraft." He clapped his hands and a suffragi appeared, bowing to take his order.

A fat young boy with a round head sat on a straw mat near the bulwark, his back towards Olivio and Anton. Totally absorbed, mumbling quietly to himself, the child ignored them. His tiny nimble fingers moved swiftly amidst the mountains of coins that rose around him. The boy glanced up, and Anton was saddened to observe that he had something of a tight, old man's face. The child had almost no neck. His arms and legs were short for his body.

"And how is my godson?" said Rider. The little lad seemed to be working at his project, not playing, as other children might. "Must be almost three," Anton added.

"Tiago Fonseca Alavedo is nearly four and a half," said the dwarf, intending no criticism by the correction.

Tiago was erecting a handsome brown tower from a pile of English coppers, Anton noticed.

"This morning the little brute is learning the value of money," said Olivio, only too aware that young dwarves never played like other children. "Every farthing counts." He had always prayed for a son, and in a way a dark side of him was pleased that the boy was so like him.

"Perhaps he can teach me," said Anton eagerly.

"I too wish that were possible." The dwarf leaned forward from his cushion, pleased to serve his friend's coffee with his own hand. As the rich odor filled his nostrils, the little man reflected on his companion's problems, knowing it was not for him to raise them directly. But how happy could a man be, living without money, or his love, or his children? Still, Anton possessed everything that he himself lacked: the health and vigor of Hector, a long future, and the ability to master any wild setting. But, in their own ways, Olivio knew, they shared one thing: the romantic ideal. At the heart of this was an enthusiasm for women, the quest for the perfect romance, a lifelong love. As to other details, the dwarf guessed that Anton in private conducted himself with that restrained simplicity peculiar to the English. When a man was young, or with a new love, passion and vigor were sufficient, but with time, harmony and ingenuity, even humor were required.

Steam rose from the copper pot as Olivio poured with the handle of its long wooden arm. He slid the small cup towards his friend, speaking quietly, restraining his intrusion.

"May I have the pleasure of assisting you with something, Mr. Anton?" The dwarf had learned to regard his few friendships as precious bottomless opportunities, as blessings to be relished and maximized. From time to time a dedicated adversary yielded similar satisfactions. As he grew older, the little man wished to be as resourceful in friendship as he had always been in competition and animosity. "What may I do?" he said.

"Well, nothing, really." Anton looked down. "But I am running a bit short just now, what with all my safaris cancelled and school fees for Denby, and . . ."

"Of course, of course." The dwarf stirred his dense coffee with deliberate circular motions, never touching the edge of the cup. Occasionally, generosity could be as satisfying as avarice. "These are unusual times."

"And I've been wondering, do you see, if I might sell my bit of that farm of yours, Olivio? The one you were kind enough to let Adam and me invest in, out by Faiyum, isn't it?"

"Al Lahun, actually. But no, it is too soon to sell. You must keep your interest." The dwarf shook his head as far as he could from side to side. For him, this farming partnership was a cloak for generosity. He spread his hands wide like the wings of a bird before he spoke.

"Already the rice shines green as emeralds. Mangoes sweeten the air. But the cotton is not ready. The irrigation is not complete. The lemon trees are young. There is always more to do. More to do." Olivio hesitated, trying to reconcile the commandments of discretion and friendship. He looked at his friend closely, thinking of the mastaba. "And who knows what this land will give to us, Mr. Anton? Who knows?"

"Still, things are getting a bit awkward . . . The hotel . . ." Cheap as it was, the Pension Agamemnon wouldn't let him stay forever if he didn't put something down on the bill.

"Of course, I now owe you and his lordship an advance on these first harvests," said the dwarf, contriving how to assist his friend without the blemish of charity. He managed to nod cheerfully as he thought of the sinking price of this season's rice, of the boll worms that toiled to destroy his cotton by day and night, of the outrageous expense of his idle workers and of the bribes and gifts required to accommodate a host of officials, worse than the rats that stole his grain. On the other hand, this war would be a blessing to a man of enterprise. "After breakfast, please permit me to give you a draft for what I owe you."

Anton watched two British soldiers descend the gangway from the Nile embankment to the deck café.

With long tan socks, khaki shorts and shirts, but no unit insignia, and dusty suede desert boots, brothel creepers not unlike his own, the two officers seemed rather informal for what was turning up in Cairo at the better caravanserais. The men ordered coffee. Anton thought he heard one mention his own name to the steward. The suffragi was well trained, however, his wits honed by fear of his master. The servant knew better than to reveal who was seated at the effendi's table.

"Excuse me, sir," said the younger officer, stepping over. "Lieutenant Hennessy. The major asks me to enquire if you might be a Mr. Anton Rider?"

"Why does he ask?" said Anton to the hearty ruddy-faced lieutenant.

"Just orders, sir. I believe Major Lagnold's been ordered to find you, if you're Mr. Rider, and ask for your advice."

"Thank you, Lieutenant. I'll be over directly after breakfast," said Anton as the steward brought a large plate and removed the hot lid with a flourish. The young soldier stared enviously at the steaming dish. Beside it, the suffragi set down a small plate covered with a vivid green mound of fresh chopped parsley.

"No, no," intervened the dwarf, always curious, and certain his friend was too naive to look after himself. "Please see that the major joins us here at my table in a few moments' time." He was concerned lest these officers awaken his friend's dormant patriotism and child-like sense of adventure.

"Do not do anything foolish, Mr. Anton," said the dwarf in a quiet voice. "This war does not need you."

"It is what I must do, my friend," said Anton. "One way or another."

Plump and moist as a fine soufflé, the omelette, more orange than most, yielded a spicy cloud when Anton pierced it and set to work.

"Allow me." The dwarf leaned forward and carefully scattered two handsful of parsley over the omelette. "A member of the carrot family, you know," he said with satisfaction. "From our farm, at Al Lahun."

"Really," said Anton, smelling the fresh bitter tang of the herb.

"Eggs of the Egyptian plover, Mr. Anton, known to the ancients as the crocodile bird. The bird that Herodotus tells us steals morsels from between the teeth of the Nile crocodile," murmured Olivio, disappointed that his friend had not enquired, but pleased as a grandmother to satisfy his appetite, and to pass along this modest lesson of avian enterprise.

"I thought the Egyptian plover was extinct here," said Anton, confident his knowledge of wildlife was better than the dwarf's.

"True," said the little man. "The Egyptian plover is no longer found in Egypt. These eggs were rushed to us from the Sudan."

The two officers joined them and put their caps on an adjoining table. Lieutenant Hennessy watched Anton sweep his plate with a crust of fried bread.

"What may I offer you?" said the dwarf.

"Pair of lemon squashes would be lovely, if we may," said Major Lagnold. He was a short wiry man with a long nose, sparse dark hair, intent eyes and a trim mustache over thin lips. He gripped Anton's hand with surprising firmness and introduced himself.

"Mr. Rider, it is my job to do a bit of what you might call specialized recruiting for this little war out here." He glanced at Olivio. "This may not be the moment for details, however. All a bit hush-hush, but . . ."

"No point trying to keep secrets from Mr. Alavedo, Major," said Anton, growing curious. "He already knows everything that's going to happen in Cairo next week."

"No doubt. No doubt," allowed the major. "So I've heard. Still . . ."

"And I'm on my way, so if you'd like to talk, we'd best do it now."

"Well, the short of it is, in confidence, we're putting together teams to go deep into the Western Desert, hundreds of miles behind Axis lines, and collect intelligence of what they've got and where it's going. Could save a lot of lives . . ."

"Ah," said Olivio, nodding. "As I thought. The Long Range Desert Group."

"How did . . ." Major Lagnold began, then stopped himself as the dwarf continued.

"But my friend is too old for the call-up, and has too many old wounds," the dwarf said, waving one hand, rambling a bit, searching for a lever to separate the two men. "Too many broken bones."

"And most of the men are pretty green out here," the major continued. "Keen enough, mind you, no problem there, but some of these chaps don't know a wadi from a tea party. I was in Palestine, myself, and managed a bit of desert mapping hereabouts, but you put these lads in a sandstorm and they'll never come out the other side."

"Why me?" asked Anton, beginning to like the sound of it.

"We understand you're a professional hunter, done your share of bush bashing, been through a scrape or two, Abyssinia or wherever, sort of chap we're after, really. One old Kenya hunter told us you're the best rifle shot in Africa."

"Could I help without actually signing up? I'm not very good at taking orders."

"That would be awkward. Couldn't have a civie learning what we're up to, you know." Lagnold raised his heavy dark eyebrows. "But we're about as relaxed and irregular as the army gets. You'd be less mucked about than anywhere else, not all that buggering around you get in the old regiments. And we need a few experienced chaps who know Africa, to choose the men, train them, lead them, sort out the equipment and all that. I'm sure you understand. Idea's to collect the best old hands we can find, then top up the ranks with whatever's available. Mostly Kiwis, looks like."

"Old hands?" said Anton. The deep tan lines crinkled around his eyes and mouth. Already he was feeling old enough. "And why the Kiwis?"

"They lost all their equipment when a ship went down on the way out from New Zealand. Now they're waiting for a new batch that's on its way from England, round the Cape. So meantime we're trying to skim off the best of 'em before they all get arrested for chucking the tarts out the windows in the Birka. Nearly as rough as the Aussies."

"My old friend has already been approached," said the dwarf, not without pride. "By some other unusual company. How many Italians and Germans do you expect him to kill?"

"I believe there will be plenty for all of us . . ." said the major, offering a lean smile for the first time. "What'd you tell the other outfit, if I might ask?"

"Said it sounded too much like hard work, especially the training."

"Our approach is a bit different. More like your old line, I should've thought."

"Could my head boy serve with me? He'll be here tomorrow."

"Bit unusual." Lagnold raised his eyebrows. "What's he called?"

"Makanyanga."

"What? Makanyanga? Where's he from?"

"Kenya. He's Wakamba."

"What can he do?"

"Track, shoot, drive, fix engines, look after weapons, spot. Best eyes in the business. Spent a lot of time in the N.F.D."

"Really? That's dry country, desert really. Interesting. Never been properly studied. Still, he'd make a strange sort of batman, and we don't really have military servants, but suppose we could put 'im down in the ranks as batman. You'll have to ask the colonel."

"Anton!" cried a female American voice from the gangway, shrill and cheerful. "Yoohoo! Anton! Olivio!"

The four men looked up and saw a long-legged girl in high heels and a tan pleated skirt, one hand holding a large straw hat in place as she tottered down the sloping ramp.

"Hullo, Harry," said Anton with enthusiasm as he stepped over to greet the lady. A taxi driver hollered after her from the embankment. Rushing forward, the woman caught one heel in the carpet that covered the gangway and stumbled down.

"Damn!" she cried as she fell forward into Anton's arms. "I've snapped off a heel."

"I say!" said the lieutenant.

"This is Mrs. von Decken," Anton said awkwardly as Harriet, one hand around his neck, bent to embrace the dwarf.

"Welcome to Cairo, Miss Harriet!" cried Olivio, casting his head back and presenting his parted lips. After the friendly greeting, he touched his lips with his thick pointed tongue and then snapped at the suffragi. "Pay off that filthy driver. No tip."

"Please give me a ring," said the major to Anton, rising and excusing himself. He tore a bit of cardboard from a packet of Senior Service, wrote on it and handed it to Rider. "Soon as you can. We need you."

"How's Ernst?" said Anton after the officer had left, recalling the mischief and adventure he had shared with Harriet before she married his old German friend from Tanganyika. Steaming out to Massawa with Harriet and her twin sister before they all went on safari in Abyssinia. The banging on his cabin door at night. Harry at the door with a bottle of champagne, restless, too excited to sleep, too naughty not to pay a call.

"Gone to join his *Volk*, I fear," said Harriet with a bit of a pout, her hand still on Anton's neck. "Must be in Libya by now. Hate to think what he's up to. And leaving me all by myself to manage on my own."

"It's very simple, really, Rider," said the colonel, stepping to the deep embrasure and staring out the window of his high-ceilinged office in the Citadel. "The blasted war's been going to hell, and we've all got to do our bit. Europe's lost. Hitler's blitzing London. Children're being evacuated. Whole damned world is falling apart. Germans and Italians and Russkies are grabbing all they can. Japs are doing the same out east. The lazy Yanks are staying out of it and counting their dollars. So it's us against the world."

The officer adjusted the dark wooden slats of the blinds and gazed down over Cairo with his back to Anton. Rider guessed it was a lecture the colonel had given more than once. Anton understood the point, but he did not like the idea of this group hunting him down and telling him what he had to do. Still, it might suit him best.

"For now, North Africa is the only place in the world where we can fight the German army. And if the Hun wins out here, we lose Iran, Iraq, all the oil of the Middle East, the largest refineries in the world, and the Canal, the short route to India and the East. Looks like they'll have one army attacking our way from Libya, and perhaps another coming down to see us through Russia and the Caucasus, sort of a pincer. Kind of thing Jerry likes. If they meet, could mean the war." The colonel turned and looked at Rider, as if to see if he had said enough. " 'Plan Orient,' they're calling it in Berlin," he added. "So it's our job to stop them here."

"Yes, sir," said Anton. Feeling awkward in his worn cotton jacket and unpressed cord trousers, he found himself already slipping into the unwelcome habit of military deference.

"The Germans understand all this too, of course. The Hun's no fool." The officer stepped over to a large wall map. "They've begun sending units over to Libya, mostly armor, to stabilize things and stiffen the wretched Eyeties before they collapse completely. Then, when they're strong enough, we reckon they'll push on east for Alex and the Delta, then take a right down to Cairo and the Canal. Meantime, we're trying to sink their stuff on the way over and drown the bastards in the Med before they get here." The colonel tapped the map. "So far, all the fighting's been back and forth along this stretch of east-west coast that runs from Tripoli to Benghazi and Tobruk and Sidi Barrani. That's where the ports are, the only roads, the airfields that control the Med, everything. Tobruk will be the key."

"Yes, sir."

The colonel turned and faced Anton, looking at him closely, pausing before he continued.

"Strange sort of crew this Lagnold's getting together. Scratched them up here and there from the Wailing Wall to Nairobi. Officers're too old, men too green."

"Yes, sir."

"How much did Lagnold tell you about himself?"

"Nothing."

"Not surprised. Typical dug-out. The war dragged him out of retirement. Chap's mad about sand. All he cares about, really. Wrote a paper, 'The Physics of Blown Sand,' or some such. Authority on sand formations, dune structures, wind patterns, desertification, all the rest of it. Spent years on his own, mapping the wastes in Saudi Arabia and out this way. Should know what he's about." The colonel pushed a slim volume across his desk. "Here's his book."

Anton lifted the book. *Libyan Sands—Travels in a Lost World.*

The colonel ignored a sharp knock at the door. "Any event, we're looking for a few men to lead reconnaissance teams, Rider, what Churchill calls 'hunter-class' volunteers. Small patrols that'll get behind German lines and watch that coast road. Motor guerrillas, you might call them. You'd be wiggling about on your belly with field glasses, rather like stagging or whatever you do out here. Then you radio us exactly what the devils've got and where it's moving. It'll be more like stalking than fighting. That's why we're after a few chaps like you. Think of it as just another safari."

"Could my head safari boy serve with me?"

"What? What sort of chap is he? Black?"

"Very. Wakamba."

"Wakamba? Kenya? What would he want to do with all this?"

"Killing Germans runs in the family. His father fought with us in the last war. Got shot in Tanganyika, near Arusha, died of head wounds. Sergeant in the K.A.R."

"King's African Rifles, eh? Take it up with Lagnold. Just the sort of problem for him."

"Yes, sir."

The door banged again.

"Anyway, we'll be counting on you." The colonel paused, waiting without success for Anton to reply before he continued.

"So there we are. Like to have you on parade at our little camp near Abbassia tomorrow at seven. Show you what we've got on and what we're trying to do. Probably give you a commission on the spot. Captain's pay, should've thought." He paused, seeing he finally had Anton's attention. "Maybe even back it up a month or two. One of the lads'll call for you at six and see you kitted out. Right you are, then, Rider." He glared at the door. "Come in, damn your eyes! I said, come in!"

"Salut, vieux pote!" said Giscard de Neuville with apparent warmth as he strode to the door of his library. *"Tu es le bienvenu, amiral."*

The center of the room was dark, the walls lit only by the slender shaded picture lights that illuminated the scenes of the emperor in Egypt: Bonaparte disembarking at Alexandria, the vanguard of 40,000 Frenchmen, the Army of the Orient, already drawn up in the harbor to receive him; the slaughter of the charging Mamluks at the *Bataille des Pyramides*; Murat's cavalry annihilating the Turks at Abuqir; and Napoleon's *savants* at their work tables, one hundred and sixty-five scholars laboring to catalogue the infinite treasures of ancient Egypt. One of these very tables, presently covered with new archeological maps and sketches, stood nearby, serving now as de Neuville's own desk.

A shortish man with a big soft face and bushy grey eyebrows and a pleated rosette in his buttonhole, Admiral Danton seemed diminished in his French suit. It had the characteristically overly short jacket and broadly sloping plank-like shoulders, details which de Neuville himself had learned to correct with the English-trained tailors of Cairo.

"Thank you for receiving me, Giscard," said his old friend from the Lycée Louis le Grand. "I was not certain which side you were on. Today, there are two Frances, perhaps more. Maybe there always were." Was de Neuville with the Free French and General de Gaulle, prepared to carry on the fight against the Germans, the admiral wondered, or did he support Vichy, the rightist government the Nazi occupiers had imposed on France? Certainly, he did not support the communist resistance.

"I am surprised to see you not in uniform, Antoine." De Neuville guided his guest to a leather chair.

"The position of our navy in Alexandria is a delicate one," said the sailor. He opened his silver cigarette case but found it empty. "The English fear we may support the Germans. They have quarantined our fleet, eight vessels, including my cruiser. To keep them under the French flag, we have agreed to demilitarize the ships by sending some of the crews to Syria and by not keeping enough oil on board to go to sea. In exchange, the British are giving us supplies and paying our sailors. So we cannot sail. We cannot fight." He shrugged. "Maybe it is for the best? *Qui sait?*"

The admiral glanced up at Giscard but received no reply. Instead de Neuville passed him a round tin of State Express cigarettes from his desk.

"May I?" asked Danton, filling his case from the tin.

"Of course," said de Neuville, not surprised. "Tell me more about Alexandria."

"The English treat us with civility, if not trust. We are allowed ashore, but when not in port, we have learned it is more prudent to be in mufti. And my *matelots* are restless, idling on board, brawling in the bars, angry that Churchill attacked our ships near Oran at Mars al-Kabir. The English killed over a thousand French sailors."

"Monsieur Churchill did not want France's warships to be added to the German fleet." Giscard shrugged. "Did you?"

Hesitating, the admiral tapped one of the English cigarettes on his case, then accepted a light before continuing.

"Most of the officers and men, including myself, support Vichy. Mostly because it is our duty to be faithful to the government of France, whatever that is, and partly because Vichy hates the Bolsheviks. We who love France must consider her well-being more than our own antipathies." Danton raised both hands for emphasis. "The Germans control all Europe." The admiral paused, as if giving Giscard time to comprehend the importance of his point. "They are building a new order." He squinted at de Neuville through the smoke before resuming.

"If Vichy cannot manage France, the German occupation will become more severe. And France includes French Africa, of course. Even today, there are one hundred and twenty thousand French soldiers in North Africa, in Tunisia, in Morocco and Algeria. Whose side will they be on? Of course, in Syria, our Army of the Levant is already cooperating with the Germans."

"*Une fine?*" de Neuville asked. "Cognac?" He was reminded of how, even in class, with his hand always raised and waving, Antoine had been too eager, too eager to lecture his classmates, and even his teachers, about what he thought he knew of history and the world. "*Pas d'excès de zèle,*" their master had once responded, an homage to Talleyrand that de Neuville had learned better than his friend.

"I am here, Giscard, to ask you to help us. To help France. To help yourself." The admiral nodded repeatedly as de Neuville poured from the carafe. "There is much that a man like you can do. Remember that it will go worse for France if the Germans judge that we are still their active enemy, that Vichy cannot be trusted to represent France as it must. These Gaullists, these 'Free Frenchmen,' can only make our country suffer. They are traitors. Yet in Egypt, here in Cairo, they are active. And this general from Djibouti, this LeGentilhomme, is now collecting here a rabble of Gaullist outcasts, from Syria, from the Lebanon, from Somaliland, Morocco, Mali, wherever, to fight with the British. Can you imagine that?"

Giscard nodded, sipping his brandy. He shared much of the admiral's view, but perhaps less of his purpose. Despising both the fascists and the communists, at bottom a bit of a monarchist who cared only for traditional France, de Neuville thought that de Gaulle and the British would lose, but that it would not be useful for the Germans to win. He recalled that at school his old friend had often accused him of indecision in choosing sides, of waiting to see which way to jump, and Danton did so now.

"I trust you do not still practise *attentisme*, Giscard? It is a personal philosophy that no Frenchman can afford today."

"You do not understand, Antoine." De Neuville shook his head. Danton still lacked the discernment to recognize a dilemma, whether moral or political. "Do not confuse detachment with bad judgment."

Admiral Danton puffed out his cheeks, as if hearing an absurdity.

Irritated, de Neuville paused. Like the Hapsburgs, his old schoolmate had forgotten nothing and learned nothing. Giscard tapped his cigarette holder against his front teeth before he spoke more slowly.

"It is a matter of what is possible, *mon cher* Antoine, a case of *le sens du praticable* . . ."

"I must know, Giscard, if you will help us," said the admiral with impatience. "One day soon the Germans will be in Cairo. Can you not understand? We must be their friends then, and now." He raised his eyebrows. "It could be important to your work, to your personal collection. And to your family in Paris."

"The situation here in Cairo is complicated, Antoine," said the archeologist, recognizing the threat, agreeing with the probabilities. His hands behind his back, a squadron of cuirassiers and the sphinx brightly lit at his shoulder, de Neuville spoke with care. "Very complicated. In Cairo, the Ambassador of France is Vichy, but most of our countrymen here support de Gaulle, notably those who manage the Canal company. But many Egyptians are with you, especially the young officers, Sadat and all the rest, wanting only to see the British driven from their country. Yet these damned English have a way of hanging on, and one must be careful. I could lose all that I have done here, all that I must do. How would that serve France?"

"One must adapt, Giscard. One must make choices, or almost choices. Times change. Consider the Mamluks." Admiral Danton rose and approached a colored engraving of a swarthy turbanned warrior on horseback, in scarlet pantaloons, curved sabre drawn, two pistols and a dagger carried on his chest, his uniform part *Grande Armée*, part Ottoman Turk.

"At first Circassian slaves, this caste of warriors ruled Egypt for five hundred years, until Bonaparte butchered them at the pyramids. Then Napoleon took eighty-five of these Mamluks into his *Garde Impériale*.

France had their sabres, but whose side were they truly on? At the end, did it matter? Regardless, with our cavalry on all sides, they charged with our Chasseurs at Jena. Of course, none went home."

"What would you have me do?"

"Just enough. Enough to help us now, and to help you later. We do not need your heart, Giscard, wherever that may be, just your conduct, like the Mamluks at Jena." Danton set down his empty glass.

"Perhaps I understand."

"Remember that before this war, and after it, our rivals outside Europe have never been the Germans. Never. Always it has been the English." The sailor's face flushed as he spoke. His hands gestured more and more rapidly. "At sea, by land. In the Caribbean, the Mediterranean. In India, North America, in Guyana, even here in Africa, at Fashoda, in Somaliland, everywhere. Forever. For centuries they even claimed part of France. *Les anglais, toujours les anglais.*"

"*Bien sûr,*" said Giscard neutrally, sympathetic enough, but bored by the hostility so many of his countrymen felt against the Anglo-Saxons and the Jews. He filled his old friend's glass, then continued.

"Tell me, Antoine. What is it about these English? Most people are coming to Cairo as refugees, to get away from the war. But the English, in all their colonial costumes, are rushing here to fight. Most aren't even really English." De Neuville twisted a State Express into his holder. He thought of Wellington, the foolish son of his lover, a youth who had never even been to England before he signed up to fight for it. With any luck that bush-mad savage Anton Rider would join up also and be killed by the Germans. "From fishing villages in Canada, bush stations in Australia, men are leaving everything, many of them forever, men who've never seen England, men for whom it is just a family idea of where someone once had come from. What are they all fighting for? What do they want?"

"That's not the point, Giscard. From 1066 to 1814, we fought thirty-two pitched battles against the English . . ."

"And lost almost all but the first." Giscard closed his eyes and nodded.

"As the Emperor said before Waterloo, we have four hundred years of insults to avenge."

"And then he lost again," said Giscard wearily. "Now it is five hundred years."

"Exactly."

Giscard leaned towards his old friend, raising his eyebrows.

"My dear Antoine, I cannot win the battle of Waterloo. What would you have me do?"

"Remember what side we must be on, at least privately. Help us to be useful to the *boches*, do it for France, for yourself. Give us information. After all, who will it hurt, but the English?" The admiral set down his glass and raised both palms before him.

"Information that will come to you with ease, Giscard, like butter with your *brioche*. Carry a bit the cross of Lorraine. Cultivate these Gaullists, the Free French. They will wish you to support them. Let them believe of you what they will want to believe. And tell me exactly what they are doing, how many they are, how they are equipped, where they will fight. The rest I will do."

"I will do what I can, because you ask me, Antoine . . . and for France." De Neuville raised his glass in toast, and drank. There was no clear course, either useful or honorable. Perhaps this would indeed be best.

"And incidentally, Giscard," said the admiral, drinking too, "should things go the other way, if I am wrong, if the Nazis never dine with you in Cairo, then your intimacy with the Free French will stand you credit, and they, too, will one day say you stood for France."

Regain the
Youthful Figure

CICUREL'S SALON

CAIRO
SHARI FUAD I

— 4 —

"Leave it to me," said Johnny Bingham, and Wellington had. The trick was to find something that two spoiled Egyptian girls had never done before, and to do it the way old Cardigan would have liked, after a glass or two, and with a dash of reckless excess.

Thirstier than after a fortnight in the desert, prepared to spend a month's pay on a three-day leave, Wellington splashed a little more champagne into his black velvet and looked down from the terrace café of Shepheard's Hotel. An empty bottle of stout rested upside-down in the ice bucket.

Honking mercilessly, herding carts and donkeys and street vendors before it, an old tan Humber pulled sharply to the curb and parked along Shari Ibrahim Pasha near the foot of the broad steps to the terrace. The faded colors of some long-gone regiment flew from the small mast on the right side of the car's bonnet. Bingham leaned out the driver's window and tossed a coin to one of the turbanned hotel doorkeepers.

"Tally ho!" he hollered at Wellington. A girl with a large hat sat beside him in the motor car.

Wellington flung some Egyptian money on the table, drained his glass and hurriedly pushed back his wicker chair.

"Steady on," said a passing senior officer as the chair banged against him.

Wellington stiffened and saluted smartly, recognizing the major-general.

"Terribly sorry, sir. Excuse me."

"Carry on," said the New Zealand commander easily. A bandage covered

64

the right side of his neck. "Just tighten your reins a bit when you're in town."

"Thank you, sir." Wellington clicked his heels and turned for the steps.

"Dear God. Wasn't that Freyberg?" whispered Bingham, nervously stroking one hand over his bald crown. He drove away as quietly as he could. "Wounded five times in the last war, and once or twice in this one, Greece or Crete or whatever. They say he still believes in the bayonet."

"That was him."

"Bonnie," said Bingham, "I brought my groom, Wellington Rider. Bonnie Wassif. I wouldn't touch his hand, if I were you, Bon-Bon. Never know where the chap's been."

"How do you do?" said Wellington, recognizing the family name, one of the most distinguished among the *Haute Copterie*, the old Christian families of Egypt. He wondered if Bonnie knew Saffron. Probably, he thought. Cairo was a small town, and she probably knew all about Mr. Alavedo, too, though her family might not welcome the little man's company.

"Cicurel's," said Wellington. "Sharp as you can. We're late already."

"You're never late if a lady's shopping at Cicurel's," said Bonnie, turning to smile at Wellington. She was a light-skinned slender girl with a pointed chin and merry eyes and short curly hair.

Saffron was waiting at the door of the store with a porter and three parcels. Wellington felt his breathing stop when he saw her. He jumped out and held the door.

"Good morning, Wellie. Hello Bonnie, Johnny." Saffron kissed Wellington lightly on the cheek and climbed into the back of the Humber. "Glad you found a driver, but where'd you get this lovely car?"

"Old staff car," answered Wellington, wanting to take her hand, to touch her. She sat a bit too far away, with a large hamper on the floor between them. "Bingham scrounged it up from the army repair shops, told them he was collecting it for the colonel of the Green Jackets. Of course they left for Singapore last year. Kind of thing Bingham's good at. He's always cadging something, you know, cigarettes or rations or whatever."

"You never seem to mind," said Bingham hotly. "Someone's got to look after you."

"Where are we going?" asked Saffron.

"Secret," Bingham said as he sped north past Heliopolis, swerving dangerously while looking at a map he took from the dashboard. "Not allowed to reveal plans in wartime. Enemy ears are everywhere."

They turned east and the military traffic thinned. Wellington took four picnic glasses and a bottle of champagne from the hamper. The wine sprayed when he opened it. A few drops fell on the top of Saffron's yellow frock. Distracted by the way her breasts filled the dress, he passed out the short glasses and poured.

"Ismailia!" cried Saffron as they drove along the famous Sweet Water Canal and approached the old town several hours later. She sat forward eagerly, pausing to finish her champagne while they motored along the Avenue de l'Impératrice. "Wonderful! I love Ismailia. I'll show you De Lesseps' *chalet*. It's still just the way he left it in 1865, his books and everything. They built this canal to provide fresh water for the new towns and the workers who were building the Suez Canal . . ."

"I'm afraid Bingham's not much on tourism and history and culture and all that," interrupted Wellington, hoping to spare himself. Saffron was beginning to sound like his mother. If they could just get a little more drink in the girls, things might go better.

"Oh, look," said Bonnie as they passed the railroad station and saw the five white cars of the royal train. "The king must be here. It's such a lovely town, full of gardens and parks and lakes, named for the Khedive Ismail, of course. It was the center of everything while De Lesseps built the Canal . . ."

"We could take a steam launch at Lake Timsah," added Saffron hopefully.

"Why don't we stop here for something cool?" said Bingham, rolling his eyes at Wellie in the mirror. He crossed the Place Champollion and parked beside a café at the top of the Rue Negrelli. Two street boys opened the doors of the Humber and they all stepped down. The air seemed cleaner but more humid than in Cairo. Wellington gave the lads a few piastres. One youth produced a rag and began to dust the car while they sat down under the canopy of the Café Chancel.

"Just time for a sharpener before the races." Bingham clapped his hands for service. "*Walad! Awziin shampanya!* Two bottles in a bucket." He smiled at Bonnie. "Gotta fight off the prickly heat," he declared, offering round a packet of Sweet Caporals.

"Races?" said Saffron. "There are no races in Ismailia."

"Sand-yachting," said Wellington, well pleased. "The RAF's been doing it out here for years. Now King Faruq's built two sand-yachts, sailboats on wheels, and he's racing this afternoon on the edge of town."

"Cheap toys, compared to his old dad," snorted Bingham. "King Fuad had a two-hundred-car garage at the palace. Used to roll about in a replica seventeenth century French carriage, with gold wheels and eight white horses. All the while coughing and barking like a dog from that bullet stuck in his throat."

"He was our king," said Saffron quietly, with annoyance in her voice. She continued before Bingham could speak again. "His great-grandfather, Muhammad Ali, mounted the heads of four hundred British soldiers on stakes in the streets of Cairo." Bonnie glanced at Saffron with admiration.

"Ah," said Wellington, "here's the champagne." Never argue with a woman, his father once had told him.

In an hour they sat on blankets under a palm tree at one end of the aerodrome. Several other parties were picnicking nearby, mostly English or South African pilots and their friends. The pilots sported long wide mustaches. Clusters of young Egyptian officers stood about in the shade of the palm trees, speaking quietly and sipping colored fruit drinks.

Mechanics were working on a flight of Hurricanes on the airstrip just behind them. A scattering of other planes was visible nearby, Marylands and Tomahawks, Bostons and Beaufighters. Their wheel struts were pegged down with ropes, their engines covered in canvas wraps against the sand. Two old Wellesleys and a Swordfish fighter appeared to have been abandoned in the distance.

Everyone stood as a shiny red Rolls Royce drove onto the hard desert in front of the palm trees. The green royal pennant, with the crescent and stars of Egypt, flew from its bonnet.

"Now you know why no one in Egypt is allowed to paint his car red," drawled Bingham.

The automobile stopped. A uniformed officer opened the door and the young king stepped down. Wearing white trousers, a double-breasted blue blazer and an open shirt with a wide collar, the handsome twenty-year-old monarch walked towards the wheeled sailboat that was being run out towards him by four handlers. The king touched his yachting cap and waved once towards the clapping guests and observers, then walked to the boat with an aide.

"That's his new one," said Bingham as they all sat again and Wellington opened a bottle of hock, precious now in Cairo as stocks of German wine were almost gone. "She's the *Almaza*, built entirely by Egyptian craftsmen and said to be much faster than his other sand-yacht, the *Agamy*, that those

Egyptian naval officers are getting into over there. The other two are the RAF boats, not nearly as fast or new. Chaps haven't had time to work on a new one. Got their hands full protecting the Canal."

Bonnie set out the spices and silver and napkins while Saffron took the jellied ducks and mangoes from the hamper.

Faruq and his first mate climbed into the *Almaza* while his staff held her steady. Perhaps eighteen feet long, with two masts, the boat had two large wheels under her bow and two small wheels connected by a rod under her stern. The large mainsail flapped briskly in the wind.

Teams of handlers wheeled the four boats to the starting line. The race master held up his fingers to test the wind. The boats were turned until the wind was at their stern. A lorry raced off ahead of them and two men set up a finish line in the distance.

The race master raised a pistol and fired one shot, then hurriedly climbed into his waiting automobile and drove to the finish.

The Egyptian officers applauded when the king's boat made a fast start. The other Egyptian sand-yacht seemed to hesitate until he was well away. The two English craft appeared to be heavier, with less sail. They moved steadily after the *Almaza*. Then the *Almaza* headed off the course, moving jerkily off-track in a race of her own. Her stern wobbled and swung from side to side. The *Agamy* veered to starboard and followed her into the open desert. The race master's car dashed after the two Egyptian boats, then waited for them ahead.

"Must be sailing back to the Abdine Palace," said Bingham loudly, gesturing with the glass in his hand. His chin was shiny with mango juice. "Haw! Haw!"

Several Egyptian officers stared down at him with cold eyes and tight faces.

Suddenly the two rear wheels of the *Almaza* came free and rolled off to port on their own. The stern of the sand-yacht crashed down onto the desert. For a time the boat continued dragging forward, slower and slower, until finally it stopped. The *Agamy* swerved to avoid her. The British vessels continued in their original direction. The pistol fired again. The race was over.

"Reckon we know who won that one," said Bingham loudly.

"Careful," said Wellington. "We're in Egypt."

Saffron smiled and helped Bonnie pack up. Her father would have agreed with Wellie. He had trained her to respect, and sometimes to use, the weaknesses of others.

A hawk-nosed Egyptian officer walked towards them, slapping his gloves against his leg as he advanced. Bingham turned to face the man.

Saffron stepped to Bingham's side, folding a blanket over one arm.

"Please excuse us," she said to the officer in Arabic when the man drew near. Her voice was firm, not conceding too much. "My friends were just being jolly. They've been at the front. We meant no disrespect."

Bingham began to speak. Wellington squeezed his upper arm.

For an instant the Egyptian looked at the two Englishmen. "Good afternoon, gentlemen," he said crisply and turned on his heel.

The sun set as they drove back to Cairo. Bonnie's head nodded, then fell forward as she slept.

"Want me to drive?" asked Wellington, leaning forward. Tonight would be their last night on leave. He hoped to dine alone with Saffron. Perhaps Celestino or the Luna Park if he could manage it. He wouldn't need any money in the desert.

"No thanks, old sport," said Bingham. "I'm better at it."

Wellington put one arm around Saffron. She sighed and rested her head on his shoulder.

"Can I take you to supper after we get back?" he whispered into her hair, loving her touch and her perfume.

"You can take me anywhere, Wellie," she said, reaching for his hand. "But let's go to Celestino's."

"They say navigation's going to be the tough one. Libyan desert's the size of India," said Hennessy with enthusiasm. The old khaki two-door Morris beat through a chaos of donkey carts and staff cars, overloaded open lorries and herds of mangy camels and fat-tailed sheep being driven to the slaughterhouse. Makanyanga was bent into the back seat, his round head sideways against the roof, a large hand pressed against either window.

"That, and petrol and water," the lieutenant continued, sticking one end of a chocolate bar in his mouth and ripping off the Cadbury wrapper as he steered with the other hand, barely missing an Arab horseman driving three camels with a long switch. The drover spat on the rear window of the Morris and cursed as his short horse capered sidewise.

"How far out do they reckon these recces will operate?" said Anton. He was finding himself already drawn into the logistics, reminded of a hundred safaris, and one or two that went badly wrong. He felt remarkably comfortable in his new uniform of khaki shirt, long baggy shorts and high wool socks, not really that different from his regular bush gear.

"Fifteen hundred miles, perhaps two thousand, they're saying now. Mostly west across the sand seas into Libya, then up to the coast, and perhaps a few patrols straight west to beat up the old Italian outposts. Should be jolly."

Finally out in the open rocky desert on the edge of Cairo, Hennessy just managed to swing the jeep through a gate formed by two large petrol drums. Their dust-tail caught up with them and swirled around the Morris as they jerked to a stop next to a column of Chevrolet one-and-a-half-tonners. "Yank thirty-cwts," the lieutenant said.

"Thank you." Anton stepped down, hoping Hennessy would not be his driver on patrol. Anton held the door as Makanyanga escaped from the back seat.

"There you are, Captain Rider," called Major Lagnold from the rear of one truck. "Just in time to sort out the new lorries. Problem is to get their weight down low enough so the engines will be able to get 'em through the sand. Means stripping off everything we don't need. Cabs, doors, windscreen, whatever, and loading 'em back up again with extra petrol tanks, water, sand channels, spare wheels, machine guns, medical supplies, radios, the lot."

Anton strode over as the major spoke, wondering if he was expected to salute. He decided to count on the unit's reputation for informality. Makanyanga stayed by the car. Nearby was a jumble of doors and windscreens. Anton saw a team of welders and oil-streaked mechanics moving from truck to truck. In the distance he heard the unmistable barking of a sergeant-major and saw lines of men crawling under wire and climbing telephone poles. Young men's games, he thought.

"How can I help, sir?"

"Help, Rider? Help? You're in charge. Hennessy'll give you a hand, if you can keep him off the grub. Fix up two trucks for starters. Strip 'em and load 'em. Then we'll have a test run. Meantime, check our supply lists. Make your own suggestions and give me a report in four days. We've got five weeks before the first three patrols mount up. Twenty-eight men, two officers, eleven trucks to a patrol. Best get on with it." Lagnold jumped down, smiled briefly and shook hands with Anton. "See you've brought your African. Looks a solid chap, all right. We can use him. Plenty to do. Any questions?"

"How many pounds were these designed to carry?" Anton clapped a hand on the fender of one Chevy.

"They've all had extra leaves fixed into the springs by the importer in Alex. Should be able to carry two tons apiece. Come and see me at tea-time and we'll chat about navigation and what not with the other patrol commanders."

Four hours later Anton wiped his face with his red diklo while he checked three sheets of paper. Then he pocketed the gypsy bandana and walked over to the large tent where Lagnold sat in a camp chair under the fly canvas, bent over a map table, measuring distances with the points of a schoolboy's compass.

Wooden cases and crates of all sizes were stacked outside along both sides of the tent. Anton slowed and read the stencilled contents and addresses as he approached: water filters and canteens from Birmingham, tea from Colombo, medical kits from Aldershot.

Twenty yards on, he saw men tightening the ropes of a makeshift boxing ring. The cables were stretched between corner posts set in forty-four-gallon gasoline drums filled with sand. Another man swept the hard gritty ground of the enclosure with a broom and kicked away the larger stones. Pairs of frayed boxing gloves dangled from the posts.

In the distance fleets of vehicles were practising flag signals and patrol formations. Columns of fine sand flared up like smokescreens as one pennant directed in-line formation, followed by another flag specifying a right column turn. The return of the age of sail, Anton thought.

"Pull up a pew, Rider," said Major Lagnold distractedly, not looking up as he twirled the compass end over end. "Just pottering about here trying to site a few supply dumps for petrol and water so we can extend our range a bit and get in where they won't expect us. Takes two and a half times the petrol to move a lorry one mile in the desert as it does on a road. We'll be getting five or six miles a gallon. Be needing 'bout three hundred fifty gallons per vehicle." He pinched his nose and looked up. "What do you have there?"

"Lists and specs for supplies, sir, broken down by vehicle and weight. I want to make each truck self-sufficient for basics, and assign the specialized stuff according to who's riding. Should cover about everything except radios and the heavier weapons."

"Really," murmured Lagnold, pushing aside a stack of logarithmic tables and celestial almanacs before he took the sheets from Anton. He nodded and scanned the lists. "Already? Looks like you've done this sort of thing before. This should save us a bit of time. Cup of tea?" Without waiting for a reply, he poured a mug and dropped in three spoons of sugar and milk from a tin.

"Thank you, sir."

"And there's one other thing I should have mentioned, Rider. We're not giving our officers regular army physicals. Too many old-timers wouldn't make it. Eyes, or livers, more likely. But we've still got to know if they're sound enough. So we're doing it our way. Other ranks, new men transferring in, get a crack at something different. Milling, we call it. Takes less time."

"Yes, sir."

"Each officer gets a choice of a morning of field exercises, including a nice run with full pack before lunch with Sergeant Murray, fellow used to mess about in some Olympic or other. Or else three rounds with old Sergeant-Major Stoner, a bit of a pug, they say, some sort of middleweight in Auckland, looks a bit heavier now. So you can make your choice, and the same will do for your Manyakanga, if you want him in."

"Makanyanga, sir. I think we'll let your Kiwi knock us about a bit," said Anton. "Makanyanga and I are getting a little old for too much running about in the sun."

"That's what I should have done myself, but I was fearful Stoner would kill me just to show the men he meant it. Ring's the only place where all ranks can get their own back and settle old scores. We always do the boxing just before dinner. It's cooler, and the men enjoy gathering about and having a shout. The Kiwis have a pool on it. Buy a round for everyone else if someone knocks Stoner down." He looked at Anton and almost smiled. "So far New Zealand's been doing all the drinking."

"I'll flip you for first go," said Anton, well trained by the gypsies in tossing coins.

"*Ndio*, bwana," said Makanyanga warily, suspicion in his eyes. "Heads."

Anton tossed up a half crown and clapped it on the back of his left hand. "Tails. Lucky for you. You'll get him before he's loosened up."

"It is always tails, bwana," said Makanyanga.

Anton chose the corner with his back to the setting sun. He and Makanyanga climbed through the ropes into the ring as the men began to gather round, smoking and chatting loudly, wiping their faces on their sleeves after a hot day's work. The New Zealanders collected behind the opposing corner, eager to face off against the Brits and Canadians, Aussies and South Africans, and all the rest of empire. Hennessy stood behind Anton's corner post with a bucket of water and a scrap of towel. Behind him, sparring lightly, two other boxers waited their turn against Stoner.

Makanyanga took off his shirt, revealing powerful sloping shoulders and a hard round belly. Nearly Anton's height, about six two, he swung his arms and flexed his shoulders as the crowd appraised him. It had been over a year since he and Rider had last sparred in camp, and Anton prayed his friend remembered not to depend only on his strength and durability.

"Proper ugly bugger," said one soldier loudly, spitting in the sand. "Worse than a bleeding Maori. Look at that neck."

The crowd parted for the sergeant-major.

"Look what's for dinner, Jock!"

"Go get 'im, Stoner! Show 'im how we play on the North Island!"

Anton laced up Makanyanga's threadbare brown gloves and looked across the ring as Stoner dropped a towel from his shoulders. He watched the sergeant-major closely.

The New Zealander, shadow-boxing, raised his fists and moved onto his toes, snapping several sets of hard right jabs as the men behind him whistled. Shorter than Makanyanga or Anton, but thick and broad and hard, with hauser-like arms and legs like tree trunks, he had a wide face with prominent scarred cheekbones and one cauliflower ear. Anton saw Stoner's second straining to pull the gloves over the sergeant's massive hands.

A young medical officer stepped into the ring and checked each fighter. "Your chap looks sound enough for now," he said to Anton with a hard Aussie accent. "Good luck to you both."

"Watch him, Makie," said Anton. "He's a lefty. Keep your own left up and in his face. You've got the reach."

"Three rounds, three minutes!" The referee called the fighters to the center of the ring, touched their gloves together and stepped back quickly as he blew the whistle that hung from his neck.

Already moving just before the whistle blew, Stoner stepped in, flat-footed, and gave Makanyanga a violent right and left to the belly.

Anton could hear the distinct powerful slam of each blow across the ring, like a smartly broken rack of pool balls. He knew what the sound meant in strength and pain.

Surprised, his fists still low at his sides, his gloves open, Makanyanga gasped and staggered forward, almost falling, as the crowd stamped and cheered. Stoner, close now, gave him a tight left uppercut, finishing with a hard right jab to the temple as the big African went down. So much for Queensbery, Anton thought.

"Next! Next!" roared a hundred Kiwi voices.

The referee, indifferent to the rushed unsporting break, bent over Makanyanga and counted ten.

Hennessy and Anton carried Makanyanga from the ring. Anton threw the bucket of water in his face and unlaced his gloves as Makanyanga sat on the sand, blinking, his back against the corner petrol drum.

"Next! Next! Next!" chanted the men. "Drinks on the Limeys!"

Anton and Hennessy climbed back through the ropes. The Englishman began to lace up the gloves while Anton watched Stoner shuffle and jab, facing into the opposing corner.

"I think he's got something in his fists," Hennessy whispered.

"Not surprised," Anton said. "Probably a roll of coins." He touched the bump on his broken nose with the thumb of one glove. He remembered his bare-knuckle fights as a boy at town carnivals and county fairs, working with the gypsy shills, shambling into the ring, then taking on all comers until some big farm lad kept him down. "Tie them tighter. Tighter."

The medical officer stepped over to Anton. "How do you feel?"

"Worried."

"Then you're still all right. What happened to these ribs?"

"Got thumped by a buff in the Aberdares. Long time ago."

"And these long scars on your collarbone?"

"Leopard in the Din Din," said Anton as Hennessy grinned. "Ethiopia."

"The rest look like bullets," said the medic, checking him once more back and front, whistling quietly. "Still, you look strong enough. Must be used to it. Little soft about the gut for this sort of work, though, but with those arms and shoulders you should be able to give old Jock a bit of sport for a change."

"Next! Next!" the crowd hollered. Anton walked slowly past the referee to the center of the ring, his hands low at his sides. He continued at the same pace, two more steps towards the opposing corner, where the sergeant-major stood wiping his face on a towel.

Anton took one more step, reaching Stoner as the New Zealander looked up and dropped the towel, squinting into the setting sun.

Anton swung low with his left, ignoring the referee's hand on his shoulder.

Astonished, Stoner moved both hands to cover his belly.

Rider's entire body exploded forward off his back foot. His right hit Stoner full in the face with all his strength.

Stoner's nose was broken. Blood flooded down his face across his mouth and chin. He fell backwards against his corner post as the crowd cursed and yelled. Anton hoped this would be enough. He recalled the incredible blinding pain when his own nose had been broken.

"Pommie bastard! Kill him! Kill him!"

The referee raised both arms and blew his whistle as Anton tried to reach around him and get in a few more.

Still game, Stoner straightened, wiping blood from his face with his gloves. The referee checked him once, lifted one eyelid with his thumb, nodded, and quickly stepped aside.

Stoner shuffled forward. He was pig-angry, his eyes tight and red above the scars on his cheekbones, squinting into the intense sunlight. He held his hands high, his head bobbing slowly from side to side. He licked the blood from his lips. Gathering strength as he advanced, he gave Rider controlled slamming lefts to the face and body. With each blow Anton felt he was being pounded with an anvil.

Anton stepped back, already short of breath. He jabbed with his left, trying to use his longer reach to keep the sergeant-major at bay. On his face and chest he felt the slick blood that Stoner had wiped onto his gloves.

"Kill the bugger, Jocko!"

Trying not to lose the freedom of the center of the ring, Anton held his ground, looking for an opening. Stoner came at him, leading with short rights, preparing to level Rider with his left. Anton gave him a right and left to the stomach. It was like punching the grill of an oncoming locomotive. He tried a right hook, just missing the New Zealander's nose, then gave him two hard jabs to the face. Stoner came in like a raging animal, ignoring the blows. Blood and sweat sprayed from his face when Anton hit him. Finally in close, Stoner snapped Anton's head back with a short right jab to the chin. Then he caught Anton's exposed raised head with a brutal left hook to the ear.

Anton staggered backwards, dazed, his head ringing.

"Kill 'im, Jock! Kill 'im, the bleedin' bastard!"

Stoner hammered him in the belly and ribs, pressing Anton into his corner. Anton felt several ribs were breaking. He struggled to protect himself with his arms and elbows. He kept both fists in front of his face, his shoulders hunched in tight. He knew he could take no more. He just hoped to get in one more punch where it would count the most.

The whistle blew to stop the round.

Stoner stepped in again and gave Anton a hard combination to the ribs while Rider sought to protect his face.

The whistle blew again and again. The referee tried to come between the two men.

Anton took a step to the right. Ignoring the whistle, he feinted with his left. Almost off his feet, he flung himself at Stoner and put his whole body behind a right hook to the nose. He felt the blow connect.

Anton fell across the referee, knocking the man down beneath him. Dizzy and exhausted, Anton scrambled to his feet, moving after Stoner in case he needed a little more.

Stoner's broken nose was flattened against his right cheek. Blood covered his chest. He collapsed backward, cracking his head violently against the petrol drum in his corner.

A dozen Kiwis stormed into the ring and pushed the referee aside.

"Stinking Pommie bastard!" they cried, going for Anton as Makanyanga and Hennessy fought to protect him.

Pumping the horn, a young lieutenant drove a truck into one side of the ring. The fighting stopped.

"All good training," said Lagnold between sips of whisky, nodding with satisfaction. "All good training." He looked up at Anton. "Ah, Rider, there you are. Looks like you could use some fodder."

"Thank you, sir." Careful not to groan, Anton sat down stiffly at the officers' mess. The long informal table was set near Lagnold's tent. Instead of regimental silver engraved with legends like Hougoumont and Sebastopol, Fontenoy and Talavera, the rough packing-case table was cluttered with cipher books and sun compasses, protractors and dividers, maps and radio parts.

"How'd you enjoy our RSM?" Lagnold poured Anton a solid whisky.

"Glad he's on our side," said Anton, his right ear deaf. He'd just shared a few free pints with the bandaged sergeant-major and a roaring gang of Kiwis. "That Stoner's a hard one to put down. Just like an old buffalo. If you don't kill him with the first shot, his adrenaline starts pumping and he'll come on forever, dead or not." Tough and jovial, the New Zealanders had welcomed Anton like one of their own, collecting him and the sergeant-major at the medical tent and clamoring for a rematch.

"They tell me Stoner wants another go," said one officer across the table. "And, if you win again, of course it'll be your job to take on all comers."

"Fair enough," said Rider, trying not to breathe too deeply lest he stretch his bandaged ribs. "But I reckon old Makanyanga deserves first crack at him."

Hennessy called from the other end of the table as he reached for the meat pie. "Where'd you learn to fight like that, sir?"

Heads turned to catch Anton's reply.

"My first time," said Anton. "Beginner's luck."

— 5 —

"What wonderful work you've done, Giscard." Gwenn entered the tent, pleased she'd come to visit the dig before it closed, and respecting the dedication that Giscard's work demanded. She brushed the dirt from her long tan skirt. "I'm sorry it's been a bit disappointing."

De Neuville leaned back from the long folding table and rubbed his eyes, reddened by the bright sunlight and sharp dust that gusted about on this escarpment above the Nile. Frowning, he picked up the long lined sheets of excavation records. He dreaded the dreary work of cataloguing secondary material.

"It's always the same, trésor," he said. "Unless you discover a virgin tomb, never found and ravaged by grave robbers and vandals, it's rare to find the artifacts and treasures that make this life worthwhile." Let alone the original vivid colors and the jewels and precious objects of which he dreamed. And virgins were rare, and every day harder to find. Too often the thieves got there first, damaging whatever they left behind. And if you were fortunate and found something unspoiled, he thought, then more sophisticated predators joined you from the Service des Antiquités.

"But what an exciting new find near that fishing village, at San al-Hagar."

"Pure luck," said de Neuville, shrugging. "After ten years, that professor from Strasbourg didn't even know what he was looking for. And it's late, twenty-first dynasty, not so important. The empire was in decay."

"Still, a gold sarcophagus," said Gwenn, "and all those lovely objects, the gold finger and toe cases, the jewelry, those little fluted gold bells on the chain . . ."

"Nonsense. The sarcophagus wasn't gold. Only the mask was gold. The body covering was gilded silver," said de Neuville quickly, shaking his head. "And the damp of the Delta had destroyed everything made of wood or leather. Only the copper lance tips and arrowheads were left from the weapons."

But envy devoured the archeologist as he thought of what it must have been like to be the first man in three thousand years to enter the anteroom through the narrow shaft and pass into the funerary chamber and come upon the huge outer sarcophagus of rose granite. Then, after breathing the haunting musty air, by torch and lamplight to prise off the lid and find the inner mummiform black granite sarcophagus containing a second of gold and silver, sculpted in the likeness of the king, his arms folded across his chest, his hands holding the sceptre and royal flail. And inside that sarcophagus, the royal mummy of King Psusennes himself. To a man of discernment, it was an opportunity worth killing for.

"Come, please, ya bey," said de Neuville's head man, bowing. "Please take final see before we close the tombs."

De Neuville put on his straw hat and light cotton work gloves. Together the three walked between the six long tables laid out under the canvas canopy. Here and there on the numbered trays set on the tables were pieces of some modest value, at least to the average collector or secondary museum: shards, a few pots and broken tools and weapons, and some yards of hieroglyphics fitted together like bits of a puzzle, some fragments faded, the best badly chipped and scratched where clumsy looters had attempted to remove them. But there was nothing worthy, nothing left to inspire a man of de Neuville's scholarship and ambition, nothing on which to build a fortune or a reputation.

They followed Hassan out past stacks of abandoned wicker baskets. The remains of the crew loitered about in the heat, shirtless, squatting on their heels or sitting on rocks wiping their faces with the ends of the cloths wrapped about their heads.

They arrived at the entrance to the tomb that was set into the rocky hillside. Hassan handed de Neuville a torch. The Frenchman took Gwenn's hand and walked into the cool dark chamber.

Walking swiftly, familiar with every inch, he scanned the floor and the north wall as they entered, then the narrow rear surface and the south wall as they left. Bare now, except for the occasional pile of screened rock and a few unclear images on the walls, this modest space had consumed six months of his life. Finally they returned to the entrance looking down towards the Nile. "The last priest must have stood here looking out before this tomb was sealed," de Neuville said, "four thousand years ago."

"That's just what I was thinking," Gwenn said, pleased to have shared his thought.

"All finish, effendi?" asked the Egyptian.

"Have the men build a frame around the entrance, Hassan, then nail on double rows of boards. Set a row of big stones against the base. You know what to do," Giscard said wearily as Gwenn released his hand and he pulled off his gloves. "And paint on the date and the government excavation number."

"What have you learned?" asked the grey-haired Frenchman two days later, suppressing his impatience as he fiddled with his ivory-handled magnifying glass. He pushed an envelope across the table.

"*Jamais assez, Monsieur,*" replied the young Egyptian, an inspector for the Department of Irrigation, pleased to demonstrate his mastery of this distinguished language. "Never enough." Admiring his host's elegant tan suit, he picked up the envelope with no word of acknowledgment. With this, he would be able to buy two thick gold bracelets for his fiancée, and a silver ring for himself. "But I have learned something."

"Yes?" said Giscard-de Neuville. He tapped the magnifying glass on the photographs of hieroglyphics that were spread on the old work table. "Yes?"

"It seems that Monsieur Alavedo's new irrigation ditch is no longer intended for irrigation. He has called off his workers, the local fellahin, and redirected their work to a new tributary canal some distance to the south, excellency. He has filed these new plans with our Department."

"Why is this information of value to me?"

"Because new laborers, very black men from Nubia, savages really, are still digging along the line of the old trench, but to a different width and depth than the former irrigation canal, and this dwarf has excluded all others from that part of his estate."

"Anything else?" The Frenchman leaned forward, his interest aroused. If this midget had found a new tomb, and was working it without disclosing it to the Service des Antiquités, it could mean opportunity for a man who shared his secret.

"Only, excellency, that they say his men are sifting rock and sand through fine screens, boring foolish work."

"I see, Gamal. You must learn more. You must learn everything." The French archeologist paused and glanced at the photograph of the woman on his desk. "Now let me give you some personal advice."

"Excellency?"

"Do not yet choose your bride."

"Why not, excellency? Already my father has spoken several times to her father." He drew a picture from his pocket. His face softened. He dusted the photograph on his cuff and passed it to de Neuville. "Already I have taken tea with the girl and her mother. I believe she loves me."

"Because if you do well in this matter for me, you will be able to afford a better one, without these teeth, without that mustache. A girl who will be lovelier, and richer, Gamal, with a proper dowry. And if you fail me, you will be too poor to marry anyone."

"I must warn you, Mr. Anton," said the dwarf, seated at his table on the poop deck, cheerful in his new maroon tarbush. He was eager to receive the guests at the reception given by the directors of the Suez Canal Company to celebrate the seventieth anniversary of the opening of the Canal. "I must warn you. All the French will be here. You know what they are like. It is their company, and this Monsieur de Neuville will be among them. Undoubtedly, Miss Gwenn will accompany him. Her French is now almost perfect."

"Is it? Maybe I'll just finish my drink and get back to camp."

"No, no, Mr. Anton!" The dwarf shook his head fiercely, the silken tassel of his tarbush flying about. He admired his friend's heart, but was alarmed by his innocence. "You must not avoid your love, or your enemies. No, no. Let Miss Gwenn see how you are, and who he is. You are so dashing in this new uniform. It speaks of honor and high principle. In her heart, Miss Gwenn knows you are doing the right thing, and that her Frenchman never will."

"Mmm, good of you," said Anton awkwardly, reaching for his gin.

"If everyone avoided his enemies, there would be no French parties, and my café would be impoverished. Tonight, Spanish fascists will dance with Greek communists, royalists will drink with Marxists, the King of Albania himself will chat with Balkan anarchists." The little man tapped the table-top with tight swollen knuckles. "Stay here by me, Mr. Anton, and I will teach you the way of the world."

As he spoke, Citroens and Bugattis, Rolls Royces and Fords and Rovers began drawing up to the embankment. With commanding gestures of his qurbash, Tariq beat back the beggars and peddlars who were swarming rat-like to the scene. At the bottom of the gangway, a tall thin Frenchman with a wide thin mustache smiled and kissed hands as the guests descended.

"Observe Monsieur Verdier, the Deputy Chairman of the Canal Company," said the dwarf to Anton. "A French gentleman who understands the limitatons of sincerity. Learn from him, Mr. Anton, please. His demeanor is his demeanor, nothing more. Five years ago, it was he who levied the fees on each Italian soldier who passed through the Canal to invade Abyssinia, even as his own brother condemned Mussolini at the League of Nations in Geneva. Even as France sold guns to the Ethiopians and Renault tanks to the Italians."

An hour later, the vessel was lower in the water. Two hundred guests devoured the delicacies of Europe and Goa and the Levant: spiced samosas and rich canapés and stout pigeons stuffed with cracked wheat and garlic and the birds' own chopped livers, hearts and gizzards. Arranged along the port gunwale were long tables presenting roasts of lamb and beef and turkey, veal tonnato and boned quail *en gelée*, shrimp and salmon and caviar, sambusak and börek, mishmishiyya and hummus and more. As noisy and crowded as the deck of a frigate fighting to repel boarders, cutlass and pike and pistol in hand, the Cataract Café trembled with the energy of conversation, scandal and romance.

Trapped against the starboard gunwale, Anton waited for Gwenn to arrive. He knew he was not in the best of moods. He always wanted to see her, but rarely enjoyed it when he did. Yet if neither of them could change, he thought, perhaps they could at least modify the way they treated each other. Or was even that too much?

As usual at Olivio's events, Anton was struck not so much by the guests as by the parade of costumes. The show was changing with the war, as it used to change with the seasons. Formerly the tailored European suits of the men had provided a neutral backdrop to the gay dresses of the ladies from the fashion houses of London and New York and the great couturiers of Paris. But now the ladies were outdone by guards officers and sirdars, wing commanders and admirals.

"Waiting for someone?" said Harriet, suddenly at his side. "Me?"

"Always," smiled Anton, kissing her cheek. Just then his eye caught Gwenn descending the gangway with her Frenchman.

Feeling hollow when he saw her, Anton forced himself to greet his wife with good cheer. Harriet turned discreetly to chat with another admirer.

"*Enchanté de vous revoir.*" The Frenchman lowered his head as Anton shook the man's soft hand.

"May I speak to you for a moment, Gwenn?" Anton asked.

Gwenn let Anton lead her aside, relieved that he was being civil. How well his uniform suited him, she thought. He looked tan and fit, better than he had for years.

He came directly to the point. "Gwenn, I'd like to spend some time with you and Denby while I've a few days on leave."

"Of course, you can see Denby whenever you'd like," she said neutrally, dreading any complications. "But what about his school fees?"

"I'm doing my best," he said, always challenged by her practicality. "But a captain's pay doesn't go far in Cairo these days. Could we have dinner later tonight?"

"I have to operate early in the morning," she said, relieved to have the excuse, yet in a way wishing she could join him. "I really can't. The hospital trains keep coming down from Alex. Every day they're longer and longer. I hardly have time to see Denby."

"You've time for all this," he said sharply, knowing he should not.

"This is the first thing I've done all week," Gwenn said, irritated, gathering herself before she continued. "Besides, I don't have to justify my behaviour to you."

She turned back towards Giscard, touching his arm and smiling, knowing he would be annoyed with the attention she had given Anton. Giscard placed his hand on hers. Gwenn was pleased to see Monsieur Verdier coming to join them.

A small ribbon of the Cross of Lorraine in his lapel, Verdier bore his Gaullism with pride. Ignoring Olivio's advice, Anton excused himself as Verdier stepped over.

"I am pleased to welcome you, Giscard," said Verdier after he bent to kiss Gwenn's hand. "We are having our first meeting tomorrow evening, the National Committee of Free France in Egypt, to discuss how to support General LeGentilhomme, to give his officers the assistance that France today cannot. There will be a captain from the Foreign Legion."

"They say that in Syria, the Legion itself is divided between Vichy and Free France," observed de Neuville.

"Will you join us tomorrow, Giscard? Are you with us at last?"

"I should like to, if I can," said de Neuville with care, handing Gwenn a glass of champagne from a passing tray. He was reluctant to be drawn deeper into the dangerous schemes of either side, not trusting the outcome, or the discretion of others. What could a committee in Cairo possibly do for Paris? "If not, I will advise you tomorrow, and see what I can do."

Verdier nodded and turned to greet other guests.

"Why didn't you offer to help?" asked Gwenn, annoyed with both Anton and her lover. "I'm surprised you haven't joined the Free French."

"I have already fought the Germans, my dear." Giscard helped himself to a layered sugared pastry. "In the last war. It was not a useful experience." He dusted his pale fingers. "And my father and grandfather fought the Germans in '14 and in 1870. Perhaps it is not something that France should do forever."

"Sometimes you confuse me, Giscard." Gwenn gripped his arm. "The Germans are occupying your country, your own house. They're slaughtering people all over Europe. You know my own son has gone to fight them." She tried to look her lover in the eye. "But it never seems to bother you, not even this Gaullist-Vichy business."

"It is complicated," he said quietly.

"Complicated?" Gwenn asked with bitterness, irritated by his tone of calm reason. "Our world is at stake."

"Very complicated," de Neuville said. Sometimes he could not fathom her moral innocence. "Please understand. For France, everything is different. It is not like England. My country is occupied. Her expatriates are divided. What do we gain by fighting each other? In this war, a New Zealander and an Englishman share more than do two Frenchmen. For most Frenchmen, Germany has already won this war. The French who are active are struggling because of who they want to rule France after everything is finished. I myself am patriotic, not quixotic. I must ask myself, what is best for France, and how will one live?"

"You just don't seem to care," she said with impatience.

"I do care, and I care about you, my dear," he said, meaning it, putting his smooth hand over hers.

"Which side are you on?"

Giscard regarded her with open untroubled eyes.

"Which side am I on?" He looked from side to side, shrugged and turned down the corners of his mouth.

"Which side am I on? I am a Frenchman."

Making his way to the crowded bar, Anton found himself elbow to elbow with a short thick-set man, a captain dressed in the dark blue uniform and red piping of the Foreign Legion. Directly in front of them, three French naval officers in summer whites and decorations laughed gaily as they held their positions at the bar, forcing others to shout drink orders over their shoulders.

The jostling crowd pressed Anton against the Legionnaire. "Excuse me," he said.

The man nodded, not unfriendly, and gave Anton a hard smile before loudly calling his order to the barman.

"Double cognac!"

When he was finally served, the Legionnaire reached between two of the French sailors to take his drink from the bartender.

Abruptly raising his hand to light a cigarette for one of his companions, the sailor in the middle knocked the brandy from the soldier's hand, spilling the drink over the third sailor.

"*Putain de merde!*" cried the sailor, his white uniform hopelessly soiled. Red-faced, he turned sharply. "*Quel con!*"

"*Quel con?*" The soldier seized the taller man by the two sides of his soiled tunic. "*Sale collabo!*" The Legionnaire slammed the sailor against the bar. "*Pédale de Pétainiste!*"

Conscious of Gwenn's presence, Anton tried to step back. He knew these things never ended well. But he was held by the press of the crowd.

The Legionnaire released the torn tunic. He pulled down the sailor's head and head-butted him twice, brow to brow, bang bang, with knocks that jarred the bar. The skin of the sailor's forehead split open in a wide horizontal line as the man cursed. Blood flooded down over his eyes. The crowd screamed and recoiled from the scene, some aghast, some amused. Anton prayed his wife was not watching.

The other two sailors, sturdier than their fallen companion, immediately attacked the Legionnaire. One man clubbed the soldier in the side of the head with a bottle of Cointreau.

Anton was struck by one of the sailor's blows, splashed with the liqueur. Sensing that they assumed he was the Legionnaire's companion and would come after him next, Anton backhanded one sailor, but controlled himself and held the stunned man against the bar until the fight was over, hoping he had helped to stop the commotion.

Then he glanced back along the deck and saw Gwenn staring at him above the crowd. De Neuville was at her side. Her face was thin-lipped, her expression set hard. He knew she would blame him for the violence. As usual, she would say, he was in the thick of it.

Anton turned back to the bar, certain it was hopeless. He might as well enjoy himself. There wouldn't be many parties in the desert.

"Nordhouse," the Legionnaire introduced himself. His handshake was hard as a freight car coupling. He wiped a smear of blood from his forehead as he and Anton took the sailors' place at the bar. *"Cognac? Un double?"*

"Thank you," said Anton. "Sound idea." He watched Tariq escort the sailors from the party.

"Thanks for your help with those Vichy bastards," said Nordhouse in reasonable English, the accent not quite the French Anton had heard in the past.

"You didn't need it," Anton said.

"I don't know your uniform," said the Legionnaire.

"New outfit," said Anton. "We're just getting started. Where're you from? I thought Legion officers had to be French."

"Only above the rank of captain. I'm from Alsace." Nordhouse raised two fingers to order more drinks. "The men are from all over. Senegal, Germany, Russia, Spain. Though some of the boches have been slipping away to join their own."

"How do you like Cairo?"

"Better than Brazza. But we just got back here after messing about with the *macaronis* near Kufra." He lifted his drink. "To Camerone!"

"Who's Camerone?"

"She's not a girl. It's a village in Mexico, where one of our companies was destroyed a hundred years ago. The last six men, rifles empty, charged two thousand Mexicans with the bayonet. We always drink to it." Nordhouse drained his glass. *"Faire Camerone,"* we say when things get bad. "What you Britishers call 'fight to the last man.'"

Back on deck the party continued. De Neuville spoke to Gwenn, who remained at his side, silent and restless.

"I see your husband is brawling again."

"Perhaps," she said. "But at least he made a choice."

— 6 —

Ernst von Decken dragged the bloody body of his dead driver out the door. He flung the man down by the side of the road and took the wheel of the Fiat 508. The damned Hurricanes climbed and droned away to the west. He used the driver's tan sun helmet to knock away the rest of the windshield and sweep the glass off the seat. He tossed the helmet onto the body and slammed the door. With the British and French closing in, it was time to leave East Africa.

Ernst wiped the blood from his left eye with the cuff of his sahariana. He ignored the cut on his forehead and drove for the nearby aerodrome at Gura. Ripped and punctured by the straffing, the torn canvas roof flapped and snapped in the wind like a loose sail.

The Free French were already approaching Massawa. The Foreign Legion was leading the attack, their ranks hardened with too many of Ernst's countrymen who knew what war was meant to be.

Most of von Decken's surviving men were back in their ships and trying to make for the open sea. Ernst knew he'd be lucky to catch a plane out of Eritrea before the British seized the airport. Swerving around abandoned Italian scout cars and ambulances, light tanks and trucks, he reflected on the fighting of the last two months. He'd been surprised by the determination of some of the Italian units, both native troops and the real spaghetti boys. For two months they'd held Eritrea's mountain passes against two Indian divisions of the British army, well-trained professional soldiers. Better in attack than defense, the Italians had fought with flashes of spirit when well led, but once things turned sour, if an

officer fell or the enemy got behind them, they melted like soft cheese in
the sun.

Von Decken's Germans had done their bit, reinforcing the Savoy Grenadiers near the Dongolaas Gorge. But a Blackshirt Legion had collapsed
on their left flank. Lightly armed, his small German unit had been overrun
by a screaming mob of Punjabis and Cameron Highlanders, typical savages
of the British Empire. Ordered to fly out and report to German headquarters in Tripoli, Ernst had directed his men to try for their ships in Massawa.
Then he and his orderly had made it back to the Fiat before the Hurricanes
caught them on the road.

Almost out of petrol, Ernst let the Fiat coast downhill to the aerodrome,
two dirt runways that crossed each other in the flat oval valley. A litter of
damaged aircraft surrounded the airstrips like a necklace, probably destroyed by British bombers, the Blenheims and Hardys and old single-
engined Wellesleys he had seen flying overhead for the past week.

As von Decken pulled up, he saw a pilot and a mechanic clipping down
the cowling of the bow engine of a Savoia-Marchetti 81. Two other Italian
pilots were at work nearby, helping several African orderlies drag a damaged aircraft from the strip. The engine and fuselage of the Breda were
still smoldering as the men hauled the fighter by the tail.

Ernst stepped down and limped to the three-engine Savoia.

"Anything still flying?" he asked the young captain of the *Regia Aeronautica*.

The flyer wiped his face on his sleeve. "Just this one, or two thirds of it
anyway. Starboard engine's dead. *Bastardi inglesi* have been bombing us
every day," he said as the other two pilots hurried over. "We're off for Libya
as soon as they've cleared the strip. Looks like right now. Who are you?"

"Captain von Decken. German Military Mission." Ernst saluted and
reached into a pocket of his sahariana. "I have priority from your headquarters on any flight out. Here's authorization from General Galtieri."

As he spoke, a fast drone rose in the west and the African troopers began
to run clear of the field. The three pilots dived into a trench at the edge
of the strip.

Ernst hesitated, watching the flight of Hurricanes close on the aero-
drome, flying low. When they were close enough for him to make out their
South African markings, he threw himself into the trench on top of the
Italians, jamming his stump against the side of the pit. The planes strafed

the far end of the strip, concentrating on the larger Italian aircraft grouped together, Capronis and twin-engined Fiats. One of Ernst's trench mates opened a canteen as the planes turned like hornets for another pass. Crammed together, covered in dust and debris, the pilots shared the grappa as the strafing drew closer.

Apparently satisfied, the South Africans turned for home, leaving three aircraft in flames and others even more damaged than before.

Ernst climbed into the back of the Savoia. The three Italian pilots, seated in the front cabin on their parachutes, revved the aircraft's port and bow engines. After refuelling at a small base near the Red Sea, the plane crossed the water and flew north over Saudi Arabia in the moonlight.

Von Decken made himself comfortable in a pile of army blankets stacked in the rear cabin of the Savoia. Ernst tapped his boot against the uninsulated metal hull as the plane flew through the night. He had thrown aside those blankets too stained with dried blood and made himself a clean nest as best he could. Even in the icy cold air he could still smell the stupefying odors of the sick and wounded who had filled the aircraft on her last flights.

Bundled against the cold, he watched as the door to the pilot's cabin opened. One of the Italians stumbled back towards him in the dim light of the single cabin bulb. The man stopped halfway, stood over a tin bucket set on the floor and urinated carelessly into it. Then he belched and buttoned up.

"We thought you could use a drink, too," said the young pilot, plainly drunk, his lips purple with wine. He handed Ernst a wicker-wrapped bottle of chianti. "Gianni thinks we're the last plane out of Eritrea, but we've still got a damned long way to go."

"Why're we flying so far east?" Ernst opened his pocketknife, cut off the foil cap and forced the cork into the bottle with the other end of the knife. He took a long pull and handed up the bottle.

"Staying away from the Sudan, and Egypt." The pilot drank and wiped his mouth. "Too much British ack-ack, fighters, who knows. We're flying up along the Saudi coast, then west along the Med to Benghazi, if we're lucky." He drank again, nearly finishing the wine before he passed the bottle back.

"It's going to be a long war, Luigi," said von Decken, forgetting the man's name. "Bring along another bottle. Perhaps a smoke?"

The Italian made his way forward and back again, steadying himself against the fuselage. He slumped down near Ernst with two bottles in one hand and an open packet of Nazionales gripped in his teeth.

"What're you going to be doing if we make it?" He tossed the crumpled cigarettes in Ernst's lap.

"Get a wash. Burn my clothes." Ernst scratched himself and lit a cigarette. "Ach. What do you greasers put in these things?" He spat and picked bits of loose tobacco from his teeth and lips. "Then a few drinks, some girls. And off to Tripoli to see how I can help kill a few more Britishers."

"You'll be just in time. The advance party of German tanks, the first *Panzers*, landed in Tripoli last month, two days after your General Rommel. Too bad they weren't in time for the real fighting." The Italian stretched out his legs on the sloping metal floor and took a bottle after Ernst opened it. "Rommel's serving under our old General Gariboldi, of course."

"Is he? Surprising. Sounds like it's your boys who need the orders," said Ernst, opening his own bottle. "Lost ten divisions up there in a few days, didn't you, Luigi? Half your quarter million men in North Africa."

"What would you know? Maybe you Krauts won't find it's so easy either," said the pilot belligerently, drinking and staring at Ernst's peg. "Everything's harder in Africa. You'll see."

"Is that right?" Ernst felt anger growing inside him. He recalled his years fighting across Africa, not to mention the risks he'd been taking recently and the countrymen he'd lost trying to help the Italians in Eritrea.

"We've been doing it all, fighting the English out here for months. I've lost a brother, and friends everywhere, the Sudan, Kenya, Eritrea," the other man said aggressively, "Somaliland, Ethiopia, Libya, and it's just beginning." His voice rose, screaming at von Decken over the roar of the engines. "You Germans don't know what it's like fighting in Africa!"

"We don't?" Ernst said, enraged. "I was killing English in Africa, and all the mess they bring with them, Rhodesians, Australians, Schwarzes, before you learned to suck spaghetti. In the last war, you damn greasers fought with the British. This time you've stabbed the French in the back."

"*Stupidaggini!*" The Italian reached over to take a cigarette from the pack next to Ernst. "And look at you. You're lucky. With that leg you'll never have a chance to learn what it's like, fighting out here."

"Lucky, Luigi?" Von Decken thought of the Italian pilot who had shot him down in Ethiopia and cost him his right foot five years before. Not satisfied with shooting down his plane, the greaser had broken the aviator's code by chasing his smoking Potez all the way down, firing the whole time, tight on his tail, finally sending him crashing into a Rift Valley lake.

"Lucky?" Ernst grabbed the flyer by the collar, his fingers inside the front of the pilot's tunic. Then he stood, forcing the smaller man to rise with him. "Lucky, am I?" With his other hand Ernst opened the hatch handle. He held the Italian against the cabin wall next to the door. Freezing air whistled in around the edges as the hatch door remained pressed against the airplane by the wind.

"Let's see how lucky you are." Von Decken shook the man against the hull of the fuselage.

"Don't be stupid," the flyer protested, seizing Ernst's arm with weak hands.

Ernst shifted the man's body until it rested against the unlocked door.

"Don't forget to open your parachute." He pushed the pilot backwards and released him.

The hatch flapped open. The Italian fell into black space. A scream rose to his lips as he dropped away, the sound unheard over the roar of the engines. Ernst glanced down before he secured the hatch. He thought he saw a white chute open in the night. Then he sat and finished both bottles of wine.

"Wake up, damn you!" A man yelled several hours later, kicking Ernst in the side. "Where's Giorgio?" The Savoia's engines throbbed steadily.

"Who's Giorgio?" Ernst yawned broadly. He gripped his pistol in his hand under the blanket beside him. "What do I know? I've been asleep."

"I said, where's Giorgio, the other pilot?"

"He was drinking. Maybe he stepped out. You're not meant to drink and fly."

The pilot drew back a foot to kick him again.

"Careful, Luigi." Ernst grabbed the man's ankle with his free hand. "Careful. Don't you do anything foolish. We need two pilots, and you've been drinking, too."

The man grunted and returned to the cabin.

It was early morning now. Out the left-hand window, looking south, Ernst saw a world of two halves. The upper, a spotless infinite blue; the lower, the endless light grey-brown of the desert. He would be in Libya soon enough.

                              *   *   *

"You were in the Schutztruppe in the last one, I'm told, Captain von
Decken, campaigning in East Africa against the British." The general
turned his back to the immense map of Cyrenaica and northern Egypt that
covered the wall behind him. He faced Ernst and clasped his hands behind
his back. "Were you not?"

"Jawohl, Herr General." Immediately Ernst recognized the high, perfectly
symmetrical forehead, the strong nose and cheekbones, the narrow mouth
and forceful chin.

"How long did you serve?" The commander appraised von Decken with
unavoidable keen blue eyes. In contrast to Ernst's filthy castaway Italian
gear and informal German markings, he was immaculate in olive tan twill
tunic, high black leather boots and breeches with red stripes running the
length of the outer edges.

"Four years, sir."

"Were you with von Lettow-Vorbeck?"

"Always."

"I have met General von Lettow twice, but briefly." Erwin Rommel's
eyes examined von Decken with increased interest. "He was the officer I
admired most in the last war. Even the British regiments he fought against
invite him to their dinners in London. Unfortunately, he declined the
Führer's appointment as ambassador to England." The general paused and
rose up and down on the toes of his boots. "What was he like in the field?"

"Resourceful. Enduring. Demanding . . ."

"And his Africans, how did they like soldiering with him?"

"Our askaris trekked with us, sir, unpaid, for four years. They never saw
their families, and they never left him. He ate what they ate. He slept
where they slept."

"In this campaign, we will have no Africans, only Italians." The general
almost smiled. "I hope they will serve as well."

"I doubt it, sir," said von Decken.

Rommel looked at Ernst more intently. "You could be right. Two weeks
ago, from Sidi Barrani to Beda Fomm, the Italians lost four hundred tanks
and a hundred and thirty thousand men, with only two thousand British
casualties."

The general's compact and sturdy figure rocked slightly on the heels of
his boots. "When we have time, Captain, I will ask you to tell me more

of those old days. And yourself, where were you wounded? Tanganyika? Kenya? On the march?"

"No, sir. Long after the war. An Italian shot up my aircraft, an old Potez, during their invasion of Ethiopia in '35."

"I, too, fought the Italians. In the Dolomites." The general continued, dismissing the point. "But now, Captain, they must march with us, all the way to Cairo and the Suez Canal."

"Excuse me, General Rommel," said an officer, clicking his heels by the arched doorway of the stately colonial building. "Your car is here, sir, to take you to inspect the new armor."

"Join me, Captain," said the general, donning his *Schirmütze*, his high-peaked general's cap with gold cording and broad-winged silver eagle. "We'll see if we can't find work for you."

They climbed into an open MB 340. As they drove, Ernst shielded his eyes from the sand and wind and sun. He tried to recall what he had heard of the energetic figure beside him. Wounded three times in the last war, a hero of the *Alpenkorps* on the Rumanian front, the young lieutenant who attacked three French soldiers in a wood with an empty rifle, Rommel was famous for capturing two thousand Bersaglieri. Said to be the very body and soul of war, he was a legend for his boldness on attack. He was a rare mixture of aggressiveness and chivalry. Between the wars he had served as commandant of the *Kriegsschule*. Never joining the party, he was whispered to dislike the Nazis, but to admire Hitler for reviving Germany. In this war, he had led his 7th Panzers, the *Gespensterdivision*, the Ghost Division, as his tanks raced from Belgium to Cherbourg. Could it all be true? Ernst wondered, hoping this would not be more of a war than he had in mind.

After thirty minutes, they pulled up in a section of desert near a Luftwaffe base. Scattered across the hard sand were what appeared to be a few broken down half-tracks and dozens of small crude-looking tanks. The car stopped beside one of the tanks.

Two soldiers with paintbrushes snapped to attention. Before anyone could assist him, Rommel opened the small triangular door of the military Mercedes and stepped down onto the footplate, squinting into the harsh sharp light of the desert.

Ernst gazed with astonishment at the tank. It was in fact a piece of canvas stretched over a wooden frame crudely built in the shape of a *Panzerkampfwagen III* and resting on top of a Volkswagen utility car. One soldier was painting the canvas field gray, with slashes of camouflage yellow. The other was painting a black and white *Wehrmacht* cross on the dry side of the 'tank.' Ernst looked at other vehicles nearby. Most were empty shells, without even the Volkswagens inside them.

"Splendid!" Rommel clapped his hands. "The Cardboard Division. Drive a tank back and forth between all these dummies to leave tracks for the Royal Air Force photographers. They'll think the 15th Panzer's already here. That should keep the pressure off us until they do arrive." He climbed into the car. The vehicle began to move almost before Ernst had hobbled over and jumped in.

"To the Luftwaffe workshops," Rommel directed.

"Without the workshops," he said to Ernst, "we will soon have no aircraft and no tanks. We will have less of everything than the British, and they can be resupplied more easily. So our planes must fly more missions, our tanks must run more miles. We must fight better. And for every machine, the sand is a second enemy. Here in the desert, we must nurse each machine like an old man in a clinic. We must be able to repair a Mark III in two days and send it back to battle."

They found the workshop in an old Italian hangar. German engineers and mechanics were installing generators and rigging overhead frames and wall racks. Steel tool chests were being laid out by colors and numbers. Heavy lathes were already bolted in place. Nearby, young officers, stripped to the waist, mosquito netting hanging from their peaked field caps, were directing gangs of Libyan laborers in building new hangars and tool sheds.

Teams of men with paintbrushes were covering sections of the outer wall of the hangar with various shades of yellow and different combinations of mottled grey and green and brown. "Sorting out the camouflage, testing," Rommel said as they passed. "Varies too much in the desert with the time of day and the light. Sand yellow seems best."

Rommel walked about rapidly, his hands clasped behind his back, his shoulders slightly arched, nodding as the young Germans paused in their work and saluted. Occasionally he stopped to ask questions. "How is the food, Lieutenant?" "How many spare engines do we have for the Heinkels?" "When is my Storch arriving?"

Behind the hangar they found three engines being removed from two damaged Junker bombers. Four battered Fiat lorries waited nearby. The fourth engine was already mounted on a metal frame secured to the rear of one truck. The large propeller faced backwards.

Had it not been General Rommel, Ernst would have asked if the trucks were meant to fly.

"Can you guess what these are for, Captain?"

"Perhaps to create sandstorms, sir, sand screens to confuse the enemy. Make him think it's a squadron of Mark IIIs or IVs, heavy armor crossing the desert."

General Rommel nodded and turned to inspect several crates of supplies captured from the British, a gift of General Gariboldi to celebrate an early Italian victory. He bent over a case of thin Perspex anti-gas goggles. He lifted out one pair, removed his cap, and tried on the glasses, squinting up towards the sun. "*Perfekt!* Put a box of these in my car," the general said to his driver. Then he secured the goggles over the brow of his cap and turned back to Ernst.

"For the moment, Captain, after you've had two days' leave and have got yourself some proper uniforms, you'll be assigned to my *Kampfstaffel,* the small combat group attached to my own headquarters. Soon we'll find you something useful to do."

— 7 —

Smooth as a snake, the slender fingers entered Ernst von Decken's trouser pocket while continuing to stroke his good leg. Without taking his eyes from the dice, the tall hard-faced German reached down with his right hand and seized the delicate wrist of the Libyan girl. He twisted her wrist like a doorknob and drew her hand from his pocket.

Biting her lip, containing her pain in silence, the Arab girl rose from the bar stool to ease the torque on her wrist. She was lucky, he thought. In some Arab countries, they'd cut off her hand.

Without releasing her, von Decken collected both dice from the board and fixed a stern eye on the Italian facing him across the corner of the bar of *Pasquali's Caffè-Pasticceria*.

"Double, Luigi?" the German said. He had to yell over the fervent Blackshirt music that flooded through the wooden shutters from the marching band across the square.

"Of course." The Italian journalist turned the ivory backgammon cube to eight. He swung his head from side to side and gaily drummed his fingers to the strains of *Giovinezza*, the Fascist anthem, the song of youth. Next to the board was a map of North Africa showing Egypt as an Italian possession.

Irritated, von Decken quickly rolled a three and a one and made another point inside his opponent's defenses.

"Our boys will be in Cairo soon," said the Italian, smiling while stirring his Cinzano with a filthy forefinger.

"Will you?" said Ernst carelessly, draining his Peroni. "All by your-

96

selves?" Still gripping the girl's wrist with his other hand, he felt the thin gold coins on her bracelet pressing into her arm like dies in a press. He laid her hand on his leg, where it belonged. He slowly released it as she began to do her duty. "I thought the Führer was sending the Panzers over here to save you."

"Rome started this campaign and we'll finish it." The Italian rolled and cursed, obliged to leave two pieces open.

"A few months ago you had two hundred and forty thousand men against thirty thousand Britishers." Von Decken snorted, knowing this would not help his adversary's game. "And they rolled you up like a prayer rug."

Red-faced, the Italian raised his voice.

"We civilized this stinking waste two thousand years ago when Germany was just a province of Rome! Barefoot German slaves ran behind our chariots in chains!" The Italian crushed his pack of Alfas in one hand. "Who do you think built these forums and baths and amphitheaters all along the coast?" The man paused and tried to calm himself. "We'll lead you into Cairo even before you'll be in London. Care to bet on it?"

"No, Luigi. You don't understand." Ernst shook his head. He recalled the tenacity of the Britishers who had hounded him and his comrades out of German East Africa in the last war. "It's going to be harder than you greasers think. Give them a chance and this filthy country will be English. Even your camels will be drinking tea. Damned *Limonen* stole a farm from my family after the last war."

"Where?"

"Down in Tanganyika, near Kilimanjaro. Luckily my American wife bought it back for me, as a wedding present, more or less."

"Where's she now?"

To his surprise, Ernst had found that he missed her. "Probably on a horse somewhere. Cairo, or Kentucky, maybe. Or else shooting something. These American girls are great killers." Aware Harriet felt that this was more than just a separation, he wondered if she was behaving herself. With the war, there would be a lot of extra men in Cairo. If it went on too long, the devil knew what she'd be up to. He considered what sort of man she'd choose. Either very young or very rich.

Ernst suddenly dropped the dice and cocked back his head.

"Here they come!" A thrill charged his spine as he heard the harsh rattle of the Panzers on the stony macadam of the street. He stood and picked up his new *Afrikamütze*, the peaked cloth field cap with its red sun lining.

"Give the girl what you owe me." He pinched her two cheeks in one hand, firmly enough to make her mouth open and her lips pucker and her eyes stare. Then he kissed her hard on the mouth, tasting her.

Von Decken paused to glance at himself in the cracked mirror above the bar. He admired his new tropical tunic. He set his cap at a smart angle over his short silver hair. No wonder the girls still liked him.

Squinting, he stepped into the hot sunlight of Tripoli's great square, banging the door behind him. Von Decken was just in time to see the first Panzer Mark III roar around the corner and turn into the piazza. Ahead of the tanks paraded a screen of Bersaglieri motorcyclists. Their dark green feathered cockades flapped proudly as Italy's finest Alpine troops lapped around the square before the German armor.

Crowds of Arabs and Italians, merchants and beggars, men in rumpled tan suits and black skull caps and thick white cloaks, and groups of women in long black robes, lined the streets and the piazza. Italian civilians, thousands strong, cheered wildly as the Bersaglieri rode past. But the entire crowd hushed and shrank back from the curbs as the German tanks approached. Gathered under the arches along one side of the square, groups of Blackshirts in sun helmets and baggy pantaloons nodded and muttered to one another.

The great machines rumbled past three by three, like immense prehistoric monsters. They were eighteen feet long and twenty-two tons of steel, all powered by the new 300-horsepower Maybach engine. The Panzers had been up-armored for the African campaign with extra plates of hardened metal and a more powerful short-barrelled Krupp 50mm cannon and two 7.9mm machine guns. Clanking and belching black fumes, the tanks shut down their right treads one by one as they came to the corner, grinding into a sharp right turn as their left treads powered them around. Two of the five crewmen were visible at the hatches in their black woolen sidecaps and metal skull-and-crossbones *Totenkopf* badges. Their black tankers' outfits had been replaced by new tropical uniforms, though the Panzers themselves were still painted in the standard German field grey. Ernst knew the old *Feldgrau* would stand out and draw fire in the desert. Crammed belowdecks, the gunner, loader and radio operator were nestled among a hundred cannon shells and four thousand rounds of machine gun bullets.

Lining two sides of the square, standing six deep, were the motorized infantry, the Panzergrenadiers. They would support the tanks in battle. Each man wore the new tropical German uniform of breeches, sun helmet, and high-lacing canvas and leather boots. Eight teams of machine gunners stood at one end of the line with their weapons and cases of belted ammunition. Limited by the Treaty of Versailles to light machine guns, the Germany army had produced the finest in the world: the deadly long-barrelled Spandau.

A double column of the new heavier Mark IVs followed the Mark IIIs up the street towards the square. Their stubby 75mm guns were elevated in salute. The light four-wheeled armored cars of the 3rd Reconnaisance Battalion followed the tanks around the square.

Ernst hobbled along behind the crowd, proud and excited as a boy. He had waited a lifetime to see the power of the new Germany in Africa. For the first time, von Decken was confident that his country would win. He followed the lead tanks to the center of the square. There General Rommel, immaculate in tall boots and leather gloves, stood beneath the palms to take the salute from his tank commanders as the 5th Panzer Regiment of the 5th Light Division ground past. Rommel's Knight's Cross and his *Pour le Mérite*, his enamel "Blue Max," were at his throat. Beside him stood Italy's Italo Gariboldi, sporting spurs and a thick white mustache. His pince-nez was caught in the heavy belt that carried his Beretta and contained his belly. The parade seemed endless.

After a time, von Decken recognized the identification number 414 on a tank he had previously noticed. The first number, he knew, stood for the company, the middle number for the platoon and the last number for the vehicle. Ernst realized why the parade seemed to go on so long. Ernst estimated that there were only one hundred and fifty tanks, perhaps eighty of them the powerful Mark IIIs and IVs.

The tanks were passing out the other side of the square, circling through the streets and coming past a second time. Rommel wished to defer a British attack until he himself was ready. Still thin on the ground until his second and heavier division arrived, the 15th Panzer, he was giving a stronger impression to the Libyans and to the enemy spies and informers scattered through the crowd. Perhaps this general would manage in Africa, Ernst thought. Von Lettow, too, had replaced strength with ruse and cunning.

"The rest didn't make it." Lagnold stared out across the desert, sitting with Anton Rider in camp chairs behind his tent.

Anton was learning to share Lagnold's affection for the empty quiet of the desert. It was always changing, like the sea. He enjoyed watching the wind stir the colors of the sandy surface and send dust and camel thorn skittering to the horizon. Lagnold had kept moving his tent to the far edge of camp as the base expanded.

"Cut up by the Luftwaffe, then by an Italian patrol, one of their Auto-Saharan Companies, with Breda 20mms, three aircraft overhead, the whole show," Lagnold added. "Mussolini set up these Auto-Saharan outfits before the war to keep down the desert tribes, Senussi and so on. It's the enemy unit most like us. Know their way around. They always work closely with aircraft. Best to stay clear of 'em."

"Sorry things went wrong, sir." Anton watched the single Chevrolet roll towards them through the shimmering desert haze.

"Got the news on their wireless before it whacked out."

Two more trucks appeared in the distance.

"My patrol's set to leave tomorrow," Anton said.

"First we'd best debrief these chaps, and see if your lot can do a little better. I'll expect you for dinner tonight, if you're free. Not required, mind you. Just a couple of drinks to send you on your way."

Anton was determined to see Gwenn before he left. "Thank you, sir, but I've laid on something in town, if you don't mind," he said. "Rather important, actually."

The first Chevy pulled up nearby at the edge of camp. Its engine coughed and died as Anton and Lagnold approached. One side of the truck was dented and charred by fire. It reminded Anton of a story he had once read about the last Carthaginian galley limping into harbor. Her sails were torn and blackened. Her deck was covered with dead. The people of Carthage watched Roman sails crowd the horizon behind her. Without a word said, every citizen realized that the long war was lost, that their great city would be destroyed.

From all over the base, men came hurrying to help and to get the news of the first patrol of the Long Range Desert Group.

The commanding officer's face was drawn and lined and burned by the sun, five years older than when he'd left three weeks before. He and two other men stepped down from the lead truck and walked to the back of the battered vehicle. There, under the torn khaki canvas, three men lay close together. All were wounded. Two were blistered with severe burns. Small sand flies clouded about their wounds. Handed a canteen, the officer held the flask to the lips of each man before finishing it himself. Then Sergeant-Major Stoner helped lift them out and set the three on stretchers before loading them into the base ambulance for the run to the hospital in Cairo. There was a hard black patch of blood in the truck where the men had lain.

"Wash up, Captain," said Major Lagnold. "Then please come 'round to my tent for a drink. Bring your maps. Sorry about your chaps."

Anton and the other patrol commanders went to wait by the table in front of Lagnold's tent. They talked until the captain returned and Lagnold asked them all to sit.

"Fine job," said Lagnold after hearing the report. "Good results against that airbase, but too expensive. Lost eight of eleven vehicles and twenty-one men captured, wounded or dead. Nine men lost at the base, twelve on the road back. Enemy patrol, strafing, exploding petrol, a mine. We'll get better at the navigation and supplies, but we can't do much about aircraft and enemy patrols. What we can do is stick to our knitting: gather information, not do the heavy fighting ourselves. That's for the SAS and the RAF. And travel more by night to reduce the risk. How'd the vehicles hold up?"

"Loved 'em, sir. These Yank thirty-cwts'll take about anything. But they need new sand filters and better condensers to cut water loss from the radiators, and recognition signs to keep the RAF off us."

"Anything else?"

"Yes, sir," said the captain. "Cut back on the radio signals when we're close in. You don't hear us well, but they do. No more checking in, except with what counts, I'd say, sir. Plus, another six-volt battery, extra water. That, and more cigarettes. Never enough fags."

"Right you are." Lagnold paused and looked at the eager faces of the other officers. "Time some of you other chaps got your knees brown. Two patrols leave tomorrow. Cranston and Rider. Cranston on road watch up by the coast. Rider to scout out Siwa for a forward base, then a quick recce along the Palificata to sus out what the Eyeties are up to, then north-west to map the approaches to Luftwaffe fields, for the SAS to hit later. While they're out, we'll work on better camouflage netting and new condensers. Now we'll redo the supply lists and get everyone properly kitted up."

Lagnold took Anton aside afterward. "By the way, the RSM will be going with your lot. Fancies himself an expert on navigation. Sun compass,

theodolites, own sketch maps, whatever. Any event, Stoner's asked to go
with you, said he needs to keep his hand in, and see how you manage out
of the ring. Hope he gets on with those new South Africans you've got."

Anton waited for Gwenn at the bar of the Semiramis. He was on his second
drink. His last evening in Cairo was precious, and he'd been hoping their
drink would turn into dinner, and dinner into a night together, their first
in two years. He was lonely, and he was determined not to leave without
making things better between them.

He remembered how it used to be, returning to Cairn Farm on the
Ewaso Ngiro, for the first time in his life feeling he was coming home.
Checking the stream for crocodile before urging Rafiki across, smelling
the bush-scented wind as they cleared the bank, galloping among giraffe
as he crossed the thorn plain. Stones flew from their hooves as the elegant creatures rocked above him like dusty hobby horses. He'd ridden
through the field of withered flax and pulled up near the tamarind tree
when he saw the distant figures setting stones in the walls of her new
house. He crossed the sheep field at a walk, then stopped and stood in
his stirrups and raised his hat. Gwenn was standing inside the walls of
the house she'd always wanted. She turned her head and saw him waving. She pulled off her gloves and wiped her face and pushed back her
hair before gathering her skirt in both hands and climbing the wall and
running to him across the field.

She'd made him feel that there was something to come back to, that
there was more than his gypsy wandering, that this special place was a
bit empty without him. Though she was older than he, he'd been
drawn to Gwenn since he'd first seen her in her cabin on the boat, naked and frightened and defiant. She'd seemed too perfect: tall and
graceful, with rounded cheekbones and eyes the color of light green apples. More than anything, he'd loved her courage. She had started almost on her own in Africa. Her soldier husband, wounded and weak
when she arrived there, had soon died. As he'd grown to know her,
he'd learned that Gwenn had what one needed to be complete: the education that came from suffering, and the spirit to carry on and be decent and optimistic despite it.

How had he managed to ruin it all?

Hungry and disappointed, Anton turned to order another as a hall boy
came to him, slow and silent as a snail in his pointed leather slippers.

"Telephone, Mr. Reader, please, sir." The old man bowed, elegant in his white gallabiyyah and lavender sash. "Number two."

"Thank you. Would you order me another gin?" Anton hurried to the second kiosk by the reception desk and closed the door.

"Can you hear me?" Gwenn asked.

"Yes." He recognized the intense exhausted preoccupation in his wife's voice. She was not calling about him.

"I'm still at the hospital. They're sending all these boys down from Alex. There's been more fighting. Their hospitals are all full up."

"Sorry. It must be terrible."

"It is," Gwenn said sharply.

"I understand. I meant it. I'm in this damn war, too."

"Have you been drinking?"

"Of course."

"Anyway, I'll be here for a bit . . ."

He paused, trying not to sound too eager. "Well, then let's meet for dinner later."

"You know I can't. I have to go to the French embassy with Giscard. They're having some big party. But why don't we have a drink or a cup of tea soon? I want to talk to you about Denby. Today he's on a school trip to some ruin or other."

"Actually, I'm off tomorrow myself."

"Oh. I suppose you can't tell me what's on, but take care of yourself."

"Of course. Give Denby my love. Goodbye."

Anton hung up, feeling empty and alone. He could accept Gwenn's preoccupations with the boys and her medical life, but not the fact that whatever she had left over for her private emotional life was dedicated to another man, not him.

Hastily, more disappointed than he wanted to feel, he swung open the door of the kiosk, bumping someone, and stepped out into the lobby.

"Anton!" Harriet von Decken cried, smiling and kissing him on the lips. "You almost knocked me down. I think you owe me a drink." An aged porter waited behind her with a pile of parcels. "Why don't you take those on up to thirty-three, Ahmed?" she said, forgetting to tip the man, who hesitated as long as he dared. "Thir-ty th-ree," she repeated slowly in a louder voice.

"Champagne," Harriet called to the barboy as she sat down. She moistened her handkerchief with her tongue and put one hand on Anton's cheek and wiped the scarlet lipstick from his mouth. "That's better," she said, before leaning close for him to light her cigarette. As he did, she cupped his hand with hers. He felt the touch of her long nails.

"What a dreadful day!" she said. "The shops were just bursting. You should have seen Cicurel's. Perfect agony."

"Sorry. It must have been terrible." Anton thought of the broad black smear of dried blood in the bottom of the Chevy. There were different kinds of bad days.

"It was," Harriet said with irritation, fanning herself rapidly with the handkerchief. "You don't understand." She put away the handkerchief and tilted her head as she looked at Anton.

"You've gotten harder," she said. "Please don't take the pleasure out of my complaints."

The young bar boy arrived with an ice bucket and two glasses. "Thirty-three, Ahmed," she said loudly, waving him off and filling their glasses herself.

"Do you remember that night I came to your cabin on the boat?" Harriet said, friendly again. As they touched glasses, her eyes shone, recalling their lovemaking five years earlier.

"Was that you?" he asked. At the time, in the dark of the cabin, with only moonlight shining through the porthole as they steamed for Eritrea, he had not been certain whether it was Harriet or her twin sister, Berna-dette. And somehow, drinking champagne from his toothbrush glass, the Red Sea shining all around them like a golden plate, it hadn't mattered.

"Was that you?" he repeated.

"Don't be horrible." Harriet stretched her lips and applied her bright lipstick, pouting and rubbing her lips together. "You've never been that nice again."

"Neither have you, Harry." Anton shook his head as he refilled their glasses. "Neither have you." But, despite being so spoiled, she had been other things as well, he thought: brave and surprisingly capable, as their safari had fled across Abyssinia with the Italian army in pursuit and Ber-nadette and her sister's fiancé both killed along the way. Courage was what Anton admired most.

Harriet looked at him before she spoke again. Perhaps she, too, was thinking of all that they had been through.

"Aren't you lovely in your new uniform. You look quite presentable. The girls would adore you in Lexington."

"Wish they adored me in Cairo." Anton poured the champagne and dropped the empty bottle upside down into the bucket.

"Let's see if they do," Harriet said. "Why don't you order the other bottle and then come up and have a drink on my terrace while I change? You can help button me up." She stood, straightening her flirty skirt. "Perhaps later we could find something to eat." Turning her head, she paused while Anton and the rest of the room admired her legs. She looked at him with big eyes and held up three fingers of each hand. "Thirty-three. Thir-ty th-ree."

Pleasantly tight on gin and champagne, Anton sat for a moment and finished his drink. It was so like Gwenn, he thought angrily, to be unyielding, not knowing when to relax her cool strength and surrender just a little. Tomorrow they could all be dead, or at least he could. He ordered the champagne and walked to the lift.

He sat on Harriet's terrace while she bathed, having a smoke and swilling champagne.

"Bring me a glass," she called from the tub.

Looking down at her, for an instant Anton thought he saw tears in her eyes, but it might just have been the water. Was it infidelity that was troubling her, he wondered, that latest loss of innocence? Did they both understand that the war was merely an excuse for selfish behaviour, to relieve loneliness and to snatch pleasure where one could, that they were all just growing a bit older and more world-weary, perhaps more cynical?

Harriet sighed and brushed her face with one hand and took the glass from him. Sipping champagne in the steam, covered in bubbles, smiling up at him in her white rubber bath cap, she leaned forward. "Would you mind soaping my back?"

Not minding, the bottle on the floor beside him, he sat on the laundry hamper by the big tub, sliding the slippery fragrant soap across her shoulders and down her back, reminded of another night by her smooth pinkish freckled skin, the skin of a redhead. He wondered why redheads always smelled different.

Harriet removed her cap and shook out her curls. Then she leaned back and closed her eyes.

Anton washed her breasts slowly one by one with both hands. He knew that women with large breasts were used to such attentions. But women with smaller, often more sensitive breasts seemed to appreciate the attention still more. Harriet's small sudsy nipples stiffened. She held out her glass for more champagne. Her other wrist was bent languidly over the side of the tub. He saw her fingers tighten.

For an instant he thought of Gwenn, and his determination to behave himself and win her back. But then he remembered how his wife had touched de Neuville's face with her fingertips when she'd kissed the Frenchman at her flat.

"Aren't you a bit scruffy?" Harriet murmured after a time. "Couldn't you use a wash, too?"

Stripping and splashing, he climbed in behind her, one leg on either side.

"Mmm. Good boy," she said, feeling him against her, reaching down behind her back with one soapy hand. "The hot water doesn't seem to bother you. Must be all that time in the desert."

She rose and turned to face him, settling onto him, playful and slick as a seal, purring and moving lazily, her arms around his neck, chest to chest, her wet cheek against his, her knees out of the water. "That's better," she whispered in his ear. He felt her heartbeat quicken. She scratched her nails along his scalp and pulled his hair as she arched her back and gasped. Then she fell forward over him, pressing his head beneath the water.

Blinking, spitting soapy water, Anton stood up in the tub, lifting Harriet by his arms under her legs. He almost slipped as he stepped from the bath and stood on the mat while she clung to him with her ankles locked behind his back and her eyes closed.

Dripping suds and water, he carried Harriet into the bedroom and dropped her on her back on the linen bedclothes. He went back for the champagne and set it in the ice bucket beside the bed. He noticed Jung's *Modern Man in Search of a Soul* on the bedside table.

Harriet lay on the bed with her eyes still closed, biting her lower lip and swinging her knees from side to side. Anton knelt on the bed and flipped her over onto her belly. On his knees between her legs, he lifted her slippery hips with both hands and pressed her against him. Her right cheek rested against the bed. Her mouth was open. Her body was pink and warm and wet as a poached salmon. He leaned down and squeezed her left breast while she reached back between his legs and helped him. Anton bent forward again and placed one hand on her left cheek. Harriet took his thumb in her mouth and sucked and nibbled it. Then he freed his hand and straightened his back.

After a few moments, pausing, Anton reached over and took the dripping cold bottle from the bucket and rested it on the small of her back. Ice cubes were stuck to the sides of the bottle.

Harriet cried out from the cold. Her body tightened around him while he pressed against her and drank champagne.

"Careful, Lieutenant," said Anton as Hennessy swerved to avoid a mound of carrots that had spilled from a broken donkey cart. Black-clad women dashed out from the curbs to collect the bright orange roots in their skirts. Behind them came two other lorries of Anton's patrol, all three heavily loaded with weapons and men and supplies. To discourage curiosity, the patrol was making its way through Cairo's crowded streets two or three vehicles at a time.

After crossing the Abbas bridge, Hennessy gained speed along the Shari al-Haram as they left Giza. Mango groves and bright green fields of rice replaced the crowded mud dwellings of the city's edge. With the pyramids five miles behind them, Anton stopped his trucks at the rendezvous point at the margin of the Western Desert. He and the men jumped down for a stretch and a smoke while they waited for the rest to join them. The sharp dry air of the desert had replaced the rich musty odors of Cairo. The morning was already warming. From here they would follow the old caravan route west towards Siwa.

"Wouldn't try it, sir," said the Regimental Sergeant-Major hours later, not disrespectfully. Cracking his thick knuckles, Stoner removed his sun goggles and squinted up at Anton. His broad face was layered in dust, his eyes centered in large pale circles like a koala bear. "That's the bleedin' Qattara Depression, that is. Two hundred miles long, hundred or more across. Say it's no place for wheels. Nor even camels. Never been mapped. Best to nip 'round the south, sir. Longer, but faster."

Anton was standing in the lead truck, a smaller 15-cwt Chevy intended as a light command vehicle for scouting ahead and swift movement. He rested his binoculars on the canvas covering of the Lewis gun and surveyed the steep decline before them. He understood why Lagnold loved the desert the way he himself loved the bush. The space, the silent freedom, the clean emptiness, the brilliant night skies. The sparkling dry air had already cleared his head.

The Depression before them was impassable, they had said at headquarters in Cairo. It was meant to be the secure southern flank of Western

Desert Force, the Eighth Army they were calling it now. Scouting to the north, they'd found the rim of the Depression dimpled with rough rocky gorges, but here the approach seemed smooth enough.

"This is Africa, Sergeant-Major, not Auckland. In Ethiopia this little dip would seem flat as a saucer. And if we can get across, it'll extend our range and get us to Siwa by tea-time tomorrow." And tell us how secure the army's flank really is, Anton thought. He lowered his glasses, flinching when his hand touched the sun-heated metal of the truck. It was early afternoon and the sky was bright as a light bulb. "Spread out the lorries over a half-mile front, Stoner, so we can find the best route across. Should also spare the lads eating each other's dust. You follow us down and do the mapping yourself."

He tapped Hennessy on the shoulder. The small truck lurched forward, the rear right wheel spinning in softer ground, skewing the Chevy sideways as Hennessy failed to take the decline straight on.

"Roll this thing and you're walking home, Lieutenant," Anton said under his breath, guessing that Stoner was hoping for just such an accident. Slipping and spinning, raising clouds of sand and dust, the truck carried on down the uneven drop, eighty or ninety feet until finally bouncing to rest on a gravelly pan at the bottom. "Let Charlie take the wheel," Rider said. The gunner and driver exchanged seats without speaking, both men relieved.

Anton turned and looked back.

Ten trucks were working their way down to left and right, some smoothly, others rocking and almost overturning as they lost control. Makanyanga, driving one of the end trucks, descended without difficulty. Immediately to Rider's right, Stoner's Chevrolet stopped dead, sand flying, digging itself in, the two rear driving wheels up to the axle. Cursing in the heat, all three men jumped down and unlimbered the two heavy sand channels from the sides of the truck. Hennessy and Charlie went over to help with shovels, digging paths for the five-foot perforated metal plates to be set in front of the rear wheels. Anton and several others joined them. They muscled the vehicle to firmer ground.

Once they were in line abreast again, the lorries began to move forward, accelerating on the flat basin of the Depression. Then off to the right three trucks began to slow, settling through a whitish crusty surface into spongey ground interspersed with clusters of spindly brown desert grass. Anton raised his hand and the other vehicles stopped. Before stepping down, he checked a thermometer: one hundred and twenty degrees. He wiped his face on his red diklo and walked over to one of the mired trucks.

"Salt marsh, sir." The Kiwi driver started to work with a shovel, his shirt already soaked. In a moment it would be dry in the parching desert air. Sometimes the sweat evaporated before it gathered on their skin.

Anton knelt and felt one of the ten-inch sand tires. "Let down the tires. Too much air."

"Sir?" said Charlie doubtfully. "I checked them all this morning."

"The heat's increased the air pressure. We want 'em as broad as possible, so they don't sink in, like the foot of a camel. Make it twenty-five pounds front, thirty-nine rear." Anton knew some of the men were beginning to feel the strain of the desert, and he looked the soldier in the eye. New Zealanders were known to dislike taking orders from any man not a Kiwi. "Get cracking."

Anton watched as they set to work on the tires.

From the north came the whirring drone of aircraft. Men still at the wheel hurried to get their trucks out of line. Those already on foot ran clear of the vehicles. Stoner and several gunners tore the canvas from their Lewis guns and Bofors and prepared to fire. Anton swung his Lewis to meet the incoming planes.

"They're ours!" one gunner yelled as the three fighters came in low. The lead aircraft wagged its wings as the men on the ground waved. "Hurricanes!"

Still, there was a lesson to be learned. Anton walked over to Stoner's vehicle.

"Whenever we stop, Sergeant-Major, before you put the men on easy, peeing and shaving and smoking, I want the vehicles scattered and two trucks with Bofors standing by on ack-ack defense. Clear?"

"Yes, sir."

"Brew-up, Captain?" asked Hennessy eagerly, once the trucks were freed. "Tiffin?"

Anton nodded, then added, "But first top up the tanks and use the casings for the fire. We're losing more petrol from these leaking cans than we're using in the engines." The grub seemed as important to these soldiers as it was to the most spoiled clients on safari. He remembered how his Africans grew surlier each day when there wasn't any fresh-shot meat. He reminded himself to be tougher about everything else, but to try to spoil the men with their rations. An extra bit of cheese or jam or even bully beef made all the difference.

All down the line, men checked radiators and filled tanks from the flimsy four-gallon petrol tins. Each leaky pair was boxed in a fragile wooden case. A signalman opened the metal panel that covered the radio mounted in his Chevy. For a moment the dance music of Glenn Miller broke through the harsh static.

Anton noticed men struggling in the sand in their heavy army boots. Many others, originally pink and pale with wintry British coloring, were already suffering from the sun. Having discarded the early-issue pith helmets as impractical, but exposed by their narrow khaki caps, the men's skin was already burnt and fiery from the sun and wind and sand. Hennessy looked as if his face and arms and hands had been grilled.

With two petrol boxes blazing, tea was soon ready. Treats appeared. Melted chocolate and cheese and Marmite, cigarettes and barley sugar. But most of all they wolfed down hardtack ration biscuits, slavered with Cooper's Oxford marmalade from a seven-pound jar. Fighting off the small determined flies, the men ate quickly, before the fine airborne sand covered the biscuits thicker than butter. Anton heard the sand grind between his teeth while he chewed.

Making coffee instead of tea, one New Zealander tightened the lid of his billy, then lifted the can by its handle and swung it over his head to settle the grounds.

Anton took his mug and walked forward into the desert on his own, wondering how things were with Wellie and the Hussars. As one of the first regiments in Egypt, the Cherrypickers would be in the thick of it, probably scouting and screening ahead for the heavy armor, the Crusaders and Matildas that were arriving from England.

He sat on the gritty ground while his tea cooled, thinking of Gwenn, and of Harriet. He felt guilty about how he'd behaved last night with his old friend's wife. He knew Ernst would be the first to understand, but he'd kill Anton for it just the same. Anton thought he wouldn't have done it if he hadn't been disappointed and mad at Gwenn, and a bit drunk, and feeling sorry for himself. But the reasons didn't matter. He was just messing up again.

"Ready when you are, Captain," called Hennessy, some yards behind him.

When the day had cooled, Anton stopped the column and they camped for the night.

The next day they climbed out of the Qattara Depression and fought their way through a fringe of steep uneven dunes that surrounded Siwa. They passed a cluster of black Bedouin tents rising from a gravel-strewn plateau broken by outcroppings of pink rock. Patches of soft and hard sand alternated as they approached the oasis. It was set, like most others, in a long east-west trough in the desert, apparently hollowed into a basin by many years of prevailing winds. Salt marshes and shallow salt lakes lay between low hills topped with small mud villages. On the flats, crumbling mud walls surrounded groves of date palms. Leaky irrigation trenches wandered here and there within the walls. A jagged rocky escarpment rose to the north.

They came to a cluster of clear pools fed by a sparkling artesian well. Here the date groves appeared healthy and well tended. A few camels dozed in the shade, tongues hanging from the corners of their thick-lipped mouths. Flies buzzed around their wrinkled bumpy knees and knobby leg sores. On the far side of the oasis clustered a few score one- and two-story mud brick and plaster buildings. In the fading light they resembled immense sand castles, some round and fanciful, others square and block-like, all the same sandy brown of the desert. A single tapering tower stood above the town, a crenellated minaret to call the faithful.

Rider noticed a few Arabs standing and watching from dark doorways. One building, low and shabby, bore the faded painted sign, Hotel Faruq.

Anton stopped the column and spoke to Hennessy. The Sergeant-Major stood nearby, dusting off the circular plate of a sun compass.

"Lieutenant, get the trucks in line, weapons uncovered, everything shipshape. We're going to drive through Siwa like Horse Guards Parade, remind these Gypsies what side they're on. Then we'll come back and laager up behind the oasis." Anton paused, guessing what Hennessy was thinking. "Should be able to buy some eggs and dates. Said to be the sweetest dates in Egypt, Lieutenant. Make sure we pay for everything, and don't let the men make a mess of the water. Get the trucks scattered under camouflage. I want every weapon cleaned and every engine checked before evening brew-up. Everything neat. No mess. Makanyanga will help lay out the camp. He knows the drill."

"Must say, sir," grumbled Stoner, "that Qattara Depression wasn't all they made it out to be."

*   *   *

Crammed into the rear seat of the Fieseler Storch, von Decken felt his gorge rise as Rommel brought the small spotter plane down sharply, parallel to the three columns of dust that marked the German advance eastward near Al Agheila.

"From the air, you will understand," Rommel had said as they walked to the aircraft. "This will be war in its purest form. Like a war at sea. No towns, no civilians."

The stocky general, a keen but unlicensed pilot, had familiarized himself with the topography and with the coastal road that ran from Tripoli east to the Egyptian border. Ernst remembered von Lettow, near the end. Limping along on his thorn-stick, blinded in one eye by elephant grass, still lean with malaria, the general had insisted on joining a patrol, to see for himself how close were the pursuing Rhodesians.

Ernst gripped the seat frame as Rommel tilted one wing and stared straight down to the side through the large windows. The broad planes of the desert, broken by long ridge lines running east-west, extended south to their right, generally for a hundred and fifty miles or more before softening into the Great Libyan Sand Sea. Below them, patches of thorny scrub occasionally gave way to *birs*, stone cisterns, or to wells surrounded by palm trees.

Swooping to the south, Rommel pointed to a German column that had wandered off track on its own. Several trucks had swastika flags lashed across their bonnets to protect them from bombardment by the Luftwaffe. The general brought the high-wing aircraft down to a fast bouncy landing beside a patch of camel thorn just ahead of the column. The tall wheel struts of the Storch flexed like the long thin legs of its namesake as it covered the brief patch of rocky desert. Dragging its fixed tail-skid, the plane stopped in under one hundred feet.

Led by a light four-wheeled Siegfried armored car, the column of eighty or ninety vehicles churned to a halt in an immense swirl of dust. An eight-wheeled Büssing scout car and a radio truck shrouded by an overhead large-frame antenna pulled up next to the Siegfried, awaiting orders. Fiat supply trucks and three-ton Opel *Blitzen*, petrol and water tankers, ambulances and half-tracks shut down their engines. Two eight-ton half-tracks anchored the rear of the column. Their four rows of seats were filled with combat engineers from a battalion of Pioneers.

The last half-track towed a long-barreled tank killer: the deadly 88mm anti-aircraft gun originally designed as an anti-balloon gun in 1916. Able to fire a twenty-one-pound armor-piercing shell two miles with great accuracy, the guns had been adapted by Rommel for anti-tank service. The *Panzerjäger*, the tank hunters, were already mobile and well trained, seeming always to fire with the desert sun behind them. But their crews sat high up, unprotected by any armor shield. When one man fell, another of the crew instantly took his place. This 88 had three white rings painted around its base to record its tank kills.

Many vehicles were camouflaged with mud instead of paint. The new rough surface blended perfectly with the mottled tones of the desert. At one camp, with paint scarce, Ernst had seen men mixing pans and buckets with the thick soupy slurry and applying it to their vehicles with bare hands and rags and brushes, desperate to conceal any large vertical surfaces that would draw fire in the desert. Most headlamps wore canvas air-raid hoods with thin light slits. The tops and right sides of many windshields were painted with mud to reduce glare from the sun. The *Afrika Korps* was learning to improvise and survive.

Rommel climbed down from the Storch. He removed his leather greatcoat and checked scarf and hurried to the lead armored car of the column that had wandered off the track. Even Ernst felt sorry for the weary-looking captain of engineers who jumped down from his Horch to salute the general. The big field car, repainted with the yellow-brown overspray favored by Rommel, had been converted to a self-propelled mount for a 20mm Flak 38.

"Where do you think you're going, *Hauptman?* Cape Town?" Rommel raised his goggles and squinted at the exhausted man. "We have no petrol to spare for these parades. If a single British tank finds these soft-skinned vehicles, there won't be one left. And if my Panzers run out of petrol because you can't keep up, we've lost Africa."

"Jawohl, Herr General!"

"There must be one man in this column who can use a compass and a radio. Meantime follow that line north. We need you and every man and drop of petrol here." Rommel looked back at the column. "Do your duty."

All down the line men had stepped down to stretch and smoke and relieve themselves. Heavy cans of water, painted with a white cross to distinguish them from petrol, were being opened and passed from vehicle to vehicle.

"Let the men drink, then move at once, before the Royal Air Force finds you," the general added, speaking quickly. "For every vehicle you have here, Hauptmann, two others have been lost on ships crossing the Mediterranean, sunk by British submarines and aircraft. The Afrika Korps has nothing to waste. Not one thing. Do you understand me?"

"Jawohl, Herr General!"

"And one other matter, Hauptman. When the time comes, make certain your storm pioneers are aggressive. They must show hardness in the face of the enemy."

Rommel saluted and climbed into the Storch, shaking his head as he caught von Decken's eye. After two months with Rommel, Ernst had some idea of how much was on the general's mind. Each day the commander of the Afrika Korps fought to clear away the rubble of politics and logistics and military jealousy that cluttered his planning, to free himself from the restraints and entanglements of the Italian *Commando Supremo* and Hitler and the German General Staff, so that he could devise bold strokes to defeat the enemy before the British grew too strong.

Ernst had learned that the Panzer parade he witnessed in Tripoli took place just one day after the vehicles were landed. Two days later, the division's reconnaisance vehicles were facing the British nearly three hundred miles to the east.

Only yesterday Rommel had received Adolf Hitler's directive ordering all German commanders to execute any prisoners who were from commando or similar special units. Muttering to himself, Rommel had shown the directive to Ernst and one other aide and ordered them to burn it. "How do they think our own men would then be treated? We must conduct war without hate," he said. *"Krieg ohne Hass."*

Landing at Sirte with his petrol running low, Rommel parked near a string of dive bombers, Junker 87s. Ernst walked over and admired one of the dreaded Stukas with the bent up-angled wings. The scourge of Allied shipping and undefended land-based targets, known to columns of refugees for the terrifying shrill scream of its sirens when it dived, the plane was nonetheless highly vulnerable to enemy fighters.

An open Luftwaffe *Kübelwagen*, with a spare wheel mounted on the bonnet, picked up the general and Ernst. Rommel's black, white and red command flag flew from one fender. The rear seat of the military Volkswagen was piled with leather and canvas dispatch cases. Von Decken immediately began to sort through the messages and pass the critical documents to Rommel.

"We've found your new posting, Captain," said the general to Ernst without looking up. "Seems some new British units are getting behind our front, possibly swinging up through the desert from the south, trying to interfere with our supply lines and petrol dumps. One group attacked a forward Luftwaffe base and knocked out six aircraft on the ground before we caught them. Could be worse than new British divisions. We can always defeat those, but without supplies we cannot fight at all. This could be the beginning of irregular warfare out here, expensive. We must extinguish it at once."

Rommel's blue eyes glinted when he turned his head and looked at Ernst, then hardened into bottomless ice as he seemed to bore into von Decken's head.

"Just the thing for you, Captain von Decken. This is what old von Lettow-Vorbeck trained you for. It is a game you will know how to play. You are in charge of learning about these British units and destroying them. That makes you a major. I congratulate you."

— 8 —

"When the test comes," said the Free French colonel, admiring two pudding-faced but buxom British nurses as they seated themselves at the next table, "France must be seen to play her part."

"There are many parts," said Giscard de Neuville. He regretted he was being dragged into a conflict probably not justified by either his own interests or those of France. What good could come of it?

Colonel Broché shook his head dismissively. "In the next battle in the desert, France must play a role that cannot be ignored. Instead of having our small units dispersed among the British troops, their sacrifices not noticed, we must gather them together to create a force that can distinguish itself." Stroking his thin mustache, the officer looked around for a waiter to take his order before continuing. An elderly suffragi, leaning against the wall of the hotel at the back of the terrace, a towel hanging from his crossed arms, appeared not to notice. "De Gaulle requires a victory for France, no matter how small. *La gloire.*"

"It's been a long time," de Neuville said dryly.

"And they've assigned me as number two in charge of the whole stew, under Koenig. The 1st Free French Brigade, we are calling it, though not much of it is French besides the name, or free, for that matter. Mostly colonial scraps and tatters, a few Jews from Palestine, and the Legion commanded by a White Russian prince."

"How many men?"

"Perhaps three, four thousand. One *Bataillon de Marche de l'Oubanghi*

Chari, black as the Congo. God knows what they eat. Another battalion of colonial infantry, *l'Infanterie de Marine*, a *Bataillon du Pacifique* from the South Seas, probably have bones in their noses. Plus two understrength battalions of the Legion to stiffen the rest. They're mostly old boche killers from the last war and Spanish *gauchistes* who lost to Franco."

"The Thirteenth *Demi-Brigade* of the Legion?" asked de Neuville. "Didn't they just fight the Sixth in Syria?"

"To the death, brother against brother," nodded the colonel. "And before that the Thirteenth was fighting the Germans in Norway and the Italians in East Africa."

The officer clapped his hands sharply and cleared his throat. The suffragi shuffled over and bowed. *"Messieurs?"*

"Present two glasses of white wine with my compliments to those ladies at the next table," said the colonel.

"Not really the best moment for that," said de Neuville, glancing at the broad steps that led to the terrace café of Shepheard's Hotel.

"Nonsense, Giscard, it is always the right moment. You know what Foch said, *'L'attaque, toujours l'attaque!'* "

"Where will the British send you?" de Neuville asked, ignoring the comment.

"Probably to garrison one of those strongpoints they're preparing to help hold the line near Tobruk, the Gazala line. Bir Hakeim, perhaps, an old oasis." The colonel bowed towards the ladies as the glasses were served. "Boxes, they're calling them. Meant to be self-contained desert fortresses. Only usually there's no fortress. A couple of old cisterns inside, if you're lucky, plus some artillery and anti-aircraft and slit trenches for the men, maybe a few light tanks, dug in, hull down into the sand, and outside, enough mines to slow the Panzers."

"I wish I were young enough to join you."

"Thank you, gentlemen." One of the girls turned her chair to the side, showing her heavy English ankles. She removed her khaki cap and ran her fingers through her dark curls and smiled at the two men. How fortunate such women were, Giscard thought. In Cairo there were ten European men for every European woman. Instead of being grateful, of course, most had grown spoiled.

"De rien." Giscard smiled and opened his silver case. "Cigarette?"

"Lovely, thank you." The girl leaned towards him and accepted a light.

"Frenchies, aren't you both?" asked the other girl in a loud jolly voice.

"Very," said Gwenn Rider, stepping to de Neuville's table, smiling, in a way relieved to catch her lover flirting with another woman.

The two men stood. The colonel kissed Gwenn's hand. Giscard pulled back a wicker chair.

"Colonel Broché is about to lead our Free French units into the Western Desert," said de Neuville hurriedly, eager to show Gwenn whose side he had taken. "They're expecting Rommel to make a major attack on Tobruk. And if Tobruk falls, the Germans will be in Alexandria for dinner, and Cairo for breakfast."

"That's what I have to talk to you about, Giscard," said Gwenn in a steady voice. "Alexandria."

The colonel sensed she wanted to speak in private. "Would you both excuse, me, please?" he said, moving his chair and glass to the next table.

"Of course, Etienne." Giscard set down his drink and looked at Gwenn. He did not like seeing her eyes so tired, her face so tight. "You wish to speak about Alexandria?"

"The Army's asked for civilian doctors, especially surgeons, to go up to Alex and work in all six hospitals, and, if things get worse, to serve in the field hospitals they're setting up along the coast near the old railway station at El Alamein. I'm wondering if I should go. I'd probably stay in Alex and work in the Anglo-Swiss, or perhaps in the Greek or French hospital. Wherever they need me most."

"No, your life is here," he said impatiently. "It'll wear you out. You're exhausted already, operating every night. Aren't there enough injured men in Cairo? How many do you need?"

"But don't you see, Giscard? That's where we're needed. It's just what I've been trained for. I keep thinking of all those wounded boys, hundreds of them, thousands, Wellington's age, not getting the care quickly when they need it most." For an instant Gwenn thought of Anton. She prayed he, too, would be safe. "They're flooding into the hospitals now, from that last frightful battle, Battleaxe, they're calling it."

"And what of me, you and I, and Denby?" said her lover, determined not to lose her either to the war or to her useless husband. "Denby needs you, too."

"Denby's busy at school. He cares more about rugger than his mother, and he can always stay with Olivio, or with you, if you'll have him." Gwenn smiled and touched his hand.

"Where is your husband?" said Giscard, suddenly bristling. "Is he in Alexandria?"

"Of course not. Don't be silly. He's somewhere off in the desert. For him it's just one more safari." Gwenn withdrew her hand, then placed it on his arm. "And Alex is only three hours away on the express. We can spend weekends together. You'll hardly know I'm gone."

"Your Saffron is such a lovely girl," said Gwenn, accepting a cup of Lapsang that Olivio poured for her. He seemed more small and bent than ever. Certain of his pain, she recalled Dr. Hänger's warning. "She and Wellie seem to get on so well," she added, not certain how her little friend felt about the friendship of their children, if that was all it was.

"Very well," he said. Too well, he thought. He was concerned lest the young couple blunder into mischief, mistaking infatuation for love, and love for life. At the same time, although he wished his children to conclude alliances rather than romances, he felt affection for the two sons of his friends. Fortunately, Saffron knew her father too well to mistake affection for approval.

"But I must ask you a favor," Gwenn said. "I'll be off shortly for Alexandria, to help with the casualties at the Anglo-Swiss, and I'm worried about leaving Denby here on his own." Once again she felt guilty for helping to scatter her family. All she'd ever wanted as a young girl growing up in her mining town in Wales was a house of her own, with a man and a family.

"My house is Denby's house." Olivio tried to bow from the waist. "If the lad is anything like his father and his brother, he should manage well enough on his own. But of course he shall stay with me, and I shall treat him like my second son. I will lock the youth upstairs to protect him from my daughters."

"It's really too much to ask." Gwenn smiled, knowing her son's shyness.

"We will speak no more of it, Miss Gwenn." The dwarf recollected how she had cared for him years ago in Kenya after he had been horribly burned in his house fire, herself cooling his burns with wet tea leaves, sponging away the bubbled skin and dead tissue and changing his leaking dressings night after night while she sat by his bed. "Now we will talk of other things."

"You never seem concerned about the war, Olivio." Gwenn sipped her tea. "Everyone I know speaks of nothing else."

"There is much foolishness in the world, my dear, and most of it should not concern us." The dwarf shrugged. "If these Germans and Italians come to Cairo, they will be just one more layer on the surface, like all the others. What can Rommel and Mussolini do here that Caesar and Napoleon did not?"

"But think of all the young men dying . . ."

"Of course, of course there are better ways to settle such things, but all involve some pain. Today the British and the Germans and the Italians are fighting each other, back and forth, east and west along the coast. Two and a half thousand years ago it was the same, with Carthage and Cyrene fighting to determine their border, somewhere west of what is now Tobruk."

"Did they settle it?"

"Forever, to this day. Without a war, just a little suffering. Both sides agreed that two runners should leave from each city, and where they met would be the border. The brothers Philaeni dashed along the coast from Carthage, and made it so far east that when they met the two racers from Cyrene, those runners claimed that the Philaeni must have cheated by leaving early. The men disputed. The Cyreneans gave the Carthaginians a choice. The Philaeni brothers were to choose between being buried alive where they stood, so setting the border where they claimed it to be, or they would all march west, and there the two Cyreneans would be buried alive to establish a more favorable border for their city."

"What happened?" said Gwenn.

"Of course," said the dwarf, astonished by the question, "the Carthaginians agreed to be buried where they stood. In answer, one of them took up a spade."

"How horrible!"

"Horrible, Miss Gwenn? How sensible. It saved many lives, and much time. And there Mussolini has erected a commemorative arch to separate the two provinces of Libya, Tripolitania and Cyrenaica. I believe British soldiers call it the 'Marble Arch.' "

"Speaking of the soldiers, I have been seeing much of your friend, Dr. Hänger, at the Scottish Hospital, and at King Fuad, operating on the wounded. He's been wonderful."

"He is my physician, my dear." The dwarf wagged one stubby finger. "Not my friend."

"Unlike you, he seems most interested in the war. Although he never speaks to the other patients, he is always questioning the boys about the war. What regiments they're from, where they're stationed, how many dead, who relieved them, how they're equipped, how the fighting's going, on and on. So unlike him, really."

The dwarf listened but did not speak.

"Sometimes I wonder why he does it. And then I remember. He says he's Swiss, of course, but I think you and I know he was really German before he moved to Zürich years ago, was he not? Do you think it's possible? Could he be on their side? Collecting information?"

"Who knows?" Olivio said neutrally. "Does it matter? Half of Cairo is on the other side, especially the Egyptian military and the French."

"Frankly, until recently I used to wonder about Giscard, what side he was on. It's so difficult for a Frenchman these days, with the Germans in Paris, and the Free French and Vichy here."

"For a Frenchman, my dear, it seems always difficult, choosing sides." Olivio looked at her with one kindly unblinking eye. She had not changed. He still feared for her innocence. "With an Englishman, or even a German, you always know. They are so simple."

"Here's Saffron now," said Gwenn, "with the twins." She watched Rosemary and Cardamom tugging at their older sister's hands as they dragged her quickly along the gangway. Then Rosemary bent down with a bit of chalk and marked a hopscotch court on the deck. If anyone else did such a thing, Olivio would hang them from the yardarm, thought Gwenn as Cardamom waved up at her father and blew a kiss.

"Have you a riding lesson now, my child?" said the dwarf as Saffron climbed to the poop deck and bent to kiss him. Her britches were tight as the skin of a pear. Another new perfume, he noticed.

"I love to ride in the afternoon," she said, smiling at Gwenn. "It's less hot, and there aren't so many flies."

"Best to take a jacket against the cool," Olivio said, disconcerted by the way his daughter's linen shirt struggled to contain her lavish figure. Saffron seemed to be revealing her gifts a trifle more than usual. Her thick dark hair shone from a thousand strokes, by her mother's lady's maid, no doubt. The dark coals of her eyes sparkled. Sensing her eagerness, alert to a woman's signals as a farmer to the weather, the dwarf smelled mischief. And for such a girl, there could only be one kind. But experience, of which a wife and six daughters were but a small part, had taught him not to interpose, lest his curiosity distance her. The best fence, he knew, was no fence. "And take your special riding crop. You never know when you will need it."

"Yes, father. Good afternoon, Mrs. Rider." Saffron walked across the deck to the bar.

She emerged carrying a riding crop and what Olivio took to be a small bag of suger lumps. Her hacking jacket hung over one arm, and Olivio thought he detected a bottle of champagne peeking out beneath it. The little man smiled to himself.

He sometimes had the sense that Saffron and he had a quiet understanding, an aptitude for sharing each other's secrets without ever speaking of them. The dwarf valued these precious connections to his different children. It was the sort of link he had always wished to have with a woman, but perhaps it was more naturally made with a special child. He himself could not live much longer, and he wished each of his children to share with him the magic details of his life and character.

Olivio raised his right hand and waggled his fingers at Saffron in a wave. As he did so, a thin current of pain ran from his arm through his short neck to his spine. He did not need this reminder that he must treat each day as a final feast.

He watched his eldest daughter mount the gangway. He was proud of her collected demeanor as she climbed at an unhurried pace, doubtless fearing his insightful instincts, and knowing he would be opposed to the rendezvous he suspected she had arranged. She blew a kiss to him before stepping into a taxicab.

Ahmad had Jezzie already saddled when Saffron arrived at the stable. A mare of a certain age, with a bit of a belly and none too swift, but with a fine narrow Arab head and always obedient to a rider who knew her, Jezebel was a treat to ride. Saffron slipped the Charles Heidsieck into a saddlebag. She checked her stirrups and mounted up. Ahmad tightened her girth and she was off.

She trotted along the hard ground between the scattered palms and soon came to a patch of scruffy desert on the edge of a poorer Cairo. Steep dunes rose to her right. Roofless broken walls and one-room mud-brick hovels stretched away to her left. Here and there piles of discarded rubbish were dusted by the ashes of old long-burning fires and shrouded with clouds of flies. Lean dark children played amidst the refuse. Lean mangy dogs fought and scrounged. Ribs showed through their patchy skin.

As the odor of the garbage greeted her, Saffron paid more attention to where she was. She gripped her ebony-handled crop more firmly. Cantering, she edged Jezzie farther to her right where the sand was softer, eager to reach the gap between the dunes where she could ride up more easily to the crest and join Wellington at the tent.

Letting Jezebel have her head and select the firmer ground to her left, Saffron approached a collapsing mud brick wall. Two dogs were fighting in its shadow. A cur with uneven yellow hairless skin had a smaller three-legged dog by the throat. The smaller animal, on its back, some sort of mongrel terrier, snapped upwards and seized the bigger dog between its hind legs. A howling mob of barefoot boys, hemming the animals in against the wall, threw stones at both dogs and bayed them on. Other dogs scampered and snarled amongst them.

One of the boys darted across Saffron's path. Almost running him down, she pulled on the reins. Jezebel slowed abruptly and skittered sideways, striking an older youth with her shoulder, knocking him down. As Saffron considered whether to stop and apologize, perhaps to offer him something, the boy rose, cursing, and threw a stone at Jezebel. The horse reared.

"Please!" Saffron yelled, keeping her seat, struggling for control. Immediately other boys turned to join their friend. Screaming with delight, they reached down for stones and hurled them at horse and rider.

One youth grabbed for the reins as Jezebel reared again. Seizing them with his left hand, the boy reached for Saffron's leg with the other. Swinging hard, angry and frightened, she leaned down and lashed him across the face with the stiff braided-leather crop. Yelling, his face marked, the boy let go just as several of his fellows grabbed the bridle and her other boot. Saffron kicked furiously. She swung with her crop, clubbing one youth in the forehead with the heavy ebony handle.

Jezebel reared up. Trying to free her head, whinnying shrilly, she kicked with her forelegs. Saffron gripped with her knees and stayed in the saddle. Several boys screamed and jumped back. Dogs snarled underfoot. One boy struck Jezebel's belly with a heavy stick. The mare went down and rolled to her right. Jumping clear, immediately on her feet, Saffron ran to the wall. Jezebel bolted for the dunes.

Saffron ran along the wall with the mob of boys haring after her. She gasped for air, her shirt and jacket torn. Stumbling in her boots, her chest heaving, she rose and put her back to the wall. The boys clustered in an arc, gathering around her as they had around the fighting dogs. They paused, excited, hesitating, not certain what to do. They jabbered one to another until the boldest caught up and pushed forward.

Saffron held the crop in her left hand and pulled on the heavy ebony handle with her other hand. A foot-long dagger, with a tapered triangular blade, came free in her right hand from the sheath that was the riding crop. Strangely calm now, facing them defiantly, she tried to think what her father would do.

The boy with the stick advanced towards her, pushed on by the youths to either side. Several others picked up stones. One threw a rock but missed her. Another threw hard, striking her in the stomach. She winced. Then she was struck again and again as others began to throw. Several dogs rushed in, yapping and snapping at her. Then the boy with the stick moved close enough to prod her, first in the belly, then the groin, showing the others her vulnerability. She struck his stick with the dagger. But he feinted and lunged and jabbed her again, striking her in the chest, tearing her shirt and scratching her breast with the point of the stick.

"My father will pay ten pounds to the boy who stops this!" Saffron screamed in Arabic, her face cut. "Ten pounds English to whoever helps me! Ten pounds!"

One or two hesitated, yelling to their fellows. Then several more paused and talked excitedly. But the others continued throwing and jabbing. Stones and sticks and dogs assaulted her in a growing frenzy.

"Bastards!" a voice roared. Like a lion rushing at a pack of jackals, Wellington burst amongst them on his horse.

He plunged into the pack of boys and dogs, leading Jezebel with his rein hand. Crying out, the youths fell and stumbled into one another in the dust. Wellington careered in a tight circle as he struck out and flayed them with his whip. Both horses on the edge of panic, his own plunging and rearing, Wellington flung the boys to the sides like froth from an eggbeater.

He jumped down beside Saffron and handed her the reins. He rushed at the boy with the big stick, the only one still aggressive. Wellington grabbed the stick before the youth could move. He tore it from the boy's hand and swung it like a cricket bat. The rising stroke caught the boy under the chin, opening his neck, almost lifting him from his feet. Wellie pursued several others, clubbing them violently as they fled. He slammed one along the side of his head and pole-axed another to his knees.

His face mottled red, his fiery hair sticking up in the air, Wellington hurried back to Saffron. Almost hysterical, she stood trembling between the horses, holding both by the bridle, gasping for air while she tried to whisper to the animals and stroked their long noses to calm them.

"Are you all right?" Wellie took Saffron's shoulders in his hands. He kissed her cheek between gasps. He could see a bruise coming up beneath a cut on her collarbone.

"I think so," she managed, still shaking. "You were wonderful."

"So were you," he said. "So were you."

He helped her to mount and they rode towards the dunes, stirrup to stirrup, easing into a gentle canter as they climbed. At the top of one dune, they found a tent. Wellington held her bridle and briefly took her in his arms as she dismounted. Her body stiffened and he released her. She stood beside her horse, clutching her arms across her chest, suddenly crying, not wanting to be touched. After a time she wiped her eyes and spoke in a quiet voice.

"There's champagne in my saddlebag," she said.

"Just the thing," said Wellington, trying to sense how she wanted him to be. He loosened the saddles and tied the horses' reins to a tent peg.

"Open it carefully." Steadier now, she handed Wellie the bottle of Heidsieck. They seated themselves on the striped rug before the tent. "It's had a rough ride."

Below spread Cairo. The lights of the city slowly brightened as the gaudy orange disc of the sun sank to the west. The tent belonged to several of his friends from the Hussars and was used for special occasions, like others on nearby dunes that belonged to various embassies and pashas. The five-posted cotton structure opened towards the city. Its interior was thick with carpets and brocaded cushions trimmed in the regimental cherry red, named for an incident in the Peninsular War when the 11th Hussars were observed picking cherries from the saddle. Wellington removed two glasses from a wicker picnic case, then slowly rocked the cork from the bottle with his thumbs. He gripped it securely as it exploded free and poured the gurgling foaming drink as best he could. Her partially exposed chest covered by the cool sweet spray, Saffron buttoned her jacket. Then she looked up at Wellington, captured by his green eyes, and smiled as she took her dripping glass.

"You saved my life, I think."

"A boiled egg?" he asked, embarrassed, rummaging in the hamper. He could feel the excitement of the violence becoming something else between them, as if a hot current had risen from the desert and wrapped around them both.

Wellington was dying to unbutton her jacket and torn shirt and kiss her breasts. Instead, he looked at her and grinned, two eggs in one hand, his glass of champagne in the other.

— 9 —

Enjoying the silence and the cold, Anton sat with his back against the rough trunk of a date tree and waited for the first light to clarify the sky and cast Siwa's shadows across the shallow sheet of the oasis.

"*Chai,* bwana?" growled the deep voice of Makanyanga.

Silent as a leopard, the Wakamba stood above him holding a steaming mug.

"Don't think I didn't hear you," said Anton, lying. He was always astonished by the big man's gift for stealth, better even than his own.

"Of course." The African squatted down beside the tree. "Do we hunt today? Italians?" His eyes brightened. "The sons of the Germans who killed the father of Makanyanga?"

"I shouldn't think so," said Anton, certain today's enemy would be the Sand Sea. "But please wake Lieutenant Hennessy and build up two fires for breakfast."

Anton heard the pigeons and pied wagtails begin to bustle about in the date grove behind him. While he stirred his tea with a long splinter from the tree, he noticed a small white flower on the low thorny bush in front of him. He leaned forward and carefully snapped off the blossom with several of its furry green leaves, then pressed it in his pocket notebook. He had the thought that Gwenn would like it.

As he sat there, he wondered if they would ever work things out. Once or twice he thought they had. But then something would intrude. Her work, or his travels, sometimes other women, or, when they were apart too long, another man, and that always seemed more serious. For him, there was truly no one else, but for her, once or twice there almost was.

Most of the time he had learned to live without her, but when someone said Gwenn's name, or he heard her voice or laughter, or when he thought he recognized something of her in another woman, something inside him froze and he wanted her to want him. Yet whenever he saw her, unable to take the risk, he protected himself too well to show her enough of what he felt to draw her from her distant manner. He knew that for Gwenn, the boys came first, as they must, but he was certain that she, too, felt always the tension of their connection. But did she still have that hidden reservoir of interest and affection, something left of that innocent romantic hope, that would give them one more chance? Did he?

The eleven vehicles drove southwest with Siwa at their backs. Smooth dunes rose before them higher and higher, like a gathering sea. With the sun still low, the ridges and dunes cast sharp shadows, helping the drivers to anticipate the pitch of their climbs and descents. As the sun rose and the shadows disappeared, though, the glaring desert appeared almost flat to the man at the wheel.

Mostly the sand was packed hard and the vehicles moved easily at a steady thirty miles an hour, but from time to time the lead truck would settle to the axle in a patch of dry quicksand. Then all hands turned to, more efficient at it now, unloading the lorry and laying out the steel sand channels and the canvas sand mats, forward or back to the closest firm ground. At every high point they left an empty petrol can as a cairn to mark the route. From time to time Anton checked the large sun compass mounted on the front of the truck. The engine and the magnetism of shifting loads made magnetic compasses less precise inside the vehicles. Travelling after dark, Anton found he always had to stop and walk a distance from the car to get an accurate reading with a hand-held compass.

All good training, he thought. He rested his arms on the wheel of his 15-cwt and wiped his dusty face with his diklo. He watched Stoner and his cursing crew free their truck. The Sergeant-Major had braked too quickly and his wheels dug themselves in. But by midday the drivers were learning to keep to the crest of the sand ridges so they could turn downhill and use the slope to get through the soft patches. Wherever possible they went for the ribbed butter-yellow sand that indicated firmer going.

When the temperature reached a hundred and five, Anton waved a blue signal flag and the column came to a halt in a gravelly patch between two dune ridges. Anton jumped down and stretched as Hennessy and Stoner came over to him.

"We're going on strict water rations from now," Anton said. "Six pints a day each man. One pint now with lime juice for lunch, two in tea in the evening, one in tea for breakfast and two in each man's water bottle to drink as he pleases. Save the rest for the trucks."

In minutes canvas shelters were slung from several lorries and the men were stretched out in the shade, opening tins of herring and cheese and biscuits while sand and dust swirled around them. Anton climbed to the top of a dune with Stoner beside him. Before them in the distance stretched a wall of sand taller than any they had seen.

"Three-hundred-footers, I'd say," grumbled the New Zealander while Anton cleaned his field glasses with his shirt tail. "Maybe four hundred, trough to crest. Should be fun, overloaded like we are, sir."

"Overloaded?" Squinting through his binoculars, Anton saw a plume of sand blowing along the distant crest like snow in the mountain tops. "Medical supplies, water, ammunition, what would you have us leave, Sergeant-Major? After we cross these dunes tonight, give me a list of what you think we don't need."

"Makanyanga," said Anton as he waited for the other trucks to catch up at the base of the tall dunes, "you take the first truck up. Go for that gap in the crest. Remember to rush it on the way up, don't stop, then slow down just before the top and turn sideways along the crest so you don't crash down the other side."

"Of course, bwana," grunted Makanyanga, rolling his eyes.

His mates gripped the sides of the truck as the Chevy plunged forward. Gaining speed, Makanyanga shifted into second as the truck started to climb, then down into first when it slowed on the steeper ascent. Two thirds of the way up, it appeared to stop. Sprays of sand were thrown up by the rear wheels while they spun in, and the vehicle slowly turned sideways to the slope. As the other men watched from below, the truck rocked on its two right wheels, then rolled over, once, twice, three times. The Lewis gun snapped from its mount. A litter of boxes, ammunition and leaking petrol tins spilled down the dunes as the four men jumped free.

Anton and the others rushed up the dune to help. One man had a broken arm. The other two helped reload the truck as Makanyanga, silent, climbed back into the driver's seat.

On his second try, Anton made it to the top in his lighter truck. Turning sharply as he reached the crest, he avoided a sixty-foot precipice that fell away down the other side where the wind had hollowed out the sand. Still moving forward, he toppled the truck gently over a milder edge of the next slope. Axle-deep in soft sand, he plowed down to the bottom in first gear. Waves of sand shot up like surf from both sides of the truck. He squinted and stared ahead across the rolling desert. He saw wavy parallel lines rippling to the horizon and sheets of water that were not there. No wonder Lagnold said it was hard to direct artillery fire in the desert when the sun was high.

Anton jumped down, then struggled back up the dune to guide the others across. He dreaded getting stuck at nightfall with half of his patrol on each side of the dune.

The patrol finally kipped down for the night in flatter country as the desert darkened. The men tormented Makanyanga about his driving and restored themselves with a thick stew of bully and tinned potatoes. Hennessy took a jar of Marmite from one pocket and an onion from another. He scraped out the crusty black residue of the relish and chopped the onion into his stew. He was celebrated for having discovered that CO_2 fire extinguishers could be used to chill beer. The men stood in line whenever he used an empty beer bottle to roll flour on a map board, watching closely as he fried little patties in margarine and stuffed them with apricot jam.

"Join the feast, chaps." Hennessy offered bits of onion to the other men of his truck.

One signalman sat by the low fire, stitching together moccasins from pieces of leather cut from the skirt of his goatskin greatcoat.

With the night sky now a sparkling rich purple above them, the men sipped a ration of rum and lime juice while Anton leaned against a truck and explained the next day's mission along the old Italian track.

"About the time you Kiwis were messing about in the woods down there slaughtering Maoris, the Eyeties were butchering the desert tribes in the country just ahead of us, mostly Senussi, filling in their wells and building fences to stop them roaming about. General Graziani used to bind their chieftains hand and foot. Then drop them out of airplanes into their own encampments." Anton paused when one of the men offered him a Victory cigarette. Rolled in India, the tobacco always flaked off onto your lips and tongue. "To help hold things in control, Mussolini laid out a desert track we'll find tomorrow, called the Palificata, with tall metal stakes to show the route after a sandstorm and the odd airstrip alongside for their flyboys to refuel at." Anton looked at the cheerful filthy faces seated on the sand around the low camp fire. The almost smokeless fire and the sweet smell of the burning acacia reminded him of home. "The first man to spot a stake tomorrow gets an extra tot of rum."

"There she is, sir!" hollered Hennessy, standing in the lead truck. One hand gripped the empty bottom frame of the windscreen, the other a map board. "Benito's Pacificata."

"Palificata," muttered Charlie beside him.

As they approached the road, another marker could be seen in the distance to either side, a half mile distant.

Anton climbed down and joined Hennessy and his crew. A ten-foot-high angle iron, one of Mussolini's *paletti di ferro*, was set into the ground, probably anchored in a sunken tub of concrete. Several feet away Anton discerned a mass of old tire tracks that defined the north-south track. He walked over and knelt to examine the freshest tracks, as if they were the spoor of an elephant or eland. "Makanyanga!" he called. "How old do you reckon these are?"

The African knelt by the widest of the fresh tracks while the other men stood around. Makanyanga trailed his fingers across the sand that had settled over them, then did the same with the ground nearby. Anton knew he would estimate the age of the tracks the same way he would a footprint: by the sharpness of the impressions and the steepness of the edges of the track marks.

"One day." Makanyanga stood and dusted off his hands. "Three lorries."

"Which way were they going?" Anton said, sensing the amazement of the men watching.

The African pointed north.

"Sergeant-Major," said Anton, "move our trucks behind those hills, about three hundred yards off the road. No fires. Have two men drag some brush across our tracks all the way back. Be certain you can't see our aerials from the road. Put two men at the base of that hill with binoculars, logging any traffic. Relieve them every two hours."

"Sorry, sir, but there isn't any brush hereabouts," said Stoner, looking up and down the road.

"Then drag the tracks with some sheepskin coats," said Anton impatiently.

By the following morning, there had been no enemy traffic. Disappointed, Anton sat under a truck canvas with Hennessy and had a smoke. "I'm off on a recce north looking for those Eyetie airstrips. I'll be taking Stoner and four trucks. Don't start anything here, just observe the traffic. Use the time to memorize the specs of all their vehicles and aircraft. If you see us coming back fast down the road, with no flag, it'll mean they're after us. Keep your heads down and let us lose them. If we're not back in five days from today, head home. Just follow the cairns."

Anton's patrol headed off. They would stay half a mile east of the Palificata, travelling a bit lighter than normal but with explosive satchels ready. The south wind picked up behind them, sending dust devils dancing before them.

After two hours of squinting through the gusting sand, Anton made out a cross on the horizon and gestured for his driver to stop. He stood and stared through his field glasses.

The fire-blackened tail of a crashed airplane stood before them like a welcoming statue in a Grecian harbor, its arms extended. Anton reached under the seat for the pamphlet identifying Italian and German armor and aircraft. A Ghibli.

They saw two wind indicators on tall iron rods: one a tattered red wind sock, and the other a red tin outline of an aircraft. As alive to the wind as a boy's kite, both moved as he watched. Anton stopped again and scanned the area with his glasses, but there was no other sign of man or machine, just a low brick shed with oil drums piled against one wall near the wreckage of the old twin-engine bomber.

"See if it's petrol or aircraft fuel," Anton said to his driver. He himself pulled a shovel from its bracket and went to break open the shed. Inside he found noting but empty straw-covered chianti bottles, a burnt out radio and an old pair of boots. But nailed to the wall were two things: a poster of Mussolini and a map. Wearing the new Italian steel helmet, his wide jaw thrust forward like an enraged hippopotamus, the Duce stood with his fists on his hips beside the statues of the Caesars on the new Avenue of the Empire in Rome. At the bottom of the poster was the slogan: 'The Life of Heroes Begins After Death.' The map was of Libya, dated 1929, but on it were marked in red and black crayon the distances and locations of Italy's desert airfields.

"A treasure map," Anton exclaimed.

"Aircraft fuel," said Charlie as Rider emerged from the shed, folded map in hand. Now he must check to see if it was real.

"Get the Miner and explosives," Anton replied as he spread the map on the warm bonnet of his truck. "And pull out those two wind socks and bring them along. Perhaps we can find a less hospitable place to plant them. See how the Italian pilots handle a tricky landing." Charlie grinned at the prospect.

Named after his old trade on the South Island, the Miner ran forward and began to set his charges while Anton studied the map. "Give us as long as you can to get away before she blows," Anton said without looking up. "We don't want the Reggia Aeronautica down on us until we've done them a little more damage."

Anton attached the Italian map to the board with two of the trouser clips Lagnold had given him as a parting gift in Cairo, together with four Thompson submachine guns. "A present from Chicago," the major had told him. " 'Bout time the Yanks gave us a hand" had been the reply.

Anton leaned forward and studied the map.

"Ninety miles to the next stop. If these marks mean anything," he said to the driver. "It should be a bigger show than this auxiliary strip. Looks like a proper aerodrome. We'll lay off nearby until nightfall, then see what kind of party we can give them." After eating and drinking in the dark, the men filled the gas tanks and checked their weapons while they waited for Anton and the Miner to return from their reconnaissance on foot.

Returning to the trucks, Anton decided it would be a useful drill to play Makanyanga's game and make a stealthy approach. Pleased there was no moon, he circled and approached the vehicles from a different direction than the airstrip.

"Sergeant-Major," he said, suddenly among the men, "why didn't your sentry challenge us coming in?"

Stoner's jaw tightened before he spoke. "Sir, I didn't expect . . ."

"Expect? The sentry's job is to prevent surprise from what you don't expect. Now let's try and surprise the Italians. They've got eleven aircraft on the ground, two Germans, Stukas, four Savoia 79s, a Ghibli and some smaller stuff, Maachis or whatever. No perimeter wire. One sentry by the fuel dump. He's Makanyanga's," Rider said, glancing at his friend. "We'll use two trucks under Stoner to create a diversion attacking the barracks. The rest of us will go for the planes and the fuel. Miner, do your chaps know where to place the charges?"

"They'll be tucking the sticky bombs right in under the armpit, sir, where the wing meets the fuselage." The Miner held up one long skinny arm and scratched himself. "Idea's to destroy the aircraft, boys, not the engine. Engine's easier to replace. We'll have about twenty minutes before the time pencils go." The Miner paused and spoke more slowly, using his hands and fingers with careful motions, as if explaining the alphabet to a child. "When the acid in the pencil eats through the wire, the wire will release a spring and set off the bomb. But the timing's a wee bit tricky. Meanwhile one of the other boys and I'll be dragging that mobile refuelling pump around trying to spray a bit on each plane before the stickies explode. They're a really nice mix of incendiary and explosive, sir, they . . ."

"Right you are, Miner. That'll do, thank you." Anton tried not to smile. He could feel the excitement of the men. "Off we go, lads. Afterwards we meet on the road two miles south of the airfield. Ten minutes after the bombs go, whoever's there is to drive back to the other trucks. Don't look back. You've all come a long way for this job, so let's do it right."

"Couldn't come no bleedin' further," grumbled a New Zealander as he climbed into his truck.

"No need to blacken 'is blasted face," whispered another Kiwi while he watched Makanyanga wrap his belt around his left fist. "Imagine 'im coming after you in the dark."

The African took out his old skinning knife and stropped the blade against the leather with swift even strokes before he set off for the fuel dump.

Twenty minutes later, Makanyanga's torch blinked twice. Stoner's vehicles, moving with their lights out under the stars, made for the barracks and two other outbuildings on the far side of the airfield. Miner and three men parked their truck near the aircraft and set to work. Anton drove to the petrol dump. Makanyanga wiped his knife on his trousers, then climbed on the Chevy and manned the Lewis gun.

"*Habari yako?*" said Anton quietly in Swahili. He stared across the airstrip at the barracks, where dim light showed through three windows. He heard music coming through the open windows from a radio or Victrola.

"*Hakuna matata.*" Makanyanga grinned in the darkness and strapped on his new German watch.

Suddenly a door opened in the barracks building. Backlit by the bright light of the doorway, two men stepped out, evidently preparing to relieve themselves just as Stoner's first vehicle reached them. The lorry's machine gun chattered and sparkled. The two men collapsed. Another appeared in the doorway firing a Spandau from the hip. The light machine gun chattered rapidly until he, too, fell as the second lorry pulled up. Two of Stoner's men jumped down and threw grenades through the windows. Dull explosions followed. The lights went out. The music stopped. A group of men, firing, emerged from one of the other buildings.

Meanwhile Anton could just make out the shadows of the Miner and his men running from plane to plane with their satchels of sticky bombs. Anton prayed they could do it safely. Then the Miner and another man began dragging the refuelling pump between the aircraft, hosing down each one as they passed. Finally the Miner flashed his torch and his men scrambled for their lorry.

"*Twende!*" said Anton and pulled away from the fuel dump. As they crossed the strip, Makanyanga swung the gun back and fired a burst of tracers into the fuel drums.

The ground trembled. An orange explosion lit the sky. Anton turned on his lights and drove quickly to the rendezvous.

Stoner was already waiting.

" 'Fraid Charlie caught it, sir," he said. "Done for. One round in the neck. We've got him in the back, and two others hit, not too bad. Only two or three still shooting at us when we left. Jerries, by the sound of 'em, and not about to give up. Must be Luftwaffe, Stuka pilots, most likely. My truck stopped a few rounds, but we're still moving."

"One minute left," yelled the Miner as his vehicle joined them.

"You go first," said Anton. "Fast as you can."

As he spoke, a Savoia exploded on the airstrip. A plume of flame ran down its length, spread in a pool around it and climbed a second plane. In a moment most of the aircraft were burning. A ripple of explosions ran from one to the other. Anton counted nine planes in flames, most of them crumpled at the base of one wing like a wounded bird. It'll never be this easy again, he said to himself. Stamping on the acclerator pedal, he sped after the others.

He caught up too quickly. Why, Anton wondered, weren't the other trucks moving faster? Behind him the fire lit the night. Occasional explosions rumbled across the desert. The rising wind pushed thick oily clouds of smoke along the ground.

Stoner's truck dragged to a halt near a metal stake. The other vehicles gathered around it.

"Light's out," Anton said as the Sergeant-Major came to him.

"She's all busted up, sir, worse than we thought. Two bullets through the rad, and something's wrong with the axle."

"Get Wilson under her with a torch for a proper look while you patch the radiator," said Anton, walking over to check the wounded men. "Meanwhile, gather all the water bottles and get ready to fill it up. Put these two lads in Miner's truck, with your radio and maps and code book, in case we have to leave the lorry." Immediately other men moved to help, bundled against the cold in heavy pullovers and sheepskin coats.

"No use, sir," said Wilson, yelling from beneath the Chevrolet. "The old cow's had it. Differential's gone and the axle won't turn."

"Sergeant-Major," said Anton, worried about pursuit, "load everything that shoots or moves into the other three trucks. You leave anything the enemy can use and you'll be carrying it yourself. Then turn her around facing north. Miner, get ready to blow her. I want a proper cremation."

In a few minutes they moved off in good order, leaving the Chevy blazing behind them.

Making fair speed south as the sky began to brighten, almost back at camp to join the others, Anton heard Makanyanga yell at him from the back seat. *"Gari!"* The African's heavy arm rested on Anton's shoulder as he pointed straight ahead.

Anton made out two points of light advancing to meet them on the Palificata, and behind these, two more. They'll assume we're friendly, Anton realized as the vehicles closed, relieved it was not yet full morning.

The advancing Italian trucks were soon within range.

He was deafened as Makanyanga began to fire the Lewis gun mounted beside him on the central pillar. Anton pulled off the road to take the enemy in the flank and permit the truck behind to add its fire.

Immediately the two large vehicles facing them stopped and began honking. Unarmed soldiers in heavy dark green coats jumped down and screamed and waved.

"*Prego! Prego!*" they cried. "*Noi arrenderse!*" One man appeared to be lightly wounded.

"What shall we do with them, sir?" Stoner walked towards the Italians with a Tommy gun while they hollered and raised their hands. "Looks like a couple of supply trucks, six tonners. They weren't expecting mischief."

"From now on they will," Anton said. "Patch up that man's shoulder and we'll leave them here with some food and water. They'll get picked up by their own people."

Stoner went to inspect the Fiat lorries.

"Looks like they've got some useful stuff here, sir," said the Sergeant-Major, standing in the back of one truck. "Military mail, new Marconi radios still in the crate, red wine, some sort of music box and enough cheese to choke Cairo."

"No time to unload it here, Sergeant-Major. We'll sort it out later. Have two men drive the Fiats. Off we go."

Last in line, with Makanyanga driving and a flag flying, Anton looked back at the Italians on the roadside. One was starting a small fire for coffee while others gathered more scraps of desert brush. The fifth squatted on his heels fiddling with an accordion.

Just as Anton turned around to check the four vehicles ahead of him, he heard a buzzing drone in the sky to the north. A single-engined aircraft, and he knew it wasn't British. Anton recognized it as a light Italian scout plane, a Maachi. The Italians beside the road jumped up and waved their arms and coats in the air. As Anton's patrol pulled away, the plane slowly circled the group of men by the road, then turned south and followed the small column of vehicles. The pilot was confused, Anton guessed, by the Italian markings on the Fiats. Was it better to fight, or to gamble on subterfuge? The plane flew past them, safely to the east, so that the sun was rising on its other side. Anton made a friendly wave. Then the Maachi banked in a broad circle and came face-on towards the column.

Horrified, Anton looked ahead to see Stoner and the Miner manning the guns as their Chevies swung out of line to left and right. With the two Italian lorries ahead of him, and the vehicles well spread out, Anton knew he could not stop his men firing in time. Now the pilot would know who they were.

He heard the pop-pop of the 37mm Bofors when Miner began firing at the Maachi. Then Stoner joined in with the heavy Vickers machine gun.

The Maachi responded by diving along the road with two guns sparkling. Anton swerved to the left and yelled for Makanyanga to use the Lewis.

Machine gun bullets raised two columns of dust up the Palificata and struck the first Fiat. Her engine began to smoke, but the vehicle continued.

Then the small plane was past and climbing north, trailing smoke from her left wing.

"Lucky," Anton muttered as the column continued on.

Another twenty minutes and he saw Lieutenant Hennessy rise like a ghost from the sand to the east of the road. He ran to meet the first lorry and jumped onto the running board as it slowed. The column stopped. The driver of the first Fiat lifted the bonnet. Flames shot up as an oil fire spread. Immediately the men doused it with buckets of sand. Anton climbed into the back of the lorry. He counted four crated radios and thirty or more black five-gallon petrol tins. He lifted one of the solid cans, noting the German stamp on the bottom and the well-designed lip for pouring. He swung it about by its heavy handle to see if it would leak. No need for wooden casings with these tins.

"Why don't we top up from these things and then destroy the truck?" said Stoner.

"No, Sergeant," said Anton. "These Jerry cans look a lot better than our flimsies. Use up ours first and chuck them out. We'll keep this lot. Looks they're solid enough to use again and again. And they don't leak."

"No news hereabouts, sir," said Hennessy. "Hardly any traffic." He sniffed and stroked the enormous wheel of parmigiana in the second Fiat as if it were a dog or child. Then he opened his pocket knife.

"Fix everyone a good hot meal while the fitters check all the trucks and we reload." Anton was pleased to see Hennessy had found some scrub and kept his vehicles well camouflaged with brush and netting. "Might as well choke down some of that Chianti once we're shipshape. Then we're back to Siwa. But keep one man on the road and another on ack-ack until we're off." Thick swirls of sand were rushing and gusting along the ground as the wind picked up. The sky was turning yellow and grey.

"Signalman," Anton said to the young South African fussing with the wireless set built into a metal cabinet on the side of one lorry. "Send H.Q. a message that we got nine planes and we're bringing in an Italian mailbag." Anton turned back to the radio man, remembering Lagnold's instructions for important messages. "Use French civilian wireless procedures and try not to use your own tempo on the dots and dashes."

Jolly and well fed, eager to be off, the men were stamping out the fire and preparing to strip the camouflage and mount up when the the road sentry whistled twice. Hennessy ran back and looked between two low dunes with his glasses. "Big column of dust on the road north, sir," he said as Anton joined him. "And here come more of them upstairs."

Three aircraft, flying high, were approaching from the north. To the west, a strange grey band obscured the sky like a curtain just above the line of the horizon.

Anton turned and quickly checked the camp. All but three of the Chevies were under camouflage, and those were tight in against one flank of the dune. Covered in sand and dust, the vehicles were exactly the broken colors of the desert. Only the two big Fiats were in the open, one abandoned down the road, the other loaded and ready for flight. Run or fight? he wondered again. He thought of his days as a hunter, scanning the bush for game. Of course: it was movement that gave one away, far more than shape or color. And it might be impossible to fight off an enemy column while also being attacked from the air. Better to go to ground like a wild hog in its hole than to flee and be pulled down like an antelope.

"Throw something over that Fiat and tell the men to keep down."

Soon everything was ready. Anton lay on his back with his body under a camouflage net, only his head sticking out. He sighted his glasses between the dunes.

Three aircraft approached and flew past to the south. He recognized two Stukas by their bent wings, the perfect planes for ground attack. The third was Italian, though he could not identify it, with the rondel of Mussolini's Italy clear on its fuselage, the fasces with its rods and axe, all in the colors of the Italian monarchy. As the Stukas growled by, heavier and more deadly than their companion, he saw for the first time the black cross and swastika of Germany.

Missing them, the planes turned around some distance to the south. They methodically began to quarter and search the ground to the west of the abandoned Fiat on the road.

"Ten minutes, and it'll be our turn," Anton called to Hennessy, who sat beside a Lewis gun under camouflage. A large wedge of cheese rested on the seat beside him, with his penknife jammed into it. "Toss some canvas or netting over those three trucks. Fast as you can."

"Yes, sir," said the lieutenant, his binoculars still aimed down the road. "About fifteen or so Eyetie lorries and armored cars coming, sir. A pair of those *Autoblinda 41s* and at least one Fiat 611 with some sort of cannon, probably 37 mm. Looks like an Auto-Sahara Company. They're just pulling up now beside the Fiat."

Anton crawled up one of the dunes and lay on his belly beneath a desert acacia. It was a long time since he had been hunted by Italians. As he lay still and adjusted his field glasses, a Painted Lady butterfly settled on his left arm. He held his breath. Then he moved his arm and she flew off in a flurry of gossamer reds and greens.

Anton saw a dozen Italian soldiers jump down from the lead truck. They looked tan and professional in boots and gaiters and khaki shorts and tunics. They were accompanied by one of the supply drivers Anton had left by the road. The men inspected the empty Fiat, then began to climb back in the truck. One man, still on foot, pointed excitedly at the ground beside the road and looked around, raising his hand to protect his eyes from the flying sand. An officer seemed to be arguing with him. The man shrugged and climbed on board, and the column set off to the south. Thank God we brushed over our tracks, Anton thought.

As the Italians sped south, the three planes completed their search to the west of the road. The light plane came first, flying low and slowly. The dive-bombers searched in sectors behind him. Anton could see the Italian pilot's face as he dipped his starboard wing and banked around the loaded and hastily camouflaged Fiat.

"Get ready to fire, Makanyanga," Anton called.

The Italian pilot seemed to look directly at them, then dipped down for a closer look. Suddenly Anton could see him pointing downward.

"Get him, Makie!" Anton hollered. "On the guns, lads! Get ready for the Stukas! Break camouflage!"

Makanyanga led the Italian plane as the pilot turned away, then opened up just before the flyer crossed his gunsight. Anton saw the plexiglass canopy shatter as the bullets stitched across it. For a second he saw a dark mess against the broken glass. The plane continued turning, the aircraft itself seemingly uninjured.

All around him, Anton's men were leaping into their trucks, manning every heavy weapon. The vehicles drove out from under their camouflage, bursting into the open between the dunes as the Stukas came for them. One lorry dragged its netting behind it like a trawler, with the Miner cursing and banging away with the Bofors mounted in the rear.

The Italian pilot crashed a mile away as the Stukas came in, diving in two parallel lines while the trucks scattered in all directions. Anton heard the whining scream of the dive-bombers and looked back. In the distance, he saw the Italian column turning and speeding north to join the battle.

The first Stuka dropped two light bombs, then opened up with two machine guns as it chased the lumbering unarmed Fiat driven by Wilson. At the last second the Fiat lurched to the left, almost rolling over. Bullets cut lines in the desert where it would have been.

Anton plunged south between two lines of dunes. He could no longer hear the firing as the shrill pitch of the diving Stukas filled the air around him. At the last moment he braked and jinked to the right. Machine gun bullets pounded the sand. Makanyanga, nearly flung out by the turn, sought to reload the Lewis.

Surprised, Anton saw no shadow race past as the Nazi bomber flew over him. He looked up and could barely see the sun. The sky had turned from blue to grey. He watched the two dive-bombers climb to the north. One trailed a thin tail of black smoke. Anton stopped the truck, then turned and put up his blue flag to rally the patrol to him. He saw Wilson jump down from the burning Fiat.

An explosion rocked the ground beside his truck. The Chevy was flipped over on its side by the blast. He saw Makanyanga pitched out, falling hard on his back.

In an instant Hennessy and his heavier lorry were beside them. "The Auto-Sahara!" the lieutenant yelled. "Armored cars."

Ten yards away he saw Miner lowering his smoking Bofors at the Italian column as it veered off the Palificata towards them. Several miles behind the Italians, a dark grey wall, perhaps six hundred feet high, was rushing towards them.

The Miner fired twice, hitting the cab of the lead armored car. Beside it, a lorry of Italian soldiers was swept end-to-end by Stoner's Vickers. The lorry crashed into the armored car. To both sides, Italian soldiers were scrambling down from trucks and moving towards them, crouching behind the two advancing armored vehicles.

Seeing Makanyanga was back on his feet, Anton grabbed the hook and cable from Hennessy's truck. He shouted close to the lieutenant's head through the din of the wind and the gunfire. "Play out the cable a few yards, then pull us forward into the slope until the incline topples us upright."

Hennessy's 30-cwt plunged forward. The cable tightened and pulled the lighter vehicle along the slope until it fell back onto its wheels. Anton and Makanyanga climbed on. Anton drove while the African tried to fire the Lewis with one hand. The sand cut their faces.

The surviving Chevies charged between the dunes in the chaos of the running fight. The air around them thickened with sand. The Italian armored cars approached, occasionally pumping off a heavy round and screening the advancing infantry. The men struggled forward against the wind and sand, sometimes kneeling to take a shot at the British as they advanced. The spare tire jammed into the truck next to Makanyanga jumped up beside him as two rounds struck it. Anton saw one Kiwi gunner fall from his truck and lie still in the sand.

Suddenly Stoner's lorry reappeared behind the armored cars, running down on them from the north. Anton saw the Vickers knock down a dozen men. The other Italians hurried back towards the road. A few men abandoned their weapons as they leaned into the blinding sand. The two armored cars turned and followed them, both taking hits before they withdrew up the Palificata with the Italian lorries.

Rider drove the few yards back to the center of the old camp between the taller dunes. He blinked his lights, exhorting the other trucks to laager round. He saw two of his men lift the fallen gunner into a Chevy. For a moment the air seemed still. Then there was a rush of wind.

The howling sky turned black. He felt the vehicle tremble as if slapped by a giant hand. Anton pulled down his sun goggles. He tied his bandana over his mouth and nose and doubled over face down on the floor of the lorry. Makanyanga did the same in the back. A column of sand struck the side of the truck like buckshot.

— 10 —

"Do not be concerned, Giscard," said Admiral Danton, seating himself comfortably and tapping a cigarette on his case. "I came in by the servants' gate."

"Does Alexandria please you?" De Neuville rose from his desk and set a bottle of mirabelle beside his old schoolmate. "I understand your cruiser is still rusting at anchor."

"I've taken an apartment ashore, in the Majestic, better for personal matters, and government business." The admiral lit his cigarette and sniffed the rich *eau-de-vie*. "As for the town, what can one expect with so many Greeks? They still think it's their city. However, there's always the Grand Trianon Café, Les Délices, the museum, one or two restaurants, but too many sporting clubs. Must be the English." The old sailor drank and wiped his lips. "All the talk is at the Muhammad Ali Club or the Cotton Exchange or the Royal Yacht Club. Of course, they've shut down the *Circolo Italiano* and the *Deutscher* Club."

"And the war, Antoine?" As always, Danton was telling Giscard more than he needed to know. He had been the same at school.

"The British have learned that what was good enough against the Italians is not good enough against the Germans." Danton waved his hands from side to side before continuing. "Now the war goes back and forth along the coast."

"In Alexandria, the *Gare du Caire* is the barometer. Whenever Rommel wins a battle or the Luftwaffe casts its shadow over the city, the station is a madhouse. Overloaded taxis and sedans battling for the curbs, baggage

143

piled to the rafters. Poles and Russians, Jews mostly, bribing the conductors and ticket sellers. They're still on the jump, but who can blame them? And the military trains, troops going north, the wounded coming back to Cairo. All you have to do is count."

The admiral stubbed out his cigarette and pulled his bushy eyebrows one after the other. "And what have you been doing for France, Giscard?"

"For France, I have been doing what you ask me. The *Gaullistes* think I am one of them."

"What news have you?"

"Rommel cannot safely advance on Alexandria, and then on to Cairo, while the British still hold Tobruk behind him. So he must take Tobruk, and the British know it. The port is already surrounded, mostly defended by South Africans and Australians, with the Royal Navy bringing in supplies."

"Yes, yes, Giscard, all this we know. But what of your new friends, the Free French, as they like to title themselves?"

"They are getting their wish, at last, their own important independent command."

"Of course. De Gaulle told Churchill he would send his troops to Russia and fight for Stalin unless they found important duty in Libya."

"I wonder how our Tahitians would enjoy the winter at Stalingrad." De Neuville almost laughed.

"So where will they go?"

"To Bir Hakeim. One of the strongpoints on the way to Tobruk. To take Tobruk, the Germans must first take Bir Hakeim."

"What is Bir Hakeim?"

De Neuville let his friend wait while he concentrated on extracting a cigarette end from his holder. Then he looked up and continued. "An old oasis and camel caravan junction in the desert, about forty miles south of Tobruk, right at the southern tip of the British mine marsh."

"Mine marsh?" Admiral Danton removed a notebook and pen from his pocket.

"The British have laid hundreds of thousands of mines between Tobruk and Bir Hakeim to stop the Panzers. And the Free French are planning to lay thousands more."

"Anything else there?"

"A small fort, useless, just like Beau Geste, and two round collapsed cisterns, or birs, covered in sand. Used to be the oasis. The men call them '*Les Mamelles*.'"

"And who will defend this box?"

"The First Free French Brigade, under Koenig . . ."

"This Koenig has already been declared a traitor, losing all his property and his rights as a citizen of France. What does this outlaw have at Bir Hakeim?"

"One brigade. Three and a half thousand men . . ."

"What that fraud, de Gaulle, has been calling a 'light division,' exaggerating, to help him bargain with the British," Danton interrupted. "Who are they?"

De Neuville resumed more slowly, speaking from careful memory.

"The Second and Third Battalions of the Legion, the Thirteenth Demi-Brigade, about a thousand men. And three more battalions, all colonial troops from Africa and the South Pacific, plus the First Artillery Regiment with the old *soixante-quinze*, imported from Syria and refitted in Beirut, and fifty-five anti-tank guns, several types, and engineer and signals detachments, and the First Fusiliers-Marins with fourteen anti-aircraft guns. Also some Jews from Palestine, and a few Roastbeefs."

De Neuville paused, recognizing he had now sealed his bargain with the devil. Men would die because of his words, some of them French. "And vehicles, but no armor except for sixty-three Bren-gun carriers."

"Well done, Giscard. It's a fine beginning. Just the sort of thing we need." Danton capped his pen and filled both glasses. "No wonder de Gaulle would've sent this rabble to the Eastern Front. Hardly a real *poilu* or *grognard* among them."

"Now you'll have to excuse me, Antoine. I have a professional matter to attend to, a matter of archeology." He had been unsuccessful in calling Gwenn in Alexandria, and it was time to try again.

"Don't forget, Giscard, we will need more as the battle approaches. Our friends will want to know where the new minefields are going, and most important, where are the paths through the mines. There is always a way out, and for the Panzers it could be a way in."

De Neuville shrugged in exasperation. "These details, I do not think . . ."

"*Vieux frère*," said the admiral. He stood and reached up to put one hand on de Neuville's shoulder. "Do not forget. Our new friends are as dangerous as our enemies. We must help them more to keep them silent. Lest they reveal your assistance. How do you think a Legionnaire would treat you after learning what you have given to his enemies?"

"The same way I will treat you if such a thing is disclosed, Antoine." De Neuville stiffened. "There is no charm in such matters. These Free French are keeping a master list for after the war, for the *règlement de compte*. The 'laundry list,' they're calling it, for a proper *ratissage*. Your family would not wish to be on it if one day de Gaulle should enter Paris."

Admiral Danton removed his hand and stepped apart. They raised their glasses and looked each other in the eye, recalling the resentments of boyhood.

"To France," both men said.

"Come in, Gamal," said de Neuville without looking up. "And sit down." He set aside his papers and sat back with his fingers laced behind his head. "What have you learned? What is this Monsieur Alavedo concealing?"

"Excellency, it has been most difficult. Those who work for the midget are too terrified to speak. The laborers, it appears, fear their supervisor, a Nubian, one Tariq, and this supervisor trembles at his master's shadow . . ."

"Difficult, you say?" interrupted de Neuville in a different tone. His pale face hardened. "You will find losing your job difficult. Instead of getting married, you will be running between the traces of a pedicab, if your health still permits it."

The Egyptian sat forward stiffly on the edge of his chair. "In fact, excellency, I have learned more than we had hoped."

"Yes?" The Frenchman raised his eyebrows.

"One laborer, some savage from the south, was injured at the midget's excavation and taken to the village clinic. There the heavy bone of his upper leg was set. I had the man moved to a dark space in the basement, where my brothers called on him at night."

"Yes?"

"Ramzi told the man that if he was in Egypt unlawfully, he would be sent to the penal quarry at Turah, where few men leave in the condition in which they arrive. But the dog was still too fearful to speak. So Ramzi was obliged to rip off his splint and shake him by his filthy foot. Finally

Munir was forced to smash the cast with a mop handle, one blow at a time."

"Seem like useful fellows, your brothers. We may have suitable work for them." De Neuville smiled. "They sound very different from you."

"I was my mother's favorite. Every millieme, every copper my father earned at the Post Office on Shari al-Baidaq, was spent on my schooling. My brothers used to stare at me across their empty plates when I received an extra portion. They were obliged to enter a harder life. I try to help them when I can, but with my marriage plans, there is not much I . . ."

"I understand, Gamal," said the Frenchman with disarming solicitude. "Now tell me everything."

"In time this injured black man spoke freely, all the while crying like a child, even more from fear than pain, I understand."

"Go on." De Neuville tapped an envelope on the table.

"It seems the midget has uncovered a treasure, some early tomb. Not a pharaoh, but some nobleman, richly prepared for the afterlife. Cedar chests, linens, alabaster vases, varnished jackals with silver claws, a wooden lion, two mummies, a model ship of the dead, and more, more than could be remembered by those who cleared the site. The details are mostly gossip passed from laborer to laborer, for the midget keeps all but this Tariq from entering the mortuary chamber itself. But one of their black women stole away and sneaked into the clinic to see the broken man, with whom she had been whoring. All of this she told him."

"Yet Alavedo has filed no report with the Service des Antiquités. He must intend to steal all this." De Neuville slid the envelope across the table. "Your new bride gift, Gamal. Have you selected her yet?"

"Thanks to your generosity, yes, excellency." Smiling eagerly, the Egyptian drew an envelope from his pocket and removed two photographs. "I have made new arrangements."

One picture, taken close-up, showed only a blurry veiled face with two enormous dark almond eyes. The other revealed the same girl seated on the edge of a chair. Her oval face and thick hair and small waist and high generous figure would torment most men. "All has been spoken of between our parents, and now, with this, it will be done."

"Remarkable how a woman's love can be made to grow," said the archeologist. Or at least most women, he thought.

*   *   *

His back to the embankment, Olivio sipped a cool mango juice and watched his son work the dials of the toy safe, recently fabricated to order at the metal market in Khan al-Khalili. Lord Penfold sat beside his host, wiping his eyes with a messy handkerchief. *The Egyptian Gazette* lay crumpled in his lap. The twins sat on the deck with their backs against the starboard rail, holding small slate drawing boards in their hands. Pieces of colored chalk were scattered around them.

"Papa!" Frustrated by the little vault, but too manly to weep, Tiago pounded both fists on the deck and stared up at his father with impatient angry eyes. "Papa!"

Rosemary and Cardamom looked down at their little brother.

The dwarf held up three fingers.

The child caressed the upper dial, turning it with slow care. Satisfied, he sat back and looked up, his fingers touching the next dial. "Papa?" he said more pleasantly, again catching his father's eye.

Olivio held up two fingers and wagged his head with a cheerful expression. He lifted a silver bell from the table beside him and rang it.

Tariq hurried across the deck.

"Master?"

"Behind me, on the embankment, beneath the royal poinciana tree, you will observe two men leaning on the parapet, watching me. You will learn what they require."

"Papa!" came the impatient cry.

Olivio glanced down. His son was still struggling with the center dial. Again the dwarf held up two fingers. "Two," he called gently but clearly. "Two."

Up the ramp, Tariq approached the two men. Both were shorter than he, but solid hard-looking men wearing coarse European trousers, shirts and belts. Shoulder to shoulder, they turned and stepped back from the embankment as Tariq approached.

"Who speaks for you?" said Tariq, standing very close, shifting his dead black eyes from one man to the other.

"What?" said the taller man.

"You have been bothering my master," the big Nubian said to him, raising both hands, palms open, his thick fingers spread. "When you bother him, you bother me." He pressed one hand against the chest of each man.

Both men stepped back against the parapet. The shorter man sought to sweep Tariq's hand from his chest but was unable to move the Nubian's arm.

"Tell me why you are here, or I will break your nose," Tariq said to the taller one, jabbing the man's chest with his fingers.

"What?"

"Tell me why you are here, or I will break your nose and throw you in the river."

"Is that midget your master?" the man replied.

"My effendi is not a midget."

Tariq slammed the heel of his right hand upwards into the man's nose. There was the crack of breaking cartilage. Blood flooded down into the man's mouth and dripped from his two silver front teeth. Tariq's left hand grabbed the Egyptian's belt and lifted him from his feet. Screaming, the man fell backwards into the Nile. As the shorter man tried to bolt, Tariq seized him by his upper arms.

"Tell me why you are here, or I will break your nose." With a hard motion, almost cuffing him, Tariq wiped the blood from his right hand onto the man's cheek.

"My brother and I came to the Café to deliver a message to your master," the man said quickly, glancing over the parapet where his brother struggled in the water, making for a distant stone stairway set into the wall of the embankment. "It is in my pocket."

"Tell me your name."

"Ramzi."

"And your brother's name?"

"Munir."

"Give me the message." Tariq eased his grip and the man handed him an envelope. Holding the man by his belt, Tariq hustled him down the gangway. "Sit over there on the deck while I present this to Mr. Alavedo." The Egyptian obeyed.

"Having fun?" said Lord Penfold when Tariq approached. He had been watching the whole time. "Old friends?"

Tariq inclined his head with deference but knew better than to reply. He handed the envelope to his master.

"Tariq makes friends quickly." The dwarf opened the envelope. He cast back his head and squinted as he read the card.

Garden City

Monsieur Alavedo,

As a matter of urgent mutual interest, I would like to call on you to discuss certain questionable antiquities recently discovered.

With my compliments,

Giscard de Neuville

"Have you a pen, my lord?" said the dwarf.

"Just my crossword pencil." Penfold removed the blunt stub from a jacket pocket. "Sorry, she's always a bit dull." He pulled a small penknife from another pocket and set to work with rare speed and precision.

"Papa! Papa!" cried Tiago, working on the third and final dial.

Penfold handed Olivio the pencil. The dwarf turned over the card and wrote a brief reply.

"Hand this to those scoundrels, Tariq, with a shilling, and tell them to give it to their master."

"Papa!" yelled Tiago joyfully, slapping open the small safe door. He plunged one hand into the safe and withdrew a shiny half-crown coin.

"Bless you, my son!" exclaimed the dwarf.

"Hooray!" cried the twins. They jumped up and kissed Tiago, tumbling him over like a doll and rolling with him on the deck.

"Useful trade," mumbled Penfold, fumbling to close his knife. "Perhaps we should drive the little blighter down to Shari al-Manakh and slip him into the Ottoman Bank."

— 11 —

"How are you, Captain?" said Major Lagnold after Anton stepped inside and dropped the tent flap behind him.

"Pretty well, sir, thank you." Washed and shaved for the first time in three weeks, looking forward to the luxuries of Cairo, Anton eagerly accepted the tall gin.

"Glad to see you so fit, Rider, and I'll tell you why later. You look ten years younger. All that swanning about in the blue must agree with you."

The major raised his glass, then glanced down at a sheet of paper. "Made it right across the Qattara Depression, did you? Should give even those headquarters chaps a fresh thought about no need to protect that southern flank. Bit of a shock for your friend Stoner, as well, if I'm right?" Lagnold glanced up at Anton.

"Hard to tell, sir."

"Damned good patrol, must say. Bag of enemy mail, at least ten aircraft, few infantry, four lorries. Two airstrips roughed up. All we could ask, really. Intelligence wallahs are especially excited with the mail. Keep those little cretins up for nights polishing their Eyetie, searching for naughty letters. And that map was the best of all. Being copied now for the next patrols. And just two men lost and three trucks. Any suggestions for us? You only get a couple, mind you."

"Yes, sir. Feet and headgear. I'd recommend either brothel creepers or heavy sandals instead of boots, something like . . ."

"Yes, yes, yes. I'm already bringing in *chapplies*, sort of thing we used

151

up on the Northern Frontier. Cool on the foot but plenty of grip." Lagnold scraped out his pipe. "What else?"

"A few men want to stick to caps, but the answer out there is to do what the Arabs do, sir. Long headcloths and rope braids. Keeps the sun off your neck and covers your face in a windstorm and warm at night."

"Of course, of course. Been wearing one all my life. We're getting them now, *kafiyas* and *aqals*. Be here tomorrow. Hear you had quite a blow out there, a proper *qibli?*"

"Took the paint right off the trucks on the windy side, sir. But it helped discourage the Eyeties, and we dug out pretty fast when it blew over."

"No doubt, no doubt. Libyan qibli's always worse than the 'Gypie *khamsin*, or even the *sharqiyas* we had in Palestine. I've seen gusts overturn trucks and tear telephone poles out of the ground. But there're usually sandstorms in the south and dust storms in the north along the coast. Sand never gets up much more'n twenty foot above the ground, of course, can't, too heavy. Proper dust storm will come in two thousand foot tall, horizon to horizon. Nothing like it. I've seen it get too dark to read at noon. Temperature drops twenty points in fifteen minutes. You were lucky yours was a bit of a mixture. Next time you'll learn to get tucked in before it gets to you."

"We were a bit busy at the time, sir . . ."

"Never mind, never mind. We'll be giving you a few new presents for your next patrol. Better wireless, the Number Eleven set, and a new 20mm Breda or two instead of the Bofors. Lot more punch and not much more weight. Picked 'em up from the Italians up north. Anything else?"

"Just one more thing, sir." Anton stepped outside the tent and came back carrying an empty German petrol can.

"What's the idea?" said Lagnold. "Planning to top up that thing with gin?"

"Petrol, sir. We captured these German tins. They're solid, don't leak, can use them over and over, don't spill when you pour . . ."

Lagnold picked up the can and examined it. "Well, my, my. Never seen anything like it. On long hauls we're losing over twenty-five percent from breakage and leakage and spillage. Those damn Egyptian *safiyhas* are built like sieves. Hmm. Leave this thing with me, if you don't mind."

"Of course, sir," said Anton, not revealing he had thirty more. He had learned one army habit: taking and keeping what he needed.

"A few things like this could win the war," said Lagnold, as if to himself, running his fingers over the word 'Wehrmacht' stamped near the bottom of the black can under the date, 1939.

"We're calling them 'jerry cans,' " said Anton, his thoughts on Gwenn and Cairo.

" 'Jerricans' eh? And look at this, will you, engraved into the side here, *'Kraftstoff 201-Feuergefährlich,'* engine fuel—inflammable. These devils don't leave much to chance."

"Will that be all, sir?" Anton wanted to stop by and visit his three wounded men in the hospital.

"All for now, Rider. I'll be briefing you Monday on your next patrol. Could be a long one. Now that you've learned a bit about the desert, we'll be finding you something a trifle more sporting. Get you out at the sharp end. See if we can do something to help hold Tobruk. Go after something the Jerries really need." He tapped the petrol can. "Like this."

"Thank you, sir." Anton glanced at his watch. A few grains of sand slid about under the glass like tiny balls of brown mercury.

"By the way," said Lagnold as Anton finished his gin. "We've got some fresh boys in camp, for the new patrols. Some of them are even rougher than your Kiwi friends. Rhodesians, mostly, and a few Guardsmen to smarten us up a bit, mostly Coldstreamers, handful of Scots. Big chaps, the Guardsmen, like to keep their leather clean. These Rhodies seem a pretty hard lot, mostly country brutes from those bush farms they have down there, don't talk to anyone for months, used to being out on their own, shoving rocks about and wrestling with crocs and rhinos and what not." Lagnold paused to suck on his pipe. "Don't take to a lot of drill . . ."

"I think I know the type." Anton turned to leave.

". . . and they've talked us into an alternative fitness test to boxing or running about with packs on."

"Please don't tell me about it, sir." Anton grinned and raised the flap of the tent. "This camp is more dangerous than the Italians."

"Well, actually, you're already signed on to be a part of it all. While you were out on your sahara safari, the lads in the mess signed up you and Stoner and that blackie of yours to challenge the best of the Rhodies. Should be fun. Some of the chaps've put a month's wages on you. Wouldn't do to let 'em down, shouldn't've thought. Too late now, really."

"Sir, I'm just off . . ."

"Milling, they call it. Milling. Seems you stand right up against the other chap, toe to toe, very thin leather mitts, driving gloves or some such, and bash each other about for two minutes, flat out, hard as you please. If you duck or bob or flinch or fall down or try to protect yourself, they keep starting the clock over again and you've got to keep at it, on and on, just to make sure everyone gets his fair share. Say the idea's to get one used to a bit of pain, so once they're in action each man knows the chap next to him will keep fighting when things get nasty. Something like that, anyway. Don't really know how it all works, but they'll set you up all right. Not to worry."

"Sir . . ."

"All good training, you know. And useful to have the men see that the officers can handle their share. So one of us has to do it. No choice, really." Lagnold struck a wooden match and held it to his pipe, sucking violently. "Can't thank you enough. Everyone in the mess agreed you were just the man for the job. Damned flattering, Rider, if I may say so." Lagnold puffed and coughed. "Only wish they thought as much of me."

"Not . . ."

"Could do it after tea this afternoon, before you head into town if I were you. Shouldn't take long." The major squinted and smiled through the smoke. "Probably best to have a crack at it while you're still in shape, if you know what I mean. We'll have a medicine man with the usual kit lounging about in case things get messy."

"Is Dr. Rider there, please?" Anton asked. "Gwenn Rider." He thought he heard a man sobbing and the clatter of a trolley in the corridor, all the noisy background of the Scottish Hospital. He set down his gin on the shelf in the telephone kiosk so that his wife wouldn't hear him drinking. Next to it lay the unopened note from Harriet von Decken that had been waiting for him at the desk of the Semiramis, Anton's usual mail drop in Cairo.

" 'Fraid not, sir. I believe Dr. Rider's off for Alexandria to work with the Army surgeons at the Anglo-Swiss. In fact she should be on her way to the station now. She's on the sleeper, I believe. Her train leaves for Alex in just under an hour. Stops for a bit along the way."

Anton jumped up and threw open the door of the kiosk and bolted across the lobby of the hotel. He had not planned to see Harriet anyway. Barely touching the steps or the railing, he dashed down the front stairs and ran to the head of the taxi queue. The taxi boy was holding open the door of the front hack as two ladies fussed over who should enter first. Ignoring their shrill protests, Rider flung himself in and pulled shut the door.

"The Main Station!" he yelled. "And drive for your life."

"Sir?" The aged turbanned driver turned stiffly to stare at his frantic client.

"The Main Station! Alexandria train. Drive for your life and I'll double the money. Go!"

Anton's stomach was tight as a clamp. Everything he should have said to Gwenn was now, at last, on his tongue. He sat back and closed his eyes, certain that if he did not see Gwenn today, he never would again. His left eye throbbed under the light dressing and black patch he'd needed after the milling.

"*Insh' Allah!*" The old man moved forward to the edge of his seat and rattled the knob of the long stick shift.

"Double the fare! Go!"

The driver swung out into the traffic as if the road were empty. Like a man diving through water, he passed between donkey carts and lorries, foot peddlars and camels and motor cars. Everything seemed to part before him. Accelerating steadily, the old Hudson achieved its maximum speed of perhaps twenty-five miles an hour and then maintained that no matter what lay before it. The strings of wooden beads that covered the rear window like the entrance to a brothel swished wildly from side to side as the venerable sedan darted left and right. Curses and prayers poured from the driver in a flooding stream of Arabic as he tore through the Mayden al-Azhar, then north past the Azbekiyya Garden. Finally the Hudson plunged across the maelstrom of the Mayden al-Mahatta, the great square before the Main Station.

Banging the rear fender of the taxi in front of him as he braked, the driver jumped down and scuttled around to open Anton's door. But Rider was already out. He thrust money into the man's hand and pushed his way across the broad crowded pavement towards the great station. Instead of taxicabs, a long row of ambulances waited against the inner curb.

"*Shukran,* ya bey!" cried the grateful man after him, ignoring the curses of the other driver as he stared into his hand. "*Ma'a salama!*"

Almost knocking down two stretcher bearers, Anton collected himself and stopped. "Excuse me," he said, ashamed as he looked down at the unconscious soldier whose head and both hands were wrapped in gauze. A nurse following the stretcher turned her head towards Rider and looked at him without expression as she passed.

The crowd struggled all around him. Most European men were in khaki, but he saw robes and uniforms and costumes of ten different countries. Baggage carts competed for space with wheelchairs and porters. Soldiers rocked along on crutches. Refugees, probably fleeing to Palestine, stood warily beside piles of boxes and cardboard cases. Men and boys sold newspapers and nuts in tiny paper cones and small sherbets from copper trays and colored drinks from fancy glass dispensers strapped to their backs.

Anton hesitated when he saw a little English boy in a school cap and crested blazer staring up, lost, pale and round-faced, both hands before him as if fearing to be knocked over, alone for a moment in the madness. Then a woman came to him and Anton hurried on.

The metal gate to the Alexandria track was open, the long platform nearly empty. The brown and tan coaches of the train must be already full. Porters walked back towards him, their numbered metal badges shiny on their arms. Empty luggage straps swung over their shoulders as they counted their tips with both hands. Passengers, women and men and children, leaned out the lowered windows to exchange goodbyes, holding hands, reaching for a kiss, sometimes waving with indifference at people they could no longer see. Running and dodging along the track, Anton looked up at the windows until he passed the restaurant car and came to the First Class carriages. Then he strode along more slowly, staring into each in turn.

A shrill whistle came from the front of the train. Then two blasts more. He heard the hinged steel footplates being slammed up as the conductors climbed on board. Puffs of white steam flooded along the side of the train. Anton hurried forward, trying to check on the front two cars. He could see the tall driving wheels of the locomotive begin to turn and the connecting rods make their stroke. The engine was lost in its own cloud. He was too late.

As the train slid past him, gathering speed, only the steps to the restaurant car were still open. Anton grabbed the vertical handrail and swung up.

The headwaiter bowed as Anton entered the empty car. A row of very dark waiters in white robes and sashes, probably Nubians, stood behind the headwaiter. Towels hung from the arms that were folded across their chests. The tables along the western side of the train were for two, those along the eastern wall for four. Pots of Marmite waited with the salt and pepper on each table.

"Sir?" said the maître d'hôtel, evidently not impressed by Anton's rank.

"Table for two, if you please." Anton reached into his pocket, glad he had collected his pay. "I'll have that one in the far corner." He could hear the first eager passengers entering the car through the door behind him. "And bring us a bottle of champagne, if you would."

"Of course, *ya basha*," said the headwaiter, his respect well rewarded. He adjusted his black tie with his free hand as he appraised the fresh arrivals.

Anton sat in the far corner facing the door and watched the restaurant car begin to fill. Cotton brokers and senior officers, war correspondents and Alexandrine Greeks pressed themselves upon the headwaiter, his power growing as the number of available tables declined. Anton watched the man hesitate, going on tiptoe and looking over the tightly packed suppli-cants, some of them uncertain whether arrogance or unctuousness would carry more influence, though of course neither was the proper coin.

Anton smoked and watched the door while the champagne waited in its bucket under a towel. Some sort of English businessman, apparently a regular, with his wife and daughter and another woman, took the table across the narrow aisle. Anton turned his eyes away and looked out the window. The slow train was still leaving the city, sliding past a parade of gardens and villas. Some of the taller monuments of Cairo were barely visible in the distance.

"You can just see the old Citadel to the west, there," explained the businessman to his companions, gesturing towards the rear view from Rider's window, "and those minarets should be the Mosque of Muhammad Ali. I'll keep you on top of it all as we move along."

"Oh, Father," said the restless, almost pretty girl, perhaps seventeen.

Saving the champagne, Anton ordered a double gin. He prayed that Gwenn would not be eating a picnic in her cabin. Trying to disregard his neighbors, he studied the menu and repeatedly put off the eager waiter.

"Qalyub will be next," the Englishman said as Cairo melted into the dusk. The windows blackened and Anton ordered another drink, not know-ing whether to feel expectant or hopeless.

He thought of how he'd first met Gwenn as a lad of eighteen on the boat to Mombasa after the end of the last war, as awkward with her then as he knew he would be now. Twenty years later, she was still the only person who could open him and take away his confidence. He remembered how impossibly fresh and perfect and daunting she'd seemed as she stood beside him at the rail of the old *Garth Castle* while for the first time they watched the morning sun touch Africa. He was dying to put his hand over hers where it rested on the rail, but dared not. As they heard the anchor chain rattle down and drop outside the reef of Kilindini Harbor, they saw the chalk-white walls and the red roofs of the Arab houses and smelled on the breeze the red earth and the coconut and mango trees. Before she climbed down the gangway to the pitching surfboat, she'd looked up at him. Her green eyes absorbed him. Impossibly bold, he'd bent and kissed her cheek.

Anton glanced down at his empty drink and felt the man's eyes studying his uniform, probably not recognizing the unusual red and blue shoulder patch of the Long Range Desert Group with the scorpion insignia, but no doubt aware that it was against security to enquire about a soldier's regiment.

"Going all the way?" the man asked him cheerfully.

"All the way?" said Anton, using a technique he admired in the dwarf.

"All the way to Alex." The man's three companions were staring at Anton.

"Yes."

"We're off at Khatatbah. I'm with Egyptian Salt and Soda. We have our own light rail line, you know, running right out to the salt lakes, there's . . ."

"Prawns or soupy, sir?" said the waiter. "Mulligatawny?"

"Soup. Soup." The man nodded eagerly and tucked his napkin into the top of his waistcoat, watching closely as the waiter set down the bowl and ladled in the steaming soup. Then he smiled at Anton. "Hope you'll not be drinking that bubbly all by yourself!"

"I certainly hope not," said Gwenn, stepping up behind the waiter.

Anton stood, speechless, and kissed her on the cheek she offered.

"What's happened to your eye?" she said, worried, raising one hand. "And the whole side of your face is so swollen. Were you wounded?"

"Nothing, really, it's going to be fine."

"Oh, good," she said, relieved, her tone changing. "Only please don't tell me it was just another brawl."

"Of course not. A training accident."

"Are you expecting someone else? This is the only seat left."

"Please, no. Sit down, of course." He was aware of the neighbors watching expectantly, uncomfortably close, as if in the very front row at the theatre.

"I'll do it, thank you," said Anton to the hovering waiter. As he opened the champagne himself, he recalled the morning Lord Penfold had taught him how to do it properly, with the palm of your left hand over the top of the cork as you give it its final liberating wiggle.

"Why are you going to Alex?" Gwenn said.

Suddenly he was shy, not wishing to be overheard. "I'm not." He filled both glasses, pausing to top up each one.

"Where are you getting off?"

"I'm not, I'm coming straight back."

"Then why . . ."

"I had to see you," he said, lifting his glass to her.

"To the boys," she said, lifting hers, happy to see him despite herself.

"To all of us," he said.

The train slowed and chattered across a large iron bridge.

"Just crossing the Damietta branch of the Nile," said the Salt and Soda man. "Railbed still pretty fair, considering old Said Pasha laid her down in . . ."

". . . 1855," contributed his daughter in a quiet voice, lifting her eyes in silent despair.

For the first time Gwenn smiled at Anton, but her green eyes were tired and he thought she'd got too slim. He watched her as she sipped her champagne.

"How was the patrol?" Gwenn said after a time.

"Not too bad. Bashed about the desert a bit, learned the game. Ran into a few Italians. I really can't say much about it."

"Tanta," the man said loudly to his family as the train slowed to a stop. "Big town. Nice clubs. Thirteenth-century mosque. All sorts of ruins and bazaars. Worse than Cairo."

Anton saw Gwenn trying not to smile. As he refilled her glass, though, her expression changed.

"Look at your right hand. Your knuckles are all scraped to the bone, as if they've just been bleeding," Gwenn said, setting down her glass. "You have been brawling, haven't you, Anton?"

"There's a war on, Gwennie," he said hotly, annoyance overwhelming affection. "Please. A lot of men are getting hurt. This is nothing. We had two chaps killed, and it might've been my fault." He tried to control himself and saw her eyes soften. "We'll be off again next week, soon as we've got our lorries fixed up and all the kit sorted out and they tell us where to go. They say it'll be a long patrol. That's why I had to see you. There's so much I want to say. I . . ."

"Oh, I'm sorry." Gwenn shook her head, knowing how hard it was for him to say this. "I'm becoming such a witch." She put her slender fingers over his, gently tapping Anton's injured knuckles. "I don't know whether it's me or this wretched war. Even Denby says I'm being hard on him."

"Gwennie," he said after a moment, reaching for her hand, "couldn't we try to work things out?"

"We have tried," she said as kindly as she could, avoiding his hand as she lifted her glass. She shook her head slowly from side to side. "We've both tried, Anton. But it doesn't ever seem to work."

"I know it's mostly been my fault," he said, those words prepared.

"Oh, Anton." She noticed again the cornflower blue of his eyes against his tanned skin, lined and harder now. "We've both done too much to spoil it. Don't you see? We don't share much now beside the boys, and they're as good as gone."

He could not answer her.

"There's only one other thing we ever really shared," she said with sadness, "and even then we weren't together."

"What do you mean?"

"Before you went to the goldfields. We'd been reading *David Copperfield* aloud together at the farm. Don't you remember? You'd been carrying it so long, it had broken in two. You gave me the first part to read while you were away, taking the rest with you. I always felt you were there when I was reading it, over and over."

"Of course I remember," he said eagerly. "Gwenn, couldn't we do better? Don't we owe it to the boys . . ."

"That's not fair . . ."

"Maybe not, but it's true. You know we could do better."

"Well, we're off here," said their neighbor, rising. "Back to the salt mines. Hope you two enjoy Alexandria. Have a drink for us at the Yacht Club. Cheerio!"

"Goodbye," said Anton. Gwenn smiled up at them, relieved by the interruption.

"That girl was already in love with you," said Gwenn, more relaxed, feeling the champagne. "She probably likes your eye patch."

"What girl?"

"Poor thing. She doesn't know she'd have to join the party."

"What party?" Anton smiled, despite himself.

She watched his eye twinkle.

Their dinner came. Grilled sardines. Roast duck and wild rice and prunes. A working claret. They talked of Wellington, and Gwenn's work, and finally of Kenya long before the war, laughing about Adam Penfold, and Olivio, and days that seemed too distant. They wondered how the farm must have grown back to virgin bush. And they thought of things they dared not say.

"I'll walk you to your Pullman," Anton said at last, as the waiters cleared the final tables. "So many Tommies about in the halls, most of them as far gone as they can manage."

"I'm afraid I'm not much better," said Gwenn. If only it wasn't Anton, she thought, though knowing she would still behave. I'm due for a little mischief, and Alex is bound to be all hell. Sex always made everything both simpler and more complicated. For a time it cleared away everything that had gone before, and gave you a fresh start. When the past was difficult, and some emotional distance had already been achieved, it could make things either far better or sadly worse. But if you let it, it could unlock everything else and bring back some innocence and help you start again.

"Well, this is you," he said nervously, opening the cabin door with the numbered key she gave him. "Fifteen." He pushed open the door without entering.

"I'd better take a look at that eye of yours," she said. As she stepped past him into the narrow room, she was not able to avoid touching him. The lower berth was already made up, the crisp top sheet turned neatly down. "You're going to need both of them when you're back in the desert."

"It's fine," he said, hesitating in the doorway, not knowing what this meant.

"Never argue with your doctor."

He closed the door and she drew down the night shade as the train crossed a canal and the lights of a small village slipped past. "Sit there."

Anton sat at the end of the bed near the reading light mounted on the cabin wall.

Gwenn washed her hands in the tiny triangular sink set into one corner. "Put your head back close to the light. Don't touch the bandage, silly, I'll take it off."

He closed both eyes and felt the touch of her hands on his face. Oh God, he thought, wanting to hug her. I don't think I'll be able to stand this.

She took off the patch, then carefully removed the dressing. "Whoever slapped this on?" she said scornfully. "Looks like a field dressing."

"One of the regimental medics at Abbassia, in camp," he said. The Rhodie he'd milled with was a cheery hairy blacksmith from Nyanga with hands like cleavers. If Anton hadn't punched him in the throat, the friendly fellow would have killed him. "They had better things to fuss with."

Slowly she washed his face, patting down the puffy bruises with a damp towel. She cleaned around the eye, then gently parted the swollen lids with the fingers of both hands.

"I'm going to put some ointment in it." She reached up and took down her medical kit from the overhead luggage rack. "Awful bruises. Few blood clots in the eye. I'd be worried about infection, but it should be all right if you look after it, this once," she added.

She taped a fresh bandage over the eye with careful, even loving fingers. "There you are." She replaced the black patch, slipping the cord over the back of his head and smoothing down his hair. "I should take another look at it in the morning."

"Thank you." Anton stood, dying to stay, but determined not to press her. "Good night." He kissed her on the cheek and opened the door.

"Good night," she said as he left.

After a few steps he turned and walked back to number fifteen. He knocked.

She opened the door a little, then wider.

"Sorry, I forgot something." Without trying to enter, he reached into his back pocket and took out his notebook. He opened it and removed a pressed flower. He handed the small white flower to her by its furry stem.

"It's lovely," Gwenn said, delighted, turning the flower in her hand. "Where did you get it?"

"In the desert, at an oasis, before we got in trouble." He hesitated. "Good night."

"Good night." She closed the door.

Anton jammed his hands into his pockets and leaned against the wall, staring out the corridor window into the blackness. Why was he so awkward with her?

He closed his eyes and leaned his forehead against the black window of the train.

Gwenn's door opened behind him.

"You don't have a cabin, do you?"

"No, but it's all right."

"Do you have a berth or a seat?"

"No. The train's full."

"Well, come back in, you can have the upper bunk. Just give me ten minutes to get in bed, then you can come in."

Anton paced up and down the corridor, pressing himself against the wall when a group of sailors stumbled past.

After fifteen minutes, he knocked.

"Come in."

Only the blue night light was on. The top bunk had been lowered from the wall. The narrow stepladder hung from its two brass hooks, the bottom braced against the floor. Anton found a hook for his jacket and leaned against the door while he unlaced his boots. He climbed up and wriggled out of his clothes before getting into bed, wondering if he should try to join her. He heard her reach up and turn off the light.

He lay there with his arms beneath his head, listening to the clicking of the wheels, once hearing the ghostly hooting of the horn. He heard Gwenn's familiar breathing when finally she fell asleep.

Some time later, waking, or dreaming, lying on his side, he felt her squeeze into the narrow berth behind him.

"I was cold," she whispered, fitting in against him in her linen nightdress. "Don't wake up. Just stay like that, please."

He did as she asked, not wanting to spoil things. As he felt her hand curl on his shoulder and her warm breath on his neck, he finally felt at peace. Perhaps in the morning, he thought as his eyes closed.

De Neuville waited for Ramzi to hurry around to his side of the black Panhard and open the door. Properly dressed in a chauffeur's dark grey suit and black cap, his new driver appeared surprisingly respectable. Since he had already performed useful service in extracting information from the midget's injured worker, the Frenchman was confident that Ramzi and his brother were not above the sort of rough work that might be required in the future.

"Is that the Nubian who savaged your brother?" said de Neuville after he alighted on the embankment. A massive figure stared up at them from the deck of the Café.

"Yes, excellency, that is the black animal who attacked my brother by surprise."

The Frenchman walked down the ramp to the Café, and Tariq led him to a doorway beside the bar. The Nubian held open the door.

De Neuville hesitated at the top of the steps before descending. Rumors had reached him of bizarre doings in the hold of this Café. Who in Cairo had not heard them? Some tales made a man of spirit wish to visit. Others led a man to cross himself. De Neuville gripped the handrail and clumsily descended the many narrow half-height steps.

At the bottom he stood and looked about him in the uneven gloom. Behind him, built into the stern of the vessel, racks of wine rose from deck to ceiling. Wooden cases from Beaune and Oporto, Pauillac and Jerez de la Frontera lay stacked before the racks. To de Neuville's left, a row of portholes cast intense beams of light across the single cavernous room. Between the portholes were shelves and vitrines crowded with objects he could not discern. Shifting slightly as the boat rocked with the swells of the Nile, the portholes illuminated scenes on the opposite wall from what seemed to be a long painting of a hieroglyphic, much like some he had seen, and yet like none other. A mortuary scene, elaborately detailed and reaching from stern to stem, it appeared to depict the entire process of embalming and mummification, the draining of each fluid, blood and marrow and mucus and urine, into its own vessel, and the removal and preservation of each organ, from brain to kidney. Every instrument and jar, every wrap and preservative, appeared with timeless colored clarity.

Fascinated, Giscard de Neuville squinted at the images, finally concluding with astonishment that this was not, after all, a painting. It was the actual hieroglyphic itself, painted on limestone about fifteen hundred years before Christ, if he was right, and the face of the stone evidently laboriously cut free from some mortuary temple and then remounted here for this macabre midget.

"Welcome to you, Monsieur de Neuville," said his host.

De Neuville turned and gazed down the length of the hold.

He saw a small man sitting in a chair, his round bald head illuminated like a fortune teller's crystal ball. The Frenchman approached.

Caught for the moment in a beam of light as the boat rocked in the wake of a passing speedboat, Olivio's single grey eye stared at him from beneath his prominent forehead. Often obliged to replace activity with imagination, and physical experience with intuition, the dwarf had learned to identify malice no matter how well it might be shrouded, as other men might recognize athleticism or good cheer.

"*Magnifique*," said the Frenchman, gesturing at the wall. "Eighteenth dynasty?"

"Indeed," nodded the dwarf, impressed but not surprised. "Thutmosis the Third." He gestured toward a rattan chair set beside the table at his side.

"I often prefer to enjoy antiquities in the privacy of personal collections," said de Neuville in precise English as he sat, "rather than in the circus of public exhibitions."

"You asked to see me," said the dwarf. He was habituated to conducting the discussion as he chose.

"Yes, but first may I say how surprising it is to find such scholarly tastes in a gentleman from Africa, or is it, I am told, India?"

"Both," said the dwarf, the patronage noted. "We Portuguese are accustomed to travel. As you know, Monsieur, we colonized western India in the fifteenth century. That was about the time your countryman, John of Burgundy, sold Joan of Arc to the English to be burned alive."

De Neuville ignored the comment. "I believe we have a number of common friends and interests . . ."

"I am aware of only one of each," said Olivio. The man was foolish, but no fool. Olivio reminded himself not to underestimate him later. But how could Miss Gwenn treat with such a man? On the other hand, who was he to disparage inappropriate liaisons?

Suddenly de Neuville was aware of a footfall just behind him.

"Serve us," said the dwarf as Tariq stepped forward in his slippers and set down a copper tray. "Coffee?"

"If you please," said de Neuville. He watched as his demitasse was filled, then helped himself to dark sugar crystals.

Tariq poured again, but this time into a skyphos that rested on the tray. The small two-handled vessel was unusual even for its type: one of the

handles was mounted vertically on one side of the cup, the other, horizon-
tally on the far side, so that a man might lift his drink in the manner he
favored. How ingenious, thought de Neuville, how Egyptian. And it was,
he knew, though uncertain of the age or provenance. Perhaps New King-
dom. If original, a treasure too priceless to be used.

Olivio Alavedo lifted the skyphos to his lips. His guest noticed the light-
figured creature depicted on its dark surface: a bald and naked leaping
dwarf, arms and legs extended straight forward and back, toes and fingers
pointed away like a dancer, testicles exposed. The immense cranium and
stumpy limbs emphasized its deformity.

Enjoying the chill of his guest's reaction, Olivio looked over the top of
the cup into the Frenchman's eyes, his gaze relentless through the steam.
Rather then be shamed by his deformities, he had learned to employ them.
Even horror had its uses. He was aware how much this ancient creature's
head resembled his own, for of course they shared the problem of hydro-
cephalus, enlargement of the skull, caused by the abnormal increase in the
amount of cerebrospinal fluid within the cavities of the brain. Fortunately,
this was one guest who knew that in ancient Egypt, despite their sufferings,
dwarves were gods, though typically depicted as naked and grotesque.

"I understand you are presently recovering some new antiquities," said
de Neuville, disgusted that this misshapen little beast could be a close
friend of his lover. When Gwenn was his again, he would see that she
terminated this embarrassing relationship.

"I am always interested in the study of antiquities," said the dwarf. He
looked forward to the unveilings of this conversation. Until now, he and
de Neuville had been fencing at a distance, by proxy. It was their minions
who had borne the wounds of conflict.

"I am speaking of your dig," said the archeologist in an impatient harder
voice. "On your farm, at Al Lahun."

"Do I speak to you of your work, and of the things you do?" The dwarf
spoke with deliberate vagueness. Every man had something he did not
wish uncovered, and he had learned some of the secrets this Frenchman
had to hide, some to do with his profession, others with his politics. Already, two of his staff were in the dwarf's employ. Alavedo permitted some
severity in his tone when he continued.

"Or of the things you do not do? Is your country not at war, Monsieur?
Is that fine gabardine your uniform? Whose medals will you wear when
this war is done?" He leaned forward. "Will you dance in Paris, or Berlin?"

There was barely a hesitation before the Frenchman replied, his voice even, as if undisturbed.

"If the Service des Antiquités knew what I know, Alavedo, you would be jailed, caged like a little monkey at the zoo, in the *maison des singes*, where creatures like you belong. All you possess in Egypt would be confiscated."

The dwarf paused before he replied, storing his resentment like treasure in a vault.

"If the government knew everything I know, Monsieur de Neuville, many men and women would be in jail, perhaps including the Inspector General. Others could be dead."

Olivio opened wide his single grey eye and stared at the Frenchman. He considered how much of his knowledge to reveal. Although he himself had little interest in politics, and still less in patriotism, he was learning that in the case of the archeologist, these could be subjects of opportunity. Even de Neuville's packer was now reporting to the dwarf. Every artifact the man packed was being compared against the Frenchman's export manifests. Of course now the shipments were to Cape Town rather than to Paris. Soon, last year's records would be checked, then the year before. Alavedo weighed the satisfaction of revelation against the wisdom of discretion. Better to learn still more. But a little fear could be a useful provocation.

"The unlicensed export of antiquities is a crime in Egypt, Monsieur," advised the dwarf.

Ignoring him, de Neuville continued. "My proposal is one you can afford, and it is very simple, with no problems of evaluation or disposal."

"If you require me to give you an answer, it, too, will be a simple one, but one that you will not be able to afford." The pleasure of anticipation was in Olivio's voice.

"If you do not wish to be exposed, Alavedo, you will choose two of your discovered artifacts, then I will select one, then you will choose two, then I will choose one, until all is divided."

The Frenchman leaned forward and raised both eyebrows, nodding with a slight superior smile, as if the dwarf were already in his snare. "Better for you to lose one third of what you are about to steal from Egypt than to lose everything that you own, no?"

Olivio looked at de Neuville and did not reply.

It was not the insult or the greed or the threat that disturbed him most. It was the implied scorn, the absence of respect, the notion that the dwarf was not to be feared. Indignation boiled in him like a secret furnace. His breath tightened. He felt his head swell with a rush of blood as he labored to control his demeanor. Did this man understand with whom he dealt? Did he confuse size with incapacity, twisted limbs with a coward's brain, appearance with reality? Did he know nothing of how Olivio Fonseca Alavedo had endured and suffered and prevailed? How he had tranformed himself from a penniless misshapen youth in Goa to a gentleman with coffee plantations in Brazil and vineyards and cork forests in Portugal, and estates in the Delta of the river Nile, rich in cotton and rice and citrus and mangoes, not to mention this magnificent Café, and his collection of treasures older than Christ?

For a brief moment the dwarf wished his worst adversaries were still alive, alive to warn this man, to testify as references, to tell the tale of Olivio Fonseca Alavedo, to establish who he was.

"We shall see," said Olivio, his voice even, his soul enraged. A monkey, was he? Always denied the physicality of violent satisfaction, the dwarf had found other methods to tilt the scales of revenge.

"Unless I hear from you first," said de Neuville, "in two weeks I will visit your farm and we can begin to make our selections."

"Is it the French habit to visit without invitation?"

De Neuville stood to leave, then bent down and lifted the skyphos in both hands and turned it, pausing to admire the squatting dancing dwarf depicted on the reverse side. "I once held the original in my hands in Paris," he said.

"The original," said the dwarf, "is in your hands now."

Wellington was eager to make the most of the last night of his three-day leave, an evening in Cairo with Saffron. It was to be a treat with some rare help from his father, a present after he'd returned from his last brief safari. Must have been a win at cards, Wellie guessed.

Waiting for her, with a secret on his mind, he was fortifying himself with a few drinks in the Long Bar at Shepheards with some chums from the 11th. The lads were a bit loud and cocky in their smart bright trousers, cranking down Joe's famous Suffering Bastards as if each one were the last drink of their lives. Every jack of them was sick with jealousy when Saffron appeared at the doorway in a cream-colored silk dress with a pleated skirt and shoulder straps, and a scarlet shawl over her shoulders.

"Good lord," said Gates, slamming down his glass. "That can't possibly be for you."

"No job for a boy," said Bingham, lifting a Senior Service from Gates' packet. Then he rubbed one hand over his head and straightened up and checked himself in the mirror behind the bar. "Better let old Bingham start things off for you."

"Good night, lads," said Wellie, tossing down a couple of Egyptian quid. "Behave yourselves."

Not permitted to enter the men's bar, tawny and dishy and promising, huge chocolate brown eyes only for him, Saffron stood near the piano between the giant potted palms, impatient to greet him with a kiss. She tapped her toe to one of her favorite dance tunes, *I'll Never Smile Again.*

Trying to be correct, but feeling like a schoolboy, Wellington took her arm and kissed her on the cheek. Her thick dark hair swept his face. Her breasts pressed against his tunic like soft melons.

"Dinner at the Auberge des Pyramides?" he said.

"Lovely," she said, "but isn't that a bit extravagant?"

"Eat, drink and be merry," Wellie said with a smile, careful not to finish the old line.

"Are any of your friends joining us? How about Johnny?"

"Uh, no. Bingham's already got something laid on," Wellington said as they walked under the colored glass dome of the Moorish Hall. "Shame, but the lads're all awfully busy. Last evening's leave and what not." Guests having late tea or drinks at small inlaid octagonal tables looked up at the young couple while Wellington guided her swiftly across the dimly lit hall towards the terrace.

"Do you think your father will catch us again?" he asked when they were in the taxi.

"Not tonight. I think Papa has some rather personal plans of his own," she said, taking Wellington's hand. "But you never know with him."

Arrived at the Auberge, well seated, surrounded by nobs and generals, they stared at each other in the candlelight before they spoke. He tried not to let her catch him looking down her dress.

"A bottle of Charles Heidsieck, please," Wellington said to the waiter, putting the large menus aside.

"That's our next to final bottle, sir," said the sommelier when he arrived with the waiter carrying the ice bucket. "The war, you know."

"Oh," said Wellington while the man popped the cork, "then would you mind bringing out the other bottle now and dropping it in the bucket for us?"

"Of course, sir, but I was holding it for General O'Connell. He always drinks Heid . . ."

"Haven't you heard? General O'Connell was captured last week, in his staff car."

Astonished, the sommelier hesitated.

"I'm sure he'd like us to drink it," Wellington added, pressing something into the man's hand. "No telling how long he'll be in Germany."

"Very good, sir."

"I'll pour the rest, thank you."

"Oh, that's awful," said Saffron quietly after the sommelier left them. "Shame on you! Fibbing like that. What'll happen if the general comes in while we're still here?"

"Don't think he will." Wellington grinned at her. "Great chap, but a German motorcycle troop captured him last week near Derna. The old commanding officer of my regiment was with him. They're probably having dinner in Berlin."

Wellington raised his glass and they looked at each other.

"To General O'Connell," he said.

"Are you teasing me?" she asked, hesitating before she drank.

"Not yet," he said.

She laughed and they touched glasses.

"Mmm. Papa still has quite a bit of this," said Saffron. "He says that's why the Café is so low in the water. Someone came 'round from the Semiramis trying to buy it all, but he said it was too soon to sell it and still plenty of time to drink it." She did not add that her father had grumbled that he'd need all of it when his five daughters finally got married.

"How is your father?" he asked, wondering how difficult Mr. Alavedo was going to be. "My mother's been a bit worried about his health."

"Well enough, but I think he's driving poor Doctor Hänger crazy. He's busier than ever. Seems to be buying and selling everything in Egypt. Says he has to do it to help with the war."

"Somebody better," said Wellie. "The Cherrypickers can't do it all, you know."

"You can't?" she said. "I think you can do anything."

He gazed at her while she spoke, feeling giddy and blessed that she was with him, and trying to think how he would say what he had to say.

"Will you order for me, please," Saffron asked at last, trained by her mother how to please a man.

He ordered, and she beamed.

The tables came and went around them while they ate and drank and talked and laughed. It was the evening for which they both had waited.

"Flaming bananas, please," said Wellington to the waiter when the time came for dessert.

"*Bananes flambées, monsieur?*" answered the Egyptian.

"That's it," said Wellington, glowing with wine and pleasure and anticipation.

Then they went to the Mena House and sat at a small round table near the band. Wellington whispered to the head waiter. The man turned and spoke to the bandleader.

"Will you dance with me, Saffron?" young Rider said as the band began to play *I'm Getting Sentimental Over You*.

"I will dance with you, Wellington." She smiled, and they danced until the band no longer played.

Finally they walked back through the bar and the old lobby, down the hotel steps and along the drive.

"Golf?" he asked, leading her across the road to the darkened course set below the pyramids.

Saffron carried her shoes in one hand and they skipped high together across the seventh fairway, holding hands. He carried their unfinished champagne in his other hand, one thumb over the top of the bottle.

They sat down on a green between a stand of palms and the decaying brick wall at the back of the course, close together on his tunic, sprayed with champagne, both conscious of the precious time.

Wellington saw the moon in Saffron's eyes when she raised her head.

"When I'm back in the desert and I see the moon," he said, "I will always think of you."

"And when I see the moon, I'll think of you," Saffron said, feeling a slight chill, as if she were already alone.

"Are you always so sloppy with champagne?" she said after a moment as they drank from the bottle.

"Only with you."

"We must behave ourselves," she said. "The sphinx is just behind those trees, watching us."

"I'll do my best," said Wellington.

He set down the bottle and put one hand on her cheek.

Saffron closed her eyes and turned her face into his hand and kissed his wrist. Slowly he ran his hand down her neck to her shoulder while he looked in her eyes and her lips parted. He could not believe the smooth warmth of her skin. He raised both hands to her cheeks and held her face and closed his eyes as he kissed her. When he drew back, her eyes were huge in the moonlight. She trembled when he kissed one corner of her neck and shoulder. Her hair covered his face. He hugged her and felt her breasts move against him as she breathed.

Then he stood and faced her and took her hand before kneeling on the stiff grass in the moonlight.

"Will you marry me, Saffron?"

For answer, she unbuttoned his collarless white shirt, then his trouser buttons, slipping the suspenders from his shoulders before she touched him and lay back, knowing he'd been waiting. The straps fell from her shoulders. He bent and put his face between her breasts, slightly sticky and sweet with champagne. He pressed them to his cheeks with both hands, then held them one by one and kissed them until he could no longer breathe. Drawing back, he gazed at her for a moment, then spoke once more.

"Will you marry me, Saffron?"

"You must ask my father," she whispered, her skirt high, her hands everywhere, her voice changing as they rolled on the grass and he lost himself. "Oh."

— *12* —

"Lower down," Ernst instructed the exhausted Berber prostitute as she massaged his back with a light Italian olive oil. "I said, lower down."

Fortunately, the young girl had not been squeamish about his missing foot. No doubt she had served worse. Short of bathing water, he thought he smelled even more foul than she did, but at least he'd doused her with the syrupy perfume that lay open on the windowsill. *Fiore di Venezia*. And, for his taste, she was a desert princess compared to the aging Italian tarts at the only German military brothel in Tripoli, a sexual mortuary designed to make a soldier pine for home. He wondered if the Italian mobile brothels could be any worse. "Raddled meat," one of his men had called the girls.

Major von Decken lay naked on his belly in the back room of the old *cantoniera*, an Italian roadhouse, the Albergo Benghazi on the Via Balbia. His head extended over the end of the rough wood-framed bed as he turned the pages of *Der Soldat in Libyen*. The seventy-page campaign booklet had been issued recently to every member of the *Deutsches Afrika Korps*. The large fold-out map lay open before him on the floor beside an empty bottle of schnapps. Ernst flipped through the pages on Libyan History, the Arab and Italian Populations, Climate and Topography, and the Identification of Enemy Armor. He paused to read the section on Health and Hygiene for Desert Living. Too late, he grumbled when he finished. I'm half drunk and I've already broken the first rule: no sex with the natives. He had not bothered with the shrivelled prophylactic provided as part of every DAK kit. *"Tropenfest,"* it said on the little envelope, "tropicalized," just like the

Panzers. But at least he'd had inoculations against cholera and typhus, the first health measures he'd taken in his forty-six years in Africa.

"Genug!" He groaned and rose from the bed. The girl pulled a dark striped robe over her head, then examined the mole under her eye in the dusty windowpane. Ernst plunged a dirty towel into the bucket of water at the foot of the bed and sponged himself down. He gave her a handful of lira and two cigarettes, then slapped her smartly on the rear. He pulled on his tunic, noting with pride the Afrika Korps cuff band on the right sleeve. Time for a coffee and a beer, then a little hunting.

Lieutenant Halder was waiting for him at a wooden table in a corner of the courtyard. He was a Pomeranian dragoon who had been transferred first to Rommel's 7th Panzer Division in France, then to the 15th Panzers in Libya. A large map of the coast lay flat on the table. Hard-boiled eggs held down its corners.

The other two tables were surrounded by noisy groups of Bersaglieri motorcycle reconnaissance troops, Italy's elite mountain soldiers. Their tan sun helmets hung from the handlebars of their bikes, or rested in the seat compartments of the sidecars. Each helmet had the traditional long dark green rooster feathers mounted on the right side and large sun goggles strapped onto the left. Cheese and bottles of chianti and square slabs of pizza bread littered their tables. The young soldiers laughed and smoked and slapped each other's shoulders as they joked and drank and told stories. At the far table, the men linked arms and rocked from side to side as they sang Giovinezza.

They reminded von Decken of the Italian soldiers, Alpini and Bersaglieri, who had hunted him in Ethiopia during the war in '35. What had happened, he wondered, to the man who'd saved him in that one after he'd lost his foot, his old friend Anton Rider.

Outside the gate of the courtyard, Ernst saw a mass of Italian and German thin-skinned vehicles, Kübelwagens and Fiats, Opel Blitzes and Lancias and captured British Bedfords and Humbers. Behind them an endless column of lorries and half-tracks crawled east towards Egypt along the Via Balbia.

Ernst rubbed his face as the harried waiter brought coffee.

"It's a big desert, Major," said Halder. A professional soldier with twenty years' service, Halder had long thin legs and a solid body unsuited to his narrow head with its short nose and bright bird-like eyes, reminding Ernst of a secretary bird. His occasional insolence was said to have held him back, but he was a dependable man with maps and vehicles. "These British desert commandos could be anywhere."

"No, Lieutenant. They can't. We won't find them deep in the desert." Ernst drained his coffee in one gulp. "They'll be where they have to be to do their job." He traced the road on the map with the handle of his spoon.

"The Via Balbia runs along the coast, here. The *Rommelbahn,* we're calling it now, instead of after that poor bastard Balbo. Only real flyer the Spaghettifresser ever had, and they shot him down themselves, by accident, some say." Von Decken paused and lit another Alfa, giving Halder time to appreciate this lesson in the miseries of the Regia Aeronautica, his old enemy from Ethiopia. "The job of these British spotters is to watch the road and radio in reports on our traffic. So many tanks, so many lorries of men, so much artillery moving east. To do that they must be lying up somewhere during the day to watch the road, then moving back into the desert at night to radio back their reports. How else could they do it? Where would you be if you were them?"

"South of the road, sir, so I could escape into the desert. During the day, I'd find a place with some cover, near enough to the road to watch the traffic, far enough to give some safety, say three, no, four, maybe five hundred yards. And it must be east of our main bases, or else they wouldn't know how much was really going to the front."

Von Decken nodded. "So they must be in a corridor within about half a mile of the road, a patch of high ground would be best, with a little brush or cover to lie up against." He cracked an egg on the edge of the table, rolled it forward and back once, and peeled off the shell. "Two or three men, with field glasses. Yes?"

"As you say, sir."

"Time for a drink," said Ernst impatiently. He looked around again for the waiter. For the first time he noticed the usual profile of Benito Mussolini painted on the wall behind the table. Below it was the legend, *"Credere, Obedire, Combattere."*

Ernst laughed out loud as he glanced across at the writing on the far wall. *"Il Duce ha sempre ragione."* He sputtered with laughter. "The Duce is always right!" he roared, slapping the table.

Two young Bersaglieri stared at the Germans, then whispered indignantly to their mates.

"If slogans won wars," grumbled von Decken loudly, gesturing over his shoulder with his thumb, "these greasers wouldn't need us to do their fighting."

"Sir," said Halder, turning his eyes to the other tables. He saw the two Bergsaglieri rising from their bench, dusty but elegant in khaki tunics and off-white linen trousers tucked into high black leather gaiters.

"Don't worry." Ernst shook his head, finishing his egg. "They can't understand and they can't fight. You should've seen this same bunch in Ethiopia in thirty-five. They didn't even know what to do with the girls, let alone how to fight the . . ."

"*Comandànte!*" said the shorter red-faced Italian. "*Apologizzare!*"

"Luigi!" Ernst said to the man in a loud voice, holding up two fingers, "*Due Peroni!*"

Shaking with rage, the Italian rested both hands on the table directly opposite von Decken and lowered his face close to the German's. Other Bersaglieri stood behind him muttering and jostling each other bravely.

A German half-track pulled up at the gate behind them.

"*Comandànte!*" shouted the Italian, growing bolder. "*Apologizzare!*"

"Put your green feathers back on and fly away," said von Decken, fluttering his left hand high in the air. "All of you."

Ernst placed his raised hand behind the Bersagliere's head and slammed the soldier's face down into the table. The Bersagliere screamed and jerked his head upright. Ernst cracked an egg against the man's forehead. Blood flooded from the Italian's nose. Ernst leaned back and started to pick the broken shell from its egg.

The Bersaglieri swarmed over Ernst. Halder jumped to his feet and yelled "*Kameraden!*" Fifteen thirsty Panzergrenadiers jumped down from the benches of the half-track. They strode into the courtyard of the albergo just in time to join the brawl.

Driving east, the sun behind them, six vehicles moved slowly in line, about fifty yards separating each machine. To their north ran the Via Balbia. To their south, over half a mile to their right, was Lieutenant Halder in von Decken's fastest desert machine, a four-wheeled armored scout car assigned to secure that flank from flight or attack, and to give them a better chance at catching the base vehicle of the enemy scout team. Between them was the crusty hard surface of the northern desert, relieved every few yards by scattered rocks and tumbling clumps of camel thorn.

In the center of the line, Ernst rode in the open round turret pit of his captured Crusader. Sitting in the gunner's high metal seat, feeling a bit stiff and bruised, he almost enjoyed the lively prick of the flying sand outside the protection of his goggles. With its damaged turret removed, relatively fast and well armored, the British tank made a fine command vehicle. It had plenty of storage space for extra fuel and ammunition. Riding English-style with a V-12 Rolls Royce engine under him made him feel good about this war. Ernst realized that he had missed the excitement and sense of purpose of the last great war in Africa. In addition, he was good at it.

The Vickers machine gun was still in place, and Ernst prayed he would get a chance to use it. He wet his lips and whistled *Haya Safari*, remembering marching across East Africa, every man carrying his own parasites with him. The guinea worms grew fat in the muscles of their legs until they were long enough to be wound around a wooden match and pulled out slowly, lest they break off. *Bwana Sakarini*, his askaris had called him in those days when he was young and fierce. The Wild One. At least this time, he was not on foot.

Von Decken looked left and right to make sure his men were staying alert, checking every yard of ground between the vehicles. He heard the thump-thump of a track pin starting to come loose on his Crusader. A curtain of dust rose like a desert storm behind them.

An hour later, with the sun at its height, a haze shimmered over the desert. Ernst halted his vehicles on the edge of a rocky slope. He wiped his face and waved at Halder, then clambered down with his stick and gimped along the line while his men got down to stretch and piss and share a smoke. He grunted a few words to keep each man on edge.

"Check that left track." "Top up the petrol." "Eyes open. A double schnapps to the man who spots them first." Ernst climbed up. With the dust now settled, he raised his field glasses and scanned around in every direction. Nothing but Africa.

They continued on for two more hours, stopping occasionally to keep the men fresh. Ernst kept searching for vantage points from which a man might watch the distant road. As their shadows lengthened, it became harder to see and von Decken considered where to laager for the night. He thought of last week's battle, another costly victory for Rommel, and one that had taken place on the day when every German soldier honored the two million countrymen who had fallen in the last war: *Totensonntag*, the Day of the Dead.

Von Decken glanced wearily to his left. He saw two men rise like genies from the rocky ground directly in front of the half-track next in line. Almost under the German vehicle, both men opened fire, one with some sort of automatic weapon, probably a Sten. Bullets pinged against the sloping armored plates of the half-track. Ernst saw the driver slump forward as the man beside him returned fire with a mounted 7.9mm. Afraid to shoot his own men, Ernst held fire as his driver swung left. One of the enemy collapsed, almost striking the half-track as he fell, nearly cut in two by the close fire of the machine gun. The other dropped his rifle and threw up his hands.

"Stop firing!" Ernst yelled. He saw the Englishman use one boot to push something under a bit of brush.

"Your prisoner, sir," the man called loudly as von Decken's Crusader rumbled to a halt beside him, enveloping them all in a swirl of sand.

Ernst climbed down, checked the dead driver, then looked at the prisoner. Copper-tan, a tight khaki wool cap pulled down to his ears, he wore a long olive-brown overcoat covered in sand and dust. He knelt and gently turned over his dead comrade, then closed his eyes and laid him straight on the ground with his hands crossed on his chest. The prisoner tussled the hair of the dead man and stood up, his jaw set.

Ernst walked over to a small hollowed-out depression where the two men must have lain against a patch of bush. He examined the place closely, then picked up two canteens that were under the bush.

"Take three *Panzerspähwagen* and fan out south with Lieutenant Halder to find this man's vehicle," von Decken said to a German soldier. "It can't be far, they've no food here."

He turned and spoke to the Britisher. "Who are you?" He handed the canteens to the prisoner as he addressed him in English.

"Lieutenant MacDonough," the man said, standing erect. "Scots Guards."

Von Decken grabbed the peaked lapels of the man's coat and spread them open with both hands. He noted the unmatching khaki shirt and corduroy trousers and the long brown scarf and the rubber-soled suede ankle boots. Then Ernst stirred about under the brush with his walking stick. He bent over and lifted a map and two small books. One booklet illustrated Italian and German vehicles. The notebook appeared to be a daily log of passing traffic, with a stroke beside each type of tank or other vehicle observed in each direction. Everything. Ambulances, artillery, estimates of the number of prisoners marching to the rear, details about troop formations, anything that might be useful to enemy intelligence in Cairo. On the last two pages he found a note about the large number of captured British vehicles, and a pencil sketch of the dead man at his feet.

"Scots Guards? Are you certain, Lieutenant? Not the Long Range Patrols, the Long Range Desert Group?" asked Ernst. "If you are not in uniform, and you are spying, you are a spy. If you are a soldier, you are obliged to tell me your true name, your rank and your unit. Do you wish to be treated by the rules?"

"Scots Guards."

From the south came the sound of automatic weapons. Von Decken watched the Scotsman trying not to turn his head and show concern.

Ernst saw a trail of dust dashing towards the horizon, with four German vehicles pursuing it, weapons firing. He heard the pop-pop as Halder's armored car opened up with her 20mm anti-aircraft cannon. Then there was an explosion, and another. A black plume rose in the distance.

"We'll wait," said Ernst. He offered the prisoner a smoke and thought of some of the Englishmen they had captured long ago in Tanganyika. Many, including Rider's old friend, Lord Penfold, had marched with the Schutztruppe for weeks, sharing their rations and their thirst and their surgeons. At first, some, especially the better educated ones, had seemed a bit soft and flippant, not serious about their soldiering. But after a time, exhausted by their unexpected determination, Ernst had realized this was their manner, not their character. They would be the same this time, irritating and dogged. He threw down his butt and stood up as the pursuit vehicles returned.

"Got the *Scheisskerle*, sir!" Halder grinned like a boy. "When we caught them, they were working on a radio mast the height of the Brandenburg Gate. But there's nothing left that's useful. All their petrol and some sort of explosives they were carrying, all of it went off like a bomb."

"Bring the prisoner to camp in your vehicle, Halder, with both the dead men," said Ernst. "We'll bury them tonight." He threw his cane into the back of a Volkswagen field car and climbed into the seat beside the driver with the captured papers in his hand. "Take me to Gambut, General Rommel's headquarters." If they got stuck along the way, the car was light enough to be muscled through the sand.

On the way they passed a party of German mechanics. The men were scavenging spare parts from derelict British vehicles abandoned in the desert.

Returning to the Via Balbia, they turned left. The road was choked with slow-moving vehicles, both lanes heading east. A good sign, Ernst thought. He directed his driver to make his way west in the dust beside the road. At least these Italians were good at public works, he thought, remembering their road gangs toiling in the mountains of Ethiopia.

They passed a mobile workshop. Sweating mechanics were repairing captured British vehicles while other men stenciled on the new palm tree and swastika insignia of the Afrika Korps.

They came to a junction where one road led off to a town directly on the coast. Vehicles were jammed together in all directions. In one corner of the chaotic intersection, Ernst was relieved to see the four long barrels of a *Vierling* 20mm flak gun pointed at the sky. Mounted on a 360° turntable, the guns were aiming east, waiting for the Hurricanes and Kittyhawks and Boston bombers. The gunner sat smoking in his firing seat.

In the center of the intersection, two Italian *carabinieri* paced about angrily, waving their arms and yelling and arguing with the passing drivers. Ernst stopped and saw a white-haired Italian colonel step from his Fiat. Enraged, the officer screamed abuse at the driver of a German tank transporter that blocked his way.

Not my problem, thought Ernst thankfully as he turned back to his Kübelwagen. He ignored an Arab who sidled up to him selling eggs. Two chickens, still alive, hung by their feet from a rope that belted the man's waist.

Just then an immense block-like vehicle pulled up beside the intersection. Painted in patterns of blue-grey camouflage, it had armored windowless sides and high-mounted headlights and fat heavy wheels like a Junkers 52. Four motorcycles and a cluster of other vehicles followed immediately behind it and parked to one side.

The door of the Mammoth swung open swiftly and Erwin Rommel jumped down.

Von Decken saluted. He could feel the general's furious impatience even before he spoke.

Rommel ignored von Decken and spoke to two junior staff officers from his *Begleitkommando*. The combat escort group was charged with seeing that his orders were immediately executed with the full force of the general's will.

"I want this road running like a machine gun in twenty minutes. Post a *Hauptfeldwebel* where those carabinieri are. Have *Feldgendarmerie* direct the traffic at every intersection and every five miles. Stand them on gasoline drums so these idiots can see who they're dealing with. All unnecessary traffic off the road." Muttering, he added, "If the RAF catches us like this, we'll never see Egypt."

"Herr General," said one of the officers in a low voice. "What about the Italians? They think it's their road."

"The Italians?" said Rommel with exasperation. "The Italians? If they're civilians, get them off the road. If they're in uniform tell them to obey orders. Ignore rank." He clenched his hands behind his back and turned to Ernst.

"Come with me, Major, and tell me your news. Looks like you've finally seen a little service. We'll have dinner in *Mammut* here. Another present from the British. What they call an ACV, an armored command vehicle."

Ernst noticed the metal outline of an elephant fixed to the driver's side of the truck.

Rommel entered the tall lorry and sat at the end of a folding map table. Two senior officers were already there.

"Gentlemen," said Rommel, glancing at his watch. "Major von Decken. Colonel Bayerlein. Major von Mellenthin, intelligence. First, we'll dine."

Von Decken had been told that Rommel ran three German and seven Italian divisions with a staff of twenty officers, a fraction of the standard in any army. He had never heard of von Mellenthin, a short man with a high forehead and hollow cheeks. Chief of the General Staff of the Afrika Korps, Bayerlein was said to be a soldier's soldier. The Knight's Cross hung at his throat. A powerful presence, he had straight black hair parted in the center and an open bronzed face with direct eyes and a broad nose and strong chin.

"Von Decken is an old hand in Africa," said Rommel, looking more tan and hard and tired than when Ernst last had seen him. "Marched with von Lettow in the last one."

Colonel Bayerlein acknowledged Ernst with interest. "We could use him in the *Sonderverband*, two battalions of our ethnic Germans we've collected from Africa and the Mediterranean."

"Germany can use him where he is, Colonel," said Rommel with what might have been a brief smile. "If he does his work."

Von Decken had been looking forward to headquarters rations, but he watched with dismay as General Rommel's orderly opened a can of pickles and four round tins of preserved Italian sausage meat. A tube of "cheese" waited beside the tins. So the stories were true. The general, unlike Italian officers, ate what his men ate. The general staff, Rommel had directed, should live and eat like a field division.

Normal rations for both Italian and German soldiers, each tin was stamped with the grim letters "AM," *Administrazione Militare*. But the greasy sausage meat was now known to all by the name Rommel had given it: *'Alte Mann,'* Old Man, though some still favored the earlier titles of *"Alte Maulesel,"* Old Mule, or *Asinus* Mussolini. To the Italians, of course, it was still *Arabo Morte*. Dead Arab.

With small gestures of traditional formality, the general's batman set tin plates before the officers. "Thank you, Günther," said Rommel.

Ernst thought a light sigh of relief escaped from Bayerlein when Günther produced some thick black *Dauerbrot* rather than the dreaded square Italian biscuits known to the men as "cement plates."

"Bayerlein," said Rommel after a moment, "review the logistics."

The Chief of Staff put down his knife and fork and wiped his mouth before speaking. His brown hands were blotched with desert sores.

"In the last thirty days, General, the British have sunk nearly forty percent of the troop ships and supplies sent to us from Italy. With some convoys, it's seventy percent or worse. That's why we lost the Winter Battle, Crusader, the British call it. Our tanks and fuel never got here. Sometimes we are reduced to bringing in petrol by glider and ammunition by submarine. The Afrika Korps is losing more men and weapons at sea than in the desert. Mostly to British submarines and aircraft based in Malta."

"Of course we should have taken Malta instead of Crete," said Rommel. "Then we could have controlled the Mediterranean traffic. Continue, Colonel."

"It's as if they know when every convoy is sailing," said Bayerlein.

"Some Italian traitor," snapped Rommel.

"But the worst is petrol. More than once, the battle won, our Panzers have run dry, unable to advance. So far, General, as you've ordered, we've often lived off captured British supply bases. Over half our lorries are

English. Our tank transporters move up with each attack just behind the Panzers. We recover every damaged tank we can salvage, ours and theirs. Our field workshops are repairing British Matildas. With a little paint, they're German. But the fuel . . ."

"The English fuel is in Tobruk, perhaps enough to get our Panzers to Alexandria." Rommel turned to the other officer. "Von Mellenthin. Tell us about the British. What do our signal interceptions tell you? What are their problems?"

"Soldiers from too many countries. Poles and Rhodesians, French and Indian, Czechs and Sudanese." Von Mellenthin spoke quickly in a crisp Prussian voice. "Long supply lines. Discontented Egyptians. And Winston Churchill."

"Churchill?" said Bayerlein.

"Yes," said von Mellenthin. "He's always interfering, pressing their generals to attack before they think they're ready. That's why they lost Battleaxe."

"Indeed," said Rommel quietly. They were all aware of the pressure from the Führer. "And their army?"

"They will only get stronger, sir. Their supply lines around the Cape are longer but safer. Their convoys get through. Ours do not. Now is a moment of relative balance, however. Except for Tobruk, you have thrown them back into Egypt with heavy losses. Yet without supplies it is hard to push further."

"Exactly so," nodded Rommel. "And we can't invade Egypt and leave the British and Australians behind in Tobruk to cut our supply lines. So we must seize Tobruk and its matériel before the enemy gets even stronger. And to take Tobruk, the best harbor in North Africa, we must first destroy these strongpoints the British are building. Von Mellenthin?"

" 'Boxes,' the British call them, General. Knightsbridge, Bir Hakeim, perhaps more. Each one's about two miles square."

"How strong are they?" asked Bayerlein.

"Somewhere between four and six thousand men each, but a lot of artillery and anti-aircraft. Not much armor, but mines, acres of minefields," said von Mellenthin. "Knightsbridge is defended by the Brigade of Guards, Scots and Coldstream, we believe. That tells you how important the British think this is. And our informants in Cairo report that Bir Hakeim, an old dried-out oasis, is defended by the French Foreign Legion, plus their usual colonial rubbish and one or two small British units, reconnaissance, anti-aircraft. And something unusual, a company of Jews from Palestine."

"So now you understand, Major." The General fixed his cold blue eyes on von Decken. "And you know why we cannot have these British patrols spying on our transport and destroying our aircraft and our fuel supplies. It is your job to stop them. What have you achieved?"

"Our enemy is the Long Range Desert Group, sir. Seem to be picked men from different regiments. Today we found and eliminated the first team of their road watchers. They were covering the Via Balbia with field glasses and counting each type of vehicle that passed. We also destroyed their communications lorry." Ernst paused and withdrew the map and two small books from his tunic pocket and handed them to General Rommel. "Now we know how they work and what they do."

There was silence at the table as Rommel examined the notebook, squinting at it closely with near-sighted eyes. "Look at this, Major," he said to von Mellenthin, tapping the notebook with his short thick fingers. "Here is a note that one group of Italians was in new uniforms and not sunburned. Concluding that they must be fresh troops. And that they had their own field cookers, so they are entire new units, not reliefs or replacements." He passed the book to the intelligence major. "The British are learning, gentlemen. Soon they will be dangerous." He nodded at von Decken to finish his report.

"Tomorrow, General, we start to hunt their fighting patrols, the ones who've been attacking our desert Luftwaffe bases."

"Tomorrow, Major von Decken? Start tonight. Now."

Still hungry, Ernst saluted and left the Mammoth. He looked around for the egg vendor, but the Arab was gone.

An *Oberleutnant* of the German field police stood on a gasoline barrel at the intersection. The shiny gorget plate of the Feldgendarmerie hung from his neck by a heavy chain, like the *tâte-vin* of a sommelier. His eyes hidden under a pale peaked field cap, the officer directed the moving traffic with sharp gestures of a long baton carrying a metal circular stop sign at its end. Man must've been in Libya since the beginning, Ernst thought, judging by the faded color of his cap, a mark of pride among early members of the Afrika Korps. Or had he bleached it with anti-gas capsules, as some of von Decken's new men were doing?

"Back to camp for some rest, sir?" asked Halder, peeling an orange by the side of the road.

"No, Lieutenant," said von Decken. "Going hunting."

— 13 —

"I'll meet you after the Culture Circle lecture," Harriet von Decken had said. "Unless you'd like to join me?" she'd added doubtfully.

"Bit of a stretch for me, Harry, I'm afraid," Rider had replied, certain he needed a drink more than insight. He'd never had formal schooling, and a lecture on Sigmund Freud sounded a bit too grave. But these American girls were always at it, sharpening themselves all the time. Of course most of them knew everything already. They also had the best legs.

After a couple of gins at the hotel bar, Anton paced up and down outside the Metropolitan while he waited for the lecture to end. No matter what Harriet had in mind, he was determined to behave himself tonight.

Catching the smell of roasted nuts, he bought a paper cone of almonds from a passing hawker and ate them on the street. A lottery vendor dozed against the wall beside him, resting back against the A-frame poster board that hung from his shoulders. 'DO YOU WANT JOY, AMUSEMENT AND A BETTER SOCIAL STANDING? THEN BUY A TICKET FOR THE ORWA EL WOSKA LOTTERY,' proclaimed the advertisement. 'FOR TWENTY PIASTRES, A FIRST PRIZE WORTH SIX THOUSAND ENGLISH POUNDS! WHY SHOULD IT NOT BE YOURS?'

A barefoot man paused beside Anton and thrust out a filthy tray that hung by strings from his neck. "Effendi?" Blackened bits of stringy meat, probably camel, were stuck to greasy scraps of old newspaper on the tray. Anton smiled and shook his head.

With the government cracking down on aggressive begging, the cries of "*baksheesh*" had grown less frequent. Many beggars had reappeared as a new lower class of itinerant food vendor. They were not the traditional aging street cooks with painted carts and charcoal braziers, providing the aroma of grilling onions and small meat puddings and fresh round flat-bread. Cairo's foreign language papers, French and English and Italian and Greek, were in full cry for the suppression of the poisonous new mendicants. Watching the man walk on, Anton wondered what the poor devils would take up next.

Even more noticeable was the growing display of the empire in uniform, as if Cairo were preparing for a coronation or a durbar. Now it seemed to be the turn of the Indian regiments. The streets were crowded with bearded turbanned Sikhs and short wiry Gurkhas and others he could not identify.

Anton leaned back from the curb as a gharry rattled past. An Australian soldier drove with the whip as the displaced owner cowered beside him on the small bench. Three other Aussies were crammed into the passenger seat. Their laps overflowed with tarbushes and turbans and veils snatched off the heads of Egyptians as they passed, a new sport at which the Australian and New Zealand troops were proud to excel. As the lathered horse approached, the Australian driving leaned out to grab the tarbush of an elderly man walking near Anton. The soldier's hand struck Anton in the head. His arm up to defend himself, Anton seized the tall slouch hat off the nearest Australian in the back seat. The leather chin strap stretched and snapped, pulling the man's head. The soldier, already leaning out, fell into the street, knocking over an old man collecting cigarette ends in a pouch hanging from his waist. The driver jerked on the reins. The three Australians leaped down and pressed back through the crowd to find their mate.

"Damn your bloody eyes!" yelled the hatless soldier. "Blinkin' Pommie poofta!" Not recognizing Anton's informal Desert Group uniform, the Australian tried to snatch back his hat.

"Steady," Anton said, holding it behind his back, knowing the Diggers were as serious about these hats as the Scots were about their kilts. "That friend of yours hit me in the head. When he's apologized and you've returned the hats and veils you stole, you'll get yours back."

Coming up behind him, not noticing Rider's captain's bars, one Australian grabbed Anton's arm behind his back. Pulling free, Rider spun to face the man. He felt himself grow hot. He cautioned himself that it was even worse for a British officer to strike a soldier than the other way around. And you never knew what these fellows had been facing in the desert. "One at a time, please, lads," Anton said as the men hesitated. "Don't you think your mate can look after himself?"

"Having fun?" Harriet drawled from the steps of the hotel.

Anton sailed the slouch hat into the crowded street, where it landed in a passing vegetable cart. The soldiers cursed and hurried after it.

"How was the lecture?" he asked, red-faced as he sought to collect himself. Thank heavens it wasn't Gwenn. Harriet seemed to enjoy this sort of thing.

"It was all about you," Harriet said brightly. She reached up and pinched his cheek with sharp red fingernails. "Suppressed emotions, excessive sexual drive, the burdens of childhood, and one or two things I shouldn't mention. No wonder men are all such babies. Hopeless, really."

"How useful. So, would you like to find a drink?"

"I've already booked. Roof garden of the Continental-Savoy. They've some sort of jazz cabaret and floor show." She took his arm as the door porter hailed a taxi and accepted a tip from Anton. "My treat. Perhaps I'll teach you how to dance."

Anton tried to ignore her when Harriet placed one hand on his leg in the taxi during the brief ride.

Arriving late at the restaurant, they bribed their way to the last table.

"If it weren't for all these lovely uniforms, and all these extra men," Harriet said, "you'd never know there was a war on. The duck and the service are better than ever."

"Wait till you see dessert," said Anton.

They were seated beneath a canopy on the wrong side of the restaurant, looking out over the rooftops towards the Muqattam Hills, rather than the Nile or the minarets in other directions. Forested with ramshackle wooden radio masts, the roofs below them were draped with laundry. Many roofs carried the makeshift shelters of the house servants of the families who lived below. The smoky glow of their fires and the thick odors of cooking gave the sense of an armed camp below the walls of a great city.

"There's a war on, all right." Anton watched a French soldier swinging along on his crutches as he made his way between the tables and the potted trees. The pinned-up cuff of one trouser leg flapped loosely.

"Are you going home?" he asked Harriet. "I see there's an Egyptian steamer leaving Port Saïd for the States, via Cape Town and Rio."

"Not yet," she said, drawing her nails across the top of Anton's hand.

He pretended not to notice. "It's still more fun here." She turned her head, apparently aware of some admirers, and called to a waiter serving another table. "Champagne! *Minfadlak*. Champagne!"

"Have you heard from Ernst?" he asked casually.

"No. It's impossible," she said, removing her hand quickly. "I think we both know we'll just have to wait and see what happens. It's as if nothing really counts right now, as if our marriage is suspended for the war. Thank God America's not in it." She paused and lowered her eyes. "You know what I mean, Anton." She lifted her pack of Craven A's and looked him in the eye as he lighted her cigarette. "And what about you? Have you seen Gwenn?"

"Yes. She was off for Alexandria to operate at the Anglo-Swiss," he said tersely, hoping that would do it.

"Won't you be going up to see her?"

"I don't think that's what she has in mind," he said. "Good Lord! Look at that, will you!"

Lord Penfold stood unsteadily at the entrance to the restaurant, like a magnificent aged eagle rocking on its perch. His craggy face was raised high-chinned above his wing collar. His grey eyebrows hung out sharply like bushes clinging to a cliffside. His watch chain swung from the vest of the new dinner jacket Olivio had given him for his birthday. He set a monocle in his right eye and stared about the crowded terrace. A shapely dowager was on his arm, not young, but still erect and womanly and presenting her attractions. Her black hair was puffed up in a crown and set with a jewelled tortoise-shell pin.

"Ah!" exclaimed Harriet. "That old dragon is Madame Pantelides, the doyenne of the Greek community," she whispered fiercely. "Look at those pearls! Just the place for them. She's got a chest like Dover." Harriet stubbed out her cigarette with quick determined movements. "And she has more money than the pharaoh. They say she consumes men like Rice Krispies."

"Hope she looks after Adam," he said doubtfully. Why was it, Anton wondered, that women, once they had the advantage, tended to overdo it? He had done the same, of course, but rarely with those he cared about.

"King Faruq complained her parties in Alexandria were upstaging the palace," continued Harriet in an intense whisper. "But Madame Pantelides told someone her people had been there since Alexander laid out the city, whereas Faruq's Albanians had swum ashore yesterday."

The headwaiter hurried to the couple and bowed, shaking his head and wringing his hands. He shrugged his shoulders hopelessly and raised both palms as he looked over the busy tables.

Hearing the lady raise her voice with some indignant protest, Anton rose and hurried to the entrance. "Won't you dine with us?" he asked.

"We wouldn't want to spoil your . . ." began Penfold.

"How lovely," said Madame Pantelides, gripping her escort's arm and firmly guiding him toward the table.

"I've been looking forward so to meeting you," said Harriet to the Greek lady when the two joined them.

"You must all be my guests next weekend," said Madame Pantelides after a time. "I've taken a coach on the Antiquities Train." Anton caught Penfold watching the lady's chest arch up and down like a bellows as she spoke. Perhaps the old boy still knew what was good for him.

"We'll sleep on the train," Madame Pantelides continued, "and have a masked dance at Luxor, ancient Thebes, you know. I'm bringing my favorite archeologist to teach us something. Even his lordship's peculiar little friend is coming, that Monsieur Alavedo, though he's insisted on taking his own cabins in the next coach."

" 'Fraid I may be out in the blue again," said Anton, turning to Harriet, but I'm sure Mrs. von Decken would love it. These American girls are great students, I mean scholars." The trip sounded too academic, or too dangerous with Harriet, or both.

Harriet kicked him under the table.

Suddenly the long shrill wails of air raid sirens tore the night.

"Black-out!" hollered a British officer.

The roof lights of the restaurant were instantly extinguished. Below them, lights dimmed and darkened as if Cairo were disappearing. The street lights and car headlamps were already dimmed with blue paint. The long wails of the black-out signals were interspersed with the short sharp signals to take cover. More sirens joined in until the sound rose around them like the screams from a vast nursery of desperate children.

Harriet slipped her stocking foot between his legs. "I used to play marbles with my toes," she once had told him. Not tonight, he thought, a little sadly, liking her too much, but surprised and rather pleased with his own resolution. It just wasn't what he wanted to do.

The all-clear sounded.

"How tedious," declared Madame Pantelides. "Just another scare."

Would she prefer a real bombing? Anton wondered.

The waiters resumed the service. Tuning up, the supper band began with *I Don't Want to Set the World on Fire*.

"Shall we dance?" said Harriet.

Covered in dust, the black Panhard drove up the packed dirt road that wound between the paddies and the young fields of green cane. Two large barrels blocked the road. Low mud walls extended to either side. The car slowed and two barefoot fellahin squatting nearby rose and rolled the barrels to the side. Behind them, a black-headed grey crane, stalking frogs and insects in a rice paddy, looked up from its hunt and bent one long knob-kneed leg. Driving on, they passed an orchard of young lemon trees. De Neuville wondered if his mistress had ever been to Al Lahun to visit her revolting friend, the midget. He thought of all he had done to introduce her to society. Now the complications of this war were entangling him and drawing them apart. Perhaps he should make the time to go to Alexandria and bring the thankless woman back.

The vehicle approached a striped tent set amidst a stand of palms. To one side stood a cluster of more modest shelters grouped around a well and an open fire. The car stopped beside the tent. Ramzi stepped down from the driver's seat and opened the door for Giscard de Neuville. Ramzi's brother, Munir, a heavy white bandage across his nose, got out and began to clean the car.

The Frenchman walked towards the tent, squinting in the bright light. A tall figure and a servant with a tray awaited him under the front canopy that was stretched between two poles.

"Water?" said Tariq, indicating the tray. His master always required him to extend this courtesy of the desert.

De Neuville shook his head and looked about him at the orderly camp, noting the stack of sieves and the stand of picks and shovels. Beside Tariq in the shade of the canopy was a table on which rested a balance scale with a set of brass weights in a wooden rack beside it. Behind the tent he saw a line of black men at work in a new orchard of young apricot trees. These must be the Nubian laborers of whom he'd heard. Some were shaping the small dirt canals that separated the rows of trees. Others scattered animal fertilizer beneath the plantings. They were not working at the slack time-devouring pace of most fellahin. This midget did not believe in idleness.

"My master will receive you in the tomb," said Tariq, his expression flat as a brick. "Come with me now. This man of yours will wait outside."

The Nubian led the way down the sloping entrance to a steep trench. At the end of the trench, a short wooden passage had been constructed outside the mastaba to provide a framework for two doors and to keep sand from blowing inside the entrance. A heavy canvas hung across the opening. Tariq held back the canvas and handed a small flashlight to the archeologist. While his eyes adjusted after the bright sunlight, de Neuville switched on the torch and followed its weak beam along the passageway.

He hesitated when he came to the stone wall, pausing to examine the dimensions of the blocks and the sophistication of the masonry. The passage descended at a modest angle as he advanced. The air grew cool and musty. He saw a dim glow of light at the end of the entrance passage. He stopped at the end and tried to examine the first chamber before entering it. Perhaps this little creature, this Alavedo, was waiting for him in the next room.

On a low platform against the wall that faced him, de Neuville saw a model of a ship of the dead. Its bow and prow were tall and narrow. Two long falcon-headed steering oars rose from the stern. The steersman knelt between them. Under an arch supported by four reed-like columns, a miniature mummy with a blue head rested on a bier in the center of the boat. Two white-robed ladies of the household stood to either side, each with her right breast exposed.

De Neuville advanced several steps to examine the painted wall behind the boat. He shivered as the air chilled him.

A flight of geese, vivid with russet heads and wing-tips, rose from tall green papyrus reeds. An ochre-skinned nobleman stood gracefully among the reeds, hurling curved throwing sticks at the fleeing birds. His wife clung to his waist; his daughter, kneeling, to his calf. A civet cat ran amidst the reeds with its head down, flushing the birds for the hunter.

Glancing to one side of the wall painting, de Neuville was astonished to see a copy of the *Egyptian Gazette* secured to the wall beside the fowling scene. Today's copy, if he was not mistaken, with a large map of the desert campaign on the front page.

"Welcome to you," said a muffled voice behind him. The words echoed off the limestone walls.

Startled, de Neuville spun around and faced the dwarf. He recoiled slightly when he saw him.

Olivio Alavedo stood on a stool. His head and torso were entirely shrouded inside the black cape of the camera that rested on a tripod before him. His right hand grasped the bulb of the camera.

A row of bulbs flashed.

"Perfect!" exclaimed the dwarf.

The Frenchman blinked repeatedly, dazzled by the flash.

"One more," said Olivio. "Just to be certain."

The bulbs flashed again before de Neuville could react. Furious, he advanced toward the dwarf. "Give me those plates!" Now he understood the purpose of the newspaper.

"Tariq will take them in his care," said the dwarf as the Nubian appeared in the chamber and stepped to the camera. "Then you and I will do our business."

The massive black man took the two film plates and looked at his master for instructions.

"Wait in the passage in case I need you, and take that newspaper with you."

"I am here to arrange the division of your plunder," said de Neuville firmly. "One third, at least." Intoxicated by what he saw, he gestured about the room with both hands at the treasures assembled around them, flagons and images, weapons and furnishings. He wondered how they were to divide the wall paintings, unusual even in the dry air of Egypt for the brilliant retention of their color. Behind the dwarf he observed a depiction of the ceremony of the Weighing of the Heart. A diaphonous-robed woman, perhaps a priestess, stood beside the left balance of the scale as her heart was weighed upon it. On the round tray of the other balance stood two figures representing truth. The baboon-god Thoth sat atop the scale table, recording the result.

"With you, Monsieur, I will share not one grain of sand." Olivio shook his head slowly. "Nothing."

"Then I will see you jailed and impoverished."

"Long before then Giscard de Neuville will be convicted for the illegal export of the national treasure of Egypt, and perhaps for other crimes." Alavedo thought of what he was learning of de Neuville's treachery with the Vichy French.

The dwarf stepped from the stool. The black photographer's cape hung from his shoulders like a monk's cowl. "My solicitor has the record of your most recent smugglings. And if you speak of me, the prosecutor will see these photographs of you here, on this date, participating in this unlicensed dig of ours, just to compound your crimes as an enemy of Egypt. I might survive such awkward disclosures. You, in your profession, will not." Olivio clasped his hands over his hard belly and stared up at the Frenchman, his eye bright as a miner's lamp. "Reveal me, reveal yourself."

"You have not seen the end of this, Alavedo." De Neuville tried to control the furious trembling of his hands as he stalked towards the passage. A voice called after him.

"One thing more, Monsieur."

De Neuville paused in the doorway. He stared down at the dwarf with contempt.

"You are not to see any more of Mrs. Anton Rider. You will leave her entirely alone."

— *14* —

"I've only a few minutes, darling, then I have to do one more operation and take the night train back to Alex." Gwenn rested a hand on Wellington's, trying to forget that she and her son were sitting at the hospital commissary and she was still in her soiled white robe. At the small tables all around them, the nurses and doctors were too exhausted to notice anyone as they hurried through their tea and coffee and sandwiches. "I just came down for two days to see Denby, and they called me in here." As Dr. Hänger had warned her, the cases were now lined up along the halls of the King Fuad.

"But there's something I have to tell you first, Mum, before I tell everyone else this afternoon."

Gwenn looked at her boy. Under the dark desert tan, he was already older and harder, confident he could take care of himself, his demeanor more like Anton's. In a way she admired him for it, for doing what he thought he had to do, as she always had, going to war twice herself, but to help people, not to kill them. Or was it somehow all the same? Was she confusing her dislike for soldiering with her fear of loss? Though she was resigned to the war, and almost to his part in it, each time she saw Wellie she felt it was a borrowed miracle.

"Saffron . . ." He stopped awkwardly.

"She's such a lovely girl."

"We're getting married, probably on my next leave, if it's all right with her family." He spoke quickly, grinning when he'd finished.

A tear came to his mother's eye.

"Oh, Mum." Wellington leaned across the narrow tea-stained table and put both arms around her shoulders.

Gwenn gathered herself and pulled back and looked at Wellington. "I'm so happy. You've known her all your life. I always thought she was in love with you when you were little."

"I hope Mr. Alavedo will be happy, too."

"Why would he not be?" she said, knowing well the answer.

"Well, I think he likes me all right, but he's so practical, and just now I've really no education or job or prospects, except for the regiment, of course."

Gwenn did not say I told you so.

"I think he'll understand," she said. "Things are always a bit different in wartime, and he adores your father, and he'll know Adam will be thrilled."

For a moment neither of them spoke.

"In a few days we're headed off to help out on the Gazala Line." Wellington hesitated. "Nothing too hot, just a bit of scouting about in the desert to the south." He saw a shadow cross his mother's eyes. "We'll be all right."

"I'm sure you will, darling. Of course you will." Gwenn squeezed his hand and stood, then hugged her son and stepped back, looking at him carefully, taking a picture with her eyes. "She's such a lucky girl."

After a couple of stiffeners with Johnny Bingham on the terrace at Shepheards, keeping a sharp eye meantime that the old bootblack wasn't leaving any polish on his spurs, Wellington Rider set off for the interview he was dreading with Mr. Alavedo. Some way to spend your leave, he thought.

"Best of luck, old boy," said Bingham as he left the hotel. "Rather face a Panzer with a bayonet, myself. I'll be here waiting."

Wellington was aware that in the mess it wasn't quite the thing to marry the Egyptian daughter of a Goan dwarf. Better some illiterate red-nosed old squire for a father-in-law, with a good shoot in Gloucestershire, a flat in Eaton Square, and, if you're lucky, a bit of fishing or stagging somewhere in the wastes up north. On the other hand, all the chaps were green about the girl, and certain allowances were always made for wartime marriages. And Saffron spoke French better than most of his chums spoke

English. Plus, Alavedo was said to have properties in Portugal and Brazil and farms all over Egypt. He probably grew enough rice and cotton to feed and clothe the army.

"Here comes the poor chap now," said Adam Penfold, spilling his tea as he folded the *Egyptian Gazette*. "Awful job. Hope you'll be nice to 'im, old boy."

"Nice?" exclaimed the dwarf. "Nice? Of course, my lord, but I must perform my duty."

Olivio sat up as erect as he could against the brocade cushion and pretended not to watch as Wellington walked across the deck, the very picture of a dashing English soldier in gleaming boots and scarlet trousers, his cap under his left arm, his fiery hair slicked down flat and parted in the middle.

"None but the brave deserve the fair," said Penfold to himself.

"What?" The dwarf put one hand to his ear.

"Dryden," Penfold said as the young man approached.

Alavedo looked at his friend and shook his head, distressed that the old gentleman seemed to be losing all understanding.

"Good morning, Mr. Alavedo, Lord Penfold." Wellington looked each man in the eye.

"And to you, dear Wellie." Penfold's craggy face crinkled with a smile as he regarded his godson with watery blue eyes. "Would you both care to excuse me?"

"Not at all, my lord," said Olivio. "What secrets could we have from you?"

"I've come to speak to you, sir," said Wellington to the dwarf with formality. His face reddened above the high tight collar of his jacket. "About your eldest daughter, sir, Saffron."

His fists full of coins, Tiago looked up from his play mat nearby. "Five," the fat child said in a clear voice before returning to his work. Sorted and stacked into high round columns stood neat pillars of piastres and shillings, francs and florins, riyals and barizas.

"Be damned," said Penfold, relieved, as always, by any distraction. "Little chap's running a counting house."

"Hopefully, my lord," said the dwarf, somewhat testily. He still had not asked Wellington to sit down. "Hopefully. A lesson from which some of us might profit, if you'll forgive my saying so. Now, my boy, do sit down and tell me what is it?"

"I've come, sir, to ask for Saffron's hand in marriage."

"Have you? I see. Well, well. I will have to think of this carefully and speak to the girl," said the dwarf, who had already done so several times. "And tell me, please, of your plans, your thoughts for the future."

"Well, we thought, in view of the war, we'd sort of tighten things up a bit, rather a short engagement, if you see what I mean, sir. Perhaps, with your permission, of course, get married on my next leave or two, something like that. Rather a small wedding, should've thought. Few chaps from the regiment, bridesmaids, that sort of thing."

"I see," said the dwarf, who had already drawn up rather different plans if such an event should come to pass. What could this boy be thinking? *Le tout Caire* must attend the marriage of any daughter of his. "But my question, Wellington, was about your future, not about a wedding."

"Oh. Well, ah, tied up with the regiment, just now, of course. Then, after this show's over, perhaps university, or some sort of job, I suppose . . ."

"Rather hard for a chap to sort all this out just now . . ." hazarded Penfold, coming to Wellington's rescue. His voice trailed off as the dwarf's hot eye glared at him balefully. Penfold blinked. "Must get some of these new smoked spectacles," he said, squinting into the sunlight.

"Would you mind if I asked another question of you?" said the dwarf, trying not to speak too harshly.

"Of course, sir," said Wellington. "Anything at all, of course."

Olivio spoke with deliberation, as if not wishing to, concerned lest there be bad luck in the words he chose. "Have you considered what would happen if you and my daughter were to marry and have a child, and then something were to happen to you?"

"Actually not, sir. No, we haven't, not at all." He was thinking only of the best to come, and this man was thinking of the worst. "Why, we . . ."

"Perhaps," said the dwarf slowly, "perhaps we could both consider all this thoughtfully, and then we could speak of it again."

"Very well, sir," said Wellington, his young voice crisp with disappointment. "Just as you say." It seemed to Penfold that the boy's face had gone pale, his cheeks hollow.

"Will you have a drink, or a cup of tea with us?" asked the dwarf. He extended one hand graciously. He knew that the interview was concluded, but he worried lest he lose the affection of both his daughter and his friends.

"Ah, no thank you, sir. I'd best be off." Gently he took the small hand of Olivio Alavedo in his own and shook it. "I quite understand. I hope we can talk again." He nodded at both men and waved a hand at Tiago. "Good-bye."

The little boy looked up at them and spoke. "Ten."

"Wellington!" hollered Bingham from the shore.

Lying on his back, Wellie's eyes were barely open. He was thinking of how it might be if Saffron were with him in the water now, slippery and excited and cool-bodied. Her chilled nipples would harden when he touched them and she reached for him under the water. For a few moments it had seemed to Wellington Rider that there was no war.

"Wellie! Come on back, you silly sod!" Reluctantly, Wellington turned his head in the clear blue water and looked ashore. Half a mile behind Bingham, at their laager on the hillside above the Mediterranean, someone ran up a blue flag on one of the new armored cars. Time to go.

Wellington flipped onto his stomach and swam for the beach. Standing naked on the shore, he shook himself like a dog, then swept water from his body with both hands and climbed wet into his khaki shorts and shirt, careful not to scrape the new tattoo of a jerboa on his upper arm. Above him, he heard the roar of engines as his troop prepared to mount up and join the squadron.

"Orders," said Bingham with excitement, hurrying up the hill with Wellington. "Seems Rommel's getting ready to start his push against the Gazala line, and before we get our leave we're meant to nip south, then do a recce west and see what he's up to. They say next he'll be going after the boxes, then Tobruk."

"You dawdlers are holding up the war," complained Gates. He was busy lashing a sack of limes to a ring at the rear of the long box-like vehicle. Made in South Africa, with Canadian chassis, British guns and American transmissions and V-8 engines, the Marmon-Harringtons were fast but lightly armored. Wellington and the other three men of his crew preferred them to the Morrises and Dingos because they were more dependable and roomier inside. Often they drove with the double rear doors open for better ventilation. Soon they should be getting their new Humbers.

The Hussars drove south from the Med across the cultivated coastal strip of Cyrenaica. They rode through grain fields and passed a crumbling Roman fort. They drove by orchards of flowering almond trees near the white plaster walls that surrounded the homesteads of the Italian settlers along the coast. Some were shell-pocked and daubed with slogans and jokes in

Italian or English or German. Powerful heads of Mussolini had been corrupted into rude caricatures by passing Aussies or South Africans.

Standing in the open turret of the Marmon-Harrington, Wellington looked left and right with astonishment as they came to the Via Balbia.

As far as he could see through the corridor of dust, the old Italian road was a solid double line of military vehicles, not driving nose to tailgate as they would be at night, but spread out a bit in deference to the Luftwaffe. Driving west to the front were troop lorries and tank transporters, water wagons and staff cars, communications trucks and mobile kitchens, armored cars and flatbeds converted into gun platforms for four-pounders and ack-ack. Passing them, heading east, were empty petrol trucks and recovery vehicles and ambulances and lorries holding the lightly wounded.

Both sides of the road were graveyards of destroyed and damaged vehicles of three armies. Burned-out trucks and armor and splintered cannons were littered for miles in both directions like charred and broken roadside fences. Across the road was a crude graveyard: rows of rough crosses and low mounds where the ground was too hard to dig. Italians, Wellie guessed. Near the cemetery, a lone message carrier was struggling to repair his Norton motorcycle.

Wellington's unit mustered near the side of the road next to the Italian marker for Mile 19. Briefly they joined a second reconnaissance squadron of the Desert Rats. A flight of Hawker Hurricanes roared overhead. A few yards down the road, a crew from the Royal Tank Regiment was track bashing, adjusting the tension of the tracks on their Matilda. Too tight, and they would snap. Too loose, and they would fall off when the tank climbed or turned. Several other tankers were examining the special fittings of a wrecked Panzer III: smokescreen dischargers set above the exhaust system, protective canvas coverings to keep sand out of the recoil mechanism of the 50mm gun, and the large metal *Rommelkiste*, or Rommel Box, mounted on the rear of the turret to hold extra equipment.

"Brew-up!" called Mosby-Brown. More efficient now, Bingham filled a cut-off petrol tin halfway with sand, then poured in a few inches of fuel and tossed on a match. He set the big kettle on top of the Benghazi burner. One man passed around a bottle of Italian cherries. Early that morning the troop had liberated a villa crammed with quartermaster supplies for the Italian officer corps: tinned tongue and beef and stews and anchovies, dried vegetables waiting to be expanded with water, and cases of wine and mineral water.

Mugs in hand, the troop car commanders gathered around the lieutenant while he spread a large map across the sloping rear plate of his armored car. "We'll be crossing the road here and following that *trigh* south along the Gazala line to Bir Hakeim," said Mosby-Brown. He pointed to one of the old tracks that wandered across the Western Desert. "And mind you keep to it. The Wops and Jerries've been planting mines all over, and our boys are putting in half a million more to strengthen the line and force their armor to go where we want it."

Soon they were following the barrel track, the line of numbered rusting petrol drums that marked the route south of the Knightsbridge box. Thousands of tires and treads had turned the thin desert crust to powder. Dust devils rose in spirals before them. The pink and yellow and grey dancers pirouetted as the sun brought each flying particle to life.

The Hussars passed two mobile workshops. The mechanics and fitters and metalworkers of the Royal Army Service Corps were laboring to repair columns of broken-down and damaged vehicles. No one spoke as they motored on past a burned-out four-engined de Havilland biplane, once fitted out for casualty evacuation. A large red cross was barely discernible on the blackened fuselage. Occasionally they passed rough wooden signs jammed into large cairns, indicating the distances to Piccadilly Circus and Berlin, Rome and Sydney.

To their right, for more than ten miles, teams of engineers and sappers, hundreds of them, were laying out minefields and planting flat round anti-tank charges in patterns in the desert. Between them were smaller anti-personnel mines, to catch the infantry that would be advancing with the tanks. The German S mines were said to be even worse. The size of a can of peas, triggered by a trip wire or a footstep, they would leap into the air and spray steel fragments in all directions.

Behind the minefield, in the box, he saw tanks already dug in, hull down. Only their turrets showed above the line of the rocky desert. Some were heavily armored 'infantry tanks,' Valentines and Matildas. Others were the new Crusaders, intended more for the old cavalry roles of speed and reconnaissance. Many Crusaders had spare tracks slung across their front plates for extra protection. The soft-skinned vehicles were inside the ring of armor, with an array of tents and fires where the Guards and the Sherwood Foresters were preparing to make their stand. Everywhere deep slits had been dug into the hard ground, some for one soldier, some for two. "Each box," Mosby-Brown had said, "is meant to be a hedgehog, able to survive isolated on its own."

Before passing Knightsbridge, the Hussars drove their armored cars inside the box to refuel at a petrol dump. Wellington strolled about while the driver filled his car.

"I'm going to slide over there and see if I can scrounge up a little tea and some grub," said Bingham as he hurried off towards a field kitchen, knowing he could depend on the usual desert hospitality.

Wellington came to two neat lines of Guards tents. Each was worn and ragged but perfectly spaced and pegged out, taut as a jib in a storm. On the last one, the words *"Nulli Secundus"* were painted in faded maroon. Even Wellie's Latin could manage that one. "Second to None."

He saw a hard-faced Coldstream sergeant, an oily rag in one hand, inspecting a collection of captured automatic weapons laid out on a canvas, Italian and German, Bredas and Mausers. "A Spandau. Best there is, MG 34, nine hundred rounds a minute, but too bloody many moving parts," growled the soldier, glancing up at Wellington. The sergeant removed the breach parts of the long-barrelled German machine gun with deft fingers and wiped each one with his cloth. Walking on, Wellie passed an officer inspecting a company of Guardsmen.

Barefoot, the big dark-faced men stood with their feet apart, boots and socks in their hands. Joking quietly, each soldier grew silent as the lieutenant came along the line, checking their pale feet one by one. Desert rot and "Gyppie foot" disabled more infantry than anything save wounds. "Remember, lads," he heard the young officer say, "every day use your last ration pint to shave in, then wash your feet with it and rub 'em down with sand. Turn your socks inside out."

"Mount up!" yelled Mosby-Brown. Bingham ran past and tossed Wellie a handful of dates.

Chewing the sugary brown fruit as they rode on, Wellington stared out from the turret and thought of Cairo and his parents. His father, he knew, would be on some sort of special operation, doing the kind of thing he was good at, managing men and guns and scouting new country. His mother would be doing what she had always wanted to do, practising surgery under crisis conditions, making a difference to many people every day. But they still wouldn't be together, as he and Denby always hoped. He wondered if somehow this war might give his parents a better chance to sort things out, to help them give each other enough of what each needed without forcing them together more than either one could bear.

Now that the war had grown so that he would have been called up anyway, at least his mother was no longer cross at him, and he prayed she no longer blamed his father. After all, she still had Denby at home to fuss over, and the war would be over before his little brother was old enough to sign up. Another year should do it.

Forty miles from the coast, riding in the third car, Wellington saw the *tricolore* flag of France rising before him in the desert. The next minute a Free French Bren carrier, mounting a .5-inch Boys anti-tank rifle instead of a machine gun, met the squadron to lead them in. Captain Blake stopped his car and exchanged a few words in French with the two black men in their *képis blancs.* The British cars left the trigh and followed the open four-ton tracked vehicle in a zigzag pattern through the minefield.

Planted atop one of two caved-in cisterns at one corner of the box, the gold-tasselled battle flag of *Le Deuxième Bataillon, La Légion Etrangère* welcomed them to Bir Hakeim with its seven-flamed grenade insignia.

The Bren led them to a patch of desert just inside the perimeter wire near two pairs of Bofors dug into shallow circular pits. Ammunition boxes were positioned like sandbags around the edges of the pits. The black gun crews, stripped to the waist and glistening with sweat, had jaunty pom-poms set in the center of their berets. The cone-shaped muzzles of the 40mm Bofors were already aimed at the western sky. Wellington thought the men seemed confident and relaxed.

Blake jumped down. His officers gathered around him.

"Right. I want a tight camp. No mess, Royal Navy style. This could be our base while we run the recces, and I want these Frogs and what not to understand who's fighting this war and how we do things."

Another Bren pulled up and a short tanned officer stepped down. He wore tall socks and khaki shorts and, at a sharp angle, an officer's blue képi with the white cloth covering removed.

"Captain Nordhouse," said the powerfully built man, saluting and introducing himself to Blake and Mosby-Brown. "*Soyez les bienvenus à Bir Hakeim!* Our old oasis that has no water. General Koenig invites you to dinner tonight at the fort. Over there, at the other end of the box from the Mamelles, as my lonely men call these round wells." Nordhouse pointed to a white rectangular structure nearly two miles away along a low ridge that ran south from the cisterns. A large French flag topped one corner of the crumbling fortress.

The fifteen cars of A Squadron laagered in a long V with a big cookfire and a latrine at the open end and patches of canvas suspended inwards from the Marmon Harringtons all along the line. When the camp was set, the cars were refuelled and the engines and weapons checked. Wellington and Bingham and Gates set off for a tour of the box. Tomorrow Blake and Mosby-Brown would be leading the rest of the squadron on patrol, leaving Wellington's troop posted at Bir Hakeim. He himself would be in charge, with the field commission of lieutenant.

"Just look at this lot, will you," said Bingham. "It's like the bloody World's Fair."

Camped between the two cisterns, groups of French soldiers were clustered by color and language. Slit trenches surrounded them like a maze. Each was four feet deep and narrow as a grave. Here and there, scattered between the two-man rifle pits, were L-shaped trenches for the machine gun teams. One of the Senegalese from the first Bren carrier waved at the three Englishmen as they passed. Two others knelt beside him skinning a goat. One man pulled back the skin while the other cut under its edge with a short bayonet. Nearby, stripped to the waist, a group of men, some with the honey-colored skin and broad faces of Polynesian islanders, were building a command bunker from fragments of the cisterns.

"*Vous êtes français?*" asked Bingham.

"*Bien sûr, mon petit brave.*" The man paused and leaned on his pick. "We come from paradise, Tahiti. The Battalion of the Pacific." The man shrugged. "*Sable pour sable, on a juste changé de plage!*"

They came to another gang of men still at work past the second cistern. The men were working in teams of three. Nothing on save boots and shorts, older than most soldiers they had seen, these men were opening boxes of British anti-tank mines, chipping out holes in the hard ground, arming the mines and gently covering them with sand and small stones. Occasionally the men paused and straightened their backs and joked and grumbled to one another in German.

"Krauts," said Bingham. "Prisoners. Why don't the Froggies have someone standing guard?"

"These are Frogs," said Wellington, nodding towards a bunch of white képis set on a rocky outcrop. "But they're Jerries, all right. That's why they call it the Foreign Legion."

"Wonder how they feel fighting other Huns," said Bingham.

"Who cares?" said Gates. "Long as they kill each other."

Other Legionnaires were digging trenches, siting 75mm anti-tank guns and dragging bales of barbed wire off a group of lorries. Supervising the work, Captain Nordhouse turned and spoke to the three young Englishmen.

"Can one of you gentlemen tell me where I'd find a Hussar called Rider?"

"That's me, sir. Wellington Rider."

"I met your father in Cairo," said the Legionnaire. "Good man with his fists. Gave me a hand with a bunch of Vichy sailors."

"Sounds like him, sir."

"Let me know if I can do anything for you. Tomorrow we'll try to entertain you. It's April 30, Camerone Day for us. Doesn't matter where we are, and my boys need to burn off a little of their desert madness, *le cafard*, we call it. Especially with no BMCs in these British boxes."

"BMC?"

"*Bordel Militaire Controlé.*" Nordhouse shrugged. "Whorehouses to you, sort of like your English boarding schools."

"I see, sir." Wellington tried not to grin.

"Meantime, I'll have Sergeant Malero take you over to the *réfectoire*, for some supper with the boys. But be sure you don't tell them your first name. Malero and his brother are a pair of old hands. Joined up after the war in Spain. Their brother and parents were butchered by the Fascists near Barcelona, and they're looking forward to a nice règlement de compte. You'll recognize the sergeant by his black képi."

To the east, the scrub and gravel of the desert darkened in the long shadowy rays of the setting sun.

Three hours later, Wellington and his friends sat around a camp fire near the cisterns, complaining about women and drinking Algerian *pinard* with a group of Spanish Legionnaires. "March or die!" toasted one soldier, knocking his tin cup against Wellies. The Germans were gathered about a different fire, and other Legionnaires were settled nearby around a third.

Wellie smelled fresh bread baking in a square tin box set in the coals. It would go nicely with the canned salmon the Hussars had brought as a contribution. Wellington looked forward to dinner. He and his muckers were tired of the usual stewed bully beef doused with Italian tomato purée.

"Your friend says you're getting married," said Malero. The Spaniard knelt by the fire while he cut up bits of garlic and dropped them into a German helmet containing a pool of sizzling olive oil.

"That's right." Bingham nodded cheerfully as he helped himself to more wine. "Soon as her family lets him do it. Poor girl doesn't know him like we do."

"Are you married, Sergeant?" said Wellie to the Spaniard.

"My brother? Of course he is," interrupted another Legionnaire, approaching the fire. He opened a rag containing a bunch of small active creatures that looked like slugs or worms, most with shells, a few without. "That's why he's here."

"Two things drive a man to the Legion." Malero speared a bit of crisp garlic with the tip of his knife and pulled it off the blade with his teeth. "The police and women."

The other Legionnaire dropped the wriggling creatures into the helmet, then passed around a new litre of the powerful inky wine.

"Here's a spare *gamelle* for you." The sergeant rummaged in his kit bag and pulled out a battered tin mess plate.

"What's in there?" Wellington pointed to the helmet.

"Desert snails." Malero lifted out two with his metal spoon. He sucked one snail from its white shell and passed the other, not quite dead, to Wellie. "They're better when they're cooked."

"My friend eats everything raw," offered Bingham. "Chap was born in Africa." He took off his beret and scratched his scalp before picking up the last tin of salmon. "But I think I'll just tuck into a bit of this fish with Sergeant Molena here, if you don't mind, Wellington."

Malero's brother pointed at Bingham's head. *"Boule à zéro!"* he yelled, bending over with laughter as the other Spaniards joined in, banging their forks on their plates.

"What's wrong with the Dagos?" drawled Bingham quietly to Wellie amidst the uproar.

"It's your friend's bald head," said Malero. "We do that to *les bleus*, the new recruits in Marseille, before they sail for Algeria. We shave their heads like an egg, but your friend's done a better job."

Later Wellie lay curled up in his slit trench, wrapped in his greatcoat, thinking of Saffron as he listened to the Legionnaires sing *Le Képi Blanc* and *La Légion Marche*. The power of their voices filled the night with the spirit of longing and fraternity. It reminded him of his mother's stories of the miners singing in the villages in Wales when she was a girl.

*   *   *

The next morning Wellington woke to French reveille at 0500 as a Legion bugler began the day. For the first three hours, the morning started routinely for soldiers in the desert. While the Hussars cleaned their weapons and serviced their vehicles, the Legionnaires continued to work on the defences. Many were digging what they called "bottle-holes," narrow-shouldered pits over which a tank could pass while one man hunkered below, waiting to rise up and slap a mine onto the back of the tank before diving back into his hole. Wellington had never seen men dig with such aggressive energy.

"We're used to it," Sergeant Malero explained. "The ground's even harder in Algeria, and for punishment the men are always digging *tombeaux*, little trenches like graves for a man to lie in baking under the sun. When that's done, they get a good slap across the head with a rifle butt to wake them up, a *coup de crosse*, before running up hills with sacks of stones on their backs."

"Sounds like your lads have a lot of fun," said Wellington.

"They're all a gang of thieves and murderers, but if a Legionnaire steals from a comrade, we flatten him down on his belly and drive a bayonet through both his hands," said the sergeant, apparently enjoying his report. "Excuse me."

Malero turned and yelled at two men, naked above the waist, who were leaning on their shovels and arguing in Spanish.

At 0800 the bugle called again. The men cheered and stacked their shovels and picks. Wellington and Bingham sat against their Marmon-Harrington as the day warmed. Then they brewed up and walked about with their mugs, watching the Legionnaires prepare to celebrate Camerone Day. The other French regiments appeared to understand, willingly undertaking the Legion's duties of reconnaissance and patrol.

Some men erected a line of makeshift sideshow booths. Others laid out lanes in the desert with rows of stones. A crude boxing ring was set up near one cistern. At noon the bugle blew again. All effort ceased as the men began to drink. Crates of beer and *bidons* of wine, formerly hidden beneath bales of wire and cases of ammunition, were carried over from the supply trucks. Bottles of unmarked alcohol appeared from rucksacks. Fires and field kitchens were frantically busy as the Legion officers joined the cooks in preparing the yearly feast.

When the afternoon cooled, the Hussars and the officers of the other French regiments were invited to visit the Legion camp.

Bottles of beer in hand, Wellington and Bingham strolled past the Legion sideshow. Behind the wooden counter shelf of each booth, between the side panels of tattered canvas, Legionnaires in motley rag-made costumes, their faces painted with charcoal, greeted the guests. Challenging the card tricks, Bingham lost shilling after shilling at two booths. "Worse than Buck's," he sniffed as he slapped down half a crown.

"Why don't you have a crack at the arm wrestling? You won't have to think," Bingham said to Wellington when they came to the next booth. "No one seems to want to take on that little chap with the scar. Probably all too drunk. These poor Froggies can't hold their spirits, you know."

Arm wrestling was one of his father's specialties, Wellington recalled, wondering if he would ever be able to beat the old boy at it. He looked down at the short thick-necked Legionnaire who waited in the booth. An empty wine bottle stood on the end of the rough board. A half-empty bottle of something else was gripped in the left hand of the squat soldier. The man's lips were black.

Wellington tossed down a rumpled Egyptian pound note and rolled up his right sleeve. He set his elbow on the splintery board and flexed his fingers. The Legionnaire stepped up onto a rock that rested behind the booth. Without looking at the English soldier, the man put his right elbow on the board while he lifted the bottle to his lips and gulped the cloudy liquid.

A gang of Legionnaires gathered round. *"Bravo! Un peu de sport,"* said one, almost knocking Bingham down when he clapped the Englishman on the shoulder. "Break his arm, Stanislas!" yelled another, knocking bottles with a companion. *"Prosit!"*

Wellington shifted his elbow and lowered his hand to meet the short arm of his opponent. The Legionnaire's breath struck him with a blast of foul air. Wellington tightened his hand just before the man seized his fingers.

Drinking as he did it, the speechless Pole slammed Wellington's hand down into the board. The crowd roared as the Legionnaire stepped down from the stone and emptied the bottle.

Wellington thought the middle knuckle on the back of his hand might be broken.

"Rather a sorry show, old boy," said Bingham as they moved on to the fortune-telling booth. There a hairy Spaniard played at being a gypsy lady and promised the young Hussars good fortune in love and confusion in battle.

The next booth was more expensive. *Lutte de Pernod* was scrawled on a board beneath the counter. A line of men from different regiments waited to compete with a series of Legionnaires in downing small mugs of some raw liquor, definitely not the namesake drink.

"Time we drank for King and Country," said Bingham when their turn came. "Been practicing for years."

He and Wellington did their manly best at this unwinnable event, finally staggering away with an arm around each other's shoulders. Sweating and gagging, the two went behind the cistern to throw up. "To France," said Bingham before he vomited again.

They joined a crowd of soldiers while two Legion champions, one lightweight and the other very heavy, took on all comers in bare-knuckle boxing. Every man but the fighters seemed to be carrying a bottle.

Shortly before dark, nearly a thousand Legionnaires, divided by company, stood along the rows of marking stones and prepared for the *marche canard* race. At the finish line, a torn truck canvas, crudely inscribed, was stretched between two poles set into piles of rocks. "*13ᵉ DBLE*," the sign read, "*Narvik à Bir Hakeim.*"

Some men, unable to stand, sat or lay at the feet of their comrades. Behind them all, the top half of the sun hovered briefly on the horizon like a flaming peach.

Sixteen men stood ready at the end of the lanes. Each lane was about a hundred yards long, as nearly as Wellington could make out.

"*A cheval!*" hollered Nordhouse, pistol in hand.

Eight men bent over with their hands on their knees. A soldier climbed onto each of their backs. Nordhouse raised his Webley and fired.

The runners dashed down the lanes, bent over with their heavy burdens screaming and kicking them for encouragement. One horse-and-rider stumbled on a bottle and fell, crashing into the team to their right. As the other six horses ran on, the dismounted teams cursed and brawled on the track behind them. At the finish, a tie was declared to unanimous protests. Bottles and stones flew. The two pairs of winners mounted up again and staggered back down the track for the decider. Cheers and brawls erupted among the spectators.

Wellington saw a pair of Brens patrolling behind the track in the distance. The narrow slits of their dimmed headlights glittered like dragons' eyes in the darkness.

Then the feasting began.

Wellington was astonished by the dinner that waited by the camp fires: fresh bread and tinned cheeses, beans and soup, pastas with rich sauce, eggs and sausages, and couscous and fresh goat and lamb roasted whole. All of it was cheerfully passed and served to the men by the Legion officers and sergeants and corporals. Wellington saw Nordhouse go from man to man with a long wooden board ripped from a medical supply case. Wellie's mouth watered. Half a lamb rested on the board. The great joint was charred and pink-fleshed, waiting to be devoured in heavy juicy pieces.

As the stars brightened, Wellington and Bingham carried Gates to a bottle-hole and dropped him in. Bingham knelt and set Gates's beret at a jaunty angle on the head of their unconscious friend. The beret peeked out just above the top of the pit.

"At least standing up in there the poor bugger can't choke to death when he pukes in his sleep," said Bingham after a belch.

"Hope one of the Brens doesn't run him over," said Wellington.

The sound of a guitar and castanets rose from a fire behind them, soon answered by an accordion and a lusty German marching song from another war. *Haya Safari*, the men sang. Then the instruments were overwhelmed as hundreds of voices sang *Le Boudin*. Attracted by a roar of cheers, Wellington and Bingham walked back and watched.

Half drunk or worse, several hundred Legionnaires, some in rags of uniforms, a few almost naked save for their boots, formed up in rough lines and marched across the race-track in the starlight, beating the powerful slow march of the Legion with their feet, slapping down their heavy nailed *brodequins* with every step while they roared out to the sky, *La Légion Marche*.

— 15 —

Olivio Fonseca Alavedo arrived early at Cairo's Main Station to avoid the hurly-burly of the rush. He disliked crowded settings that he could not control, where his stature could not be offset by influence and planning. It had been a long time since he had made such an expedition, but he thought the change might do him good, and there were always new secrets to study in the Valley of the Kings.

With Tariq at one elbow, and his Nubian cousin Abduh at the other, the dwarf entered the station at a stately pace. One of the new motorized baggage carts awaited him inside. A low bench was already mounted on its platform. Tariq gave a brief firm instruction to the driver, then sat on the bench facing backwards with his master on his knee between his arms. The cart parted the crowd like a royal barge. Abduh followed just behind, carrying the dwarf's satchel. His master's baggage and travelling companion were already on board.

"No, wait," Olivio said to Tariq. He was fascinated by the wartime bustle, suddenly excited as a schoolboy on an outing. "We will venture slowly. I wish to see the station." Tariq squeezed the driver's shoulder and gave him new instructions.

They paused opposite a long bulletin board hung above the benches beside the ticket windows. Blown-up photographs of the war covered the board: a column of Bren-gun carriers churning across the Western Desert, a crowd of Italian prisoners near Sollum, acres of them, a troop ship unloading at Suez with a regimental band waiting on the dock, and a flight of Hurricanes in the dark sky above Big Ben.

Nearby, young English soldiers, flaxen-haired and brown and dusty from the desert, cheerfully lined up and ordered sticky buns and mugs of tea from the new canteen staffed by English ladies in white overalls. How much better these boys look now, the dwarf observed, than when they first come out. Not as weedy and pale and timid, and without the grey spirit of their island cities.

"There you are, dear," said a white-haired volunteer, handing two hard-boiled eggs and a cucumber sandwich to a Tommy, perhaps eighteen. "That's one piastre, if you please."

For the first time the dwarf felt the war was close, that his own concerns might not be sufficient.

"Jump to it, lads, we're off," a man cried from behind Olivio's cart.

There was a stampede of khaki as the soldiers grabbed the food and bolted for their train. Several young women hurried after them carrying trays with sandwiches and mugs and jugs of tea and milk.

"After them!" Olivio said excitedly. Tariq struck the driver and pointed over the man's shoulder.

They followed to the soldiers' platform beneath the gate for Alexandria and the war. A whistle blew. Moved, the dwarf watched as if at the theatre or the opera.

He saw the men throw in their gear and climb on board. A volunteer from the canteen, a stout English woman in her fifties, trotted up, puffing and red-faced. She handed up a tray of doughnuts and passed it through a window. Others passed up mugs and sandwiches. The young men smiled and waved and cheered thanks as the train pulled out.

"Back to the canteen," snapped the dwarf in a husky voice.

"Abduh," he said once there, "take one, no, two thousand piastres from my satchel and present them to that lady. Do not say from whom it comes. If one millieme sticks to your filthy fingers, I will have your hand."

The dwarf had positioned himself early in the way that pleased him, so that arriving friends must come to him rather than pity him as he struggled along the moving train. He adjusted the cushion beneath him while he reviewed his schemes. Tariq waited nearby. His arms folded, the Nubian leaned against the corridor wall of the passage that led to the entrance of the dining car.

Opposite Olivio, sipping tea, sat Jamila, perhaps more lovely and provoking than he had ever seen her. His mouth opened with expectation as he watched her. His thick tongue quivered between his lips like a lizard's. Truly, she had the face and hair and color, even the nose, of a wild Nefertiti. Tonight she wore not a robe, but a mauve Norman Hartnell suit and, over one eye, a hat by Lily Dache with a lace veil covering the top of her face. The flared pleated skirt, cut to the knee in the latest style, no doubt was seventeen inches off the ground, as Paris required. It must now rest high on her leg, he thought. The jacket, open at the throat with a wide peaked collar, could not conceal her magnificence. On her right wrist Jamila wore a priceless ancient band of gold and lapis lazuli.

"*Ah, bon soir!*" said Madame Pantelides in her loud but educated voice. "No need to stand, we'll just sit here across the aisle." Lord Penfold greeted them cheerfully and held his companion's chair.

No doubt this Greek hag doesn't want his lordship sitting too close to my young Jamila, thought the dwarf.

The door opened again and Giscard de Neuville entered the dining car. Tariq loomed behind him in the doorway.

"*Quelle plaisir! Mon professeur!*" cried Madame Pantalides. "Giscard, surely you know everyone?"

De Neuville kissed her hand and acknowledged the others. He looked with admiration at Jamila, lingering over her hand. The archeologist stared with astonishment at her bracelet.

The dwarf nodded imperceptibly. Jamila lowered her eyes.

"Giscard is going to give us little lectures once we get to Luxor," said the Greek lady. "He knows everything."

Too much for his own well-being, thought the dwarf as the Frenchman passed on to another table.

Olivio's first day in Luxor had been a physical and moral trial such as the dwarf could no longer endure. He was reminded of his penniless boyhood in Goa, when each day had been a test, a feat of guile and determination. A struggle against the gangs of street boys who ridiculed and robbed him until, through craft and violence, he became their master. A struggle against the incapacities of size and the absence of all family and support. And a struggle against those who resisted him as he advanced. First against the jealous stewards and houseboys of the brothel where he toiled and learned the mysteries of pleasuring even the most jaded woman, then against the merchants and traders and blackmailers who sought to swindle from him the gains he had extracted from others like a tooth from the mouth of a tiger.

After breakfast in the dining car, the party had motored to Karnak.

While the dwarf toured in a cushioned donkey cart, the Pantelides guests had paraded around the Temple of Amun, lost amidst the massive columns of the Hypostyle Hall. Periodically the guests clustered about de Neuville while the archeologist lectured at them. Olivio rolled past, with Tariq holding the head of his donkey.

Annoyed by the patronizing prattle of the Frenchman, Alavedo was pleased to leave the company for a private ride up the unexcavated Avenue of Sphinxes. The limitation of his own scholarship was always supplemented by the intimacy of his sensibilites with this magic past. The dwarf savored his favorite bas-reliefs: the display of the triumphs over the inhabitants of Palestine and Libya, with the pharaoh in his victory chariot and the losers in their chains, and the depiction of the water separating Africa and Asia, in which long black crocodiles swam amidst the waving reeds. Like dwarfs, he recalled, these dark creatures, too, were gods to the brilliant ancients.

Finally it was back to the Winter Palace for a late buffet lunch.

"Of course," declared de Neuville, "the Table of the Kings, a list of the Egyptian monarchs from earliest times to the Eighteenth Dynasty, was removed from Karnak to the *Bibliothèque Nationale* in 1843." He sipped a Meursault while the others picked over the cold duck and stewed artichokes, the casserole of perch and the pigeons stuffed with giblets and green wheat.

"Giscard knows absolutely everything," said Madame Pantelides to Penfold in a loud whisper, doubtless trying to make her English suitor jealous, thought the dwarf.

"Do you suppose they have a bit of chutney?" replied Penfold, glancing around, oblivious to learning. "Or perhaps a little Marmite?"

Tomorrow will be still worse, Olivio reflected later. He lay on his back on his berth, feeling as if he had been trampled by the Camel Corps. The next day would be physically arduous and socially irritating. An early ferry boat across the Nile, with lunch baskets from the Winter Palace and carriages and donkey carts waiting on the west bank. Then on to the Tombs of the Kings, Ramses after Ramses and Thutmosis after Thutmosis, too many of each, every tomb with its sloping passages and side galleries, its airless hidden chambers and flights of awkward steps. All to be followed by a picnic near the Temple of Dayr al-Bahari. And always with de Neuville holding forth.

Perhaps he could avoid all this and instead pass a quiet day at the Necropolis, a site for gentlemen. There he could contemplate the complex arrangement of all the edifices that it served: stables for the sacrificial animals, prisons and barracks, lodgings for the masons and painters of the mortuary temples, and, above all, the quarter of the ultimate craftsmen, the embalmers. Then back to the hotel for the Pantelides Masked Ball, a costume party for which Cairo's most costly tailors and *fournisseurs* had labored through many nights. The dwarf himself would be Napoleon, with Jamila attending him as Katherine the Great.

Olivio closed his eyes and moaned at the thought of it all. As it was, he was journeying in defiance of Dr. Hänger's orders.

At last he heard a bolt slide back. The cabin door opened. Not the door to the public corridor, but the side door to the adjoining cabin. A fresh sweetness entered the room, some new perfume which had not yet seduced him. Resisting all temptation, the dwarf kept his eye squeezed shut. He knew that, like the best of lovers, Jamila would make his pleasure hers. Bored by convention, she would relish the gift of his unusual intimacies, particularly when, her own energies exhausted, she waited for his tiny oiled hand to open inside her, the smooth nail-less fingers rioting within her like puppies in a pen.

He heard her place two bottles on the night shelf. He smelled the musky odor as she opened one. This reminded him of long afternoons of private service on the Malabar Coast so many years ago. He felt her warmth as she bent over him and removed the slippers from his aching feet and undid the sash that bound his paisley silk robe. And he tasted the metallic flavor of the kohl that covered one long pointed nipple as she lowered it to his mouth by way of introduction. A generous lover, the little man sucked and nibbled until he was obliged to pause and gasp for air.

Then she filled the small corner sink with hot water and bathed him with a scented sponge. She took each foot and squeezed and kneaded it, grinding her knuckles into the ball and the arch until the stiff bent toes no longer curled inwards but wriggled freely like baby chicks in a nest. He heard her refill the sink and pour in some liquid. She wrung out a hot towel and doubled it to make it thick and slapped him with it from toe to neck and neck to toe, hard, sparing nothing. His small stinging reddened body tingled and vibrated like a tuning fork. Her hair swept along his face and body as she bent over him and dried him, patting him down and powdering him like a baby before she turned him over on his belly onto the damp bed. When she was finished, she lifted Olivio Alavedo in her arms and carried him into the other cabin. She slammed the door behind her with the heel of one foot.

There, in her own cabin, Jamila laid Olivio on his back and raised his legs. She snared his little feet in the netting that hung on the wall over the head of the bed, intended as a secure holder for small personal necessaries. Gently she performed for him the most intimate of his bedtime ceremonies: spreading his hairless left eyelid with delicate fingers and removing the ivory ball from the dead socket, which was now hot and dry and irritated after too long a day. In the morning, after rinsing it, Jamila would warm and lubricate this eyeball in the arousing womanly way that gave them both such private pleasure.

The dwarf opened his eye. He saw nothing but the darkness of total intimacy when, wet as the Nile, the woman lowered herself above his face. Her knees pinned his arms to his sides while he feasted inside her like a ferret in a mole tunnel. Trained as he was, he thought he could carry on no longer when finally she groaned and raised herself and turned around and sat on him as the gods intended, her belly thrashing and rippling and drawing him in until he thought he must have reached her navel.

A low building ululation rose from her as from a parade of professional mourners. Just as her tone passed from low to shrill, there was a deafening explosion.

Blown from its hinges, the splintered side door smashed against Jamila. A flash blinded Olivio as smoke filled the cabin.

Tariq was leaning against the corridor wall with his arms folded across his chest. He bowed when Anton approached the open door to the dwarf's room in the Anglo-American Hospital.

"Ya bey," said the black man. "I failed my master."

"No, Tariq, you did not." Anton shook his hard hand, recalling all he had been through with Tariq's stalwart brother in Abyssinia five years before. "And Mr. Alavedo was fortunate he was not in his own cabin when the grenade exploded."

"Tell me what I must do, effendi."

"Perhaps you could find the steward of the sleeping car and learn how someone got the key to Mr. Alavedo's cabin."

"Keep still out there!" snapped a harsh voice with a German accent. "Ve must have complete quiet, Herr Rider." Dr. Hänger stepped into the hall and closed the door behind him. "I am surprised your vife has not taught you this."

"How is he, Doctor?" asked Anton, restraining himself, knowing the pressure under which Cairo's physicians now worked.

"How is he?" Dr. Hänger removed his rectangular spectacles and pinched the bridge of his high hooked nose. His black eyes stared up at Anton while he considered his reply.

"Herr Alavedo should have been dead long before this. And now he has been bombed. He is blinded, I hope temporarily, in his remaining eye. By the blast. But the voman, most unusual. She protected him. Her body saved him, taking the explosion first and the door that killed her. The doorknob into her temple like a cannonball. But his right side, from his shoulder to his ankle, has received splinters from the door and shrapnel from the bomb. We must have many small operations. He feels much pain, but I think my patient has found something else to keep him still to live."

"Something else?" said Anton, seeing Saffron come up the corridor with flowers in her hand. "You mean his children?"

The physician shook his head. "More than that."

"Love?"

"Something more enduring. Revenge."

Saffron kissed Anton on the cheek. The doctor gave one further admonition before departing. "You have one minute with my patient." He held up one forefinger. "He must have peace, and I must examine the soldiers in the wards. There are so many battles."

"Who is it?" said the dwarf in a frail distant voice after they entered his room.

"It's Saffron, Father, and Uncle Anton."

The girl leaned over the bed. Olivio raised his left hand to touch his daughter's face as she kissed him. Swaddled in bandages like a mummified child, his head wrapped in gauze above the nose, the dwarf sat erect against the pillows.

The wall facing his bed was covered with large maps of his farms and plantations. The double window to his left looked out onto the golf links and polo fields of the Gezira Club. From the other window one could see the long curve of the racetrack. A cabinet filled with books and ancient objects stood in one corner beside a chamber pot.

"You have already made yourself at home, I see," said Anton while Saffron arranged the lillies in a vase.

"I am preparing for the day when I will see again." The dwarf spoke very slowly. "When my farm managers call on me for instructions, I must remind them whose farms these are." And the worse my condition, the more authority I must demonstrate, he thought.

"You won't be here that long, Father."

The dwarf spoke in a weaker voice. "But in the meantime, child, you must leave me now with Mr. Anton."

Saffron kissed her father and fussed with his pillows before departing. Anton saw a tear in her eye as she left.

"How fortunate are you and I, Mr. Anton," said the dwarf after the door closed. "Nothing can deepen a friendship more than a common enemy."

"We've had a few of those."

"We have one now."

"Who do you mean?"

"A Frenchman."

"De Neuville?"

"Who else? The rogue is after your wife and my property. I should say our property, for you and his lordship are partners with me in the farm where he covets my possessions."

"I don't . . ."

"Look on the wall behind you at the farm at Al Lahun, near Faiyum. Have you found it?"

"Yes, there we are."

"Do you see the new orchard of the apricots?"

"Yes."

"Just beside it I have found an ancient tomb. Not a pharaoh, or a prince, but some nobleman, I would say, and a gentleman of taste and rich possessions. This is a secret I have not shared even with you or with his lordship. I wished to spare you both my irregularities, though a share of the profits will be yours. Nor is it a secret I have shared with those thieving devils at the Service des Antiquités, which puts me now at peril." The dwarf's voice fell off as he grew faint. Anton saw his legs tremble and guessed he must be in cruel pain. He rose from his chair.

"May I get you some morphine?"

"Not yet. Just a little lime and water. I must tell you more."

Anton took the drink from the bedside table and held the bent glass straw to the lips of his friend.

"Thank you. But this de Neuville, who is concluding a licensed but ungratifying dig at his own property nearby, with such trifling thefts as he can manage, he has learned of our little excavation and he has threatened me with exposure unless I give him one third of our treasure."

Anton smiled at the thought. "I need not guess what you replied."

"Indeed, and I threatened to expose his own misdeeds, and I implicated him in mine."

"So you think he was behind this bombing?" Anton saw the hands of the little man clench and twist his bedsheet.

"With the life I have enjoyed, I have too many enemies to be certain," said Olivio, not without pride. "The timing, of course, suggests it. But I must be certain." Whoever it was would endure a calvary that would bring a respectful smile to the thin lips of de Torquemada himself. Possibly it would be time to employ the neck press that, for amusement, Alavedo had once had modelled from the hieroglyphics at Beni Hassan-al-Chorouk. Or possibly the Maiden's Winch, the unspeakable gift of a lonely planter from Sao Paulo.

Anton tried not to notice as the dwarf, still preferring the clarity of pain to the ease of euphoria, gathered himself before pursuing his thought. His little fingers were white and knotted.

"I do not mind punishing the wrong enemy, Mr. Anton. But I do not want to let the right one go unpunished. If they knew that, they would all be after me."

"I have asked Tariq to learn who got the key to your cabin."

"A useful step, but there is more to be done."

"What can I do?"

"Whilst I am here, you must see that no one robs our tomb. Now it is at risk, for any thief knows we could not complain to the authorities."

"Have you ever thought of getting psychoanalyzed?" asked Harriet as she and Anton motored down to Al Lahun the next day in one of Olivio's green Sunbeams. She turned and glanced at him as she spoke, taking one hand from the wheel and pinching his right ear.

"I wouldn't know how to spell it," said Anton, annoyed at the suggestion. He filled his glass from the ice bucket that rested on the floor between his feet. Harriet seemed more interested in him since he had declined her advances following their bathtub fling. "And you?"

"I can't wait, it'll be so fascinating. Give me a chance to think about myself for a change."

"At last."

"No, really, it's true. But I never seem to be ready for it. I don't know whether it's too early or too late." One hand lightly on the wheel, Harriet looked at Anton. "And imagine spending all that time with one man."

She held out her glass for more champagne. "Don't drink it all."

"Watch out!" he screamed as a donkey cart backed onto the road in front of them.

"Don't be silly." Harriet swerved and carried on calmly. "You know I'm a good driver."

"There are two kinds of woman drivers," Anton said. "Good is not one of them."

Instead of answering, Harriet took a drink and put her foot down. Clouds of dust flew from the road. Fellahin jumped back as they sped through the mud village of Maidum.

"One kind drives like bad women drivers, nervous, tense, hunched forward, too frightened to handle a crisis." Anton paused and emptied the bottle. "The other kind, like you, Harry, drives like bad men drivers, fast, aggressive, over-confident."

"I did all right in Ethiopia, thank you." She braked hard as they came to Al Lahun. "Which way?"

"Right," he said, thinking of the safari that had turned brutal as they fled from the Italian army. "Ethiopia was different, and you were better on a horse, and with a gun."

"I still think of Berny every day," Harriet said in a different voice, speaking of her twin, murdered by the Italians. "I just want to turn my head and see her there."

"Sorry," he said, touching Harriet's shoulder, speaking gently. "I'm sure you do. We all miss Bernadette. Turn in here, please. We're there."

Waiting for them by the striped tent, the farm manager opened the driver's door.

"All well, Youssef?" said Anton.

"You come too late, effendi," said the Egyptian, a doubled-barrelled shotgun in his left hand. "The thieves came last night. They stole . . ."

"What happened?" asked Harriet.

"They killed one of the Nubians and stole much before I came from the farmhouse and fired two *cartouches* and we drove them off."

"What did they steal?" said Anton.

"How much I am not certain, but they had a large lorry, a Ford, I think, black as the night, and they took the boat of the dead, some ornaments and weapons, and a mummy, the one with the golden vest. Only the other is left." The man groaned and raised his dark eyes to the sky. "My master will be most angry."

"Show us," said Anton. Harriet followed him as Youssef collected a torch from the tent and led them to the tomb.

"I must not wake him," repeated the small wrinkled woman in her black house robe, shaking her narrow head fiercely. Peering out, she held the cracked wooden door barely open with one hand and held a black *tarha* over her thin white hair with the other. "All night my husband worked on the Alexandria train, serving the *farangi*. If I wake him, Salah will beat me."

"Do not wake him." Tariq put one foot across the threshold. "I will wake him."

"No!" the woman cried, attempting to close the door. "As Allah preserves us, you will not come in this house!"

A rag dealer's cart was jammed in the narrow alleyway behind Tariq. Above the Nubian's head, the second floor of the woman's house nearly touched the narrow shuttered balcony of the dwelling across the alley. Cords covered in laundry were strung like banners back and forth across the passage. A small crowd began to gather. The woman's neighbors muttered ominously.

Tariq glowered down at the small woman and ignored the mob. "If I do not wake Salah this morning, the police will wake him tomorrow."

"Who is this man?" the woman screamed as Tariq took the edge of the door in his right hand. "Will no one help me?"

The shutters of the opposite balcony slammed open. A heavy white-haired crone leaned out and screamed. Spittle flew and her tarha flapped wildly as she gestured with both hands. "Leave her alone, you black devil! Stop this man!"

Tariq felt the old burn scars on his face begin to throb. Trying to mask the discreet violence of his act, he slowly forced the door inwards. Then he stepped inside the narrow house and slammed the door behind him.

The single downstairs room was dark, save for an oil lamp burning in a niche in one wall. Hanging neatly on a hanger on a peg in the center of the wall opposite was the dark uniform of a railroad conductor. Light glinted from the polished badge of the Egyptian State Railway. An old clothes brush hung from a string beside the uniform. The back of the room gave onto a small open-air kitchen where a charcoal brazier burned with low coals. Tariq smelled onions and the greasy odor of old mutton. These railroad men lived like pashas, he thought, frowning.

He walked over to the brazier and looked down at the steaming pot. He saw a sheep's head, the skull split lengthwise in the proper way, simmering in a sea of onions, carrots and celery stalks. Cardamom seeds and a bay leaf danced on the boiling broth. Tariq took a knife from his pocket. Ignoring the scalding water, he gripped one ear and lifted half the head against the edge of the pot and cut off the end of the tongue.

As he chewed, Tariq tried to think how his master would manage such an interview. Find what they care about, and pretend to give them a choice, he thought.

Tariq removed the hanger from the wall and lifted the lamp from its niche. He climbed the stairs while the woman protested and wrung her hands. He turned on the narrow steps and spoke to her. "If you and your husband do not make trouble, all should be well and you will be paid. Keep quiet and stay where you are."

"What is this noise, Dunya?" demanded a man's angry voice from upstairs. "Be still, woman."

Tariq climbed the few remaining steps. The stairs creaked beneath his weight.

Thin bands of light filtered into the upstairs room through heavy wooden shutters. The noise of the alley had quieted to the customary clamor. Hazy beams of light entered through cracks in the low wooden roof. An old man, bone thin, either dead or asleep, lay on a narrow cot against the far wall. On a bed in the center of the room, a heavy bald soft-bodied man, dressed only in a pair of shabby grey trousers, sat up and lowered his feet to the floor. His chest and thick belly were covered in white hair. "Who are you?" he said, his tone both nervous and aggressive. "Why are you in my house?"

"Salah!" called the woman, her voice shrill and anxious. "Salah!"

The man began to rise from the bed. Tariq pushed him back down, using the hand that held the clothes.

"If you answer my questions," said Tariq, "you will keep your job and your house, and your freedom and your health." He rested the oil lamp unevenly on the bed. Oil pooled at the bottom edge of the lamp, almost dripping onto the rumpled bedclothes.

The man reached to steady the lamp, but Tariq slapped his arm aside with a sharp blow. He wiped the lamb grease from his lips with one sleeve of the uniform jacket. Then he threw the jacket on the floor and drew the dark blue trousers from the hanger.

"How long have you worked for the railway?" asked Tariq.

"Who are you?"

Tariq held the cuffs of the trousers over the flame. "How long have you worked for the railway?"

"Twenty-two years," said the man quickly. He reached tentatively for his trousers. "I started as a cleaner."

"Then in three years you will retire with a handsome pension to support you and your wife as you grow old and more fat." Tariq held the trousers aside. "Unless you go to prison or lose your job for some misdeed."

"Misdeed?"

"Three nights ago a bomb exploded in a cabin in your car. A lady died."

"I . . ." the man began.

"Speak."

"I was asleep."

"How did the villain get a key?" Tariq swung the garment across the flame.

One cuff began to smoke.

"I cannot work without my uniform," implored the man. He leaned over and reached across the bed.

Tariq backhanded him across the face. He heard something crack in the man's neck or back. A few drops of warm oil spilled onto the bedclothes. The old man on the cot groaned.

"How did the villain get the key?" A small flame flickered amidst the smoke rising from the cloth. It shot up one trouser leg in a long orange streak. Tariq held on as the fire approached his hand.

"I . . ." the man began, then stopped again. He rocked back and forth on the edge of the bed, both hands pressed to the sides of his face.

The flames reached Tariq's hand. He dropped the trousers onto the bed. The fire spread along the dark cloth as the man watched, his mouth trembling, his hands clutched together. "My wife, my father," he said, his eyes fixed on the pool of spilled oil.

"Smoke!" screamed Dunya from downstairs. "What is that smoke?"

"You will not rise from that bed until you tell me." Tariq pointed to his own face. "See? I have already been burned once before. You will not like it."

"A man paid me and threatened to kill me if I did not lend him the key. I knew nothing." The conductor coughed and tried to wave the rising smoke from his face. "But I swear it, master, I did not know what he was going to do."

Tariq pulled the patched waistband of the trousers towards the oil. "Who was this man? What did he look like?"

"He was rich. He had two silver teeth, here." The man raised his upper lip and pointed to his yellow front teeth. "I do not know his name. And he was with another man, his brother, I believe."

"What was this brother called?"

"Munir."

"As I thought." Tariq reached down and lifted the jacket of the uniform. First he used it to smother the guttering lamp and snuff the wick. Then he slapped it down onto the trousers, extinguishing the flames, leaving only a few sparkling edges where the cloth smoldered on into the bedclothes without igniting. As the conductor rose, Tariq took the smoking oily jacket and pressed it into the man's face, forcing him back down. The Nubian bent over the struggling man and continued to hold the jacket against his face while he thrashed and coughed and gagged.

Tariq stood and straightened his gallabiyyah. "You will not speak of this," he said, dropping a handful of silver riyals on the blanket. The conductor lay gasping on his bed. Small flames blossomed beside the man.

Tariq walked down the stairs and said one word to the wailing woman as he approached the door. "*Mayya.*" Water.

— 16 —

"Time we got you back out in the blue, Rider." Major Lagnold stood and walked to the large map rack mounted at the back of his tent. "You look like you've forgotten how to sleep. Bucketing about the desert seems to agree with you a deal more than all this town life. Looked a damned sight sharper after your boxing match."

"Can't disagree with you, sir." Anton covered his yawn and tried not to remember the final stop on last night's low-life Cairo crawl. It had started innocently enough. Anton was determined to behave himself. First, before the Kit Kat Club, a tea dance at Shepheard's, Harriet turning too many heads as the Continental Cabaret Orchestra played her old favoites. But these rich girls liked to slum. He thought of the photograph she'd folded and slipped into his army picture wallet: two champagne bottles upside down in the bucket, the ashtray full of butts, Harry's hand on his leg as she leaned across the tiny table to kiss him in an all-night belly dancer dive called Turkish Delight. Fortunately that was as far as he had let things go.

"War's a lot simpler, sir," Anton added, feeling horribly sick. During the war, everything was so intense, and nothing seemed to matter, or did it matter more?

"Must be why these Jerry prisoners always look so bloody hard and fit," said Lagnold. "They've got nowhere to go on leave. Few nights in Cairo and they wouldn't be able to button their shorts."

"Perhaps we could send them a few busloads of bints from the Birka, sir. Some of those extra tarts that are always sitting there fanning them-sleves on their little balconies," said Anton. "Rather the way the Germans shipped old Lenin back north to help soften up the Russians in the last war. Reckon some of these dollies could do anything he could do."

"Maybe." Lagnold pulled the stem from his pipe and tapped out the muck. "We've got more brothel casualties than battle casualties. All seven VD centers are overloaded. Fortunately the officers aren't allowed to use the same bordellos as the men. Otherwise they'd be killing each other."

"I see, sir."

"Good, Rider. Now it's your turn to do a little damage." Lagnold tapped the map of Libya with the stem of his pipe. "It's fourteen hundred miles from their base at Tripoli to ours at Alexandria, and neither side seems able to make it more than half way without getting over-extended and weaker as the defending side gets stronger. Tobruk's shaping up as the big test. Rommel can't attack Egypt unless he takes Tobruk. And he's got to do it before we get any stronger. And there's one thing he must have to keep moving: petrol. We think he needs six hundred tons a day just to keep going, and he's getting less than half that."

"Yes, sir," said Anton wearily.

"Do I have your attention, Rider? Good. Anyway, they're getting better at hiding the stuff. Both small caches of jerricans buried under the sand, and big camouflaged dumps up near the coast, usually near an air base or the Via Balbia. Your job's to locate the forward petrol dumps for his big push on Tobruk." Lagnold tapped the map. "This area between Benghazi and Derna, down here. Map them, radio them in if you can, then come back and tell us about it. But be careful. This time they'll be waiting for you."

"May we do a little mischief ourselves, sir?" said Rider, brightening. "Keep our hand in?"

" 'Fraid that's not our assignment. That's for the SAS and the RAF. But if you knock one out on your way back, HQ wouldn't complain, once your job's done."

"When do we leave, sir?"

"Morning after tomorrow, Rider." Lagnold polished the bowl of his pipe along the side of his long nose and squinted at Anton as if staring across the desert. "Should I tell you how to spend your time until then?"

"No need, sir, thank you."

*   *   *

"He who defends everything defends nothing," von Decken heard the hard clear voice state to General Barbasetti. "If we defend every Italian settlement in North Africa, I cannot concentrate the forces to take Tobruk."

The Italian protested, speaking rapidly as his voice rose.

"And one other thing, General," said Rommel. "Henceforth, I will expect the immediate execution, in the field, of any officer who shows cowardice in the face of the enemy."

"Impossible!" roared Barbasetti. "Who is to say what is cowardice?"

Waiting outside Rommel's tent, Ernst and two other German officers pretended not to listen. Barbasetti's immaculate aide paced about near his general's Fiat 508, occasionally pausing, despite the heat, to sip expresso from a thermos in the general's hamper.

Near von Decken stood Major-General Ramcke, commander of the recently arrived First Parachute Brigade, and a major from the 361st Grenadiers, the unit formed from two thousand German veterans of the French Foreign Legion.

Beyond the tent, Ernst saw the young soldiers, the *Feldgrauen* of this new war. Soon they would be proper Africans, like the Schutztruppe. Perhaps half his age, they were lean and tan and cheerful in their shorts and shirts and sun-bleached field caps. Some had cut off the tops of their high lace-up canvas and leather boots to make comfortable ankle boots. A few wore bits of English uniform. Several were washing their clothes in gasoline, then rubbing them clean with dry sand. One soldier, shirtless, was winning a wager with a comrade by slowly frying four eggs on the sun-heated armor of a Mark III. Others sat in a circle, throwing down playing cards, gambling on a game of skat. A couple were reading *Die Oase*, the field newspaper of the Afrika Korps. A young officer whistled "We Are Marching for England" while he cleaned his Luger and reloaded.

Most of the men, von Decken knew, were suffering from the desert and their diet: bowel diseases, scurvy, ulcerating skin sores, diphtheria, jaundice, small wounds festering, gums bleeding, teeth lost.

Ernst thought of the chiggers that had burrowed beneath his toenails during the long East African campaign. The females preferred to burrow into the scrotum and the armpits. There they would ovulate beneath the skin, then feed off the damaged tissue they had manufactured. He remembered the men pissing blood in thick inky spurts when they came down with blackwater fever.

Here in Libya, with no water for bathing and no hope of leave, every man was afflicted with lice, wonderfully vicious and tenacious, said to be carried by the Italians and the Arabs. Some men wiped themselves with kerosene to kill the little creatures. Early this morning Rommel himself had stood by and watched, his hands behind his back, while Günther burned all his bedclothes with gasoline. By his order, the narrow metal bedframe stood in the flames in order to purge it thoroughly. "Just like the English," the general had muttered. "You can win every battle but you still can't get rid of them."

In this camp the lucky men had double tents, one above the other. The two layers of canvas kept them cooler by day and warmer at night. Many of the tents, well dispersed, were pitched near sangars, small barricades of rocks and sandbags that provided protection from the RAF without the men having to dig shelters in the hard ground.

Some men were in line beside the "goulash cannon," the black chimney of the mobile field kitchen that was serving up a mixture of disgusting Italian rations as well as the luxury of rice captured from the 10th Indian Division. Often there were so many flies on the food that it was impossible not to eat them. Other men were shaving in the remains of their morning drinks, in deference to their commander's preference. Ernst had heard Rommel tell a film crew that he wanted his men to look clean and young and fit. Most older men could not take the hardship of this campaign. Rommel was sending home any man over thirty-three, save senior officers or a few special old hands like von Decken. And he'd sent a few generals home as well, "on their camels" as Rommel called it, including one he caught still breakfasting at six-thirty. He wanted every man ready for duty before sunrise.

"We've already pushed the British back a thousand miles," Rommel added impatiently to Barbasetti. "*Schwerpunkt*, General. Concentration!" Receiving no reply, he switched to his intense awkward Italian. "*Concentrazióne. Concentraménto di truppe!*" He pointed to the opening of the tent. "Now you must excuse me. And please thank Rome for the medal."

Rommel's aide stood aside as the Italian left, then directed the waiting German officers into the tent. Without looking at it, Rommel snapped shut the presentation case containing Italy's Order of the Colonial Star and handed it to Günther. "*Ochsenkopf,*" he muttered. Blockhead.

Ernst looked at the map of the Eastern Front that hung from a board. Thick blue arrows were aimed at Moscow and Grozny. Both were nearly surrounded by thickets of smaller red arrows. Dates were marked in green. The general had been at work with his colored pencils.

"Ramcke," said Rommel with a near smile. His skin was slightly yellow beneath his tan. His lips were burnt and cracked. For a week, on his physician's orders, he had eaten nothing but rice and condensed milk. "Welcome to Africa. I'm glad you survived Crete."

The tall lean-faced officer saluted with a snap and clicked the heels of his polished paratroop boots. Distinguished by their tight-fitting rounded helmets, his thirteen hundred men were the best equipped Germans in Libya.

Rommel pointed at a map of the coast with his calipers. "I want you and your men to surprise the British and cut the coastal road farther to the east. And don't ask me for more support."

"Jawohl, Herr General," said Ramcke, revealing two rows of metal teeth. He saluted and left as the general turned to the waiting Grenadier.

"The Three Hundred Sixty-First, Major, will join the Ninetieth Light Division. You'll be flanking the British, swinging south through the desert. Should be like home to your old Legionnaires." He tapped the map south of Bir Hakeim.

"Aldinger," Rommel said to his adjutant immediately after the Grenadier major left the tent. "Quick now, Aldinger, watch that those French-trained devils don't steal our spare tires while they're hanging about headquarters. These ex-Legionnaires thieve even better than they fight."

The general turned to von Decken, noting his attention to the map.

"That is why we don't have enough men and supplies." He tapped Moscow, then Leningrad. "*Die Ostfront.* The Russians are devouring the Luftwaffe and our Panzers. And we still have not taken Sevastopol and the Caucasus. Two hundred divisions on the Eastern Front, and we have three for Africa, understrength and without supplies. Two more divisions here, two, and we'd be dining by the Sphinx, and the Canal and the Persian oil fields would be ours."

"Yes, sir." Ernst recalled the famous tale that when, after the invasion of Poland, the Führer asked Rommel what he wanted, the officer had replied, "command of a Panzer division." Hitler had obliged him, and Rommel had cut France in two. Now he just wanted a couple more of the same and he'd cut the British Empire in two.

"We've no time now, von Decken. Join me in the Kübel and we'll talk as we drive. There's a bit of a sandstorm blowing up. Some of the men use gas masks when the storms get bad."

Sand flooded down the windscreen like waves of water as the headquarters company pushed southeast through the wind. The Mammoth lumbered behind at the end of the little column. Four dispatch riders rode their motorcycles, squinting through their goggles. Their coat collars were turned up. Their exposed skin was like leather covered with hard grey dust. The sidecars of the BMWs were packed with supplies bundled in canvas.

Squeezed into the back seat of the Volkswagen, Ernst hunched forward, his head between Rommel's and the driver's as he tried to listen to the general over the noise of the engine and the flying sand.

"Let your number two take charge for a few days, Major," yelled Rommel. "I want you to tell me about fighting the British in Africa. Teach me what von Lettow learned twenty years ago. What odds did he face?"

"Ten to one, sir."

"It's about four to one against us, if you don't count the Italians. But von Lettow was always on the run. We must attack. I'm damned if I'll end up like him. Hounded across Africa from country to country."

The car slowed. Talking became easier.

"Who were their best troops?"

"I'd say the Rhodesians and South Africans, sir. They understood the country. But by the end, ninety percent of the men on both sides were black, fighting our European war."

"And supplies?"

"To East Africa, Herr General?" Ernst grunted. "It was impossible, worse than now. Berlin sent one cruiser to help us, the *Königsberg*, but the Britishers sank her in the mangrove swamps. So we recovered her cannons, four-inch guns, mounted them on railroad wheels and dragged them through the bush for a year."

"That was it?"

"Not quite. Berlin tried once more. They sent a dirigible from Bulgaria to Tanganyika, the longest balloon flight in history. She was designed to be taken apart and everything used. The struts for radio masts, the skin for bandages, the treads for boot leather. But the lying British sent her a radio message that we'd surrendered, and she turned back over the Sudan."

There was a violent crash. Von Decken plunged into the front seat. Rommel hit the windscreen with both arms.

Blood running from his nostrils, the driver staggered from the car, followed by the two officers. The front left wheel of the Kübel had plunged into a slit trench. The general tried to help Ernst lift the corner of the light vehicle, but the rest of the convoy soon gathered around and other men rushed to assist. Rommel himself took the driver's seat, but found the steering column had snapped. Impatient, he strode back to the Mammoth with Ernst. Two days earlier, his command truck had been attacked from the air. Rommel's driver had been killed before the man could close the battle shutters. A metal splinter had ripped the heel off the general's left boot. The previous week, a battalion of Bersaglieri had fired on Rommel's Storch. Ernst wondered if the general himself would survive this war.

In an hour they came to the camp of the Afrika Korps' radio intercept company.

Camouflaged with lashed-on bunches of camel thorn and brown, yellow and grey netting, the seven vehicles were laagered between two bony outcroppings of black basaltic slabs. The trucks of their supply train were scattered nearby. Several were hidden up to their windows in deep pits. Others were surrounded by sangars. As the storm ended, two men were adjusting the guy wires that secured a fifty-foot radio mast. A shorter star antenna rose from the rear of one truck.

"Have you news for me, Hauptmann Seebohm?" called Rommel as he approached the radio truck. The astonished intelligence officer stepped down from the three-ton Opel Blitz, his earphone headset in his left hand.

"British claim they've sunk another convoy just off Tripoli, Herr General, six of seven ships lost, all Italian. And the Second South African Division is preparing to defend Tobruk."

"Captain, can you direct us to the Ariete Division?" said Rommel, ignoring the bad news. "Time I called on the Italians."

"Their rear units should be just over the horizon, sir."

"Carry on, Seebohm, and have the Luftwaffe drop me the latest photographs of Bir Hakeim."

"Yes, sir. And here's a wireless for you from Berlin." Captain Seebohm handed Rommel an envelope. "Seems they're having trouble finding you, sir."

Von Decken stumped after the general as he returned to the Mammoth.

"You know, von Decken," said Rommel as the heavy vehicle lumbered forward. "The General Staff complains I should be at headquarters, but in Africa you must lead from the front. Those old desk soldiers do not understand. This isn't static trench warfare. Here no battle plan holds good after the first day. The desert is like the ocean. No admiral ever won a battle from a shore base." The general paused, almost shivering, as if with fever. "Here the boldest decision is the best decision, but you cannot make it unless you are there. Already we've lost the commanders of all three of my divisions. In the last war two German generals died in action."

Rommel set his desert glasses on the front of his cap and tore open the envelope. He grunted with contempt and handed it to Ernst. "Now you see what we're dealing with," he said. "Destroy this in our next camp fire and never speak of it."

Ernst read the message.

It is reported that many German refugees are fighting with the French. The Führer has ordered that they are to be terminated with extreme prejudice. They are to be liquidated mercilessly in combat. Where they are not, they are to be shot afterward, immediately, on the orders of the nearest German officer, insofar as they are not temporarily reprieved for the extraction of intelligence. The communication of this order in writing is forbidden. Commanders are to be given oral briefing.

Von Decken put the message in a pocket of his tunic as General Rommel said, "If we capture men from their Palestine Battalion at Bir Hakeim, we must mix them up with the other prisoners."

"Good men, this division, especially the artillery. Never abandon their guns, but there aren't enough of them," said Rommel an hour later as he and von Decken strolled about the Italian camp. "My generals tell me that one British soldier is worth twelve Italians. But there are no bad soldiers, von Decken, only bad officers."

"I know exactly what you mean, sir. In Ethiopia," said Ernst, "the Italians had three different grades of food for officers and men. The men often had no field kitchens, while the officers were eating Parma ham off linen and silver. Even here I've seen their soldiers, sometimes with no boots, begging our men for food."

Groups of men waved at the general and cheered as they passed.

"The Ariete's the only Italian division I can depend on," Rommel said to Ernst. "That and the Folgore, the paratroopers, trained by us, of course.

The officers are better, know their men. Most Italian soldiers have never seen a general in the field. And we need them. We have to hold a broad front, and we can't do it without the Italians and our minefields."

"*Mangiare, Generalissimo?*" called one soldier, kneeling by a steaming pot.

Rommel and Ernst walked over.

"*Grazie,*" said Rommel.

The Italian soldiers stood awkwardly, saluting and smiling. One man drew a large can marked *Estratto di Pomodoro* from the edge of the coals. He opened the tin with a bayonet and spread the tomato extract over the macaroni that another dropped onto two battered tin plates. Tiny sand flies swarmed around the food. Rommel and Ernst sat on a rocky ledge and ate with the men. The round black leather helmets of the Italian tankers rested on the rock behind them.

As they were scraping their plates, a Lancia artillery tractor and a Fiat Toppolino pulled up. A colonel stepped down from the small touring car and saluted Rommel.

"*Colonello,*" said Rommel at once, "we have to make the British think your artillery is even stronger than it is. I'm sending you three lorries of telephone poles. You must make dummy cannons, with empty shell cases nearby and scraps of camouflage over them. Bit of paint. Make them look like eighty-eights. Put them behind the minefields to draw fire so we can use your real artillery where we need it. And we'll give you a few of the seventy-six millimeter anti-tank guns we captured in Russia. Use them well."

As Rommel went back to the Mammoth, he slowed his pace to allow for Ernst's bad leg. He entered the vehicle and collected his field glasses. Then he climbed up through the hatch and took his favorite seat on the broad roof. He lowered his peaked cap and pulled down his sun goggles. His legs dangled through the open hatch.

"Only in artillery and mines are we as well equipped as the British," said the general when von Decken joined him. "On the offensive it must be *Sturm, Swung, Wucht.* Attack, impetus, weight." He raised his field glasses and scanned the horizon while he spoke.

"But on defense, Major, it must be defense in depth. To hold the line where we are understrength, we are building false minefields sprayed with scrap metal, alternating with real mines, and booby traps, artillery and interlocking fields of fire. I'm having Buelowius, he's a genius, the Beethoven of mines, supervise the minelaying."

"I saw Buelowius two weeks ago, sir, near Bardia," said Ernst with satisfaction. "He was teaching his men to take a tire from a captured enemy vehicle and roll it along right next to one of our big Teller mines so the British would see the track and think it was safe to drive there. He said none of the English would live to warn the next man."

Driving on, they came to an abandoned group of German lorries. Two appeared to have been blown by mines. Disgusted, Rommel jumped down and inspected the empty vehicles himself. He checked two of the petrol tanks and shook his head.

"Mine belt, sir," said the driver, taking a few careful steps forward from the Mammoth. "Their crews were probably taken prisoner."

"Siphon the fuel from those trucks," Rommel told the driver as he returned to the Mammoth for a bayonet.

Kneeling, the general gently scraped the sand from the top of one mine with the edge of the blade. Then he removed the igniter, lifted the plate-shaped mine and set it aside. Before he looked up, his staff had joined him from the other vehicles. Soon a lane was cleared and the convoy advanced.

"This one's too good to miss," whispered Anton to Hennessy and Makanyanga. Their patrol had found five fuel dumps and logistics centers and radioed in the locations. One vehicle had broken down. Two men were almost useless with dysentery, but the rest of Rider's men were impatient for action. Like the best hunting clients, he would need to hold them back a bit.

Lying in a shallow wadi, their hats and faces the colors of the desert, the three peered over the edge of the dry streambed with the sun setting behind them. As Anton adjusted his glasses, he smelled the oily fishy odor of the tin of sardines that Hennessy was opening at his elbow. Hennessy passed the can around, then ate his share before drinking the olive oil with one gulp.

"Tell me, Lieutenant," said Anton quietly. He licked his fingers and turned and leaned on one elbow. "Why do you always drink that disgusting salt water at the bottom of the potato and vegetable tins? Nobody else can stand it, thirsty or not."

"Saves me from having those unhealing desert sores, sir, that all the rest of the squaddies have got, that're always getting infected, sir, and spreading all over. Worse than getting creased."

"I don't have any sores," said Makanyanga.

Anton chuckled and stared through his glasses. It was the time of evening when sometimes the desert blushed pink just before the sun was lost.

Centered in the lenses he saw the ninth German transport land on the rough airstrip half a mile away. Already the ground crew was swarming around the first aircraft. Efficient as ants, they opened the wide hatch of the loading bay just behind the ribbed wing of the long narrow Junker 52, the workhorse of the Luftwaffe. Anton assumed the three-engined planes would take off at once, flying back to Crete or Italy by night to avoid the British fighters based in Egypt and Malta.

"Petrol," said Makanyanga as the first drum was rolled out onto the platform formed by the bottom of the Junker's opened hatch. In minutes Anton counted eighty large petrol drums rolled to the edge of the airstrip. The Germans must be desperate, he thought, if they were bringing in petrol by air instead of by sea. He scanned the airfield with his binoculars. He spotted occasional Italian sentries, and one German armored car and a line of trucks parked under camouflage. Old Renaults, doubtless supplied by the Vichy forces in Algeria and Morocco. Soon they'd be trucking the gasoline out to the thirsty Panzers. He saw a group of stretchers being loaded into the last plane.

Anton turned on his back and slid to the bottom of the wadi. The three men ran along the bottom of the long curving depression until they came to the forward trucks of their patrol. Stoner and the others greeted them eagerly.

"Quick scoff now," said Anton. It was time to do the job. "Biscuits and rum. No fire. Be ready to move the minute it's dark. Soon as you hear the first Junker warming its engines, Stoner, take your Chevy with the Bofors and run out past the end of the airstrip. Try to shoot them in the belly while they're still climbing. Skip the last one, it's full of wounded." He paused and spoke more slowly. "Don't try to get them all if it gets hot. When you have too much company, let the others go and dash back to our last camp and get the rest of the patrol moving south. As soon as you start firing, I'll take the other two Chevies and go after the petrol and the lorries. When it's over, we'll come after you. Don't wait for anyone."

In half an hour it was dark and cool. Waiting in the trucks, camouflage stripped and stowed, the men pulled on heavy sweaters and sheepskin coats as a wind rose and whined through the wadi. Clouds of sand and dust gusted before it. Another hour and the men were stiff and cold.

"Sure the bastards're taking off tonight, sir?" asked Stoner, standing beside Anton's Chevy.

"Back in your truck, Sergeant-Major. You'll miss the first plane."

Perhaps, after a long flight, the Luftwaffe pilots were waiting till morning, when they could get an escort of Messerschmitt 109s to the coast. After that, Anton knew, they'd be on their own crossing the Med. Or perhaps they'd be off in the middle of the night, so as to leave in darkness and land in daylight.

Anton was reminded of poaching in the woods in England as a boy. He grinned at the memory. Learning to wait in silence, and to listen, for the snap of a snare the instant before a rabbit rose squealing in the air, or for the rush of a pheasant through the brush, or for the tread of a gamekeeper as he hunted for poachers. Though never welcome, the gypsy caravan would try to camp near villages where the locals were more tolerant, and where there was a market for their horses and farm crowds for their gambling and fortune-telling.

The crack of an engine misfire cut the night. Then again, as the engine grumbled twice and caught. Then another and another. Stoner's Chevy lurched forward up a slope in the wadi. The other two lorries followed, then waited on the edge of the dry streambed with their engines running. Anton could just make out the black mass of Stoner's vehicle as it headed off beyond the far end of the runway.

All he could hear was the thunder of twenty-seven engines as the transports prepared to take off. Sparks and a fury of heat glowed at the edges of the nacelles as the aircraft began to move. Two ground crew stood at each end of the crude runway, beckoning the dark planes forward with circular motions of their torches. The first Junker turned about at the near end of the strip and stopped, then revved its motors and began to move. Free of cargo, it accelerated rapidly and began a swift climb. Hope Stoner hasn't driven too far, Anton thought. The first plane disappeared into the starry sky.

The second plane followed, lifting off quickly. Just as it began to climb, a pop-pop-pop and three flashes erupted near the end of the runway as the Bofors fired. The Junker's bow engine exploded. Flames sheathed its fuselage as the plane continued to climb. At the same time, Anton saw Stoner's machine gunner open up on the next aircraft just before it took off. The remaining transports were rushing down the runway behind it. The German armored car raced along beside them. He hadn't expected it to be in action so quickly.

Anton hollered at Hennessy. The two Chevies, moving by starlight, made for the petrol dump.

To their right, they saw the third transport begin to rise, then crash in a pool of fire. Stoner's truck, silhouetted against the blaze, stood motionless. Anton could see each man in action. Two served the Bofors. One, probably Stoner, fired the Bren and another the light Thompson. The Bofors was still turned on the line of climbing Junkers. Anton prayed the truck wouldn't stay too long. Now Stoner had turned his fire at the onrushing armored car. Anton glanced up and saw the second plane receding into the night. At least one engine still worked, but the body of the aircraft was lit like a meteor from nose to tail. He watched it burst into pieces. Each part fell glowing to earth.

Tracer machine gun fire swept Stoner's vehicle. Both men fell from the Bofors. Four planes were rushing down the airstrip. Anton, almost at the petrol drums, cut down two sentries with his Bren. He saw Stoner climb into the driver's seat as the Thompson gunner fell from his truck. The lorry moved towards the dwindling line of aircraft. Another took off. Then Stoner crashed his Chevy into the next Junker. Plane and truck vanished in a ball of fire.

Cursing, Anton fired into the waiting row of drums. Pools of fire ran from them before they exploded in a roar that rolled across the desert. Anton felt the searing shock of hot wind as the explosive wave struck their truck.

Then he was past the drums and following Hennessy towards the Renaults. Scores of men were breaking from a line of tents and rushing about firing weapons. The armored car was turning at the far end of the strip.

Nose to tail, the two vehicles of the Long Range Desert Group drove rapidly past the row of parked lorries, sweeping them with machine gun fire. Anton's driver was hit twice in the chest. Crying out, he fell over the wheel. Anton pushed him aside and grabbed the wheel just as they swerved and grazed a Renault. The driver, dead, fell from the truck. Makanyanga, his shoulder bloody, was firing from the back seat.

"Drop the attack! Clear out!" Rider yelled at Hennessy, knowing he could not be heard. Anton pulled away across the airstrip just as the last plane rose.

Coughing, Anton looked back through the orange flames and black oily smoke of the petrol fire. He saw Hennessy following them. One gunner was slumped in the back of his vehicle. Two planes were burning on the ground. In the distance, one Junker was still flying with a wing engine on fire. Anton turned on the lights and accelerated across the bumpy desert. Looking back again, he saw the armored car coming after them, its heavy machine gun firing at Hennessy's vehicle. In the distance, two truckloads of enemy soldiers were following the armored car, illuminated by the blazing petrol fire as they left the airfield.

Coming to a rocky mound, Anton turned off his lights, braked and swung sharply behind the hillock. Hennessy went rushing past, his remaining gunner firing at the pursuing armored vehicle.

"The armored car!" Anton yelled to Makanyanga as the six-wheeler approached. Anton pulled the pin from a Mills bomb. Makanyanga fired the Bren as the big machine raced past the mound with its cannon firing. Anton hurled the grenade. He saw a round from the armored car strike Hennessy's truck. The Chevy went down on one wheel, then rolled over and caught fire.

The grenade exploded under the front of the armored car. Almost lifted by the explosion, the front of the car plunged to the ground, scraping forward across the desert like the cowcatcher of a locomotive.

For a moment no one seemed to move. Then a machine gun fired from the rear of the armored car. Too late, Anton went into first gear. He felt a line of bullets saw into the front of his truck. He and Makanyanga jumped down into the darkness. The machine gun continued to fire. Anton ran to his left, then closed on the car and threw another grenade as Makanyanga fired a Thompson from the right. The grenade hit the top edge of the vehicle and exploded. Anton lay flat on the ground. Behind him he could hear steam hissing from the Chevy's radiator. The ammunition and bombs on the truck exploded. He heard men scream as Hennessy's truck blazed.

"Bwana?" called Makanyanga. His deep voice seemed lost in the oily smoke and the explosions that filled the night. He called again, with less strength. "Bwana!"

"I'm waiting for Dr. Hänger," replied Saffron Alavedo to the middle-aged nurse. The heavy olive-skinned woman looked at her with exhausted eyes that had seen too much.

"Then, please, wait right here by the side of the door, Miss, until the doctor has finished. There is no visiting now and he is very busy. We're expecting another train."

"Is there anything I can do to help while I'm waiting?"

"I don't think so." The nurse, Greek, Saffron guessed, stared at her smart green dress and matching high-heeled shoes before she turned and walked rapidly down the corridor past a line of empty gurneys.

Sensing that the men in the nearby beds were staring at her, Saffron put her back against the wall and folded her arms across her chest. She thought of Wellie and what the war was doing to all these boys. She glanced down the long ward and saw her father's physician slowly working his way towards her, talking to his patients one by one. Behind Dr. Hänger, two ladies of the Auxiliary were passing through the ward with the library and cigarette carts. The metal beds, perhaps forty or fifty of them, were no more than three feet apart. Several were surrounded by white cotton screens. Many had chamber pots beneath them. Some men had one or more limbs suspended from cords stretched above their beds. Low groans rose here and there, and occasionally a laugh amidst the quiet chatter. Although two windows were open, the room had that peculiar smell of all crowded institutions, no matter the disinfectant and the care.

From the open door of a private room at the end of the corridor, Saffron

238

heard the voice of Vera Lynn. A scratchy gramophone played two tunes over and over, heartbreakers, the familiar wartime songs of separation and loss and longing.

The boy on the nearest bed kept staring up at Saffron with awkward dropping eyes. On the wall beside the soldier's bed was one of the new anti-espionage security placards. STARVE HIM WITH SILENCE, it demanded. A long-tailed rat, wearing Goebbels-like spectacles and with a white swastika branded in its fur, nibbled at a sack of food labelled "War Secrets."

Saffron took an envelope from her purse and opened the letter she knew by heart.

My darling love . . .

I cannot tell you where we are but you are with me here. If there is sand in this letter it is because there is sand in everything, even in the tins and jars when we open them. In the morning our eyes are stuck shut with sand and grit. I think about you always, especially when I'm on watch at night. Bingham and Gates tease me when they catch me staring at your picture, almost every day, but I know they're only jealous. When I think about you I can't believe how beautiful you are. I can't wait. . . .

Glancing up, almost crying, Saffron caught the young man's eyes on hers. It could be him, she thought.

"Sorry," the boy said quietly.

"That's all right," she said, trying not to look at the dressing that covered the stub of his left arm. "Can I get you anything?"

"Everything," he said, smiling at last.

"My dear," Dr. Hänger interrupted, his voice stern. "You are waiting to see me?"

"Yes," Saffron said, holding out her hand.

"Pardon," he bowed stiffly. "I do not shake hands before I operate."

"Perhaps you don't remember me, Doctor. I am Saffron Alavedo, one of Olivio Alavedo's daughters . . ."

"Ah, yes, of course, child, forgive me." His demeanor adjusted. His black eyes almost smiled. "What may I do for you?"

"May we speak privately?"

"If you wish to, briefly. There is a room just here, now free. Zuch a complicated case, too complicated." He led her to a room off the corridor where a young Egyptian orderly was stripping the bed. Hänger motioned with his head. The man left the room and closed the door.

"I have a personal problem, Doctor, and I don't know who else to talk to."

"Perhaps it is not for me . . ." August Hänger removed his rectangular gold spectacles. He pinched the two red marks on his beaked nose. "It is not my practice to involve myself in personal problems."

"I think I'm pregnant, Dr. Hänger, and I'm not married," she said quickly. "I couldn't go to our family doctor, because he would tell my . . ."

"Your father will not like this, young lady," said Dr. Hänger with concern. He breathed on the lenses of his spectacles one by one, staring closely at each before dusting it against the left cuff of his white coat. This secret was too dangerous to keep from Mr. Alavedo, thought the doctor, not eager to make an enemy of his fierce patient. He recalled hearing it whispered that one of the dwarf's adversaries had perished hideously at the camel abattoir.

"Please help me, Doctor, I just don't know what else to do."

"Very well, my dear. You will come to me at three this afternoon. But I cannot do what may not be done, nor what your father would not wish to be done."

"No, no, it's not that." Saffron straightened her shoulders and looked the surgeon straight in the eye. "I really want this baby. My fiancé, the father, and I are getting married as soon as he gets his leave. But before I tell my family, I just want to make certain that everything is all right, without upsetting anyone."

"At three, then." Dr. Hänger replaced his glasses and stepped to the door. He looked at her for a moment, his eyes larger again. "It will be my pleasure to examine you."

"You seem uneasy, Giscard," said Admiral Danton as he sat in front of de Neuville's desk sipping his calvados.

"I have a number of problems besides this war, Antoine." De Neuville tapped his cigarette holder on his desk. He thought of his mistress, fled to Alexandria, recent government enquiries concerning his antiquities exports, and certain initiatives he feared the vile midget might have under way. At least a few of the treasures from the tomb were now in his possession, but the little *monstre* was still alive, and dangerous.

"We all have problems, Giscard. *La vie, et ses petites crises personnelles.* Who does not?" The admiral scratched his rumpled eyebrows. "But France must come first."

"Help yourself, won't you?" De Neuville gestured at the carafe.

"In case you are hesitating, Giscard, let me remind you that this General de Gaulle has now himself been condemned to death by a French military court." The admiral leaned forward and drummed his fingers on the carafe. "He is officially a traitor to France."

"So I am told," said de Neuville neutrally.

"And here, in Cairo, the Egyptians are screaming Rommel's name in the streets. Their young officers are studying German, waiting for the moment to rise up against the British. King Faruq himself drank champagne when the *Queen Elizabeth* was sunk in Alexandria harbor."

"So they say," de Neuville said. Although he had chosen sides, more or less, he still had forebodings that things might not end well.

"What have you learned of the defenses of Bir Hakeim?"

De Neuville leaned forward. His pale features became alert. "I have talked twice more to Colonel Broché and done him certain favors that we need not mention. Yesterday he returned to Bir Hakeim."

"What have you learned?"

"Now they have four thousand men. Broché says the minefields and the entrenchments are very strong, but they are always short of water, and of transport if they wish to break out. He believes the British do that to make them hold. But his men will fight, especially the Legion. Those old *canailles* love a desert siege."

"I asked you to learn about the minefields . . ."

"Altogether, they say the Gazala Line has more mines than ever before seen in war. Perhaps one million. Broché says the Free French themselves have laid fifty thousand around Bir Hakeim."

"Is there no way in?"

"That was more than I could learn. But the supplies come from the northeast, so perhaps there . . ."

"Giscard, this is war. 'Perhaps' is dangerous . . ."

De Neuville nodded. "But the colonel worries that the box is weakest to the south. Fewer mines, weaker regiments, furthest from all British support."

Admiral Danton put down his glass. "Now that, Giscard, that is something our Nazi friends will understand. But *les chleuhs*, the Germans, always want more, and you must do your duty."

"Glad to see you a trifle more sound, old boy." Adam Penfold took the glass of apricot nectar from the hands of his friend. "Looking more like your old self."

"I'm not sure that is how I wish to look," said the dwarf, rocking from side to side with a touch of merriment, unaware of his orange mustache. A gauze bandage still covered the crown of his head, but the bracing disciplines of vanity had returned, and a red tarbush rested atop it. His short legs, one still bandaged, were extended on the wicker chaise longue on which he reposed. A brocade blanket of Turkish design was wrapped about his shoulders.

"Are those spectacles comfortable?" asked Penfold, concerned that the overly large sunglasses were slipping from the dwarf's tiny nose, made even smaller by the fire he had endured many years ago. "Perhaps I should read to you." He lifted a copy of the *Gazette* from the table that rested between them on the poop deck.

"No thank you, my lord, no need." The dwarf peered across the river, proud of the new shaded glasses that protected his healing eye. He was aware that they brought a dash of adventure to his look, and added even more of the inscrutable to his appearance. "They are made from Perspex, the new material used in the canopies of fighter aircraft, you see. Spitfires and other new machines of war." The dwarf's countenance was barely visible behind the broad tinted lenses. "How do you like them, eh?"

"Why, certainly. Most flattering, actually."

"They are the same glasses worn by that German general in all the photographs, the very 'body and soul of war,' they call him," added Olivio.

"Yes, the Desert Fox. Seems to be rather the best sort of Hun, if you know what I mean. No end to mischief, though, when those devils finally find a good one." Penfold tapped his right foot with his cane. "Rommel reminds me of old von Lettow-Vorbeck in the Kaiser's War, the chap who gave me the bits of shrapnel I'm still carrying around in this game leg. Far enough from the home front that he doesn't have to act like a real German, what?"

"My lord," began the dwarf. His tone had changed. He was keen to end this frivolity and get to the bone of the business: the intertwined needs for safety, profit and vengeance. With his only other friend and partner away at the war, he would need his lordship, despite his unsuitability for the harsher strokes of life. At least the old fencer still carried his sword cane.

"Look at this will you! THE LIFE OF A GAME: IS CRICKET LOSING GROUND?" read Penfold, wondering why the world could not just slow down. "What rubbish! MANY PEOPLE BELIEVE THAT THE PEAK OF CRICKET HAS ALREADY BEEN REACHED AND PASSED. . . . TIMES CHANGE. . . . WE CANNOT NOW EXPECT TO ENJOY BEARBAITING . . . THE ELIZABETHAN GAME OF COURT TENNIS OR ROYAL TENNIS, ONCE SO POPULAR IN FRANCE THAT THE WORKS OF MOLIÈRE WERE EVERYWHERE PERFORMED WITHIN THE WALLS OF TENNIS COURTS . . ."

"If you please . . ." The dwarf tried to conceal his exasperation. Court tennis? Molière? One day he would punish his old master by reading to him in Portuguese the religious notices from the *Anglo Lusitano*, the Goan newspaper published in Bombay.

"VON RIBBENTROP HAS PRIVATE AUDIENCE WITH THE POPE. Deserve each other, should've thought. U-BOATS . . . 500TH ANNIVERSARY OF ETON COLLEGE . . . RAF BOMBS BERLIN . . . JAPANESE BATTLE AMERICANS IN THE PHILIPPINES. Too much going on, really, can't read it all. CUBA LOOKS TO GENERAL BATISTA . . . ROOSEVELT PROCLAIMS AMERICA THE ARSENAL OF DEMOCRACY. . . . COSSASKS STORM GERMAN BASE . . ."

"Please, my lord, we have enemies closer than Russia." Olivio stared at the embankment where Tariq patrolled up and down with his qurbash. "Our property has been looted. I have been bombed. Our friends are fighting in the desert. Must we worry over Cuba?" The dwarf wrung his hands with impatience, trying to think how to make this kind man understand the world. "Remember Voltaire."

"What? The old Frenchy?"

"Indeed, sir. He said in times of trouble, each of us must cultivate his own garden."

"How French."

"Speaking of the French, my lord. In order to protect us from any wickedness by that de Neuville, I have now filed an antiquities discovery report with the government." After removing a few modest treasures, thought the dwarf.

"Well done. Much the best, you know, to do these things properly. Must say, I was sorry you'd neglected to do it earlier . . ."

"With a little help from a friendly clerk, the matter of the date will be uncertain." The dwarf licked away his mustache with his thick pointed tongue. "And wartime provides opportunities for confusion. Even now the British are building fortifications near the pyramids, and the Museum is boxing its finest treasures. What does our little find mean at such a time?" Too much to some, thought Olivio.

"But there is one troubling matter. In my haste to do the right thing, my lord, and with my eye still cloudy, our report indicated that we have two mummies in the tomb, instead of just the one we still possess. The other, as you know, was thieved from us by the dog de Neuville or his agents. He is the same man who seeks to steal the heart of Miss Gwenn, while Mr. Anton is at war defending us all." That should keep his lordship's honest gaze staring in the right direction, thought Olivio.

"Damned rascal." Penfold did his best to follow, but wished his friend would leave off business and instead give him the advice he needed: what to do about Mme. Pantelides. It seemed these Greek women liked to have a man to manage. Having lavished upon him her purse and body, to the point of embarrassing exhaustion, she was now pressing forcefully into the deepest corners of his privacy. Was he still grieving for Lady Penfold, whose long neck finally had been broken in a hunting accident two years before? A sentiment that had never occurred to him. Did he intend to continue living in Mr. Alavedo's guest house? Englishmen liked extended visits. Would he ever be inclined to take a second Lady Penfold? Good God.

"May I ask your lordship to assist me in recovering what the Frenchman has stolen from us, and from Egypt?"

"Can't think how I could help, really . . ."

"I wish to call on Monsieur de Neuville. If things are to be arranged without too much distress, he must first take me seriously. But he looks down at me, Gallic hauteur, or worse. But at you, he must look up. In his heart, you see, every Frenchman wishes he were an English gentleman."

"You don't say?" Penfold opened his eyes wide and shook his head. "Hopeless, really. Certainly explains a lot."

"And it is known you went to school with the ambassador, the most powerful man in Egypt."

"Never much took to him. Bit too big and sporty. Too many fancy waistcoats." Penfold turned and looked at the gangway. "But here's a better sight."

Saffron waved as she approached along the embankment with the twins. The younger girls left her at the end of the gangway and ran into the bar while she climbed to the poop deck. Saffron kissed both men and sat at the foot of her father's chaise.

"How are you today, Papa?"

"Better, child, thank you."

"Oh, good," Saffron said happily. "Can we talk about Wellington again, please? You promised me you'd think about it."

"Of course, my dear, and I have." He took her hand and smiled.

Adam Penfold tried to look uninterested. He glanced across the river, then waved at Rosemary and Cardamom as the twins sat down on the deck below with a plate of tea cakes. Tiago crouched beside them with the tray from the money drawer in the bar.

"I've thought of all you've said about this boy," added Olivio in his most weighty voice, "and how well we know what Wellington is like, and how much his parents have cared for us."

The dwarf paused. His heart was heavy as he looked at his lovely daughter. He understood the reason for her urgency, and knew the pain of her secret. What choice had he now but to make the best of it? Not daring to risk his wrath, Dr. Hänger had shared Saffron's secret. Did she know he would? the dwarf wondered, admiring the gift for indirection that this daughter sometimes shared with him. He smiled and continued.

"But you are both so young, and Wellington's future is so uncertain. Yet, war or not, we must take the opportunities of life. So, yes, you have my blessing, child, always." Olivio's eye glistened as his daughter jumped up.

"Oh, Father!" she cried, bending and kissing him, hugging him with both arms, nearly pulling him from his seat. "Oh, Father, Father!"

"By Jove!" said Penfold, waving down at the twins and Tariq. "Champagne!" he called. The twins squealed and ran up the steps to the poop deck.

"I'm getting married," Saffron said to her sisters, taking each by the hand.

"Of course," said Cardamom and Rosemary, kissing her, then their father, then Lord Penfold. "We knew that. When are you going to do it?"

Saffron looked at Olivio before replying. "If it's all right with Father, perhaps we could hold the wedding on Wellie's next leave, as soon as possible. Would that be all right?" she asked with excitement.

"Of course, my dearest, but this ceremony is not to be the modest,

hideaway affair of which your young man spoke. No, no. When the Ala-
vedos play music, le tout Caire must dance. Ha! Ha!" The little man
clapped his hands as Tariq set down a bucket with two bottles of champagne. "And bring up Tiago, Tariq, and a glass for the little lad as well.
My son must drink to his family's good fortune." Olivio spread his arms
wide as he explained his plans.

"Four hundred invitation notices are already at the printer, with the date
to follow, in the wartime way," announced the dwarf, not revealing that
the invitations would be sent out in sprinklings, fifty one day, forty another, and so on, to excite gossip and sharpen the envy of those not yet
invited. The perfect opportunity for a little social vengeance, the chance
to reopen a few old wounds. Sometimes exclusion was more satisfying than
hospitality. He caught his breath and continued as Tariq opened the Heidsieck.

"The Basilique d'Héliopolis will be an arbor. The guests will vie for
places while the organ and trumpets play old German music and the pigeons soar about in the eaves. The bishop himself will unite you." For a
price, Olivio thought bitterly. And a further price to disregard the fact
that this groom was not a Holy Roman, that his spiritual spring was not
the Vatican, but Henry VIII.

Olivio saw Saffron's shining eyes and steepled his fingers together and
leaned forward as best he could, invigorated by the excitement of the spec-
tacle.

"Then the swords of His Majesty's Hussars will cross above your heads
on the steps as the maids shower you with rose petals and you enter the
Daimler to drive down the Avenue des Pyramides to the party. Finally a
feast to gorge all Cairo! Cymbals and tumblers. Dancers with tiers of candles flaming on their heads. Tents not seen since Alexander. The fruits of
our farms, delicacies and sweetmeats, the canapés of Europe and the *mazzah*
of the Levant, great bleeding roasts and baked fishes and stuffed fowls, and
all the treats of ancient Goa, especially *feni*, patiently brewed from the sap
of palm trees, and, for a few true friends, *fontainhas*, cashew feni, the elixir
of the gods . . ."

The dwarf stopped, exhausted, hoping he had transformed his daughter's
anxiety into happy anticipation.

"Father! Father!" Saffron leaned close to him and took his small stiff
hands in hers and kissed his cheek while the twins clapped and Tiago
dipped one hand in his champagne.

"Yum yum. Sounds splendid," said Penfold, smiling. "Should do this sort of thing more often. Good thing you have four more daughters."

"His excellency will see you now." Munir stood well back from the doorway to let Tariq carry his master into the library. For an instant the massive Nubian pinned Munir with hard eyes as he passed.

Excellency? thought Penfold. This jumped-up Frog has become an excellency? What was happening to the world? There was so little left that he still understood. Even personal relationships, with a few exceptions, had become so difficult that he was learning to isolate himself.

Tariq entered the room like a conquistador and gently rested Olivio Alavedo in the leather armchair facing de Neuville's desk. He took his place behind his master's chair while the old Englishman crossed the room with smart taps of his cane. To Penfold's eye, their host, in his overly pressed grey suit, was dressed with the tight formality of a clerk, not a gentleman.

"Good morning, Baron Penfold, Mr. Alavedo." De Neuville stepped around his desk. He shook the Englishman's hand and nodded down at the dwarf. "Your servant may leave us. May I offer you coffee or a glass of wine? Perhaps a cigar."

Though tempted, keen for a drink, Penfold declined but accepted a cigar. Olivio shook his head and gestured for Tariq to leave. The Nubian left and closed the door.

"Exciting days in Cairo," said de Neuville. "I understand they are burning stacks of secret papers on the roof of the British Embassy, in case the Germans find their way. Half-burned papers, all the secrets of empire, are floating down in the streets. Ash Wednesday, they're calling it." The Frenchman paused to enjoy the point. "The peanut vendors are making their paper cones from the charred scraps of secret British documents."

"In Berlin and Paris and Vienna," said Penfold with rare annoyance, "they burn books and papers every day." He drew out his half-hunter to check that they were precisely on time, wondering why his little friend had been so unusually strict on this point.

"We hear of plans for the British to abandon Egypt," pursued de Neuville. "Half your army to flee to the Sudan, the other half to Palestine."

"I believe old Bonaparte over there abandoned Egypt back in 1799, not to mention his army," said Penfold with persistence, using the head of his cane to gesture at the painting of Napoleon in Alexandria. He restrained

himself from mentioning that France's greatest general had deserted his
armies in the snows of Russia, in the sands of Egypt, in the mountains of
Iberia, and finally in the fields of Belgium.

"We have come to offer you an opportunity," interrupted the dwarf,
disappointed that his friend had revealed his irritation. He himself was
dressed like an Ottoman gentleman of business, in dark trousers and a
stambouline. The small black frock coat set off a white wing collar and
silk tie, held in place by a large grey pearl that matched his eye. A narrow
white bandage circled his head like a bandana. In the chair beside him,
Penfold was searching for the smoldering tip of his wooden match. It had
fallen onto his magnificent new chalk-stripe suit, the first reward of the
early yields from their farm at Al Lahun.

"To offer me an opportunity?" De Neuville settled back easily behind
his desk. He gazed down at his small guest. How had this hideous midget
survived such an explosion? He recalled seeing the little beast's magnificent
companion in the dining car of the Antiquities Train. Much as women
were drawn by money and influence, could there be enough of either in
the world to lure a lady to such a creature, or was it possible that he had
some other, more sordid charm? He tried to imagine Alavedo being saved
by the woman's naked body, but the notion of it was too revolting.

"An opportunity to retain your reputation and your freedom and your
collection in Egypt," said Olivio. "If you return the boat of the dead, the
missing mummy and the other stolen artifacts, we will consider our affairs
settled and your professional life will be undisturbed. Then only one other
matter will remain between us."

"And that?"

"The delicate matter of Mrs. Rider . . ."

The Frenchman stared at the little man before replying. How dare this
bastard midget even speak of his personal life? Of course, the war had
complicated his affair and confused the Englishwoman, temporarily giving
her penniless gypsy husband a presentable way of life in Egypt. But he
would recover his mistress in due time. This damned creature before him
could go to hell. Perhaps he should motor to Alexandria and bring Gwenn
back. He missed her, and was increasingly troubled by the suspicion that
things would be different between them when she returned to Cairo.

"Monsieur Alavedo," he began just as the telephone rang on his desk.
De Neuville looked at the instrument and hesitated.

"Please," said Penfold, checking his watch again. Was this the cause for punctuality? He gestured towards the telephone. "By all means."

De Neuville lifted the receiver. A few words from the telephone could be heard in the quiet room.

"Monsieur de Neuville? . . . archeology . . . problems . . . export manifests . . ."

"Yes, Inspector," said de Neuville, pressing the receiver tightly against his ear, trying to interrupt what might be overheard as the loud voice spoke. "Of course, Mustafa Bey. I will review the reports at once. An oversight, perhaps, my staff. May I ring you back? Yes . . . Goodbye, sir."

De Neuville set down the phone. He stared at the dwarf through the cigar smoke. His lips were thin as razors.

Olivio's grey eye, round and open as an owl's, did not blink. At last, this arrogant Frenchman was beginning to learn with whom he was dealing. Soon, the dwarf thought, he must give the archeologist his favorite present: the gift of a new enemy. It was almost time to let the Free French learn, indirectly, of course, of this man's duplicities.

De Neuville heard a noise in the hallway outside but ignored it. He glanced up at the wall at one of Napoleon's Mamluks.

"But before we leave," said Alavedo, "if you do not accept the opportunity we bring, we will take it as declined.

"Ridiculous. I have stolen nothing. How can I return what is not in my possession?"

"Then the Inspector General will call again, and after him, the National Police." The dwarf touched his stickpin and raised his voice. "Tariq!"

The door opened at once. Tariq entered and lifted his master from his seat. Olivio's dark grey trousers and small black English shoes, their toe caps polished bright as Caesar's shield, hung down over the Nubian's right arm.

"Goodbye, gentlemen," called de Neuville from his desk.

As Penfold followed into the hallway, brushing ash from his lapel, he saw the unconscious body of Munir sitting in a chair at the far end of the passage. His mouth was open, two silver teeth visible.

— *18* —

"Von Decken," said the general. His tone was vigorous but his expression was drawn as he squinted into the rising sun. His eyes were sunken with jaundice and fatigue. "We have lost more petrol and aircraft to these English desert raiders. While their big units blunder about or bury themselves in fixed positions, these hornets are killing us. For every Stuka or Messerschmitt they destroy on the ground, there will be more British tanks to fight my Panzers, more British warplanes to bomb our columns, more comrades who will be killed." The general was wearing his checked scarf. His long dark-olive leather overcoat was open, the peaked collar raised. "I will give you more men and transport, but you must finish this job."

"Jawohl, Herr General."

"Join us here for a moment. I wish you to understand." Rommel turned and walked under the broad canvas tarpaulin that stretched from the top of his Mammoth. On the other side of the canvas was an eight-wheeled Büssing armored car from the general's Kampfstaffel. A large-frame antenna shrouded over it like the stays of an umbrella.

Colonel Bayerlein and three other senior officers acknowledged Major von Decken as he joined them beside the map table in the shade of the canvas. Bayerlein made an introduction.

"General von Bismarck, this is Major von Decken, assigned to special operations."

Ernst saluted the tall bullet-headed general with close-cropped hair, already celebrated for leading his 21st Panzer Division into battle from the sidecar of a motorcycle after a band played old Prussian marches to encourage the Panzergrenadiers as they mounted up.

Rommel set down his field glasses and placed both hands on the table.

"We cannot let our war of maneuvre become their war of attrition. Once your opponent is one pawn up, gentlemen, you cannot afford a game of exchange." He paused and examined the tanned hard faces gathered around the map.

"So far our Panzers have won because our doctrine of concentration of armor, speed and attack has prevailed over the British concept of scattering their tanks around to probe the enemy and provide support for the infantry. And we have done a better job of coordinating our Panzers with other arms, the infantry and air support. At the beginning, the British were still driven by obsolete experiences from the last war, and even by their nostalgia for cavalry. But the enemy is learning. So each time we must do better, with less. And with America and Japan in the war, it's time we concluded this campaign."

Von Decken thought of what his own driver had said the day before. That Rommel had a sixth sense for war. *Fingerspitzengefühl*, an instinct in his fingertips.

The general swept one hand along the map. "The battle for North Africa will be won or lost somewhere between here and Alexandria or El Alamein. And if we take Egypt, we get the Middle East and all the oil we need to win the war." The commander looked up and stared at von Decken as he banged the map with his knuckles.

"For the enemy, we must make this strip of Africa into a devil's garden. Mines, artillery, booby traps, tanks, aircraft, shock troops must work together so that at the point of conflict we are always stronger. They will be stronger everywhere else, so we must choose where to fight."

Rommel paused and rubbed his eyes, blood-red from the sand and sun. His prominent cheekbones stood out like white knobs against the darker skin around them.

"And to maintain the advantage when we fight, we must conceal our intentions until it is too late for the enemy to adjust."

Before continuing, Rommel stopped and read a wireless message handed him by Aldinger.

"But first there is still Tobruk. We cannot attack Egypt unless we take Tobruk. Our early attempts have failed. The first time we tried, last year, the Australians counterattacked every night. The new garrison, Indians and South Africans mostly, is not so vigorous. The British resupply them from the sea. To carry the attack, we must flank the Gazala Line and begin by destroying these British boxes. First, Bir Hakeim, then Knightsbridge. While our Panzers sweep further south, the Italians of the Ariete Division will take Bir Hakeim after we clear a path through the mines. Most of the defenders are Foreign Legion. The Thirteenth Half-Brigade. They will be stubborn. Some are from the Fatherland."

Same bastards who fought us in Massawa, thought Ernst, growing more interested.

"When do we march?" asked von Bismarck without taking his eyes from the map.

"At night, so the RAF cannot warn them or attack. The next full moon. Soon. Operation Venezia. Everything we have will be on the move: both Panzer divisions and the Ninetieth Light, the entire Italian *Corpo di Manovra*, and our 'hump' of supply trucks. Thousands of vehicles crossing the desert at night at eight miles per hour. We must pre-position petrol dumps. If any tank turrets have been jammed by the sandstorms, dismantle them and clean them now. Take enough water for four days: three quarts for each man per day, four for every truck, eight for every tank."

The general looked at his officers one by one. Ernst's stomach tightened. He felt Rommel's intense blue eyes drill into him before the general resumed.

"The Pioneers will line the route with shaded lamps set inside cut-out petrol tins. Sappers will clear paths through the minefields. The day before, to the north along the Gazala Line, we will confuse them with smoke generators, dust clouds from our propeller trucks, aerial attacks and columns of lorries moving in false directions. As an old Italian soldier said, those enterprises are best which can be concealed until the moment of their fullfilment. Questions, gentlemen?"

"*Nein*, Herr General," said von Bismarck. The other officers shook their heads.

"Very well," said Rommel. "By first light, the Afrika Korps must be in position to surprise the enemy with ten thousand vehicles behind their lines to the south, around Bir Hakeim. Then, gentlemen, if you give me Tobruk, I will give you Africa."

Ernst felt a chill shoot down his spine. This was the moment he had awaited for over twenty years.

* * *

All three of their trucks were destroyed. Anton and Makanyanga lay shoulder to shoulder in the little depression and watched the line of German vehicles and Italian infantry search the desert in the moonlight. Once or twice the headlight of a turning truck or armored car swept across them as they pressed their heads into the hard ground.

"I'm afraid no one else made it," said Anton as the enemy moved back towards the burning air base. He thought the fault was mostly his. But at least he'd split the patrol before the attack. The rest of the men should be all right. "Time to move." He picked up the Thompson and stood and stretched. "We better get as far from here as we can before daylight."

Makanyanga groaned as he rose.

"Are you all right?"

Makanyanga grinned. "Once again my bwana has led me into danger." He flinched as Anton pulled off his long coat and shirt and examined the African's left shoulder as best he could.

"Not too bad," Anton said. "Deep, no bullet, but I think the wound's filthy with threads and muck. Stay here while I check our wrecks for water or a medical kit."

Hennessy's truck, upside down and smoldering, was black and still hot from end to end. He tried to free Hennessy's charred body, but it and two others were trapped beneath the vehicle. Singeing one hand, Anton freed the long leather strap of a compass case from one man's shoulder, whose he could not tell. He crept around his own burned-out Chevy, unable to recover anything useful. Nearby he stumbled across a canteen and a knapsack apparently thrown free by the explosion. The pack contained a sweater and shirt, a pocket torch, cigarettes, two tins of sardines and a housewife. Anton checked that the little hold-all was properly equipped with a needle and thread. Better than nothing. But he found no sulfonamide with which to powder the wound against infection.

Anton washed Makanyanga's wound with water and tore the clean shirt in strips to bind it. This was the kind of infecting wound that might kill a white man, but the Africans he'd known seemed to survive them better. He put the half-empty canteen in the pack and the pack on his back. He knelt and retied Makanyanga's boot laces, and his own. Then he checked the compass, and the two men began to walk east. The half moon followed them across the sky.

When the orange disc of the sun finally edged up over the horizon,

Anton paused and leaned the Thompson on his pack on the ground. He stared around in all directions. Nothing. It was going to be a hot one.

"Are you going to feed me, bwana?"

"Lie down on this, Makie, and get some rest." Anton removed his sheepskin coat and spread it on the ground. Makanyanga sat and Anton saw that the binding of his wound was dark and wet. He handed Makanyanga his service revolver and picked up the Thompson. "I'll see what I can find." He began walking into the sun.

He tried exploring several wadis for water, digging at the lowest point the way thirsty elephants do with their tusks. In one wadi he found a cactus. He broke off a thick leaf and pulped it between two rocks. He sucked the pulp. It was bitter and painful to his throat.

Farther on, Anton saw a distant desert gazelle outlined against the sun like a child's cutout against a light box. Hopeless, he knew, with the short-range Thompson. As he advanced, the small antelope fled.

When he returned, Makanyanga, sweating and feverish, was already not himself.

Anton sat on the coat beside the African and took a tin of sardines from the knapsack. He opened it with his pocketknife and shared the fish one by one. They sucked the oil from the tin. Anton opened the canteen.

"Take two sips, and then we'll see if you can walk a bit."

Makanyanga sipped slowly, and Rider wet his lips. Anton pulled his friend to his feet, then steadied him before they started off. They walked for two hours, pausing often. Occasionally Anton took the big man's good arm across his own shoulder.

When the sun was nearly at its height, they stopped near a patch of thorn bush. Makanyanga slumped down in the sketchy shade. Anton placed the revolver on the coat beside his friend. The hard surface of the desert burned Rider's hand when he touched it. The ground was the hottest he could remember, perhaps a hundred and thirty degrees or more.

Staring down near his feet, shielding his eyes from the sun, Anton thought he saw a small patch of crusty desert stir as if moved by a miniature earthquake. A swarm of Saharan silver ants poured from a hole like tiny bits of lava, pushing grains of sand to the side.

Anton watched the ants separate and dart off in different directions, scavenging the desert for nourishment. Their legs moved quickly, barely touching the hot ground. No other creature, he was certain, could tolerate such high surface temperatures. Like beachgoers hopping on scorching sand, trying to touch the ground as little as possible, some of the ants ran with two of their six legs raised in the air. Others seemed alternately to sprint and tumble and hop. Some ants, returning from their sortie, climbed the thorn bush, apparently in search of the higher cooler air. There they extended their bodies skyward from the ends of the thin branches and reached upward into the fresher air with their long front legs. Finally returning to its hole, each silver ant dragged a few grains of sand down after it to help close the entrance to the nest.

Anton stood and set out again on his own. After an hour he became dizzy and collapsed briefly in a small patch of shade near a spindly cactus. After three hours he had found neither food nor water.

As Anton returned, his face burned and blistered, he saw a thin wisp of white smoke rising near Makanyanga.

Sweating heavily, his eyes hot red circles, the African was sharpening his knife on his belt. A dead lizard lay on a flat stone beside him. Anton sat and watched. The spicy smell of the burning tamarisk bush made him still hungrier.

Makanyanga turned the lizard onto its mottled brown back, then carefully cut its pale throat. He pinched the small wound in his fingers and lifted the long-bodied reptile to offer the first drink to Anton. Rider shook his head. Makanyanga sucked the body dry. Then he skinned it, spitted it on a thorn branch and held the white body over the low fire. They ate eagerly, enjoying the flesh, crisp and firmer than chicken.

"How did you find the lizard?" said Anton hoarsely when he felt able to speak.

"I didn't, bwana. He came for the ants," whispered Makanyanga. "Did you not see his burrow? They are always near the nest holes."

Anton shook his head, too exhausted to smile.

"Soon the ants will come out again," Makanyanga added, "to eat the skin of the lizard."

The afternoon cooled. They each took a sip of water, then continued walking east.

"*Pole, pole,*" muttered Makanyanga from time to time. Slowly, slowly. Anton's own feet were cracked and blistered with desert sores. He considered the old trick of cutting out the toecaps and heels of his boots, but left them as they were.

While the light was still clear, Anton made Makanyanga sit and permit him to examine his shoulder. He considered trying to sew it up, but knew the wound was far too dirty. Open and sticky, the deep cut was thick with pus. Flies tried to settle on the lips of the wound. Anton rubbed the bandages with sand to clean them, then retied the strips of khaki shirting.

The two men rose and struggled on for another hour. Just as Anton was considering stopping for the night, he saw a bird circling high above in the distance. A desert hawk, he guessed, scouting for the wagtails and doves and other migratory birds on which it feasted.

"Come on, Makie, you damn lazy African." Anton took Makanyanga's right arm across his shoulder and tried to carry all the weight he could. After a time he made out a battered truck, abandoned in the desert like the carcass of some desiccated animal. With fresh energy, the two pushed forward.

As they approached, a small animal lifted its tan and white head from something near the vehicle and gazed towards them, raising its pointed nose to catch their scent.

"*Bweha!*" whispered Makanyanga.

Anton dropped Makanyanga's arm and gripped the short Thompson as he advanced. Long-legged and dog-like, with a yellowish brown coat mixed with red and black, the animal sneezed twice, then double-barked several times in growing excitement. Its snout was bloody. Anton raised the Thompson. The animal turned to run. He fired one short burst, aiming high to allow for the range. Untouched, the jackal growled once and loped off.

The vehicle was a Fiat. The long bed and cab were both empty, probably cleaned out by the Senussi or some other desert tribe, Anton reckoned. Both doors were open. The windshield and hood had been drilled by two rows of bullets from the air. On the rocky ground beside the driver's door was the almost naked body of a young Italian soldier. Though evidently wounded first, it was a cut to the throat that had killed him. One side of the man's belly was torn open where the jackal had been at work.

Makanyanga rested on the passenger seat while Anton searched for something to eat or drink. He raised the hood and took the cap off the radiator. He could see no water, or reach any with his finger. He dropped in a pebble and heard a splash.

"Nearly finished," he told Makanyanga, handing him the canteen. "No need to spoil our last water if the stuff in there's no good." Makanyanga drank and passed the canteen to Anton, who drained it, tasting the chlorine at the bottom. He then took down the short pick that was mounted on the side of the open truck. He climbed under the lorry with the pick and the canteen. Banging with the pick, he knocked the rusty bung off the base of the radiator. A rush of water flushed out into the waiting canteen. The instant it was filled, Anton put his head under the drain hole and gulped the last rusty water that ran out.

Feeling stronger, Anton took off his own boots and socks and Makanyanga's. He threw away the socks. They only made things worse once one's feet began to bleed. The walking had turned the usual unhealing desert sores into filthy weeping blisters. He crawled under the Fiat and opened the oil pan, draining the waste motor oil into his cupped hands. He bathed his own feet thoroughly with the oil, then did the same for Makanyanga. He spread some over the burns on his face. Finally he rubbed their feet clean with sand and put their boots back on.

The sun fell quickly. Anton packed Makanyanga as comfortably as he could in the cab for the night, wrapping him in the sheepskin coat. He walked around the truck and dragged the body of the Italian into the desert. He took the sweater from the knapsack and lay down in the bed of the truck.

Trembling with cold, he woke before sunrise and climbed down and lit a Springbok, despite the renewed dryness of his mouth. He looked up, found Orion and Gemini, still bright and sharp and cool in the desert night. Again he thought of the men he had been responsible for, Hennessy and Stoner and the seven others who had died. Had he killed them? With that aggressive instinct about which Gwenn always complained? Or was it just war, and bad luck, and what was bound to happen?

The early sun hit the shattered windscreen and Makanyanga began to stir. Anton opened the driver's door and tried to speak to his shivering friend, but heard little that was coherent in reply. At the top of the canteen there was a slight skim of frozen water. Anton wet his own lips, then held it to his friend's mouth, but Makanyanga would not drink. Anton pulled him from the cab and tried to get him to stand and walk. The African opened his eyes and leaned away from the truck. "*Habari*, bwana?"

"We must walk, Makie. Take my arm."

After an hour they saw several low huts in the distance and struggled on.

They found a dozen crumbling huts, abandoned, made of mud and brush with palm-thatch roofs, gathered around what appeared to be a deep-set well. Anton left Makanyanga sitting on a rock outside one of the huts. The entrance to the well was cut into the ground in a small sheltered depression between two hillocks. Nearby, Anton spotted the split-hooved tracks of a small antelope. He knelt and traced the sculpted impressions with his fingertips. Probably a Dorcas gazelle, he reckoned. He stood and prayed for a shot.

He hurried down the rough steps, perhaps centuries old, that were cut in a narrowing spiral that descended sixty feet to the mouth of the well.

Halfway down, as his fingers traced the stone to his left, Rider noticed a series of worn engravings cut into the limestone wall of the descent. He made out an antelope and two ostriches. They were drawn simply with a few spare lines. But some ancient hand had caught the essence of each animal's shape and movement.

He found that the well had been filled in with a hardened slurry of some cement-like material, now cracked and dried into fragments but still serving to block the opening. He clawed at the cement with the tips of his fingers. Damned Wops, he thought. He closed his eyes and slowly climbed back up the worn steps. He followed the gazelle tracks until he lost them on a long stone outcrop. Then he walked back to Makanyanga.

"Sorry, Makie, but the Italians got here first," he said hoarsely. "Probably old Marshall Badoglio in their first war out here."

Anton made a small fire. After finishing the sardines, they huddled together in silence before he helped Makanyanga to lie down in one of the huts. Another day or two, he thought, and they would be drinking their own urine.

In the morning a harsh qibli was blowing. Long violent gusts drove sand through the decaying walls of their hut. Anton lay beside his friend with his coat spread over both of them, scratching himself, trying to kill the lice or other insects that had found them in the night. He wondered if he smelled as bad as Makanyanga. His tongue was swollen, his mouth too parched to speak.

When the wind died, the light brightened to full day. Makanyanga was delirious with thirst and fever. Using his knife, Anton cut up the knapsack and fashioned a cap with a flap hanging down his neck, like an old Foreign Legionnaire. He shook the canteen and wet Makanyanga's lips. He took a mouthful himself and set off with the Thompson, leaving the pistol and canteen behind with Makanyanga. He had to find help or his friend would die.

He walked until he could no longer stand. Parched and dizzy, he paused frequently, then set off again. After a while he could not discern the horizon in the noon-time light. The hovering bands of wavy light that created mirages and made gunnery difficult at midday turned his sight to jelly.

Near delirium, he let the Thompson fall from his shoulder and slumped down beside a clump of camel thorn. He saw a green sand viper slither away as he collapsed. Glancing up, blinking, his dreamy eyes observed a trembling grey-brown image that resembled first an oncoming elephant or rhino, he thought, then perhaps a train or truck.

He rose on his knees, then stumbled to his feet as the half-track bore down on him. Too late, he made out the German markings and reached for the submachine gun.

Waiting for the dinner ration, Anton sat with his back to the sun and shared a precious smoke with two other prisoners. They were in a small compound, kept aside from the mass of fenced prisoners with other men from the RAF and the SAS and the Long Range Desert Group. Fifty yards away were two huge barbed wire pens, each filled with thousands of British Empire prisoners taken during Battleaxe and Crusader and the other early battles. Italian sentries, relaxed in long floppy coats, rifles slung barrel-down over their shoulders, patrolled outside between the different fences.

Rider was barefoot, his legs extended on the ground before him. His feet were still swollen. His boots rested at his side.

He was lucky, Anton thought. He'd survived once more, luckier than many other men of his patrol. He still felt sick about the men he'd lost. Hennessy and Stoner, and all the others. All for a few aircraft and some petrol. But their signalman had radioed back masses of information, and perhaps what they'd done had saved a lot more lives. At least every man had known what to expect.

"What'd they do with your mate?" a young pilot asked him, fixing his dirty white scarf around his throat.

"Took him off to the prison hospital at Derna," Anton said, passing back the V cigarette. He was confident that Makanyanga would survive once more.

"Lucky bloke," said the third man, his left arm in a sling. "That's where I started. Grub's a lot better. When I was there, bleedin' Rommel himself came by, just to be sure we was gettin' treated proper."

Anton thought of the first meal his German captors had fed to him and Makanyanga in the desert, the finest breakfast he'd ever had: porridge and goat's milk.

"Should be coming for you any time now," said the pilot to Anton. "Probably before scoff. They always come to question any new prisoner in this cage, once they've had a chance to look through your kit and any papers. When they can, they use someone who knows about your line of work. Luftwaffe intelligence for us. Very good at it they are, and not too nasty, thanks to Harry, the Desert Fox."

Anton turned his head as the fence gate swung open. An open-bed Fiat drove into the compound, like the one he and Makanyanga had found in the desert. The prisoners stood quickly and formed a line beside it, grumbling as they waited for their food.

"Any surprises?" called one from the end of the line. "Roast lamb? Red currant jelly?"

"Same as yesterday," another hollered back. "Wop hardtack and these meat tins the burial parties filled up on the Russian front. If we give 'em your watch, we'll get some Chianti to drown it in."

The Italian driver and several prisoners laughed as the truck pulled out.

An open Volkswagen field car swung through the gate.

Ernst von Decken jumped down, his sidearm in a holster. He stalked about the pen, limping heavily on his stump in the sandy ground.

Their eyes met. Anton jumped up, grinning.

"Mein Engländer!" Ernst roared, clapping him violently on both arms. "Get in. We must talk."

Anton grabbed his boots and climbed into the Kübelwagen. Ernst sped out through the gate.

They drove east for half an hour as fast as the car would go. It was impossible to talk. Anton squeezed into his boots and tied them loosely. Ernst turned to look at him and shook his head. The Volkswagen bounced and jarred wildly on the rough trigh that ran parallel to the crowded Via Balbia. Ernst banged on the horn as they passed occasional Italian and German vehicles masked in clouds of dust.

Finally they stopped at the top of one of the rocky escarpments that rose along the plateau behind the coast.

"That's my camp down there." Ernst pointed to a collection of armored and soft-skinned vehicles, many of them British, that were scattered under camouflage across a small depression. He got out and opened a hinged wooden box in the back seat. He took out a packet of cigarettes and two bottles of red wine and two tin cups.

Anton thought of Ernst and old man von Decken taking him on his first safari twenty years earlier. He tried not to think of his stupid behaviour with Harriet in Cairo.

"Grab the pizza bread and that salami," Ernst said as he pulled the corks. He handed Anton a bottle and the two men sat down on the edge of the escarpment and looked at Africa.

"Before we have too much to drink," von Decken said, "put this back in your pocket. Then you can tell me whatever you're allowed to." He handed Anton his British army photo-holder. Made of stiff khaki cloth, intended to hold the bearer's identification and personal photographs, the small flat folder opened to show two transparent windows. One displayed his officer's identity card. Anton left the wallet closed and slipped it into a pocket, guessing it still contained pictures of Gwenn and Wellie and Denby, and one very old letter from Gwenn, and perhaps one other thing, a souvenir photo that should have been removed.

"Thank you." Anton lifted his cup and banged it against Ernst's. "Now tell me about your war."

"Much the same as the last two." Ernst emptied his cup. "Too much knocking about in the veldt. Not enough good food or women." He shrugged and rubbed the top of his bristly head with one hand. "What does it matter whether I'm killing Italians in Ethiopia and Eritrea, or Englishmen in Tanganyika and Libya?" He looked at Anton, then spat to one side. "But this time I'd like to win."

"That won't be easy."

"No," said Ernst, "it won't. But this time it's possible. And my job is to stop the Long Range Desert Group." He punched Anton in the shoulder. "You. You damned scorpions. Your outfit is causing too much trouble."

"Not nearly enough." Anton shook his head and filled his cup.

"What can you tell me about them?" Ernst cut thick slices of salami with his belt knife and passed a couple to Anton on the point of the blade.

"You'd like them."

"What else?"

"Nothing, my friend. Really, nothing. You already know more than I'm allowed to tell you." He turned and looked at his oldest friend. How little he had changed. Perhaps a little heavier in the body, but his short silvery hair was still thick, his arms and neck big and solid. "Want to try a little torture?"

"Perhaps I'll get you drunk and then you'll tell me everything." Ernst emptied his bottle into his cup.

"Please try." Anton wondered if he should smash von Decken on the head and steal his car. His escape might mean less trouble for his friend if there had been a little violence.

"I'd like you to tell me one useful thing, and then I'll let you go," said the German. "I owe you that from Ethiopia. You saved my life, twice."

"More than that."

"You saved my wife's life, too," Ernst said in a different voice as he stood and went back to the box. He handed Anton another bottle of wine and poured some from his own second bottle.

Anton felt guilty again, but pleased he had behaved himself after that one foolish night at the hotel.

"Do you remember the first time I picked you up, outside Dar?" Ernst said. "My God, you were green. But you knew how to throw a knife."

"On the road in Tanganyika? That was my second day in Africa. I was eighteen."

"You still are, you damned stupid boy. You never did know when to stop."

"That's what my wife says."

"Gwenn's right. How is she?"

"Better without me, she thinks. She's working in a hospital in Alexandria. The more busy and dangerous the better. You know how she is. Surrounded by suffering, doing all she can. More, if possible. Now she says she was always too old for me, after all."

"Everybody's too old for you. And what's happened to your little *Zwerg?*" Ernst gave a hard chuckle and shook his head. "Your dwarf. Still getting smaller and smarter and richer every day?"

Anton grinned. "That's what he does."

"Now just tell me what happened to your patrol."

"We did as much damage as we could, the rest got killed, and Makanyanga and I stumbled into the desert."

"That old bastard," Ernst said admiringly, taking a long slug of wine. "He's a hard one to kill."

"I hope so."

"Your turn, Engländer. Stand up and get us the other bottle." Ernst belched and finished the salami. He wiped his knife on a cuff and put it back in his belt. "And don't think of anything smart while you're up. Don't forget, I'm meaner and stronger than you are."

"Maybe." Anton came back with the last bottle.

Neither man spoke for a while. They passed the bottle back and forth. The sun was dropping. The first chill gust reached them as the wind swept along the escarpment.

"You know," said Ernst, looking down at his stump, "war's not the same anymore. Too much heavy stuff you can't watch out for. Doesn't matter what you do. You and I'll be lucky if we make it through this one."

"I know," said Anton. "Wellington, too."

Ernst turned his head and looked at Anton. "Wellington's already in it?"

Anton nodded. "And Denby can't wait for his turn. Hopes it'll last a couple more years so he can join up."

Von Decken frowned and rubbed his forehead. "They're too young, and we're too old."

"I've got an idea," said Anton. "Why don't I smash you on the head with this bottle and steal your car. You can stagger down to camp and tell them I went the other way. Then we'll be square, and next time you can shoot me."

"Next time, I will. But it's all a good idea, except you can't have the car. With my leg, I need it more than you do." Ernst stood up and spat. He tossed the empty bottles down the slope. "Get in. I'll drive you east until it's dark. Then you're out and on your own. I'll say I gave you back to the spaghetti boys. They never know who they've got or where they're going."

They climbed in and Ernst drove swiftly with the sun setting behind them. They passed several camps and a line of dug-in 88s. Their long barrels pointed not at the sky, in their anti-aircraft role, but low and east, waiting to stop the British armor.

"The best thing we've got," yelled Ernst. "Tank killers. Their shells drill a four-inch hole in your tanks before exploding. Krupp first built them in '16 to shoot down your observation balloons." Von Decken grunted. "Old wars can be useful."

Neither man spoke again as they hunched forward in the cold. In an hour Ernst stopped as the full moon rose.

"Thank you." Anton shook his hard hand before he got down. The German handed him a canteen and a salami and his knife.

"You'll need these. The sausage is for you. The knife's for the Italian sentries."

"Thanks, again."

"Goodbye, Engländer." He leaned towards Anton and gripped his shoulder, staring hard into his eyes in the bright moonlight. "The next time I see you, I'll kill you. And you know why."

The German turned the car and drove away, his lights masked to tiny beams.

Anton watched him leave, covering his face against the dust. Then he sat down on the trigh. He opened his photograph wallet. By the light of the moon he peered into the pocket behind the picture of Denby. The folded photograph of Harriet von Decken kissing him at the cabaret was missing.

He found the going easier than he'd thought. Anton walked east for two nights and lay up in the desert for two days. The desert south of the Via Balbia was littered with the wreckage of the see-saw battle for the coast. Clusters of blackened bodies, brewed-up tanks, broken guns and trucks. Occasionally the lonely wreckage of a Hurricane or Stuka. Formidable in the sky, the aircraft seemed strangely pathetic burned-out and broken on the ground, like the empty shells of turtles on a beach.

For two hours Anton had been watching what appeared to be a party of Italian deserters as they struggled to repair an abandoned British lorry. They seemed to have no weapons.

Finally, with night falling, they appeared to have the job done. Three times they turned on the engine and let it run before returning to their camp. The four men gathered by a small fire perhaps fifty yards from the truck.

His stomach grumbling, his teeth grinding sand, Anton reminded himself of the first lesson of his gypsy mentor: patience is the hunter's greatest weapon.

He crawled forward, wishing the moon were not full. But at least it allowed him to watch the four lie down, each man wrapped up, as close as he could get to the dying flames. Anton stopped, waiting for the fire to darken.

Circling into the desert, he crawled to the off-side of the truck, away from the sleeping Italians. As he approached, he saw that the battered 15-cwt Bedford had seen a lot of service. He crouched to open the passenger door, but the door was jammed shut in the bent frame. He crawled under the truck to the other side and climbed in the open door, pulling the door after him until it was almost closed. He pumped the gas pedal four times and pulled out the choke. He put the floor gearshift into first and kept the clutch pedal down. Then he turned the key and pressed the ignition button.

There was no sound. He pushed the button again and the engine chattered to life. Anton gave it more gas. The engine coughed and died. He glanced out the window and pressed the button again. Two of the Italians were already standing. A third was pulling on his boots. One man was pointing at the lorry and hollering. Two men began running towards the truck, then all four.

Again the engine started and died. Anton cursed. Just as the first two Italians reached the lorry, the engine caught. He released the clutch pedal and the truck lurched forward, knocking down one Italian with the left fender. Anton heard him scream. The second man jumped onto the running board on the driver's side, gripping the frame of the door through the open window.

"*Bastardo!*" he cried, grabbing at Anton's throat with his free hand. Anton felt he was being atttacked by an animal. He struggled to brush the man off at the same time as he groped for the headlights and tried to shift into second. With a secure grip on Anton's neck, the powerful man released the door frame and tried to strangle him with both hands. Dizzy, but trying to steer as they roared across the desert in the moonlight, Anton turned sideways on the seat and kicked against the door with both legs. The door slammed open, knocking the Italian off the running board. But he still hung on to Anton's neck like a terrier. Anton clung to the wheel and kicked again. The man lost his grip and fell free. His mouth was open in a wailing yell as he disappeared.

Regaining control of the Bedford, Anton looked through the cracked windscreen. The headlamps, evidently shaded to narrow slits for road convoy duty, provided little visibility. The petrol gauge, below empty, told him nothing. He glanced back at the vanishing camp of the Italians.

For two hours he drove slowly eastwards, figuring that he was about fifteen miles south of the Via Balbia and perhaps approaching the no-man's-land of the broken front line. He thought of von Decken. He knew that Ernst had let him go even after getting a good idea of what Anton had

been up to with his wife. How ironic that on the night of the photograph
he had behaved himself.

Flashes of light erupted over the horizon to his left. Anton thought he
heard the crump-crump of German Pak 38s, the long-barrelled 50mm tank
killers. He turned further south. In a few minutes a score of flares, British
Very lights, he guessed, illuminated the sky. Perhaps the Germans were
moving up behind him. Or were the British advancing towards him? He
realized there would be nothing for it but to make a break for the British
lines and pray for the best.

In the flaring light, he saw a tangle of British vehicles, armored cars and
trucks and Bren-gun carriers, moving south across his route. He turned to
the right on a converging path, hoping to join their ranks without being
fired on.

Suddenly Anton's heavy lorry seemed to rise in the air. There was a
blinding flash beneath him. He felt a rush of pain as he was blown through
the door.

Squinting at her picture by the light of the brightest moon he had ever
seen, Wellington kissed the photo twice and put it back inside Saffron's
letter. He wondered if Mr. Alavedo was going to reconsider. Saffron said
she was going to keep trying and that she guessed he might. He thought
of what the wedding would be like. Even though it wasn't on, Bingham
and Gates were already badgering him about the bridesmaids. He tried to
calculate how much honeymoon he'd get. A week would be lucky. The
first night at Shepheard's, perhaps the Sultan's Suite, then up the Nile to
Luxor for a little spoiling at the Winter Palace, or possibly the Auberge
du Lac at Faiyum.

Trying to stay awake, he stood and looked back at the small camp. One
more hour on stag and it was his turn to get some kip. The three new
Humbers, assigned to forward patrolling and reconnaissance south-east of
the Bir Hakeim box, were laagered tightly together, the men's bivvies side-
by-side in the center. There was no fire. It had been biscuits and bully beef
and salty water, with no brew-up in the dark. The camp was death-still
under the moonlight. Wellington was proud that, even here, in this tiny
laager, his troop of Cherrypickers had held to the tradition of calling Last
Post at 9:50 in the evening, the moment of death of Lord Cardigan, the
colonel of their regiment who had led the Light Brigade charge into the
Russian guns at Balaclava.

Wellington turned around, facing north. He raised his collar and sat down and lit his last Senior Service to keep awake. Nodding, he let the burning stub of the cigarette slip from his fingers.

Waking after a bit, bone cold, he shivered and rubbed his hands together. Something had woken him.

Ever so gently, a low rumble beneath him, the ground seemed to be shaking. He pressed both his palms flat against the hard desert and held his breath.

A growing disturbance shook the ground. He stood and listened, his mouth open in disbelief. His blood chilled. Then he ran forward to the rocky ridge that broke the slope of the desert before him. He collapsed there on his knees.

He gazed across the desert, clear now, shimmering like a shallow lake under the full moon. He could almost see the stars reflected. He lifted his field glasses to his eyes.

Ant-like, crossing his sight at a ninety-degree south-west angle, Wellington stared at the greatest mass of transport he had ever seen.

Three or more abreast, some seeming to touch in the distance, motorcycles and light reconnaissance vehicles, trucks and tankers, command and signal lorries bristling with antennas and aerials, armored cars and half-tracks and tractor-drawn artillery, and Panzers, scores, perhaps hundreds of them, ground along in line, as far as he could see in both directions.

Wellington heard the squeaky rattle of hundreds of tracked vehicles slowly advancing in the distance. He wondered if Rommel himself was leading the column. Staring harder, he made out tiny figures swinging their arms in circles, snapping their elbows back and forth, small lights occasionally visible, sparkling in their hands. The Afrika Korps.

— 19 —

"No, no, my treasures. That car is busy." Olivio wagged his round head as his four younger daughters gathered about him on the poop deck, smart in their matching green school pinafores. Their Portuguese governess waited patiently on the deck below.

"Saffron and your mother have taken your car to go for a fitting for her bridal dress, and then to the shoemaker and the other wedding fournisseurs." He thought of the prodigious expense of it all. But why not? Why not? For what other purpose the cruel labors of a lifetime? Why else had he squeezed every millieme from his sweating fellahin, every escudo from his estates in Brazil and Portugal, every piastre from the cotton contracts in the Alexandria bourse?

"Oh, Papa," moaned Ginger, the oldest of the four. "If we're late, we'll miss the pony jumps." She held Rosemary and Cardamom by the hand. The twins strained to pull her in two directions. Cinnamon, the youngest, was on her knees playing Banco with Tiago. Frowning, his eyes fixed on the board in a fury of concentration, his short stubby fingers hovering above the squares, the small boy competed with his sister for the best space to place his coin.

Seeing his children all together, Olivio thought of the daughter he had lost. Clove would have been twenty-one.

"But you may take my car instead, the other green Sunbeam," continued the dwarf, pleased that his son, though younger and far smaller, was winning this important contest. "Mine is identical, except for its tinted windows, and is fresh back from the shop today, working like a jewel, as the engineers of Coventry intended, no doubt. Umar, Tariq's cousin, will drive you all to the gymkhana."

"Can Tiago come, too, Papa?" asked Rosemary, touching her father's arm. "Please," implored Cardamom with big eyes.

"No, my sweets." Olivio smiled, in his way, and shook his head. He knew the value of denial. "Tiago will remain at his father's side." Olivio had a meeting scheduled with his farm managers. He liked to have his heir with him to absorb the atmosphere of leadership and to learn whatever else he might. The boy bore the burdens of his father's deformities. Best, in the struggle of life, that he also have the benefit of his advantages. The lad must be nimble instead of swift, shrewd instead of strong, charming instead of handsome, a fox, not a lion.

Sometimes the dwarf felt guilty, a rare sentiment, guilty that he took pleasure that his son shared with him the isolated world of little men. But if other fathers could take pride in the mundane inherited qualities of their sons, why could not he do the same for a different, more precious distinction shared by Tiago and himself?

While the girls and Olivio spoke, Tiago took advantage of Cinnamon's inattention to place his sixpence on the corner space.

Olivio's Sunbeam, OFA1 read the numberplate, drew up on the embankment. The governess led her charges to the automobile and sat in the front seat. Umar held the back door for the girls, then climbed in and pulled away. The sisters chattered and fussed behind him, crowded together in the back seat, tussling and pulling pigtails under the monogrammed motoring blanket. The river flowed gently to their left as they drove north along the Nile. From time to time the Portuguese lady attempted to quiet the girls.

Umar drove with special care, as his master required when the children were aboard. Today the embankment and its tributaries were more frantic than usual. The busier streets were always a chaotic mixture of London and a Nile village. Powerful trucks and motorcars jostled with camels and donkey carts and herds of goats being hustled to the slaughterhouse. But now the road also bore the traffic of war. Columns of lorries and even the occasional troop of armored cars sought to stay together while staff cars and ambulances plunged in and out like rugger players chasing a loose ball. Whenever the horns and sirens paused, the usual clamor of yells and curses and the brays of animals filled the air. The Mayden al-Hami was choked with unmoving traffic. Umar pulled on the handbrake and watched calmly as two British military policemen and two officers of the Egyptian Police worked together attempting to break the jam where a large farm cart, loaded with a mountain of onions and *birsiim*, had been hit by a military lorry. The cart had lost two wheels on one side and lay crumpled on its edge. The farmer sat on the curb, patient and accepting. The man held the lead ropes of his two unharnessed donkeys while the animals feasted on the bright green forage that had tumbled from the wagon. After a time the army truck went on its way and the traffic struggled forward.

Approaching the left turn for the island of Gezira, Umar slowed, then mounted the gently sloping bridge. Relieved by the lighter traffic, he glanced to his left at the wide vista of the Nile. Gezira was always a relief from the relative density of Cairo. The generous grounds of Al-Kubri garden, the Gezira Palace, the Casino, the Fish Garden and the Sporting Club all presented a welcome sense of space.

Suddenly Umar was aware of a massive lorry crowding him as he finished the turn onto the bridge. The large black vehicle pressed him from the right. He edged left, but the big Ford struck him across the right front fender. Umar lost control. The Sunbeam veered to the left and mounted the narrow pedestrian sidewalk before striking the light stone parapet. The girls screamed. Sparks flew as the Sunbeam scraped along against the stonework before Umar could regain control. Just as he recovered and brought the car's left wheels off the walkway, the truck hit the Sunbeam again, harder, at a sharper angle. Its left front corner slammed against the right rear door of the Sunbeam. Grinding along against each other side by side, their metalwork screaming, the Ford forced the green Sunbeam into the wall.

The old parapet crumbled and gave way. For an instant the Sunbeam hesitated on the edge of the bridge, its left front wheel spinning freely as it hung suspended above the water. The lorry gave it a final knock. The motorcar slid forward and plunged nose down into the river.

The car righted itself, floating on the surface. The governess was unconscious, her head bleeding where she had struck the windscreen. Umar forced open his door. He freed himself while water rushed into the front seat. He grabbed the right rear door as the Sunbeam sank. He braced one foot against the narrow running board and forced open the door. Her eyes staring into the water, her cheeks puffed wide as she held her breath, Ginger glided through the doorway, drawing Cinnamon after her by her pigtail. With his last breath, Umar reached inside for Rosemary and Cardamom, tangled in the sodden blanket. The car rolled to the right as it sank, tumbling slowly in the water, taking the governess and Umar and the twins to the bottom of the Nile.

*   *   *

"Here we are, sir," said the Deputy Superintendent with professional crisp-
ness as the launch of the River Police approached the bridge. "Here is
where the accident took place." His voice softened, but not enough to invite
a shared commiseration. "Most dreadfully sorry, sir. Unspeakable tragedy."

Olivio Alavedo was desolate. His eye was grey as stone. He stared up at
the broken parapet of the Qasr al-Nil bridge. For the first time in years,
his mind, his spirit, his very soul, ached more than his body, and for this
they always would.

Three daughters lost on this ancient stream. First, his eldest, Clove, five
years before, in the boat fire that destroyed his old Café. Now his beloved
twins, their love and smiles stolen forever. The dwarf crossed himself.
Thank God his son had not been with them.

The launch slowed. Crowds stared down from the embankment and the
bridge. A passing felucca slowed and drifted with the current, her crew
peering across the water with curiosity.

"Tomorrow we will be back, Mr. Alavedo, with divers and the crane barge,
and we'll have it up. And we'll find that lorry. The witnesses said it was a
black Ford. Don't worry, we'll hang the bastard. You have my word."

But the dwarf knew it would never be. The police were overwhelmed.
Axis spies, all Cairo restless, wild soldiers crowding the streets, crime raging, there was already more than they could manage. Any justice must be
his own.

"Thank you, Superintendent," he said quietly. Some man would pay, in
a currency that had no price. "Now I'd be obliged if you would take me
back to the Café."

"Accident," the man had said, not knowing Olivio's world. Long ago,
as a boy struggling with his adversaries in Goa, the dwarf had learned not
to believe in coincidence and accident. Wherever he'd lived, in India, in
Kenya, here in Egypt, he'd always had too many enemies to leave time or
place for accident. Of course, one of his enemies had known whose car the
Sunbeam was, and, with the windows tinted, could not have seen that the
little man was not inside.

Tariq carried his master from the launch to the Café.

"Take me downstairs," said Olivio in a lonely empty voice. "Leave me
in the hold." He reached out to touch his servant's sleeve as the Nubian
set him down on his divan. "I am sorry for your cousin, Umar. His son
will be provided for."

Tariq nodded and left the little man.

The dwarf sat alone, weeping in the darkness as the evening fell. The light of the river disappeared from the portholes.

Wearing old sandals and a rough gallabiyah, Tariq met his nephew and passed with him through several crowded alleys. Barbers sharpened razors and shaved heads in narrow stalls open to the street. Dervishes sold water flavored with raisins, licorice and orange blossoms. They passed a public fountain in a small square where a turbanned school master chivied his pupils with sharp blows of a long switch. Tariq was pleased to hear the boys recite the first chapter of the Koran while they bent over their wooden writing tablets and swayed in unison to left and right, an exercise known to strengthen their memories to enable them to learn the ninety-nine prayers of the Mohammedan rosary.

Finally they entered the dusty curving street of the automotive repair shops. Here a man could buy the pieces to build an automobile entirely from stolen parts. And some had done so, building unrecognizable automotive Frankensteins: the lamps from Stuttgart, the bodies from Detroit, the electrics from Oxford and the tires from France. In three hours a car could be painted or dissected, cannibalized or rebuilt. The street was divided into rough quarters, here the electricians, there the bodyworkers, further along the painters.

Tariq's nephew, Muhammad, carried a ship's spanner, a one-and-a-half-inch wrench, which identified him as a man from a heavy lorry repair shop. Less tall than Tariq, short-armed, but exceptionally thick and burly, the youth's dark hands and forearms were covered in a grime of oil and mechanical dust.

Muhammad led his uncle into a long barn-like shed, open at both ends, with a large yard behind it. Here Ford trucks of several generations lay about in pieces. Men were busy stripping fenders, building box-bodies, replacing windscreens.

"*As-salamu aleikum*, Muhammad," said the proprietor from a stool set against one wall of the shed.

"And with you be health and Allah's blessing," said Muhammad. "This is my worthy uncle, Tariq. He carries a great reward for the honest man who helps us. Enough to buy a new Ford truck, and a wife as well. Or an old Ford and a young wife."

"Sit." The proprietor gestured with his hand at the bench beside him. "May I offer you a coffee, or the *nargila?*"

"With pleasure." Tariq seated himself and took the long stem of the water pipe. He drew on it and nodded with careful appeciation before he spoke.

"We seek a large Ford lorry, from last year or the year before, closed at the back, black but bearing fresh marks of green paint and scratches or dents on the left side."

"It has not come to me."

"Where would you take such a truck if you wished to have it repainted at once, and the dents removed before the day is finished?"

"Here, if you were a wise man. If not, to the thieving rogue who is two shops down, on this side of the road."

"Thank you," said Muhammad. "We will be back."

They left and walked to the other shop.

"My uncle wishes to buy a used truck, but not too old. Perhaps a Ford," said Muhammad to a white-haired man in a skullcap seated behind a rough wooden table covered in gaskets and filthy parts catalogues. "May we see what is here?"

"We have all you could wish." The man shrugged with thin shoulders. "Some are mine, and almost all could be yours. Look about and then speak to me."

In the yard behind the workshop they found it. One man was washing the black Ford while another worked on the dents. A can of black paint rested nearby. The left front fender and the left side bore vivid slashes of green paint. The left headlight was smashed.

"Perhaps we will buy that battered black Ford in the back," said Tariq to the old man.

"That one is not mine, but perhaps I can help to make it yours."

"When is the owner coming back?"

"Soon. He has paid me to repair it quickly. He may come today, insh' Allah!"

They found a small café squeezed between two second-hand parts shops across the street. The odors of spices and tobacco and coffee welcomed them. They entered the narrow wooden arch of the café and sat on one of three raised benches made of brick and covered with mats. Tariq ordered coffees and a *tumbak* of Persian tobacco in a coconut water pipe.

The two Nubians remained there for hours, watching the street, waiting for the owner of the truck to return. They played backgammon on a small wooden board with one pair of dice. They sipped coffee and nibbled *sambusak*. While he chewed the spinach turnovers, Tariq watched closely, nodding from time to time as the cook, just outside the café, fried white broad beans in oil with onions, parsley, coriander and cumin.

As the day darkened, Tariq and Muhammad saw men leave the workshop. Finally the old proprietor swung out two wide wood and metal doors. He fitted them together and secured them with a chain and lock.

Back for breakfast, Tariq and Muhammad ordered and ate slowly in order to stretch out the morning while they waited for the driver to return for his Ford. First they enjoyed their thick coffee, then whole wheat round bread sprinkled with a thin layer of bran, followed by fried eggs with white cheese and *ful*. After prolonged stewing, the dry fava beans were properly mashed with olive oil, lemon, salt and garlic under Tariq's demanding eye. The ship's spanner rested on the brake bench beside Tariq.

The lorry, evidently ready, stood in the unpaved street in front of the garage workshop.

Tariq belched and called for the backgammon board and tea. As Muhammad placed the board on the bench between them, Tariq looked across the street. He threw a handful of piastres on the board and rose from the bench. "Come, nephew." He took the heavy wrench in one hand.

A man stepped from the workshop and climbed into the Ford as the old proprietor in the skullcap held the door for him. Tariq and Muhammad approached the truck from the rear.

The engine started to turn. Tariq opened the passenger door and climbed in. Muhammad jumped onto the running board beside the driver.

"*Sabah el-kheir*, good morning, Ramzi," said Tariq. "Stop the truck. My nephew wishes to drive."

Ramzi pressed down his right foot. The truck lunged forward.

Tariq slammed the wrench down on the driver's knee.

Ramzi screamed. His foot jumped from the accelerator.

"Stop the truck." Tariq raised the spanner.

Sobbing and groaning with pain, Ramzi pressed the brake with his left foot. His hand shook as he reached for the clutch knob and shifted into neutral. "*Ana fi 'ardak!* I am under thy protection, save me!"

Muhammad opened the driver's door and forced Ramzi into the middle of the bench seat before climbing in.

"*Qarafah al-Khalifa*," directed Tariq. The City of the Dead.

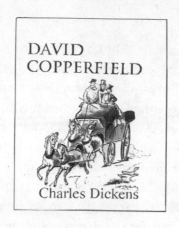

DAVID
COPPERFIELD

Charles Dickens

— 20 —

There was no sound like it. Gwenn Rider had heard it only twice before.
Once in Ethiopia, five years ago, when the mountain valley near Harrar
was filled with wounded men. Hundreds, thousands, acres of wounded. All
their agonies surging together in one vast low moan. The screams, the
gargling coughs, the aching groans all joined in a tide of suffering that
flooded down the valley in one common wave of pain.

And before that, as an ambulance driver in Belgium in '17. On the third
day of the Passchendaele offensive, her little convoy had struggled forward
through a quagmire of rain and shell holes. Stepping down from the ambulance into the boot-sucking mud, she found herself surrounded by fields
of dying men lying in the grey swamp of battle, the first of Passchendaele's
300,000 dead and wounded. She had promised herself that once the Great
War was over, she would become a doctor, but would never again hear
such a keening mass of unrelieved suffering. Today was the first time she
had heard a whisper of that evil echo.

The area around the railhead at El Alamein had become a vast scattered
depot for fuel and equipment and motor repair centers and reinforcements,
and an immense field hospital for the wounded of the 8th Army. Painted
gasoline drums marked the rough tracks that led from place to place.

Teams of doctors and nurses from the army and from Alexandria's six
hospitals worked in colonies of khaki tents. Rows of stretchers, and men
lying on blankets and ground sheets, were gathered around the tents.
Nearby, the men were unloaded from trucks and ambulances and from
Bren-gun carriers converted to field rescue. The walking wounded and

those in stable condition were sent on by train to Alexandria, and then to Cairo. The cars of the Egyptian State Railway now smelled like ancient airless butcher shops. The rest of the men, those fatally wounded and those requiring immediate surgery, were examined briefly, then carried to a tent. The lucky ones faced surgery. When things were busy, those hopelessly, mortally wounded lay in triple rows, dopey with morphine. Sometimes a dead man lay on the cot or blanket beside them.

Most days, the medical processing worked well enough, in the rough efficient way of an open-air market. But today hundreds were coming in at once from the Gazala battles to the west. Rommel's siege of Tobruk was tightening. The fortified boxes were under attack.

Followed by stretcher bearers from the Royal Army Medical Corps, Gwenn Rider and five other doctors were going from convoy to convoy examining and assigning the men. Better prepared than in earlier days, the RAMC bearers had straps hanging from their belts to hold the handles of the stretchers, particularly useful devices when crawling along under fire with a casualty slung in the middle.

The Gazala fighting had become so confused and violent, she'd heard, that German and British field dressing stations were treating Italian and British and German casualties impartially as they joined the lines of wounded. German tank recovery teams were said to have given hot drinks and blankets to wounded British tank crews lying beside their burned-out vehicles.

Gwenn came to a group of four Brens. She always checked them first. Straight from the fighting, they often carried the worst cases, men who had received no care whatever. The first one carried two dead men. The driver, himself lightly wounded, was too dazed to speak. She looked at the wounded on the other three carriers. One man in particular caught her attention. Wrapped in a blood-soaked army blanket, he was strapped to a sand channel secured across the top of the carrier. Good idea, she thought. Perfectly rigid if a back or organ injury, although unyielding and very painful with the shock of movement. She paused and watched the driver free the sand channel. Gwenn shivered and stared at the wounded man: Anton.

"He's all yours now, ma'am." The exhausted driver shook his head. "Poor chap's about done. Got blown out of his lorry. Lost lots of blood. Can't say he'll make it."

She stood frozen, almost collapsing. "Thank you for looking after him,"

Gwenn said. She gripped Anton's wrist, feeling the sand and sweat and blood under her hand. He was unconscious, barely breathing, his pulse weak. Immediately she forgot who he was and forced herself into her professional thinking.

"Quickly, boys," she said to two Indian stretcher bearers. "Take this man to our surgical tent and get him on the table. Gently, now."

Anxious about Anton but wanting to do her duty, she cleared the other two Brens and hurried after the stretcher.

Anton was naked on the table. Her staff was cleaning his wounds and pumping in the plasma, but his blood pressure was down to fifty-five over twenty-eight, less than half what it should be.

The right leg was broken in two places. His right collarbone and four ribs were fractured. Fragments of shrapnel and clothing, and perhaps bits of truck metal, were embedded deeply in both legs. She prayed she could save them. The right side of his face had a long gash from his hairline past his ear to his chin. There seemed to be no organ damage. A mine, she was certain, but perhaps only an anti-personnel mine. Otherwise the explosion would have killed him.

Her mind raced back to all Anton had done when she was nearly killed in Ethiopia, bombed by the Italians at her field hospital. Once again, without hesitation, he'd risked himself for her, staying behind to look after her while the rest of his safari struggled on towards Kenya.

If he lived, she thought, at least this would keep him out of the war. She washed her hands in a tin basin and set to work.

"Your husband's doing better, Dr. Rider," said a young nurse's aide when Gwenn entered the Anglo-Swiss three days later. "Seems quite a sturdy sort."

"He always was." Gwenn was no longer accustomed to thinking of herself as married, but she found she did not mind the sound of it.

Exhausted by long hours of surgery, her rounds almost finished, she walked down the busy hall and looked in the door of Anton's room. Designed as a double, with the intimacy of wartime it now held four beds.

Anton was asleep. Heavily wrapped, his right leg was suspended by a chain and triangular frame. The problem had been the debridement, cleaning out the dead tissue and scraps of clothing and getting out the shrapnel while setting the two breaks and controlling the bleeding. She'd done her best at the field hospital, but she knew it had not been enough. Once the leg was set and stronger, they'd need to have another go at the shrapnel, and perhaps a third try for the smaller stuff after that. Otherwise the fragments would be in there forever, shifting about amidst the damaged muscle and nerves, driving even a man like Anton crazy with pain and sleeplessness. Then it would be a lifetime of morphine and alcohol, or both. The other leg was all right, or would be soon, and the ribs as well. She hoped his facial cut would heal nicely. He was such a good-looking man. Cut up and covered as he was, he was still the most attractive man she knew. Unfortunately, too many other women thought so too.

"Morning, nurse," said a Tommy in the next bed as she entered. A bandage covered half of the upper part of his face. "I mean, Doctor." He blushed. "Sorry, ma'am."

"Good morning, Williams," Gwenn said quietly, smiling as she lifted his chart. How could you be angry at a boy who'd just lost an eye?

She examined the other two men. One, though he'd need a cane for the rest of his life, was on the mend, and cheerful enough. The other, she feared, was becoming a different sort of patient. A tanker, with burn scars forming smooth as cooling glass on the left side of his face and body, the red-haired boy had not spoken since he was carried into the hospital three weeks before. But each night he screamed in his sleep, and cried when he awoke, leaving the other men in his room troubled and sleepless. His hair and youth reminded her of Wellie.

Gwenn leaned against the window sill by Anton's bed, almost too tired to concentrate as she made notes in the records on her clipboard. But she was very aware of Anton's body close beside her.

Turning to the window, she glanced down to the right at the Rond Point, then across the Rue Sign al-Hadra to the municipal prison, nearly as handsome as the building she stood in, originally the German Deaconess' Hospital. She wondered why all the public sites in Alex seemed to be referred to in French, even though there were far larger colonies of Greeks and English and Italians. It reminded her of Giscard, and she put that thought behind her. Somehow he seemed far away and long ago, although she was certain she had not heard the end of him. During her last visit to Cairo, Gwenn's housekeeper had warned her that Monsieur de Neuville had turned up twice, insistent and demanding to see her and to learn exactly where she was.

Gwenn took from one corner the small folding chair she had brought yesterday. Relieved to be off her feet, she sat down and looked at her husband. Anton's left shoulder was bare. He already had too many scars. She hoped these new ones would be the last. His face was nut-brown against the bandages, though drawn and worn. His two arms, still tan and strong, lay extended over the white top sheet. She sighed and shook her head. She used to dream of how they would grow old together, sitting on the verandah at the farm, talking and reading Dickens aloud as the sun went down. For a moment Gwenn wondered if they should try again. Or would there always be that imbalance between the things that drew them together and those that pulled them apart?

She heard a bell tinkle in the hall. The tea trolley. Two of the other three men looked eagerly to the door. Was it the scones, Gwenn wondered, or the tea girl? Or just the attention that men always seemed to need?

The Coptic women of Alexandria had organized themselves to look after the soldiers at the hospitals, especially the junior officers from the better regiments. The younger ladies had never had so many suitors. Not just at the Anglo-Swiss, but at the Egyptian, European, Jewish, Greek and Italian hospitals it was a season for medical debutantes. Whether in bed, or on crutches in the halls, or being wheeled on the promenades by the Mediterranean, or gimping about on canes at tea parties, the young soldiers were more interested in courtship than the war.

"Morning, Gertie!" said two of the patients as a statuesque young lady entered with her creaking trolley.

"Tea, gentlemen?" she asked with smiling brown eyes. "Muffins?"

"Ladies first," said Williams smoothly.

"Thank you." Gwenn took a cup and set it on the window sill. She opened the window and let in the sea, one of the blessings of Alexandria, a town she had always found more gay and cosmopolitan than Cairo.

Though she was more than used to it, Gwenn hated all the smells of hospital. Not just the locked-in smells of ether and vomit and urine, but all the others: the honest naked smells of death and suffering, blood and discarded flesh and bone and the charred stink of burned men, as well as the clean-up odors of disinfectant and bleach and alcohol and ammonia.

She rubbed her eyes and removed a book from the pocket of her white coat, glad that Anton was still asleep. Not surprisingly, the circulating library of the British Book Club was out of Dickens. She'd been obliged to stop at Spiros Grivas' crowded store. First she thought she'd try one they had not read together, perhaps *Pickwick* or *Great Expectations*, but she'd stopped herself. For once, she had bought what he'd like rather than what she knew was best.

"Goodbye, boys," said Gertrude with a wave. "See you all tomorrow."

"Bye, Gertie!"

Gwenn suppressed a yawn and took a sip of tea, then opened the book. A nice way to wake up, she thought, aware that Anton knew every word. She remembered the first time she'd seen him reading it, twenty years ago on the steamer to Mombasa.

Though she spoke quietly, just for Anton, two of his roommates stopped talking, as if touched by a sense of homesick longing awakened by the writer of their boyhood. They stared at her as Gwenn turned to the title page and read.

"*The Personal History, Experience and Observation of David Copperfield the Younger of Blunderstone Rookery, Which He Never Meant to Be Published On Any Account . . .*"

"You're a damned lucky chap," said the officer in the wheelchair beside him as Anton opened the letter. "Wife like that, and here every day to look after you."

"Too good for me." Anton tried to shift his position in bed. "That's the trouble."

"Glad me wife's not here," said a sergeant. Stiff in his neck brace, he leaned heavily on his crutches as he squinted out the bright windows of the solarium. "She's where she belongs. Night shift in an ack-ack factory in Leeds. Just the thing for Mavis."

Anton drew out the note.

> *Muhammad Ali Club*
> *The Cotton Exchange, 2 Rue Chérif Pacha*
> *Alexandria*
>
> *My Dear Captain Rider,*
>
> *It is my honour to represent the interests of Sr. Olivio Fonseca Alavedo on the Cotton Bourse, and on other matters here in Alexandria, including the most delicate.*

I am instructed by Sr. Alavedo to extend to you every courtesy whilst you are here in hospital, and more than that. Whatever you "may wish or require" were his words. You will, sir, disappoint him and embarrass me if you do not call on me for every service.

Y'r obed't servant,

Dimitri Kotsilibas

"Love letter?" said Gwenn, resting one hand on the head of Anton's bed and bending to kiss him on the cheek.

"Of course." Anton handed her the note, sorry to see the deepening circles under her eyes.

"Olivio," she smiled. "What an angel."

"Angel?" said Anton, trying not to laugh lest it hurt his ribs. "Most people think he's the devil, and that's the way he likes it."

"He's already sent you all these flowers and every day fresh fruit from his farms, not to mention thermoses of that spinach soup he swears will cure anything. Shame you wouldn't try it."

"Chap in the next bed drank a bucket of it, and they cut off his leg anyway."

"The whole hospital's eating your presents. Just look. He's made this place into a greenhouse." Thanks to Olivio, she thought, this is the only room that doesn't smell like a hospital. Instead, it was jasmine and oleander that gave the room their scent. The dogbane seemed perfect from the dwarf. Lovely to the eye and nose, but poisonous if consumed.

"What do you suppose he means by delicate?" said Anton.

"Most delicate." Gwenn smiled.

"No doubt," said Anton, handing her a letter of his own. "Please be sure and put this in the post to Colonel Lagnold in Cairo. I'm telling him that the Eyeties are holding Makanyanga in Derna and asking the colonel to try to swap him out in the next exchange. Should be worth a dozen Italians, maybe more."

"Of course. If Makie's still alive, he should make it back. They say things are getting awfully busy on the Gazala Line, and at all the boxes. I hope Wellie's still all right."

Anton looked her in the eye and nodded, not wanting to alarm her, but knowing the Cherrypickers would be out front in the thick of it, scouting and skirmishing.

"I pray for him every day," she said. Anton took her hand and smiled.

Gwenn leaned down and parted Anton's hair with the fingers of both hands, knowing she was embarrassing him. "Be good."

"Instead of spoiling him so, ma'am, couldn't you read to us, please?" asked the officer in the wheelchair. The sergeant struggled to pull over a chair for her and set its back to the window. Other men, perhaps a score or more, moved closer as best they could. She was pleased to see the red-haired boy turning his head towards her as she lifted the book.

"I'd love to," said Gwenn, glancing first at Anton, wishing she could just lie down beside him and close her eyes. Instead, she sat down and began to read.

It was his first day out. Older couples, apparently Greek and Italian, paraded slowly past them near the parapet of the Avenue Promenade de la Reine Nazli. Nearby a group of uniformed French children from the Lycée played hopscotch, or some game like it. Here and there along the long curve of the Promenade, other soldiers, recuperating, walked or wheeled themselves along as they gazed out over the Grand Port des Anciens. Less importuning than in Cairo, a few beggars and purveyors of ices and postcards sought what business they could.

Double mounts of Bofors anti-aircraft guns were pointed skyward at both ends of the harbor. The Regia Aeronautica and the Luftwaffe had already bombed Alexandria, though not severely. Just enough to bring the war to the city. Every time bombs fell, the lines grew longer at Barclay's as Alexandrines withdrew their money and prepared to flee. If Rommel took Tobruk, the Panzers would soon be at the gates. The town butchers were making their own preparations: converting *saucisson* and bangers into *Wursts* for the restaurants that would be hosting the hungry officers of the Afrika Korps.

Anchored in the distance was the quarantined fleet of France. A salty sea breeze cooled the heat of the afternoon.

Anton was seated in a heavy wooden wheelchair, his right leg extended straight forward like a ram. Gwenn wheeled him slowly towards the fort of Qait Bey at the mouth of the harbor. Purring along the Corniche, a few yards behind them, was the old slate-grey Daimler of Dimitri Kotsilibas, probably the only motorcar in Alexandria capacious enough to permit Anton to be moved in and out without distress. With its wide door and tall roof, it was like entering a drawing room. A burly attendant, needed to lift Anton, sat beside the driver. A Cypriot with lively eyes and a full head of short-cropped white hair, said to be a former seaman, Taki smoked dark cigarettes and played with his heavy amber worry beads while he watched his charges on the Promenade.

"That fifteenth-century fort is built on the ruins of the old lighthouse," said Gwenn, wondering how much of this she could get away with. "The lighthouse of Pharos, built by Ptolemy the Second, the father of Philadelphus, in the third century before Christ."

"I see," said Anton carelessly.

"Don't be such a Philistine. It was one of the seven wonders of the ancient world, and it was right here. You might as well learn something while you have the chance."

"Yes, dear."

"It was white limestone. Nearly four hundred feet tall." He wasn't even looking. She pinched his left cheek. "You should be taking notes."

"I don't have a pencil."

"Tomorrow, after I operate, we'll see Pompey's Pillar, and perhaps the Catacombs. When you get better, we can try the Museum of Antiquities, if you're not good."

Gwenn saw an automobile parked facing them by the curb ahead. A uniformed driver was wiping the front grille with a long shammy cloth. She stopped wheeling the chair as her heart chilled.

The driver opened the back door of the black Panhard. Giscard de Neuville stepped down and walked towards them.

"Good afternoon, my dear." De Neuville lifted Gwenn's limp hand and kissed it. The chauffeur took his position a few feet behind his employer. "You don't look yourself, Mr. Rider."

"You won't either if you don't leave us alone," said Anton evenly. Galled by the incapacity of the infirm, he strained forward in his chair.

"Please, Giscard," said Gwenn, stepping between them. "Not now. You can't." She found herself strangely frightened. "Tell me where you're staying, and I'll call you later."

"Munir," said de Neuville. "Take Mr. Rider for a walk."

Munir seized the high rail at the back of the wheelchair and began to push it swiftly forward.

"Giscard!" Gwenn cried, trying to follow the chair and restrain Munir. "Stop it! You can't do this!"

"I'm taking you home, Gwenn." De Neuville grabbed her firmly by the upper arm. "I must talk to you. You don't know what you've been doing, and you do not understand what I have had to do."

Gwenn screamed and kicked and fought him with her hands as he dragged her towards the Panhard.

Behind her, Anton grabbed the wheels of his chair with both hands. Munir continued pushing. The chair braked and tipped forward. Anton screamed when his right foot hit the pavement. Blinded with pain, he fell on his side.

His worry beads still wrapped around his fingers, Taki struck Munir across the face with all his strength. The Egyptian fell back against the parapet. His jaw was broken. Blood streamed from his eye socket. The marks of the small square stones were cut in rows across his cheeks. Taki bent and lifted Munir in both hands like a Graeco-Roman wrestler. He slammed him to the pavement, then hurried to Anton and resettled him in his chair. Anton sat with his eyes closed, biting the side of his hand, trying not to scream.

The driver of the Daimler ran to Gwenn. Several British soldiers hobbled towards her and the Frenchman.

De Neuville released Gwenn and stared at her. Recovering his composure, he raised his chin and jerked his head from side to side and adjusted the collar of his jacket.

"You will not leave me," he said in a cold low voice. Then de Neuville turned and walked to his car. He climbed into the driver's seat and pulled away, leaving Munir where he lay.

It was several days later and Gwenn was happy to be taking some precious leave. Neither spoke of it but both knew this short outing to Ramleh would be their last day together before Anton left for Cairo. They sat in the back of the Daimler. Anton's bad leg rested on the jump seat. Gwenn tried to ignore the minefield-clearance school and a vast field depot of the Royal Army Ordnance Corps as they motored by.

"Thank you, for everything," Anton said to her. He was not certain how far to press things, but was anxious to leave with a better understanding. For the first time in years, he had felt loved. It was the most precious feeling that he knew.

Gwenn turned her head to look at him. For once, he had let her feel needed.

"Just doing my job."

"That's not what the fellows in my room think." He took her hand and smiled at her.

"Don't they think I'm too old for you?"

"Apparently not, but they might think I'm too young and foolish for you, or for anybody else, for that matter."

"You always will be," she said, stroking his fingers. "But maybe I'm getting used to that." She hesitated. "And I'd like you to know that I'm sorry for some of the things I said in Cairo."

"Oh, that's . . ."

"No, it's true. It wasn't your fault that Wellie signed up. At least, not really. All the other boys have gone now. And I know those fights and things aren't all your fault, you're just the way you are. I knew you were hopelessly scrappy when I married you." She smiled a bit. "I just thought I could help you grow up."

They passed the Chatby-les-Bains station of the tramway and the race course of the Sporting Club, then motored on past fig plantations and the bathing beach at Stanley Bay before they came to the lavish villas of the Alexandrians and Cairenes who made Ramleh their favorite escape.

"Just a bit further along, and we could see the Bay of Abuqir," Gwenn said. "Where Nelson won the Battle of the Nile."

"Really," Anton said, trying to shift his leg.

"The French flagship, the *Orient*, was filled with the treasures Napoleon stole from the Knights of Malta, and gold from Switzerland to pay his Army of the Nile. When the *Orient* exploded, silver dinner forks stolen from Malta rained down on the English ships."

"Wonder what happened to the gold."

The Daimler slowed and entered a stone gate and continued along a dusty alley of eucalyptus trees that led to a broad white villa set on a small promontory by the sea. Taki stepped around to open the door. Followed by two suffragis, a *bawab* in a white gallabiyyah hurried down the steps of the house to assist them.

Anton put his left arm around Taki's shoulder. The old seaman helped him out and carried him around the house to a stone terrace above the Mediterranean.

"Mr. Kotsilibas presents his regrets," said the Egyptian butler as Gwenn and Anton settled themselves. "But he is detained at the Bourse and cannot be here himself to entertain you at lunch, or at dinner, should you stay. Your rooms are prepared on the first floor, in case you wish to rest from your journey, or to retire after lunch." While he spoke, the other servant opened a bottle of chilled Boutari and filled their glasses.

"Heaven." Gwenn cast back her head and closed her eyes.

They raised their glasses, and looked out over the turquoise sea. There was no war.

"I'm so happy about Wellie," Gwenn said. "Saffron's just the sort of girl he deserves."

"They're a lucky pair." Anton hoped it would be true.

They ate olives and drank and laughed and chatted, about the boys, and Kenya, and Cairo and their friends. Gwenn could not remember when she had felt so relaxed, especially with Anton. Twice they heard aircraft. Once they saw a British destroyer sailing west along the coast, but they did not speak of it.

"Lunch is ready, sir." The butler and another man carried a round wooden table to Anton and covered it with a flowered linen cloth and set an umbrella beside it.

Hungry and at ease, they relished all that followed: sea urchin coral, stuffed artichokes, grilled lamb and young okra, melons and baklava drowning in thick dark honey.

"No coffee, thank you," said Gwenn to the butler. "But could you please help Captain Rider to his room? He must have his nap."

"Gwennie," he complained. "Please."

"Doctor's orders."

She helped Anton into bed, undressing him like a child while he protested. She opened the windows wide and drew the shutters of the corner seaside room.

Full of wine and fatigue and sea air, Anton soon fell asleep. Gwenn took off her shoes and put her legs up and watched him from a chaise longue in the corner. Soon he began to grunt and gently snore.

Gwenn stood and regarded herself in the mirror while she removed her clothes. Still a flat stomach and a schoolgirl's small high breasts, and a slightly bony lower chest, and slender arms and legs. She raised her chin and ran her fingers through her short tawny hair and shook her head from side to side. Not so bad for forty-seven, except for those circles under her eyes. She entered the spacious bathroom and drew a deep bubbly bath.

Later she slipped into bed and lay on her side close to Anton and waited for him to waken.

But Gwenn fell asleep herself, one hand and cheek resting on his left shoulder.

"Careful," she said when he woke her with a young man's ambitions. "You'll hurt yourself." She did her best to help. "Mmm. That's better. There. Let me."

Afterwards, they stayed over, like lovers, with dinner and candle lanterns on the terrace, and the moon just past full. Twice they heard bursts of ack-ack to the west.

"Do you think Mr. Kotsilibas always intended to leave us here alone like this?" asked Gwenn.

"He is a friend of Olivio's." Anton smiled.

"I'm glad we didn't disappoint him."

In the early morning they had Greek yoghurt and honey and coffee on the terrace.

Driving back, Gwenn closed her eyes and slept in the car, falling against Anton's shoulder. But as they drove, he passed from contented to anxious, eager to make their future like this day at Ramleh.

She awoke suddenly as the Daimler braked in the traffic of the Rue du Prince Abd al-Moneim. A military convoy choked the road beside them.

"Gwennie," he said when she sat up. "I hope we can go on like this."

"I hope so too, but I'm not sure," she said, dreading another disappointment. "We'll have to see." She drew Anton's face to her and closed her eyes and kissed him. The car drew up at the Gare du Caire. The war was waiting for them once more. She did not want to cry. "We'll talk about it after Wellie's wedding."

Anton started to speak, but Taki leaned into the car to help him. It was too late to say he loved her.

— *21* —

Cresting the low ridge south-west of Bir Hakeim, Wellington saw a fiery glow rising from the desert stronghold. Desperate to get back to report the advancing German column, he watched the fortress sparkle like a jewel box in the darkness of the huge desert night.

"Stop the car!" he yelled at his driver. The three Humbers paused. He ordered the wireless operator to try and make the radio report once more.

Like ghostly black shadows, a flight of German bombers sailed across the blue-black sky. Either Heinkel 111s or Junker 88s, the three aircraft seemed to glide slowly over the blazing base. Shocks shook the ground as their incendiary bombs flared up and lit the box. Below them, Wellington recognized the bright blue-white flashes of anti-aircraft fire as the Bofors popped away and the Fusiliers-Marins fired into the night.

When the raid was over, the armored cars zigzagged their way along one of the three paths through the minefields. Wellington found General Koenig in his command bunker with his senior officers. Nordhouse nodded when Wellie entered.

"Yes, Lieutenant?" The commander stroked the thick dark mustache that filled his sallow face beneath its long hooked nose. His high forehead stood out in the dim light of two lamps suspended from the roof.

"Sir," said Wellington. "The Panzers. We've just spotted at least a division swinging around Bir Hakeim to the south. Tanks, lorries, half-tracks, the lot, sir. We counted two hundred tanks, over a thousand other vehicles, and more still coming."

"Sounds like it's our turn." Koenig dropped a telephone into its cradle.

"The land lines have just been cut. But if Fritz wants Bir Hakeim, we will make him pay for it."

The lights shook. Shadows danced across the bunker as shells landed nearby. The general stood and buckled on his sidearm. "To your posts, *mes braves*. And remember to have your men shave their beards. We have reports they're using gas on the Eastern Front, and the men must be able to wear their masks if we need them."

"Italians, Captain Nordhouse, by the look of it." Wellington passed his glasses to the French officer. It was 0530 and the early light was brightening in the east. They were standing near a battery of six quick-firing French 75s dug in next to the Mamelles. The broken-down cisterns, half covered in sand, now provided shelter instead of water. Two miles to the south, at the other end of the box, was the crumbling fort from the old days of colonial desert outposts.

The Foreign Legion officer kept silent while he studied the moving formations through the shimmering haze and the clouds of dust raised by the enemy vehicles.

"Looks better than their usual *foule paysanne*," Nordhouse said at last. "Can you guess which division? You boys have been doing all the reconnaissance."

"From the tanks and pennants and the order they're in, sir, I'd say it's the Ariete." Wellington took back the glasses. "The best they've got."

"I see they finally have some heavier armor. Not just those old Fiat coffins."

"Those'd be their new Semoventes. Seventy-five millimeter self-propelled guns, fourteen tonners." Wellington was excited to be doing his job.

Nordhouse lowered the glasses and glanced at the young soldier. "Damn *pizzayolas* are already looking for a way through the minefields. They've got sappers moving up in teams under the artillery fire, followed by tanks and infantry." The captain turned to his spotter and gave him new coordinates. "Minefield's no use without guns to protect it, and we've got interlocking arcs of fire covering most of them, but if you lay down too much fire you destroy your own mines."

"I'd better get back, sir." Wellington was anxious to confer with Bingham and Gates about their next recce.

"Well," said Nordhouse, "Rommel has to break us here before he takes

Tobruk. And without Tobruk, they can't get to Alexandria and the flesh-pots of the Delta. So we'd better expect the worst. Just time now for a round of pinard and a little *casse-croûte* for the boys before we take care of this first wave." The captain gave instructions to his Algerian orderly. Two men went around distributing long loaves of stale bread and pouring inky wine from goatskin bags into the tin mug of each Legionnaire.

Wellington hitched a ride on a camouflaged water wagon back to his troop's laager near the old fort. *"Vous êtes anglais?"* asked the Senegalese driver.

"More or less," said Wellington cheerfully. They stopped several times so men could gather round and draw water from the truck. Everywhere he looked, Wellington saw fire trenches, vehicle pits, dugouts and command posts honeycombing the box. Nordhouse had told him that Bir Hakeim's four thousand defenders had prepared over a thousand trenches, outposts and strongpoints. Men were still digging with picks and shovels while others laid camouflage and wire.

Approaching the laager, he found Johnny Bingham and his crew work-ing on their car while the rest of the troop built rough shelters around the three vehicles.

"Time you got your hands dirty," Wellington said to Bingham. "Finally some use from all that time messing about with those silly roadsters."

"Damned Rootes never could build a motor," grumbled Bingham. Grease and engine oil mixed with the dirt on his arms and face.

"We'd better leave the Frenchies to this rubbish and drive you back to Cairo to try and get you married." Bingham lifted his beret and scratched his scalp, making it look like greasy camouflage. "That girl won't wait for you much longer. Far too good for you, anyway." He grinned and wiped his hands with sand. "And her girlfriends are restless and desperate for Gates and me."

Wellington smiled and walked past the laager to a slight rise in the ground. He saw a line of dust approaching from the east and raised his glasses. Bingham hurried after him, squinting into the desert.

"Good Lord," said Bingham. "Here they come."

Suddenly the southern edge of the camp came alive with gunfire, first from the sentries and outposts along the wire that began at the inside of the minefield, then from the mortars and heavier weapons sited deeper inside the fortress. A shell landed nearby. For an instant nothing happened, then a deafening blast almost lifted Wellington off his feet. He jumped into a slit trench and watched the Italians advance as Bingham dropped in beside him. A canteen and a tin helmet rested on the floor of the narrow L-shaped trench. Flies swarmed where someone had defecated at one end of the trench.

"Damned filthy French," said Bingham. He slapped the helmet on Wellington's head. "Your red hair needs this more than I do."

Scores of medium tanks, the old *Medio* 13/40s, followed the sappers towards the wire. Many carried sandbags lashed across their thin armor plates. Open *Camionettas Saharianas* came behind the tanks, loaded with men. Italian infantry hung back in the distance, well dispersed to avoid attracting fire. Wellington made out the baggy shape of their trousers above the tight wrapping of their puttees. Cones of dust and pillars of flame rose between the tanks when French artillery fire landed all around them. The gunners cursed as the midday shimmer and mirror-like reflections of the desert made shooting difficult. Famously underpowered, the fourteen-ton tanks rumbled slowly forward, returning fire with their cannon as they advanced.

In front of Wellington, just as it reached the wire, one tank took a direct hit. The front armor plating split open. Black smoke poured from the vehicle when its shells and petrol tank exploded.

"Poor buggers," said Bingham. "Every tanker's nightmare, and our tin cans won't be any bloody better when it's our turn."

Another M13 roared through the smoke and broke through the wire firing its machine guns. One side of the tank lifted off the desert, then crashed down as a mine blew off its left tread. The right tread was still engaged. The tank spun around, broadside to the wire and took a hit in the side of the turret. The metal plating cracked like an egg. The turret separated from the body of the tank.

Further back, Wellington saw a section of Italian infantry tossed in the air by a mine in a geyser of smoke and dust. Several men crashed down on their backs with their limbs crumpled around them. Another lay sprawled across a stretch of wire.

Wellington smelled cordite and hot dust and burning gasoline. He watched more tanks rumble towards them. A few yards to his right, well dug in, their guns lowered to point-blank range, a Bofors crew fired at the Italians over open sights.

The turret hatch of one damaged tank opened. An officer jumped down and climbed onto another M13. He fired the turret machine gun of the new tank as it rattled forward. Italian armor was pressing ahead all along the line. Wellington heard the dull clang of solid shot hitting steel.

"These Eyeties are sportier than they told us," Bingham yelled at Wellington as splinters of rock and shell fragments whistled over the trench. Bits of hot metal glowed and smoldered nearby.

Wellington waited for a moment, then raised his head. The Bofors crew were lying around their guns. One gunner had lost both legs. Wellie saw a Legionnaire rise and attempt to serve the remaining Bofors by himself. The man's shirt was smoking. Wellington leaped from the trench and ran to the gun emplacement.

Bingham hurried past him and climbed his Humber, joining another trooper as they fired the car's Besa machine gun at the advancing Italians.

"Get down!" Wellington shouted at his friends. Too exposed on top of the seven-foot-tall vehicle, the upper bodies of the two Hussars stood out like silhouettes in a shooting range.

Wellington passed a shell to the Legionnaire gunner. "Here you go!" he yelled as he handed him another, cutting his right wrist when he removed the next shell from its case. His eyes smarted from the cordite. The Frenchman coughed and spat black mucus. His face dark with burns, his hair singed, he sighted the gun while Wellington passed him the ammunition.

Squinting through the smoke and dust, Wellington saw a wedge of Italian tanks pressing forward past the blackened hulls that had preceded them. The front plates of some of the dead tanks glowed red. Again an officer climbed from the hatch of a broken tank and took command of another. The same man, Wellie guessed.

The Legionnaire screamed something that Wellington could not hear over the racket of the machine guns and shells and the clanking of the tanks. He looked up from his loading and saw an Italian tank crash through the wire directly before them. Then it stopped, caught in an anti-tank ditch, its treads grinding, but the tank motionless with its bow high in the air. A heavy round caught it between the treads. It fell back as if speared in the belly. Flames flared from every opening of the wounded vehicle. The hull shook as the bullets and shells inside exploded. Beneath the tank, Wellington knew, molten metal would be dripping like blood onto the desert, hardening in small clots. Black smoke rose as the oil and the rubber gaskets caught fire. A charred body lay folded across the open hatch.

Suddenly six more tanks appeared through the smoke and chaos, no more than fifteen yards from a Legion command post to Wellington's left.

One took a direct hit from a French 75. Others exchanged fire with the Bofors. An Italian shell went through the roof of the command post. A line of Legion *voltigeurs* rose from their trenches and swarmed over the tanks. A cloud of Italian infantry came forward to meet them. Wellington saw Captain Nordhouse lead a shock company past the cistern towards the attackers. Without hesitation, the *compagnie d'appui* ran forward through the smoke as the captain screamed, "*À l'assaut!*" Nordhouse climbed onto a tank and emptied his revolver through the observation slit.

Soon an uncanny quiet settled on the box as the gunfire ceased. Columns of black smoke rose from the brewed-up tanks, joining in a stinking pyre to form oily dark clouds that spread across the sky. Men climbed from their bunkers and gun pits and gazed about the battle scene. Wellington looked over to see how Bingham had done on the Humber.

Relieved, he saw Bingham wipe his face with his silk scarf before taking off his rust-colored beret and waving at Wellie from the top of the armored car. The trooper beside him was busy reloading the heavy Besa. Wellington raised one arm and returned the wave.

The Legion gunner looked once at Wellington and nodded his appreciation. His forearms were covered in black blisters. His friends lay all around him. The man turned and offered Wellington his open canteen. For the first time Wellington looked at the gunner's hands. Both were burned to the wrist, scorched red, raw almost to the bone. Wellington drank and thanked him.

He paused to watch a French medical team extricate a wounded Italian from his tank. The man screamed with every movement. The two medics stood atop the turret. They were lifting the burned tanker out by two stretcher slings attached to his shoulders under his arms.

Shaking, suddenly realizing what he'd been through, Wellington hurried to his troop's laager. Gates's car had been hit, but apparently with no one in it.

The firing started again as he approached. Wellington threw himself down, losing his helmet as bullets and shrapnel splintered the rocky desert around him. Squinting up through the dust, crawling to a slit trench, he saw Bingham swept from the Humber by machine gun fire.

The shooting stopped and Wellington ran to his friend. Gates was immediately at his side, jamming the bayonet of a rifle into the ground. Wellington knelt and gently turned Bingham over onto his back. His right shoulder and arm had been shot away, almost severed from his body. Another trooper ran up with a medical pack. Gates hung a bottle of plasma from the rifle butt. Wellington looked up with dead eyes. "Too late," he said. A clear tube hung uselessly from the bottle.

Wellington stood and turned and leaned against Bingham's Humber with both hands. His head hung down between his arms. He scarcely felt the scorching metal plating that burned his hands. He closed his eyes. After a time he felt Gates's arm around his shoulder. Then he vomited and retched and retched.

They lay Bingham on the desert, stretched out on his sheepskin great-coat. The white wool lining of the coat was matted and slick with blood. Flies settled over the blood like raisins on a pudding. Bingham's dusty beret lay beside him. Its red band was torn.

Wellington collapsed onto the ground beside his friend. He took Bing-ham's head between his hands and pressed it against his own cheek, rocking back and forth as he held him. He felt Gates's hand grip his shoulder. He sat back, unable to cry.

After a time, Wellington stood and looked across the camp. His friend's blood was drying on his shirt. He saw General Koenig moving slowly towards them in a Bren, stopping to speak with the men in each position. Medical teams and burial parties were at work.

When the wind changed, Wellington smelled the pork-like odor of the burned Italian tankers whose bodies lay near their dead machines. Their blackened tanks still smoked and smoldered. Broken tracks lay spread around them on the ground like the bones of animals. Long lines and crossed patterns of tread marks extended back into the desert like the strands of giant spider webs.

"Next time it won't be so easy, Lieutenant," said Nordhouse. "Whenever the greasers can't get it done, they give the job to the chleuhs to finish." He leaned back against the side of the Humber and gulped his share of the whisky he was drinking with the Cherrypickers. Nearby were two ham bones and empty jars of fruit preserves, the remains of the supplies retrieved from the Italian tanks, together with blankets and bottles of eau-de-cologne.

"We're away in a few minutes." Wellington glanced up at the moon, no longer quite full. "We're meant to meet tonight's supply convoy and lead them in. Then they're off again before first light. Food and water and ammunition in, prisoners and wounded out, including several of ours."

Wellington heard music behind him. The inevitable strains of *Lili Marlene* came from a German forces radio station picked up by a signalman's wireless, probably from Radio Belgrade.

"Remember that *macaroni* you saw leaping from tank to tank?" said Nordhouse. "That was the colonel commanding their regiment. Not much of it left. He's a prisoner, wounded. Changed tanks three times. He's dining now with Koenig."

"He deserves it," said Wellington. He and Gates and the others mounted up.

"Mind if I come with you?" Nordhouse looked up at Wellington as the engines warmed. "Gives me a chance to check our defenses from the other side, and you Roastbeefs might need a Frenchman to get you back in."

"Who wants to get back in?" said Wellington.

Nordhouse looked young Rider in the eye and did not answer. He swung up and settled himself against one of the sandbags lashed to the armored cars.

They waved at the sentries and the two Humbers slipped out along the southern pass through the minefields. Wellington counted the last of the thirty-two Italian tanks that had died around the box, now low black shapes scattered in the desert.

The second day began early. Wellington woke with his head aching and his eyelids glued together with sand. Two flights of Dorniers bombed the box at first light. Mountains of smoke and dust towered in the sky after the explosions. As the bombers banked and turned back west, three Stukas came in from the east at about five thousand feet with the sun rising behind them. The camouflaged planes started to roll, then dropped into a seventy-degree dive with their sirens wailing, finally levelling out at two thousand feet, leaving clouds of exploding dust behind them.

Wellington was back in a slit trench with Gates. They covered their eyes and pressed themselves against the rough wall while the aircraft screamed down. Wellington heard the barking rattle of machine gun fire as the dive bombers strafed, then the sharp bursts of bombs exploding nearby. Heat pulsed towards him from two trucks burning behind their trench. The blaze seemed to suck up the air all around them.

"Where's the bloody RAF?" shouted Gates through the din.

"Swilling gin and peach juice with the skirts at Shepheard's," Wellie hollered back.

All day the French worked on the defenses: digging, laying mines, siting artillery, distributing ammunition. Wellington and the Cherrypickers cleaned their weapons and checked the remaining vehicles. They stacked more rocks and sandbags and ammunition boxes around their vehicle pits. Whenever an Axis convoy came within range, the long guns of the fortress opened up. When night fell, he watched the Brens sally out to harrass the German supply lines. Another relief convoy made it through, with two water trucks and mail and forty tons of ammunition for the 75s. After the trucks left, Wellie joined a few men gathered in the dark with torches, sorting the letters, hoping they had mail. No luck for him.

Counting each one, Wellie found the third and fourth days and nights were much the same.

About noon on the fourth day the wind rose and blew steadily from the south-west, hot thick air dense with fine desert dust. Soon the dust was in everything, weapons and engines, eyes and mouths, and in every wound before it was dressed and in every tin of food before it was fully opened. Wellington and Gates tied their scarves over their mouths and sat silently in their slit. The small cut on Wellie's wrist had developed into a festering desert sore. Now it was swollen and crusty. When he bumped it on the edge of the trench, the sore leaked pus that became pasty and gritty as it mixed with the dust.

On the fifth day the Italians and Germans held their fire while six hundred unarmed Indian soldiers staggered up to the wire. Even at a distance, the exhausted men were recognizable by their turbans and gaiters. Several had been killed crossing the minefield. The Cherrypickers were called over to speak to them in English.

"What unit are you from?" Wellington asked one bearded soldier.

"Third Indian Motor Brigade, sir," answered the Sikh, gulping water from the canteen Gates handed him. "All our English officers are dead or wounded."

"How did you find us here?" asked Wellington.

"The Germans captured us, sir, but they had not food or water for themselves, and nothing for us. They said their supply trucks could not keep up with their advance," the Sikh replied, eager to talk. "They told us Rommel he is drinking half one cup a day, like the men. Foul water, sir, dark and salty and lot of chemical. So they turned us loose here for you to take care of us, and said they would see us again when they capture you in two days' time, sir."

"We'll see," said Wellie, almost amused. "General Koenig ordered me to tell you that we'll try to get you lot out of here on tonight's convoy with the Italian prisoners and our wounded. Gates here will be leading you out."

"The Indians made it out," said Gates early the next morning, "and you have mail, you lucky bugger." He sailed a blue envelope at Wellington. "Might as well read it out loud. You know you'll be needing my advice."

Wellington caught the envelope in the air and shook his head as he opened it. He cut the letter open with his father's choori and read it quickly. Then he stood and bit his lip and got a mug of tea. He walked to the old fort and sat down against the rough white wall. Twice more he read it.

My darling Wellie . . .

I have such news for you. My Father has thought about it and says he approves after all and we can go ahead. I'm so happy. And we're going to have a baby . . . a bit before we'd planned, I'm afraid . . . so you'd best hurry and get some leave. I so hope you don't mind. If it's a boy, I thought we'd call him Adam, if you'd like that. It's such a lovely name, and Lord P has always missed a son. He once told my Papa he'd always wanted a boy just like you . . .

That afternoon two Italian officers presented themselves at a Legion outpost under a white flag. Wellington saw them being escorted blindfolded to Koenig's command post. The Italians carried a handwritten message from Rommel asking for the surrender of the box. The French general did not reply. Instead he wrote to each of his unit commanders.

Wellington and Gates read the message: "It is my order and wish that every man will do his duty unflinchingly, either at his post or isolated from his comrades. Our mission is to hold the ground, whatever the cost. Good luck to you all."

Dossing down for the night, lying on his back in a slit trench under his greatcoat, his muscles finally relaxing, Wellington realized how simple and intensified everything had become. Even life and death were not his choice. A drink of water was a lordly pleasure. One hour's peace at night was more refreshing than a holiday.

* * *

On stag as the sun was about to rise, Wellington leaned against an ammunition case and thought of Saffron, and Cairo, and his future. He took
the letter from the pocket of his shirt and read it again by the scant light.
He thought of the baby and his responsibilities. He felt more thrilled and
alive than he ever had. One day he would walk idly with his child and
pause for a game of duck-on-a-rock. Perhaps his father or Denby would be
with them. Slowly, quietly, Wellington began to cry. Why, he did not
know. His mother and father would be so happy. He rubbed his eyes and
carefully unfolded the blue envelope and began to write on it to Saffron.

But he could not keep his mind from Johnny Bingham. He still saw his
friend's body lying torn open like a lion kill in the bush. They had buried
Bingham by his car, in the new tradition of the Desert Rats.

For the first time Wellie worried about his father. He'd always seemed
so indestructible, but now Wellington had seen what war could do. Thank
God it would be over before Denby could join up, unless the little blighter
tried to sign up early. Wellington stood and put the unfinished letter in
his pocket. He'd finish it tomorrow. He stretched and lit a smoke, wondering what the day and the night would bring.

A deep-throated blast rumbled in the distance, then two, three, more.
Heavy explosions shook the ground all around him.

He knew at once that this was not the fire of the usual 75s. Nor did it
have the dreaded whip-crack report of the high-velocity 88s. It had to be
heavy German field guns, tractor-drawn, the 105mm howitzers. The real
siege had begun.

All day the stonking, the steady heavy shelling, continued. Wellington
felt the explosions pounding in his lungs like drums. His ears ached. The
air itself seemed hard with shock waves. Shells fell from the Mamelles all
the way to the southern tip of the box. Bunkers were stoved in, artillery
smashed in the pits, trenches obliterated, ammunition dumps destroyed.
He saw men torn by shrapnel and blown to pieces.

A French officer from a colonial regiment knelt by Wellington's trench
and used the barrel of his revolver to tighten the tourniquet on his left
arm. Flies gathered on his wrist like a bracelet. Before Wellington could
collect himself and offer to help, the officer rose and stumbled off through
the clouds of dust and sand.

Wellie and his mates cheered when nine Hurricanes appeared from the west. After losing two aircraft, they were beaten off by flights of Messer-schmitt 109s. Then, with the Me 109s flying protection, the Stukas came again, diving and strafing and bombing in relays. Four were shot down by the Bofors of the Fusiliers-Marins, but the Stukas visited Bir Hakeim three times that day. Wellington knew he would never forget the scream of their sirens as they dove, nor the leopard markings of their mottled desert cam-ouflage as they came in low to strafe.

When it grew dark, the Cherrypickers gathered for a brew-up: tea, tinned peas and bully beef. Several men leaned against their vehicles, read-ing old letters.

"Thank God the fighting's always in the desert," said Gates. "Can you imagine what it'd be like if this was in a city, like Stalingrad or Warsaw?"

"Or London, with the Blitz and the underground full of children," said one trooper, handing round a flask of gin.

Wellington tried not to notice Gates's hand shaking when he passed him the flask.

"To Bingham," Wellie said. He looked at the stars as he cast back his head and drank.

"Be careful," said Nordhouse before the Hussars left later to meet that night's convoy. "The noose is tightening."

The two armored cars drove out through the narrow path, and then another two miles into the blue. They turned the cars around at the usual rendezvous, a shallow wadi near a ridge in the desert, and switched off their engines. Immediately the gunners and drivers started cleaning out the fresh sand and dust that was beginning to clog the gun breeches and motor engines.

"Nothing's changed," grumbled Gates. "Chaps used to have to feed and water the horses even before you took a wee. Now it's the same with the Humbers."

From time to time they heard explosions in the distance. Occasionally there were flashes on the horizon and a rumble like far-off rolling thunder. But no convoy appeared.

At 0200, chilled and worried, Wellington walked over to Gates.

"Another fifteen minutes and we're off," he said, picking at the messy wound on his wrist. "Back to camp and catch some kip."

"Must be that fighting in the Cauldron." Gates stamped his feet and shrugged. "Radio said the Panzers overran Seventh Army Headquarters. We lost a hundred and fifty tanks and the box at Sidi Muftah. Apparently Rommel led the first Grenadier platoon himself."

Wellington nodded, wondering what tomorrow would be like. "Not much to stop the bastards now," he said.

That day they saw the first German soldiers: lean bronzed figures in the threadbare faded tan of the Afrika Korps. Light flak units unlimbered and set up at the edge of the minefield. Batteries of Pak anti-tank guns opened up and shelled the bunkers. Squads of Pioneers and Panzergrenadiers began to work their way between the mines. The Pioneers had wire-cutters and sacks of stick grenades hanging from their shoulders. A few carried flame throwers, making them immediate targets for the French riflemen who hunted them with their bolt-action St. Etiennes. Wearing cloth-covered helmets or pale lime-green field caps, the Panzergrenadiers carried rifles and machine pistols. The Germans advanced efficiently, well spread out. They moved like soldiers who did not need orders. Like men who had done this sort of thing before.

"The damned chleuhs seem to know where the paths are through the minefields," Nordhouse growled to Wellington. Behind him a squad of Legionnaires was adjusting a Vickers on its tripod. The corrugated barrel jacket of the machine gun was steaming from extended firing. Short of water, one *tireur* urinated into the cooling compartment of the metal jacket. "In the last war, they used wine," muttered the French captain.

Wellington and Nordhouse stood back against the wall of the fort to let parties of stretcher bearers pass. The whole evil parade of crying moaning men: bandaged stumps, raw burns, painful belly shots, and, worst of all, the deep head wounds that usually guaranteed both mutilation and mental incapacity. Some men were carried on improvised stretchers made from two rifles and scraps of canvas. Others were borne on three-point carries. Two men clasped their right hands together beneath the wounded man's back, while their left hands supported his neck and knees. One soldier, his face a gory mask, had shrapnel through both cheeks.

Wellington watched the French mortars and shells from the 75s fall among the German infantry when they got about 1500 yards from the perimeter. Men fell here and there. But Rommel's "Africans" kept coming. Wellie saw their three-man machine gun teams run forward, steady and determined. Crouching low, the first man carried the Spandau, the long-barrelled MG 34s with their short bipods mounted near the muzzle. The other two followed with the spare barrels and cases of belted ammunition. When one man fell, the remainder of his crew recovered what he had carried. Badly shot up, the teams finally fell back. They slung their weapons and dragged their wounded with them.

They're just like us, Wellington thought, watching them struggle. They're really fighting for each other, for the men they muck with.

In the next two hours the Stukas bombed Bir Hakeim four times. Three more were shot down, but the Bataillon du Pacifique took heavy losses. Wellington saw lines of men waiting outside their hospital bunker when the fourth attack came in.

Two bombs exploded at the mouth of the bunker and stove it in. Wellington's stomach hardened like a stone when he watched the roof collapse in a mass of sand and rubble. As the airplanes peeled away, Wellington and the Cherrypickers joined the men running from all over the camp, digging and clawing at the wreckage. Wellington saw a medic lying on a stretcher, his pelvis smashed to pulp, the mess of his body and his uniform inseparable. The man beside him had frothy red bubbles on his lips and an open sucking wound in his chest. As the shellfire resumed overhead and all around him, the dying medic instructed the stretcher bearers how to care for the nearby wounded.

That evening a new sound joined the bombardment: German 155mm guns, their heaviest. "Probably on their way to Tobruk," said Wellington, "but diverted here because these Frogs have been so stubborn."

"Hardly a real Froggie here," scoffed Gates. His cheeks were hollow in his brown grimy face. "Except the officers. The rest of 'em are islanders or Africans, or Jews or Krauts who don't dare surrender."

Outranged and short of ammunition, the French 75s could not reply to the big guns. Nordhouse prepared to lead a party of artillery outside the perimeter to set up a counter-battery position to reach the German guns. "Care to join us?" he asked Wellington that evening.

"Why not?" said Wellington after an instant's hesitation.

"No, no, boy," replied the captain, slapping him on the shoulder. "You've got your own job." For two days Nordhouse and his men succeeded, keeping the heavy German pieces from closing in, but down to five hundred rounds for the 75s, the French finally pulled in their guns.

Late that afternoon, completing his daily tour of the defenses, General Koenig rattled up to the small camp of the Hussars in his Bren.

"Tea, sir?" said Wellington after saluting the French commander. He sensed that the general was struggling to disregard his own exhaustion. Wellington had heard it said that war at the front was a young man's game. "Tea?" he asked again.

"*Avec plaisir.*" Koenig accepted a mug. His right eyelid seemed to be twitching, but it might have been the dust. "How many vehicles do you still have working?"

"Two runners, sir, more or less. And we're trying to patch up another."

"You and your men have done your work here, Lieutenant. Now we know where Fritz is, and what he's trying to do. This can't last much longer for the rest of us, and I want you to consider yourselves free to break out and rejoin your regiment whenever you judge it best. I'd suggest you leave tonight." The general paused and drank some tea, giving Wellington time to decide. "Things will not get better."

Wellington glanced at his men working on the armored car. Hopeless, he reckoned. The blasted thing would fly before it would roll. Maybe it was time to saddle up and fight another day, while they had two cars still running. Then he thought of Bingham. What had Johnny died for if the rest of them were to cut and run? And he thought of his father teaching him to hunt, telling him never to shoot unless he was prepared to finish the job.

Wellington looked back at General Koenig and caught his eye.

"With your permission, sir," the young man said, "I think we'll just hang on for a bit and see it through."

*   *   *

Ordered to rejoin the commander-in-chief, for two days Ernst von Decken and his small column of mixed vehicles had forced their way south through the *Hexenkessel*, the Witches' Cauldron of the Gazala battlefields that stretched from Knightsbridge towards Bir Hakeim.

Clusters of smoldering machines marked the great tank battles of the last week. Everywhere the desert was criss-crossed with the track marks of armored vehicles. Like a Manyemwesi following animal spoor in the bush, Ernst could now distinguish one armored footprint from another.

Von Decken yelled at his driver and his vehicles pulled up in an informal laager to refuel.

Two hundred yards to the west, like the dried bones of a dinosaur, a line of burned-out soft-skinned machines lay along a rocky escarpment where the RAF had caught them undefended. Tankers, ambulances, tank-recovery vehicles had died together.

While Ernst's men unloaded their last petrol tins and refueled, von Decken watched the eastern sky. Then he turned and looked back from the turret of his Crusader.

A curtain of oily smoke rose to the horizon. Some German, he thought, but most of it British. Despite being surprised and outgunned by the new American Grant tanks, the Panzers and the 88s had won most of the armored battles. But they had lost more than they could afford. The day before, Ernst had seen a line of broken-down Panzers towed into position along a ridge to draw British attacks, like bait for a leopard. A battery of 88s had waited behind the derelicts and soon destroyed the attacking Grants.

During the earlier fighting, when the 21st Panzer had broken through and smashed the British armor and then stopped for lack of petrol, Rommel himself had led a long supply column through the Cauldron to resupply his troops.

Driving on, spitting dust, von Decken came to a group of German vehicles, a squadron of armored cars with a radio car and a few support trucks in the center.

The familiar forceful stocky figure stood on the sloping hood of a half-track. Field glasses were set to his eyes under the visor of his peaked cap.

Ernst straightened his shoulders and gimped over and saluted. "Herr General."

"Ah, von Decken, at last." Rommel lowered his glasses before continuing. His voice was low and hoarse. "Did you bring us any water?"

"Nein, Herr General," said Ernst. "But we can spare a gallon or two," he added quickly.

Rommel climbed down and lifted a map case from the seat of his vehicle. "For the moment, the path to Tobruk is almost clear, once we've cleaned up this thorn of Bir Hakeim." Columns of dark smoke rose where the general pointed with his glasses across the next stony ridge towards the two broken cisterns that identified the desert fortress.

"Those wretched wells have become the devil's own oasis. We could pass by Bir Hakeim and just move on, but I can't afford to have the French cut our supply lines if we leave this fort alive behind us."

The commander wiped the dust from his cracked lips with the back of one hand. "They surprise me, these French. They are dying for a scrap of desert. They never fought like this for Cherbourg."

Von Decken nodded. Exhilerated by participating in the attack, Rommel seemed stronger, healthier than when Ernst last had seen him. In the battles of the Cauldron, the general had led those swift turning movements that for him were the essence of desert warfare.

"So I have no choice but to stop and smash Bir Hakeim," the commander continued. "By this time tomorrow, Bir Hakeim will be destroyed. Then it's Tobruk, and probably one last battle somewhere on the way to Cairo, probably near Alexandria. With the British, the fighting is never over."

"Yes, Herr General." Von Decken watched Rommel clean the lenses of his field glasses on his checked scarf. His face was a mask of dust.

"The Italians were meant to take Bir Hakeim for us. The Ariete, but they never got past the mines."

"*Natürlich*, General."

"Look after your men and machines, von Decken, then join my reconnaissance squadron. After the last week, we need replacements. See that you share your water with my men. In two hours we'll be moving up to support the attack. The sun should be setting in their eyes."

Ernst saluted and positioned his machines beside the armored cars of Rommel's Kampfstaffel. He spotted one thirsty soldier surreptitiously siphoning water from the radiator of an armored car. God help the man if Rommel saw him. Ernst stepped to one of his own vehicles and rapped his knuckles on a petrol tin marked with a white cross. "Still half full," he said to the driver. "Give this water to the general's men."

Von Decken sat on the side of his tank, cooler now in the late afternoon. He pulled up his trouser cuff and restrapped his wooden leg. In the alternating heat and cold of the desert, with sand always working its way between flesh and cloth and wood, the hard puckered skin of his stump had grown soft and raw.

He drank chianti from a canteen with two of his officers while they opened ancient tins of Alte Mann. He wished they had a few cans of the captured bully beef that some of his men had been sending home to Germany as a wartime luxury. Yet when they read the mail of British soldiers, to them the bully was disgusting fodder.

While he chewed the greasy mess, Ernst thought of his wife, and Anton Rider. He was not certain which of the two he cared for most and disliked the most. He thought of the photograph that was in his knapsack. He did not doubt that Harriet, spoiled and bored on her own in Cairo, and resenting her abandonment, had been eager for whatever mischief Rider had provided. She had always had a weakness for his foolish friend. "But damn you, you stupid Engländer," Ernst said aloud, spitting out a bit of fat, "you should have known better. You're even worse than I am."

He was pleased to hear friendly artillery open up on both flanks, the pump-pump of the Pak 38s, the fast whistle of the 88s, and the heavy boom of the field guns. In the distance, he heard the occasional reply of the defenders' weapons. Ernst's men stood and waved and cheered when flights of Stukas screamed down to blast passages through the minefields.

Suddenly nine Hurricanes appeared from the east. As the British fighters attacked the slower Stukas, three dots grew rapidly in the western sky. One Stuka spiraled down in a column of black smoke.

"Seille! Seille!" men cried as the three Me 109s flew in over Bir Hakeim.

The Hurricanes gathered in a circle flying nose to tail to cover each other as the Messerschmitts climbed above them.

"Seille! Seille!" Ernst's men hollered, waving their weapons at the sky as they called out Rommel's nickname for Joachim Marseille, the 'Southern Star' of the Luftwaffe, the twenty-one-year-old aerobatic ace who had shot down over one hundred British aircraft.

As Ernst stared up and watched the Me 109s dive into the Hurricanes, he recalled a morning at an airstrip near Al Agheila. There Ernst had seen Mathias, Marseille's black servant from the Transvaal, set a handkerchief on a patch of soft sand. While his fellow aviators cheered from a nearby dune, the Southern Star dove and picked up the handkerchief with one wingtip of his 109, like a diving hawk ripping a snake from the ground without even touching the earth.

Two Hurricanes went down as the others fled to the east.

Later, as the armored cars and half-tracks ground forward through a chain of wadis, with Rommel in the lead, they passed groups of crouching soldiers, infantry stormtroopers and combat engineers. Some were retying their boots or leggings. Others were preparing their weapons and equipment: mine detectors and flame throwers, wire cutters and smoke-screen candles. Thinking of von Lettow and the last war, von Decken watched Rommel nod to left and right as he passed between his Africans. For a moment, it was 1915 again. It was going to be another long war.

* * *

On the tenth day Wellie was at a Legion outpost when a German truck flying a white flag pulled up. A major, gaunt and erect in his faded uniform, stepped down and asked to parley. The sentry replied in German that negotiations were forbidden by his commander. It was time to 'faire Camerone.' The officer's truck drove off and hit a mine. He and his driver walked back to the enemy lines, the wounded driver leaning on the major's shoulder.

Again the Stukas came all day. The air spotters estimated the Luftwaffe was flying at least one hundred and fifty sorties a day against the box. That night the Luftwaffe dropped magnesium parachute flares and the German artillery maintained its fire.

Wellington awoke to a morning of thick fog.

"Might as well be in Cambridge," he grumbled as he stood and stretched. He could not see the old fort. He kicked Gates awake and walked with him to the edge of the perimeter. They heard the eerie rattle of tank tracks and the shouts and curses of German infantry. They stumbled onto the body of a black signalman with his telephone still pressed to his ear. An unmanned French 75 stood nearby like a ghost in the fog. The mouth of its barrel was split open like the petals of a tulip.

Walking close to the perimeter, they heard the snip-snip of heavy wire cutters. Wellington raised one hand. He and Gates both stopped.

"Let's get one for Johnny," Gates whispered, tightening his scarf.

They drew their new revolvers. Wellington stopped Gates from firing until they both lay down. Snip-snip came the sound again. They emptied their Enfields and a man screamed in the fog. Immediately there came the chattering bark of a Schmeisser machine pistol. Bullets whined over their heads.

As the wind rose and the mist cleared, the Panzergrenadiers struggled forward through the minefield while Stukas machine-gunned the defenses.

Nordhouse, touring the perimeter, knelt beside Wellington and scanned the enemy with his field glasses. He followed the movements of a single half-track topped with a large-frame antenna.

"That's the end," he said. "It's Rommel."

The Africans of the Bataillon de Marche took the first assault. The Ubangis held on grimly yard by yard. When the Germans broke their line, a dozen Legion Bren-gun carriers rushed to their aid and plugged the hole. They knocked back the German infantry with machine guns and anti-tank rifles. Finally sixty Stukas attacked at once, bathing every position in gunfire and explosives.

Stumbling and constantly thirsty, Wellington helped carry one of his men to a medical station.

"No more water left to wash the wounds," an exhausted medical officer told him, bending over the unconscious Hussar and shaking his head.

"Anesthetic's all gone," said an orderly, "and the plasma and sulfonamide are about done." Wellington tried not to breathe when he smelled the overripe stench of the open wounds. As he set down the wounded signalman and turned away, he saw a Legionnaire stagger to the dressing station, his right hand missing. The man held the end of the dangling open vein of his arm in his teeth.

It was no longer possible to bury the dead. Caught on the perimeter wire, the bodies of German and Italian soldiers were bloated and swollen tight inside their uniforms.

General Koenig ordered that instead of being driven back by the German tanks, all units should let themselves be overrun by the enemy armor and should then rise up and destroy the Panzergrenadiers who would be advancing with the tanks. Without their screen of infantry, the tanks would be more vulnerable.

The defenders had no more mortar shells. The 75s were almost out of ammunition.

In the next attack, one German combat group lost ten of its eleven tanks. But by nightfall the Afrika Korps had broken the line in several places. Their tank recovery teams were loading the damaged tanks onto transporters, hurrying the casualties back to the mobile workshops. Two infantry *Kampfgruppen* had stormed the high ground that looked down on the most important French positions. Now their Grenadiers and combat engineers were digging in two hundred yards from the old fort. Wellington heard the crump-crump of their three-inch mortars and the sustained fire and recognizable fast cadence of their Spandaus, twice the rate of fire of the heavier Vickers with their steady rat-tat-tat. There was the sharp crash of hand grenades before the enemy made each new push.

As the German infantry pressed the night attack on the ground, three Junker 88s, ten Me 110s and about forty-five Stukas bombed and attacked the box, escorted by over fifty Me 109s. Flares and bombs and red tracer fire lit the fortress.

Koenig called a midnight meeting of all unit commanders. One of two Englishmen present, Wellington represented the small troop of Cherry-pickers. Nordhouse was barely able to stand. He was suffering from a head wound and had one arm in a sling. Many of the gaunt officers had not slept in days. All looked at their general with hard sunken eyes.

"The Thirteenth Demi-Brigade can do no more," said the general. His lips were cracked. His eyes looked like two holes burned in a blanket. "Annihilation would not be victory. France needs us to fight again. Now it will be up to Tobruk to hold the enemy. Tomorrow night we will break out and rendezvous with a British relief column of lorries and ambulances waiting for us five miles to the south-west. Should be the 7th Motor Bri-gade, the same dependable unit who've been running the night convoys."

His voice scratchy, the general paused and looked around him at the ghostly faces of his officers. "First we must open a new path through the mines, where they do not expect us. Two companies will stay behind to keep the enemy engaged. Once we start out, no one will stop. No matter what happens. *Bonne chance*." Instead of saluting, Koenig shook hands with each of the officers as they left his bunker.

The next morning, while every unit worked to ready its remaining vehicles, one hundred and ten aircraft assaulted Bir Hakeim in a single attack. The wreckage of downed planes littered the fortress and the minefields. The defenders now tallied the score in the air at fifty-eight lost by the Axis and seventy-six lost by the RAF. A downed Italian pilot told the garrison that one German flyer had shot down six South African fighters in one day over Bir Hakeim. When his cannon jammed, he'd fought on with his machine guns.

Wellington Rider was no longer the eager fresh young man he had been two weeks before.

He lay in his slit trench, a borrowed tin hat on his head. For two hours the ground shook and burst around him. Cries and gunfire and bombs joined in one endless shriek, louder and louder. Deafened, at times he could not remember where he was. The air grew hot and filled with dust and smoke and shrapnel. Now he understood the deserters who were said to be hiding in Upper Egypt in great numbers. He thought of Cairo. The letter to Saffron was still unfinished in his pocket.

When he climbed out, Wellington found none of his remaining five men seriously wounded, but only one armored car still operational. They worked on it all afternoon, stealing petrol from the broken cars and going over every moving part. They taped over the headlights to thin slits. Gates tied a Union Jack to the aerial.

All day the Germans kept up the attack on the perimeter. Low-angle shells pounded the bunkers and trenches. Whenever the artillery or the Stukas paused, the Panzergrenadiers pressed forward through the smoke. Prisoners said Rommel himself had led the last attack with three battalions, including his personal combat group. Occasionally the general's command car was visible to the French artillery.

The muster at 2030 hours started better than it ended.

Faster and quieter than the Brens, four trucks with mounted machine guns were to lead the convoy out. The Cherrypickers would be with them. Once through the minefield, their armored car was to scout ahead and locate the waiting British column. The French battalions, all short of transport, would follow as best they could.

While Legion sappers cleared a new path through the mines, Wellington and his mates helped load two hundred and fifty wounded into lorries scattered around the camp. When they were all ready, the trucks gathered near the old fort. The mine-clearing parties returned, some men still trembling from the effort. Wellington checked his watch. It was time for the breakout.

"Saddle up, lads," he said cheerfully. "Get out your whips." Gates and the other four men scrambled aboard the Humber while he closed the battle shutters to protect the engine from gunfire. Then Wellington took his place on the outside of the overloaded armored car. Scattered behind them on the desert was the usual battlefield litter of shell casings and ration packs and old bandages, letters and snapshots, souvenirs and torn rucksacks.

As soon as they heard the diversionary fire from the other end of camp, the convoy started through the perimeter two by two. Just as the last ambulance truck entered the minefield with the Cherrypickers beside it, German flares lit the night. The perimeter exploded with fire. Every remaining French gun discharged its last rounds as the Panzergrenadiers pressed forward.

The heavily loaded trucks followed the path through the mines. The survivors of the Bataillon du Pacifique came first, then the Africans of the

Bataillon de Marche. The Fusiliers-Marins held up the line as they struggled to withdraw with their remaining artillery. Last came the Legion.
Men fired from their lorries as they fled.

Wellington looked back and saw machine gun fire strike the driver's
cab of the truck behind him. Glass shattered. He watched the three men
in the seat jump and shake like dolls as the heavy bullets cut through
them. Sickened, Wellington saw the old Bedford veer to the left, wandering on its own, careening crazily as it lurched onto two wheels. It trembled
and rose in the air when a heavy mine went off beneath it. Wounded men
fell and struggled from the lorry, crawling like crabs into the darkness.

As the lead elements of the convoy cleared the minefield, he heard en-
gines roar and saw headlights flash to both sides of the retreating trucks.
Rommel must have been waiting for our breakout, Wellington thought.
That blasted German fox.

Standing close beside his driver, gripping the top frame of the turret
with one hand and the machine gun mount with the other, Wellington
ordered the man to pull out to the right and speed up and pass the trucks
ahead. He was anxious to get in front and find the British convoy. For an
instant he glanced up at the waning moon and thought of Saffron and the
baby.

Soon the armored car was running along the flat bottom of a long wadi,
bouncing over rocks and crashing through thorn bush. Wellington
squinted ahead into the darkness, following the thin beams of the lights.
The lorries were rumbling along behind them, protected by the higher
ground to either side.

Suddenly Wellington could not see.

Like a volcano, the night erupted into dazzling light. Two parachute
flares burst right before him. They fluttered down, sparkling brilliantly,
swinging and flashing brighter and brighter. Pairs of headlights flicked on
directly ahead.

The last thing Wellie saw was two German half-tracks charging at them
down the wadi. The armored vehicles came at them with the unstoppable
head-down violence of an enraged rhinoceros. Their machine guns blazed.
Other weapons opened up on the steep banks ahead.

Wellington felt a blow and was overwhelmed by a flash of blinding
light.

— *22* —

"E*n garde!*" cried Adam Penfold. He raised the short blade of his sword cane and bent his right leg as best he could. Twenty years of gin and idleness had not prepared him for this. He wished he had a proper foil. The length would be useful to keep the little brute at bay, and he'd always preferred foils, finding sabres too hearty, and epées too French and fussy. He'd never won his Blue, but for a time he'd been quite handy. He tried to recall his schoolday drills as he faced the diminutive demon.

Tiago Alavedo stared up at the tall Englishman through the oval grill of his fencing mask. Behind the mask was his father's sallow, almost yellow skin, and the same intense grey eyes. With murder in his heart, the boy raised the rounded tip of his epée and saluted his tall opponent. He seemed annoyed that his enemy's sword tip was covered in a champagne cork, and that the match would not draw blood.

The two blades clashed furiously. The small six-year-old stamped his right foot forward. He lunged and attacked along the narrow Turkish carpet that lay across the waist of the Cataract Café. Only Penfold's reach and experience saved him as the boy came after him like an angry hornet.

Olivio gazed down at the two figures from the poop deck. What more could a man ask? His oldest friend, an English lord, no less, was teaching his son the lessons of survival. What better sport to teach this precious youth the lessons of agility and concentration, self-reliance and timing, and the indivisibility of attack and defense? Not to mention the need to put a blade through the heart of your adversary. And who better to instruct his heir, apart from Douglas Fairbanks, Jr., the greatest swordsman and actor in the world?

Olivio was wearing a handsome English chalk-stripe, certain that the bold spacing of the broad lines made him appear even more confident and substantial. Two black silk bands circled his left arm to proclaim the grief that still devoured him.

A large dark saloon drew up along the quay. Tariq opened a door. The Inspector General of the Service des Antiquités stepped down and proceeded to the covered gangway.

"Good morning to you, Mustafa Bey," said the dwarf with a slight bow as the heavy stooping Egyptian met him on the poop deck. His guest's face was flushed from the exertion of the ascent. "My Café is honored by your visit. What may we serve you? A coffee? Or perhaps something cool?" Olivio gestured at the waiting ice bucket. "A glass of champagne?"

"That would be agreeable, Senhor Alavedo."

"Champagne for his excellency, Tariq. Champagne!" The dwarf clapped his hands. "I trust your dear lady received the earrings my wife sent for her birthday?"

"Ah, yes. She asked me to thank Senhora Alavedo should I see her."

"Nothing at all." The dwarf shrugged. Six costly pearls, set and mounted in gold in the French fashion, all for a woman with the pendulous jowls and balloon lips of a dromedary. But what choice had he? In Cairo, extortion was one price of success. "Perhaps your wife will honor us by wearing these trifles to our daughter's wedding?"

Mustáfa Bey Hafiz leaned forward and helped himself to a sugared pastry. As Tariq poured the Heidsieck, the Inspector watched closely, checking the label with narrow eyes. From below came the sharp rattle of sword-play. The official stared over the railing as he drank his wine.

"Can that be your son?"

Olivio was pleased the boy was suitably kitted out in the trim white fencing jacket that was strapped between his legs. He had taught his son already that in matters of dress he must replace stature with perfect tailoring.

"Yes. Tiago is taking instruction from Baron Penfold." The little man spoke casually. His guest was not aware that, even when young, dwarves did not play like other children. They were never carefree. "The lord fenced in England, with Ambassador Lampson, you know."

"Some time ago, I should think." The Egyptian held out his glass and Tariq stepped forward. "The boy seems quite fierce."

"Thank you."

Startled by the response, Mustafa Bey finished his glass before continuing.

"I thought it best to call on you here, Senhor Alavedo, because we must speak freely of matters that require some discretion, and at the Ministry there is no privacy. Especially in these uncertain days, with the Germans at the gates and so many of our young officers eager to draw their swords to assist them."

"It is my pleasure, Inspector, to be at your service wherever you may wish."

"About this new tomb on your farm, at Al Lahun." Mustafa Bey lifted a honeyed almond cake from the platter. "Your discovery report is on my desk, but there are certain details . . ."

"If my clerks made any errors in their haste to file the report, Inspector, I would be pleased to have it corrected in accordance with your wishes . . ."

"For the moment we will overlook the matter of timing, the question of compliance with the reporting deadlines, you understand." The Inspector's lips glistened with champagne as he set down his empty glass.

"As you say." The dwarf tapped his glass. Tariq poured, and prepared a second bottle.

"More significant is the matter of completeness. On this there is not much that I can do. The Minister to whom I must report has heard there may be treasures missing. A ship of the dead, I believe he said, some smaller precious artifacts, and most important, a mummy, one of two found at your dig. That mummy cannot be lost." The Inspector wiped his face with a large white handkerchief. "The Minister charged me personally with verifying that the record is complete."

Mustafa Bey paused again and brushed fine powdered sugar from his stambouline. "How the Minister heard these things, I cannot say. We have a few days, for the Service is absorbed with packing at the Museum and preparing inventories. But somehow, Senhor Alavedo, you must account for these unreported treasures, or the Minister will be obliged to make an example of you. And you know what that could mean." He gestured with both hands towards the two ends of the vessel, as if embracing all the Egyptian possessions that the dwarf might forfeit.

Olivio wondered if there were other approaches he might pursue at the Service des Antiquités. Perhaps the Inspector General or the Minister himself, jaded by most bribes, could be seduced by more elevated, more carnal offerings. He had heard that this Minister had personal tastes that flowed in even darker streams than his own.

The dwarf was presently engaged in the arduous task of selecting a replacement for Jamila. Then would come the period of training and physical and moral integration, while he taught the new creature to replace her sense of obligation with sincere delight. Of course, it was her state of mind that would fulfill the match, not her arts or skills, essential as those were. When young and poor, without the seducing blessings of money and power, the dwarf had learned to approach women intent on their pleasure, not on his own. This few men did, especially Englishmen. The more revolting a woman found him, the more skilled and pleasing Olivio had learned to be, astonishing each one with the extension of her own appetites. Finally, when she was limp and moist as an uncooked pudding, he would slip his small oiled hand inside her vagina, pausing while she trembled with this unspeakable delight. Then his hand opened like a tropical night flower and his tiny active fingers gave her life. Of course the equation of effort had changed as he grew rich and richer, but his early lessons continued to bear young fruit.

Perhaps, the dwarf thought, he had already found Jamila's successor. Another Circassian, always his favorites, Mango was young, very young, but apt and tireless. Named for the smoothness of her skin and for the rosy hues that seemed to blush within it, Mango had that luscious ripeness of a succulent fruit about to burst from its skin, at that point of perfection when the flesh is both firm and soft.

"*Touché!*" exclaimed Penfold from the deck below. Olivio glanced down and saw his lordship stagger back. Exhausted, the elderly man slapped his left hand against his chest and leaned against the deck rail. "Touché!"

Tiago tore off his mask and stared up at his father, craving his acknowledgment. His small round face shined with sweat. His eyes blazed with the energy of victory. Olivio nodded and clapped twice. What he saw in his son's eyes should carry him through life. The boy beamed and let Penfold shake his hand.

Meanwhile the dwarf turned over the difficulties in his mind. If he disclosed the Frenchman's theft, he himself would be accountable for a second offense: failure to report the crime to the National Police. How much to reveal now? Down which path to guide the suspicions of the Service des Antiquités? Perhaps it was best to embroil Mustafa Bey Hafiz in the problem itself, to burden him with the truth, or some of it, so that later the Inspector could less easily turn against Olivio Alavedo.

"We must have that missing mummy," insisted the Inspector General once more. "That is essential."

For a mummy, you require a body, thought the dwarf.

"Mustafa Bey," Alavedo replied as the champagne was poured, "we live in testing times. Nothing is as it should be. I myself have been grievously ill, in the hospital, unable to see with even one eye. In this difficult time my staff and clerks have acted for me, doing their best, more or less. Apparently there was a theft, a robbery, at our little dig, though what was taken, it is hard for me to say, as I was not there and could not see." He squinted at Mustafa Bey Hafiz but found no sympathy in the toad-like man. "I have initiated enquiries, but these things take time. You and I have the same purpose, Inspector, to secure these treasures and to record them. If we recover them, it will serve well for both of us. Give me two weeks."

"One." Mustafa Bey stood with a pastry in his fingers and looked across the Nile. He put it in his mouth. "Not one day more. Then I must file my report with the Minister and nothing can be changed."

Mustafa Bey Hafiz turned and walked heavily to the gangway. Without looking back, the Inspector General waved as he climbed to the quay where Tariq was setting a case of champagne into the trunk of his car.

"Chap just came in says there's heavy news from the front," said Penfold with rare urgency when he rejoined Olivio Alavedo at a corner table in the P'tit Coin de France. The restaurant was a center of Free French intrigue. The air was heavy with smoke and loud French conversation. Tariq waited outside in the Sunbeam.

"Indeed, your lordship?" said the dwarf distantly, intent on his own purpose amidst the hubbub.

"Tobruk has fallen," said Penfold.

"Tobruk?" For once, Olivio was interested. "Are you certain?"

"They say Rommel himself was in one of the lead Panzers. He's taken thirty-five thousand prisoners, two thousand vehicles, great stores of petrol and rations. The devil's already pushing east for Alexandria. Looks like they're setting up for the final battle at a rail stop called El Alamein. Eighth

Army's digging in. Hitler's just made Rommel a field marshal. One more win and the Hun could have Suez, the oil of the Middle East, the whole show."

Olivio considered for a moment before he replied. It was not this war that mattered, of course, but rather a suitable settling of accounts with the French villain who had taken from him his twin daughters and his mistress.

"This Rommel is not here yet, my lord." The dwarf gestured at the bottle of claret and Penfold filled his own glass. "Here in Cairo, on the Nile, life will continue."

"Mussolini has flown his white charger to Derna, so he can lead the Axis victory parade into Cairo," added the Englishman, pausing to drink. "Can't imagine he's much at the jumps."

"No wonder all these French are so excited." Alavedo glanced around the establishment at the clamorous energetic diners. His eye smarted from the smoke.

Rarely comfortable at tables not his own, the dwarf nonetheless enjoyed the fresh organs presented on traditional Gallic menus: brains and liver, kidneys and sweetbreads. He appreciated the lack of waste and the earthy realism of traditional cuisines, including the Arabic appetite for each part of the camel, down to one of his own flavorful favorites, camel foot soup. Occasionally this restaurant offered the classic French dish of broiled horsemeat to remind the soldiers of their kitchens in Picardy and Normandy. Today, to the disgust of his English friend, the dwarf himself had enjoyed sautéed sweetbreads. He sprinkled them with chopped parsley as he ate. A bit of garlic in the rich sauce had enhanced the calf's thymus, that seemingly useless gland of the animal that was put to such fine use by man. Satisfied with the fortifying dish, Olivio slid his tongue over each lip. He clasped his hands over his hard belly and looked about him.

"May I join you?" asked the red-faced proprietor. He beamed at his clients, grateful for the dwarf's early financing, and recently for the precious supplies he had been receiving from the little man's farms. He sat down and uncorked an old bottle of poire. Penfold brightened and accepted a glass. Olivio, who declined to drink it, admired the decaying pear trapped within the bottle. But he rarely took the time to chatter over drinks.

"How may I be of service?" the Frenchman asked, aware of the infrequency of Alavedo's outings.

"What can you tell me of Giscard de Neuville?" asked the dwarf.

The Frenchman stiffened and forced the cork back into the bottle. "That man no longer dines here."

"Please tell me what you can. In deep confidence, of course." The dwarf was eager to discover if his discreet revelations of de Neuville's treachery were now known amongst the Free French. Had he succeeded in giving his adversary new enemies?

"Some say he is with Vichy, though at first he seemed to be with us. But I know little of what he does, and less of what he thinks."

"Can you learn more, quickly?"

"What I can do, I will." The proprietor sniffed his drink. "But yesterday another man was here, asking after him as well."

"And who was that?"

"A Legionnaire, a captain, banged up, his head in bandages. A real *dur*. Fresh back from the desert. He told one of our regulars that de Neuville had passed on to Vichy details of our defenses at Bir Hakeim, I think. Says it probably cost a lot of men."

"Where can we find this soldier?" asked the dwarf, scenting a useful motivation.

"He is here now. I'll bring him to you."

The Legionnaire joined them, his blue officer's kepi under his left arm. Olivio studied the tough lined face, worn and exhausted under the dark tan and the bandage that crossed his scalp and covered one eye and ear.

"Jacques Nordhouse." The soldier set his kepi on the table. "*Un autre*, Ricard," he called to the suffragi before studying Alavedo with tired eyes. "Our host says we have much to discuss."

"Enough to make us instant friends," said the dwarf. He admired the red top of the Frenchman's hat with its cross of gold braid. "May I recommend the sweetbreads?"

"Perfect," said Nordhouse. The waiter set down a partly filled glass, a bottle of water and a small bowl of ice. The Legionnaire dropped in a cube and poured a splash of water. The glass clouded and the Frenchman drank.

The three men spoke of de Neuville and what he owed them. When the conversation became ominous, Penfold excused himself and stepped to the bar for another poire while Olivio and the soldier made their plans.

"Aren't you both friends of Anton Rider?" asked Nordhouse later as he finished his second plate.

"Indeed we are, Captain," said Penfold, having rejoined the table. "He's meant to be back in Cairo any day. Been in hospital in Alex."

"Well, I think I've got some very bad news." Nordhouse saw Penfold and the dwarf lose their animation. "No, it's not him. Didn't even know where he was. It's Rider's son, young Wellington."

Penfold stopped breathing and set down his glass while Nordhouse continued.

"I'm afraid he caught it on the way out of Bir Hakeim. His armored car was shot up. It was the last of his troop of Hussars."

"Dear God," said Penfold, white-faced, feeling he had just lost the son he'd never had. "Dear God." His pale eyes glazed over as he clenched his drink. His hand shook.

The dwarf thought of Saffron. All his life he had learned to suffer, and had mastered that, but the pain of his children was almost more than he could bear. He thought of all his daughter's plans and how she had been waiting to build a life with her young man. Now there would be a service, but not a wedding, and a child, without a father.

Anton stood at the entrance to the platform, resting on his crutches. Smoking, leaning on the shafts of their furled stretchers, a crowd of bearers was waiting behind him. Trainloads of civilians were departing Cairo for Palestine from the next platforms. With Rommel at the gates, even the Royal Navy had abandoned Alexandria, leaving demolition parties to blow up the docks.

Anton had not slept since he had heard the news of Wellington. He felt that the best of him had died. He knew this would be the hardest thing he had ever had to do, telling Gwenn that they had lost a son.

Finally he saw the long Alexandria train pull into the Main Station like a snake. It curled along the track, then straightened as it slid along the platform behind the puffing locomotive. He knew that every car would be overloaded.

Filled with dread, Anton was certain that Gwenn would always blame him. Yet he needed her comfort as she would need his. He was numb to the noisy frenzied bustle of the station, the yells of porters and greeters, even the grinding of the braking wheels and the sighing of the expiring engine.

The metal gate was folded back. The steam cleared. The crowd rushed past him to greet the descending passengers. Anton waited where he stood.

After a moment, he saw Gwenn coming towards him carrying a small case, now visible, now lost as she walked down the platform through the hurrying crowd of soldiers and porters and friends and families. She was slim and erect. Her face was drawn. He took one rocking step forward, then another.

Gwenn stopped and looked up at his face. In an instant she knew.

Her green eyes filled.

"Oh, Anton," she said. She dropped the case and slipped her arms inside his crutches and hugged him. He felt her sobs echo through his body. "Oh, God, no!" she screamed. "No!" She sobbed once more and collapsed in his arms.

"Come in," said the impatient voice in French, "and put the tray on the table by the leather chair."

The door to de Neuville's library swung open, banging violently against the panelling between the bookshelves. The painting of Napoleon at Alexandria fell from the wall.

Captain Nordhouse strode in and flung the dinner tray onto de Neuville's desk. Two plates cracked. Hot soup splashed onto the desk and sprayed the archeologist's silk shirt. A half bottle of Bordeaux dropped to the floor and spilled.

De Neuville jumped to his feet. Fear and outrage mingled in his face. "Who are you?" he demanded. He did not recognize the hard-faced bandaged officer.

"Captain Nordhouse, *Deuxième Bataillon*." There was no need to name the regiment. Every Frenchman knew the colors and uniform of the Legion. "We have met once before."

"I think not," said de Neuville distantly.

"Yes," said Nordhouse. "With Monsieur Verdier and others, at a meeting of the National Committee of Free France in Egypt."

As Nordhouse continued, Anton entered the room slowly on his crutches. A third man, dark and thickly built, also in the dark blue of the Foreign Legion, accompanied him.

"I believe you know Mr. Rider," said the French officer. "And this is Sergeant Malero of my battalion." The sergeant's right arm was in a sling.

"This is not a military hospital, Captain," said de Neuville, collecting himself, wondering what had happened to his staff.

"No, Monsieur de Neuville, it is not a hospital," said Nordhouse, shaking his head. "Think of it as a military court."

"A court?" De Neuville began to edge around the side of his desk away from the Legion officer.

"A court of your country, a court of Free France. We have found you guilty of treason."

"Treason?" De Neuville raised his eyebrows and tapped his chest. "Me?"

"You passed French military secrets to Vichy and to the boches, and you cost the Legion many lives at Bir Hakeim, including the brother and several comrades of Sergeant Malero here." Nordhouse paused and looked at the dark-faced soldier beside him. "The Sergeant is a Catalan, and they never forget these things. Am I right, Malero?"

"*Si, Capitano.*" Malero took a step forward, though he still stood between de Neuville and the doorway. He put his left hand on the handle of the bayonet that hung from his belt.

"Bir Hakeim? I know nothing of Bir Hakeim." De Neuville shrugged nervously. Things were turning out exactly as he had always feared. "And what has this misunderstanding to do with this crippled English adventurer? Is he here from jealousy, because his wife loves me?"

"My son also was at Bir Hakeim," said Anton, his heart cold, scarcely caring what happened to the man before him. "And you killed two daughters of my friend."

"The children of that wretched midget?" De Neuville raised both palms in the air. Now he thought he understood why Munir had never returned with the Ford. "Everyone knows that was an accident."

"An accident that you did not kill Mr. Alavedo as well," said Anton.

"Soon, Monsieur de Neuville, it will be your turn to have an accident," said Nordhouse. "Put on your coat. You are coming with us to Mr. Alavedo's farm at Al Lahun. Our small friend has found a use for you. He says it will take some time to prepare you."

Anton stood back against the picture of Murat charging at Abuqir. He smelled the Frenchman's fear as de Neuville stepped past him to take his jacket from the back of the door. Sergeant Malero waited in the doorway.

With Nordhouse a step behind, de Neuville reached behind the door and removed his jacket from a hook. Suddenly there was a gun in his hand. He fired twice into the chest of the sergeant.

The Spaniard fell. De Neuville stepped quickly over his body.

Anton seized de Neuville's left wrist as the archeologist made for the hall.

Unable to free himself, De Neuville spun around. He turned his pistol on Anton.

Rider lost his balance on his crutches and fell to the floor, still gripping de Neuville's arm. The weapon went off as the Frenchman fell with him.

Nordhouse threw himself on de Neuville's back. He forced one knee against de Neuville's spine and grabbed the man's head with both hands. He twisted violently. Anton heard the neck snap. Nordhouse twisted the head in the other direction and the neck cracked again. A long gargling sound, almost a sigh, came from the dying man, as if he wished to say a final word. He twitched violently and was still.

"Quicker than a hanging," said the Legionnaire to Anton. "But your dwarf will be upset." He brushed his hands together and stood. "Are you all right?"

"I'm much better." Anton rose on one crutch. The other had been shattered by the bullet, which had torn his right sleeve but left him unharmed.

Nordhouse lifted the dead body of Malero. He placed the sergeant's body erect in the leather chair before de Neuville's desk. He put Malero's kepi on his lap. He closed the sergeant's eyes and made the sign of the cross over his face. He drew the Legionnaire's bayonet and cut the Cross of Lorraine into the savant's work table that had been de Neuville's desk. Then he stabbed the weapon deep into the wood. "That should teach the bastard's Vichy friends a lesson."

Nordhouse gripped the back of de Neuville's collar and dragged him down the hall. Limping on one crutch, Anton followed.

The old farmhouse always seemed cold and lonely at night. Even with Lord Penfold asleep upstairs and Tariq and August Hänger here with him in the sitting room, the house seemed empty.

The dwarf sat in a tall-backed wicker wheelchair. Tariq stood near his master with his back turned, watching out the window. The wall behind Olivio was covered with the nearly black skin of a giant leopard. He enjoyed the atmosphere of vigor and danger that the African specimens added to his country house. Like all his trophies, this one was a gift from Anton Rider. The leopard was a melanistic creature from the Din Din forest of Ethiopia. The sable rosettes that were its spots were a very dark chocolate brown and touched each other edge to edge. The huge animal, the size and weight of a lioness, had nearly killed Rider, attacking him after being shot in one shoulder.

"May I ask again why you have brought me here?" The doctor glanced up at the massive dark head of the record Cape buffalo that hung over his head. "There is so much to do in Cairo."

"Have I not always rewarded you well?"

"Indeed you have, Herr Alavedo. But you directed me to bring my surgical case, and I do not understand the need. You seem as well as might be expected, considering everything, especially your unwillingness to follow my regime. Zo stubborn you are, if I may say, zo stubborn . . ."

"Soon I will have an unusual request, indeed an unusual opportunity for you, Doctor, in view of your fascination with the ancient arts of Egypt, particularly surgery and embalming."

"I do not understand." The doctor sipped from his drink of hot water mixed with vinegar and lemon juice. It had been served to him in the Russian way, the warm glass contained in a fitted silver holder with a handle.

"Let us say you will be doing the sort of thing you do best, Doctor. Soon a motorcar will arrive, carrying a specimen for your attention. When we see the lights, you will go to our small slaughterhouse where we kill and clean the sheep and the chickens and the goats. It may be necessary to sweep away some feathers and remains."

"I do not think this is something that I will wish to do." The surgeon's small black eyes narrowed behind his spectacles.

"You will do it, wish or not," said the dwarf in a different voice. "I am aware, Doctor, of your German background before you moved to Zürich. And I understand that in the hospital every day you gather military information from the wounded soldiers. Why do you do this, knowing it is against the wartime regulations?"

Dr. Hänger opened his mouth but did not speak.

"I do not care about this foolish war, Doctor, or whose side you are on, or what you do about it," said the dwarf. "Mussolini and Stalin, Rommel and Montgomery are all the same to me. What do I care for whom you spy?" The little man paused to let the word of treachery linger in the air between them. "I care only about my friends and the welfare of my family."

Olivio's single eye burned like a hot coal. "But about that I care. More than you can understand." The dwarf trembled ever so slightly. "I will not report your treason, Doctor, or trouble your life. But you owe me this night. Tonight you will do what I say."

In due time, of course, he would see that this doctor, too, received his punishment, but it would be not political, but personal, not for treason, but rather for helping the enemies of Olivio's friends.

As the dwarf continued, Tariq turned to face the surgeon. He stared down at the doctor and crossed his arms over his chest. His face was dark as the black window behind him.

"In the slaughterhouse you will find canopic jars, real ones, that in ancient times, and in the tomb of my discoveries, contained the preserved organs of the dead. And there you will find long linen wrappings, as close as we could come to those that wrap the mummies. And you will find a few yards of actual mummy bindings to wrap around the outside, no matter how lacey-thin and worn and fragile they may be." The bleeding, he thought, would go better were the body still alive.

"I . . ." began the physician.

"Tariq will help you to undress the specimen." Olivio paused, then spoke more slowly, seizing the attention of the doctor like a nocturnal animal caught in the bright white light of a lamp.

"Tonight you will operate and eviscerate like a surgeon of the pharoah. You will drain and empty the body and fill those jars in the ancient way and seal them with brown wax. You will create a new mummy. Then that mummy and a second, an ancient one, will be boxed like twins and sent to Cairo in one crate, to complete an inventory for the Service des Antiquités. They are too busy now at the Museum to examine with care what they receive. But we must send them two mummies, and we will." At last, thought the dwarf, despite the too easy death of the Frenchman, I have found a way to immortalize my vengeance, to make it endure for as long as the crimes of my enemy.

August Hänger removed his spectacles using both hands. He stared at his patient. The assignment was not without interest.

They heard the sound of an automobile on the driveway.

"They are here, master," said Tariq. He wheeled Olivio towards the door.

The three men met the car in the courtyard. Tariq walked back to the farmhouse to collect the surgeon's case. The driver's door opened and Captain Nordhouse stepped down. He opened the boot of the car and dragged out the stiff corpse of Giscard de Neuville. It appeared that his legs had been broken to fit him into the trunk.

"Where would you like him?" the soldier asked.

Olivio gestured toward a small brick building across the courtyard.

Slightly chilled, the dwarf sat alone in the darkness, his hands folded in his lap. He watched Tariq and the surgeon and Nordhouse walk to the slaughterhouse. Tariq carried the body across his shoulders. He held an ankle in one hand and the surgical case in the other.

The dwarf raised his eye to the stars. He thought of all the suffering, and of all that had been taken from his friends and from him, and then of the blessings that they still possessed. He thought of his lost daughters, feeling their presence in the night, as if the twins might come running to him now, and call him Papa, and kiss him once again on either cheek. He sniffed and inhaled the crisp night air of the Western Desert. He thought of Saffron's cruel loss, and the courage she would need, and how her child would have no father, though none would have a better family or friends. And he thought of Mr. Anton and Miss Gwenn. What loss could be more cruel than theirs? When Olivio had looked into the eyes of his friend, the hunter, it was as if Anton Rider had died himself.

— 23 —

Saffron sat behind her younger sister, braiding the girl's thick dark hair with slow listless motions. Only concern for her baby had kept Saffron functioning at all. But she was still her father's daughter, and she was determined to carry herself as best she could.

"Keep still, Cinnie," she said quietly. "I'm almost finished." She pulled a rubber band twice around the bottom of the second pigtail and snapped it tight. Then Saffron sat back and stared across the river at the rising moon.

Her father watched her, proud of her fortitude, saddened that so young she had to endure the cruel suffering that made one either weaker or stronger. Now she would be obliged to grow up too fast. But he knew the baby would help her face life again.

Adam Penfold sat beside the dwarf at the table on the poop deck. His saucer was full of tea. Fortunately it was time for drinks. He tried to refold several copies of the *Gazette* into less messy creases. Hopelessly uncomfortable with emotional distress, he sought to distract his friends as best he could. He glanced at a photo of the new Italian victory medal already struck to celebrate the conquest of Egypt. On one side was an impression of Mussolini and the pyramids; on the other the motto SUMMA VIRTUS ET AUDACIA. Penfold chuckled and turned the page.

"Only look at these headlines, will you," he said. "LUFTWAFFE'S GOERING KEEPS TWENTY AMERICAN BISON AT KARIN HALL. Should've thought he had enough to do, what with that film star of his and blitzing London and Stalingrad. U.S. WILL REMAIN NEUTRAL, DECLARES ROOSEVELT. Typ-

325

ical Dutchman. Must be an old paper." Penfold squinted at the date and turned to a different edition. "NAZIS CALL PETAIN THE 'FRENCH FÜHRER.' DE GAULLE ASKS—HOW DO YOU EXPECT FRANCE TO RISE AGAIN BENEATH THE GERMAN JACKBOOT AND THE ITALIAN DANCING SLIPPER? Good question. Suppose it's up to us again. FROM STALINGRAD TO SUEZ—CIVILIZATION ON THE EDGE."

"Aha." Olivio nodded, oblivious.

Saffron, silent, looked down at the quay, pleased to see Mr. and Mrs. Rider making their way towards the gangplank. They were the only ones who shared the loss she felt. Anton Rider was moving carefully on his crutches. He did not resemble the strong and graceful man she had known all her life. But she knew how happy Wellie would have been to see his parents together once more. She wondered if that would last.

"Here they are," said Saffron to her father. She hurried down to greet them, waiting at the bottom of the ramp as Anton descended slowly, leaning on the rail. Gwenn held his crutches and gripped his left arm with her other hand. Saffron hugged Gwenn and felt Anton's hand squeeze her shoulder. She closed her eyes and began to cry, though she had thought that she could cry no more.

Olivio and Adam Penfold stared down at them from the poop deck.

Although he had his three children with him and his best friends were now all here, the dwarf did not feel like the fortunate man he knew himself still to be.

"Let's hope that losing Wellington is the end of it," said Penfold quietly. The German advance had stalled at El Alamein, just sixty miles from Alexandria. Now both sides were building up for the final push. In Alex, shopkeepers were putting up signs welcoming the Germans. Italian women were forming a reception committee. One more battle might do it, might be the beginning of the end for England, or for Germany. The world was on the edge, Penfold thought before he spoke again.

"Looks like we have one last chance to stop Rommel, somewhere near El Alamein. One more win, and that rascal will have Egypt and the Middle East. His Panzers are just a hundred and fifty miles from Cairo." Penfold folded the paper and put it in his pocket. "This wretched war can't go on forever."

"Perhaps not," said Olivio. He moved his gaze away and stared across the broad river, his attention taken by a qayyasa sailing low in the water with a cargo of barrels and crates. At least business continued. The river hurried along as it always did in the summer, the water brown and fertile with the rising of the Nile. The pungent dust of the city filtered through the aromatic trees that lined the limestone embankment and mixed with the river air that cooled his deck café. Along the embankment, the unceasing energy of the traffic poured down the Shari al-Nil towards the Pont des Anglais and central Cairo. At moments like this on the river, it seemed that the war was far away, that not much had changed, and that victory in the struggle of life would not elude him after all. But today the calm of the river was mere background, not relief.

Anton pulled himself up the steps. In a few minutes they all sat around Olivio's table on the poop deck. Tiago squatted cross-legged on the deck beneath the table, counting a pile of coins. Occasionally he tried to shuffle them like a croupier. Tariq moved around the table, serving cold white wine and lemonade.

Anton lifted a glass of wine. He was annoyed by the effort it had taken him to cross the boat and climb to the poop deck. He thought of Wellington. He promised himself that he would behave with Gwenn and Saffron the way his son would have wished. It was time to make the most of things, to rebuild what they could have together.

"To us all," Anton said. Before drinking, he looked his wife in the eye and thought he saw what he had hoped to find. Gwenn seemed to take pleasure again in looking after him and to believe that he would try to do his best.

Saffron turned to her father and spoke in a quiet even voice.

"I have something to tell you all," she said. "I'm going to have a baby. I feel very lucky. At least now, part of Wellie will not be lost."

There was no sound but the traffic on the embankment and the clink of coins beneath the table. Cinnamon stared at her sister with open brown eyes.

"I'd written Wellington and told him . . ." Saffron stopped again, then gathered herself while she spread the wrinkled blue envelope that she clutched in her left hand. An officer of the Hussars had brought it to her yesterday, explaining that after the battle Rommel had permitted a burial party to enter Bir Hakeim. The officer had also brought a letter from the colonel of the regiment. She wondered how many he had written.

Saffron continued in a steadier voice.

"Wellie was writing me about it the night before the breakout, but he never got a chance to finish. I'd like you all to read it so you know how happy he was before . . ." She had planned to read his letter aloud herself, but knew she could not. "And we must all remember, please, that Wellie was doing what he wanted to do, with the friends he wanted to be with." She passed the letter to her father. Her eyes filled as Gwenn took her hand.

Then Saffron handed Anton his old choori in its worn leather sheath. "Wellie would have wanted you to have your knife back," she said. He drew out the blade and tested it against his thumbnail. His boy had kept it sharp.

The dwarf took the letter and held it to his eye. He had already told Gwenn and Anton that his daughter was pregnant.

Anton tried not to look at Saffron as she turned her head and wiped her eyes with a napkin. He was looking forward to a grandchild, keen to do more than he had for his own two sons. But he did not know what the rest of this war would hold for him, or what he would do when it was over.

Gwenn caught Anton's eye and gave him a slight tight-lipped smile. She understood, he thought, and no longer blamed him. He hoped he would be as understanding. Perhaps now they could help each other do what each of them had to do. She had her duty, and he had his. Anton wanted to find the best way to let her know that, for him, the war was still not over.

The dwarf nodded when he finished reading, and passed the letter to Adam Penfold. Gwenn put her hand over Anton's where it rested on the table. She felt him turn his wrist as he glanced at his watch.

"Do you have to go somewhere?" she said.

"I thought I'd just run down to Abbassia," he said, warmed by her touch. "I want to ask the major if there's anything I should be doing while I'm on the mend."

"What could you possibly do?" Gwenn said, dismayed, sharpness in her voice. "There's no reason for you to go."

"Oh, there's always something one can do." Anton shrugged, praying she would understand. "Briefing the new chaps, let them know what to expect. Perhaps help a bit with training." He felt her hand stiffen. "I've got a few ideas for new equipment."

Olivio looked from one to the other, hoping Gwenn could accept what his friend felt he must do. "Take my Sunbeam, Mr. Anton," he said. "Tariq can wait and bring you back."

"Best, really, if he doesn't wait," said Anton. "It might take some time. I want the chaps to see that I'll be coming back."

"Back?" said Gwenn. "Back? I know the army. They won't expect you back after those wounds. What's the point?"

"I have to do it, Gwennie," he said, gripping her fingers when she began to draw her hand away. "I must. Please. They need me. I can't have what's left of my patrol going back out again without me. A few more weeks and I'll be fine. All we do is drive about in the desert."

Saffron caught his eye and forced a smile.

She understands, Anton thought. She knows what Wellie would have done.

"Here we are!" said the dwarf brightly as a suffragi passed a plate of steaming samosas and set down a small dish of spicy green sauce. "Stuffed with peas and chopped hens' livers from our farm. Just the thing."

Anton felt Gwenn's hand relax. He knew she'd taken her leave to be with him. "I'll be back for dinner," he said to her.

"I know it's a bit early," said Penfold to his host, setting down his empty wine glass. "But do you mind if I have something a trifle stronger?"

"Of course, your lordship." Olivio clapped his hands and turned to look at the departing suffragi. "Ah," said the dwarf, "here comes young Denby."

Anton looked down and saw Denby crossing the deck as the boy hurried to join them. Every day the lad seemed taller and stronger. Several of his friends, sixteen or seventeen, had lied about their age and signed up for the war. He knew Gwenn could barely speak about it. Just then, Denby caught his eye and waved. God, no, not now, Anton thought, certain what the approaching boy had in mind.

One of the awkward surprises in researching military history is the inconsistency between authorities, even when those authorities have been first-hand participants. This is true both as to such significant points as the number of combatants and the armament of Panzers, and relatively minor ones, such as how General Rommel got his trademark sun-and-sand goggles. I found this true with the desert battle of Bir Hakeim, including references to the composition of the garrison, the number of casualties, and especially as to the breakout on the night of June 10–11, 1942. So, if military scholars find details in this novel with which to cavil, you may well be correct, but please be assured that there is authority available for the background facts as presented here.

Two men were particularly helpful in verifying matters relating to the British forces and to the French Foreign Legion. My first cousin, Major M. Matthew Bull, M.B.E., of the Coldstream Guards, reviewed the manuscript with his usual crisp regimental eye. (Years ago, when Matthew was in New York commanding a British army tattoo at Madison Square Garden, a radio interviewer asked him if he did not feel strange to be leading a British regiment in New York. "Not at all," Major Bull replied, "the Coldstream captured Manhattan twice before, from the Dutch in the seventeenth century, and from George Washington in the eighteenth.") With the energetic efficiency characteristic of the former commander of the Guards Parachute Company, Matthew verified details for me with such resources as the archivists of the Royal Armoured Corps and the Royal Air Force Museum. By coincidence, Matthew had once trained with paratroopers of the 2nd Battalion of the Foreign Legion, the same unit that was at Bir Hakeim many years before.

The redoubtable Simon Murray, who served for five years with the Foreign Legion in North Africa with the requisite *honneur et fidélité*, taught me much about the Legion through the pages of his splendid autobiography, *Legionnaire*, soon to be republished in a handsome new edition. In addition, he kindly read my manuscript to verify details regarding the Legion.

The authority I most would have liked to have read the manuscript was not available: my late father Bartle B. Bull, who fought in the North African campaign as a captain in the 3rd Battalion of the Coldstream Guards. He was gravely wounded near Sidi Barrani, but later rejoined his battalion in the Knightsbridge box in the Western Desert, twenty miles from Bir Hakeim. (As the Coldstream war history put it, "A welcome reinforcement at this juncture was the quite irregular return of Bartle Bull, M.P., who had been sent away once already as unfit after receiving a wound which would have killed most people, but who now thought the tempo of the battle warranted his desertion from a staff appointment in Cairo some seven hundred miles away.") The 3rd Battalion was then besieged at Knightsbridge for eighteen days. Two days after the fall of Bir Hakeim, the battalion withdrew from Knightsbridge to join the 35,000-man garrison at Tobruk. On July 21, 1942, the last day of the Tobruk siege, 200 Coldstreamers, joined by a few Sherwood Foresters, constituted the only unit to reject the order to surrender and instead cut their way out of Tobruk as an organized formation. As King George VI put it, "I have learned with pride of the splendid exploit of the 3rd Battalion Coldstream Guards fighting their way out of Tobruk."

I am indebted to that dashing North African veteran Major Ned Cook and to General Sir Charles Guthrie, Chief of the Defense Staff, for securing my father's wartime records. Although an officer of the U.S. Army Air Corps, Major Cook served as a copilot with the British Tactical Desert Air Force. When thanking General Guthrie, I had the opportunity to tell him how proud I was to have seen how the Cheshire Regiment protected the refugees in Bosnia in the brutal winter of 1993. In a small mountain village on a bitter Christmas morning, I had seen the band of the Cheshires, at risk from Serb snipers, sling their rifles down their backs and march through the narrow streets playing their instruments in order to bring Christmas to the hungry refugee children.

The capture of Tobruk is often considered the high point of Germany's military success in World War II. Shortly thereafter, the British 8th Army broke the Afrika Korps at El Alamein in October 1942. The Soviets destroyed the German 6th Army at Stalingrad three months later. El Alamein was the hinge. It became both the beginning of the end for Nazi Germany and the high point of the "British" war. Thereafter, with increasing American involvement, the war became an Allied campaign in North Africa and elsewhere. After El Alamein and Stalingrad, with disjointed moments of exception, Germany essentially went over to the defensive, first in Africa and Russia, then in western Europe, and finally in Germany itself.

The Luftwaffe ace Joachim Marseille, known as the "Eagle of the Desert" to the British and the "Southern Star" to the Germans, died on September

30, 1942, at the age of 22, shortly before the German defeat at El Alamein. Still undefeated in the air, with 158 confirmed kills, Marseille died when his Me 109 suffered engine failure and his parachute failed to open over the desert.

The diaries of Lieutenant Heinz Werner Schmidt of the Afrika Korps, like the diaries of Rommel himself, were extremely useful to my research. Schmidt participated in the early campaigning in Eritrea in 1941 and later served on Rommel's personal staff in North Africa. Ernst von Decken shares several of Schmidt's adventures. To acquire a sense of life in Cairo during the war, I read three years of the city's daily English language newspaper, the *Egyptian Gazette*. I am indebted to its journalists and editors for making me feel that I was with them on the Nile.

I am also painfully obligated to John Rodenbeck of Cairo, Haut Languedoc, and the Oriental Club for that professor's merciless editing and implacable scholarship in attempting to purge this work of any error, as he saw it. For some of the happier details, I am grateful to the late Douglas Fairbanks, Jr., and to Bobby Short, who advised me regarding period films and music. Andrew Carduner, an expert on the history of motor vehicles, again shared his knowledge, as did my friend Rosario Italia on certain Italian details. Dr. Thomas R. Kuhns, an eminent surgeon, assisted me with medical points and shared his scholarship of World War II. My French friends Laurence Heilbronn and Louis Trébuchet, and an old Francophile friend too modest to be mentioned here, were all most helpful in correcting and enhancing the details of the French participation in this novel. I apologize to them for the nationality of my villain. Edward Gilly, whose father was a leading Free French admiral, also reviewed the manuscript and provided insightful assistance. Terry Mathews, now a prominent sculptor of African wildlife and once a professional hunter who took Ernest Hemingway on safari, once again helped me with various naturalist details.

The Makanyanga of this story is named after two Kenyan hunters, one a friend, the other a historical figure. On safari in Tanzania in 1987 with Robin Hurt, "the hunter's hunter," Ted Roosevelt and I had the pleasure of long hard days spent stalking with Robin and Makanyanga in the Moyowosi Swamp and along the Ruvu Escarpment. Having shared with Makanyanga his favorite dish, raw still-warm buffalo liver dipped in the spicy grass in the animal's stomach and offered on the tip of his skinning knife, I can testify that Makanyanga, a true gentleman of the bush, is a tracker of the old school. The other Makanyanga was a celebrated tracker and elephant hunter in Nyasaland (now Malawi) in the years immediately after 1900.

I have taken a few liberties. The Major Lagnold of my novel is drawn after Major Ralph A. Bagnold, the desert cartographer and founder of the Long Range Patrols, later the Long Range Desert Group. King Faruq is said to have drunk champagne after a German submarine sank the British aircraft carrier *Ark Royal*, rather than when Italian torpedomen disabled the *Queen Elizabeth* in Alexandria harbor. The General O'Connell mentioned in Chapter 11 is a reference to that vigorous and distinguished soldier, General Richard O'Connor, who won the battle of Beda Fomm but was captured by German motorcyclists in April 1941. Not being able to document whether O'Connor enjoyed Charles Heidsieck champagne, I changed his name to O'Connell. The name of Sergeant Malero is an *hommage* I drew from an article in the *Egyptian Gazette* of March 14, 1943, which reported that a Legionnaire named Manuel Malero fired his revolver into the air while celebrating on leave in Cairo, accidentally wounding a Syrian engineer and resulting in Malero's trial for attempted murder before the Mixed Courts. I thought Malero deserved to be remembered.

I retained the actual name of Field Marshall Rommel's mine-laying genius, Karl Buelowius, who assisted Rommel with this specialized defensive work both in North Africa and later along the "Atlantic Wall" when Rommel was directing preparations against the forthcoming allied invasion of Europe. (Interned in Tennessee at the end of the war, the always-resourceful Buelowius hanged himself with a luggage strap.)

It is impossible to study the war in North Africa without admiring Erwin Rommel as a man and a soldier, as did his British adversaries. Speaking in the House of Commons, Winston Churchill described Rommel as "a very daring and skillful opponent . . . and may I say across the havoc of war, a great general." As that splendid British historian Brigadier John Strawson put it: "Rommel, whom the British soldiers admired not only because of his dash and habit of commanding from the front, but because of his chivalrous attitude to the whole desert conflict." Having refused to join the Nazi party, and suspected of being indirectly involved in the July 1944 plot to kill Hitler, Rommel is thought to have been forced to commit suicide on October 14, 1944. Rommel shared with Admiral Nelson the habit of disregarding orders himself while demanding strict obedience from his own officers. Brigadier Strawson observed, "Rommel . . . like Nelson did not believe in looking too far ahead but in bringing about a pell-mell battle." Others, like General Sir David Fraser, compare Rommel to Wellington in terms of his personal fearlessness and his devotion to the wounded of both sides. Both Wellington and Rommel insisted that wounded soldiers be given the same care as officers. Rommel himself waited in line for medical treatment.

General Koenig, the resolute French commander at Bir Hakeim, survived the war and afterwards became the military governor of the French Occupied Zone of Germany.

One of the satisfactions of researching the war in North Africa has been to come across the honored names of my father's Coldstream friends in that campaign, notably Robin Gurdon, Roddie Faure Walker, George Boscawen, John Fox-Strangways, and Ralph Lucas. Reading about these cheerful soldiers and studying their desert photographs helped teach me what the world was like when they were young, though Boscawen has said that at the time they joined the regiment, he and my father (then 37) were the two oldest subalterns (lieutenants) in the British Army. Famously irrepressible, Fox-Strangways, too wounded to be moved, was captured, operated on in the field, and later exchanged for a famously large number of Italian prisoners. After the war, still badly lame, he was noted for kicking a member of the Socialist cabinet down the steps of White's in London. Fox-Strangways did not think that that was the England for which he had been fighting. One of my first memories as a child is visiting Fox-Strangways in the hospital where he was enduring yet another operation on his legs. Ralph Lucas was a fine sporting shot. According to the regimental war history, "Bartle Bull, wounded, was saved by Ralph Lucas, who had the rare experience of killing three of the enemy in hand-to-hand fighting with three successive revolver shots."

Robin Gurdon served with both the Coldstream and the Long Range Desert Group. He shared a flat with my father in Cairo, and his sister married my father's youngest brother during the war. His son and I are friends. Gurdon participated in several important missions, escorting the SAS into action and taking David Sterling, Fitzroy Maclean, and Randolph Churchill on the celebrated Benghazi raid. Gurdon was mortally wounded during an Italian air attack on his truck. As Gurdon died, he ordered his men to ignore his condition and continue with their raid. Robin Gurdon's father, Lord Cranworth, was a distinguished East African pioneer. With Berkeley Cole, he had founded the White Rhino Hotel in Nyeri, Kenya, in 1910. I took the name of that hotel for the title of my first novel. When

I was a boy in England, while playing croquet with him, Lord Cranworth once told me that my late father had said that the Coldstream Regimental Sergeant Major, C. L. Smy, was the bravest man he had ever seen, and that Smy had said the same of him. Later known as "the Voice" when he served at the Royal Military College at Sandhurst as the senior R.S.M. in the British army, Smy was said to be as fearsome on the parade ground as he had been in Africa.

I should also mention that splendid Egyptian lady Gertrude Wissa, a legend of hospitality in wartime Egypt, who was most kind to my father while he was in the hospital in Cairo. The Gertie of this book, in the hospital in Alexandria, is a small reminder of her good heart.

Irritating as they sometimes were, I must extend my thanks to the following intelligent readers, each of whom made *The Devil's Oasis* a better book: my son, Bartle B. Bull; the distinguished editor Betty Kelly; Connie Roosevelt; my agent, Carl D. Brandt; my editor, Kent Carroll; Cissie Chatwin, who listened to most of it; and my patient and acute friends, Winfield P. Jones and Dimitri Sevastopoulo.

Writing fiction tends to be lonely work, but the friends mentioned made it a pleasure, as did my gifted illustrator, Indre Bileris. Our weekly dawn breakfasts at the Victoria Diner gave me the refreshing opportunity to correct the work of someone else for a change.

B.B.